DEVIL CALLS THE TUNE

Chris Maddox

Theogony Books
Virginia Beach, VA

Copyright © 2020 by Chris Maddox.

All rights reserved. No part of this publication may be reproduced, distributed or transmitted in any form or by any means, including photocopying, recording, or other electronic or mechanical methods, without the prior written permission of the publisher, except in the case of brief quotations embodied in critical reviews and certain other noncommercial uses permitted by copyright law. For permission requests, write to the publisher, addressed "Attention: Permissions Coordinator," at the address below.

Chris Kennedy/Theogony Books
2052 Bierce Dr.
Virginia Beach, VA 23454
http://chriskennedypublishing.com/

Publisher's Note: This is a work of fiction. Names, characters, places, and incidents are a product of the author's imagination. Locales and public names are sometimes used for atmospheric purposes. Any resemblance to actual people, living or dead, or to businesses, companies, events, institutions, or locales is completely coincidental.

Cover art by J Caled Design.

Ordering Information:
Quantity sales. Special discounts are available on quantity purchases by corporations, associations, and others. For details, contact the "Special Sales Department" at the address above.

Devil Calls the Tune/Chris Maddox -- 1st ed.
ISBN: 978-1950420865

To my wife, Christine.

Thanks for listening to my endless supply of stories.

Book 1: A Devil of a Predicament

Prologue

A communications beacon does not spend its day wondering if it will receive a signal that harbingers an empire-ending invasion or relay a simple message that begins, "Hi Mom, sorry I haven't written lately." It doesn't care whether it is busy every day, processing thousands of exabytes of data or sending a single picture of someone's cat. Machines do not, as a general rule, get bored.

The communications Wiemaster/Husker InterSpacial Comm Relay (WHISCR) beacon at the hyper limit of the Aberdeen System did not get excited at the approach of a vessel from a vector that it normally did not see. The beacon floated in interstellar space more or less "facing" the Caledon system some ten light years distant. Aberdeen was what was referred to in navigation as a dead-end system. Caledon was the only inhabited star system on a close navigational vector. You could navigate to other star systems by taking other vectors, but between the deep space hazards like grav anomalies, black holes, supernovae remnants, et cetera, and interstellar distances, actually traveling to any of them was more trouble than just vectoring to Caledon before moving on to another destination.

The beacon did not even notice the vessel as such. The vessel was not using grav propulsion and thus had no grav footprint that would trigger the beacon's computers to query the vessel for identification and then log said vessel. Plus, it came in on an unusual vector for any kind of shipping traffic.

It slowed its approach before coming to rest several kilometers away from the beacon. Once at rest relative to the beacon, a small thruster sled detached from the unknown ship and approached the beacon.

Again, the beacon gave no notice of its presence. Staying well out of the beacon's magnetic detection sphere, a pair of suited individuals exited the sled and traversed the final kilometers to the surface of the beacon.

One suited figure attached a device to the access hatch on the beacon's main structure and input several commands.

"Are you sure you got this?" the second figure asked via comms.

"This is nothing," said the first. It was a woman's voice, clearly used to the question. "I was hacking door locks in grade school. This sucks! But yeah, I got it." The airlock telltale above the hatchway changed from red to green and opened. "See?"

The suited figures entered the airlock.

Two hours later, they exited the beacon and flew back to their sled, which then returned to the ship. The inertial engine thrust the ship past the beacon onto a course leading toward the inner system.

The beacon hung in the blackness of space, not remembering it had detected an object approaching, not remembering anyone had entered it, and not remembering anything entering the Aberdeen System.

* * *

Lieutenant Gerald Nivens was bored. The midnight watch, or midwatch, on any vessel was not exactly what you would call a hub of activity. Nivens cycled through his screens one more time, yawned, and scratched his belly. Another hour and he could go to bed and sleep the sleep of the righteous.

HMS *Barclay* was on picket duty in the Aberdeen System, providing overwatch and protection for…well, Nivens wasn't sure what they were providing overwatch and protection for.

The settlement on the surface of the fourth planet was pretty much like any other settlement Nivens had ever seen, as far as he knew. They had contact with the surface once a week, and that was just voice only. No one from *Barclay* ever went down to the surface, and no one ever came up.

Scuttlebutt, what there was of it, said the settlers were from some fundy religious group and "just wanted to be left alone." Which was fine as far as Gerald Nivens was concerned, but it didn't even begin to explain why *Barclay* was pulling picket duty.

He couldn't imagine pirates or raiders coming to a backwater's backwater like Aberdeen for any reason. There wasn't anything here, and the settlers only inhabited one little ring valley on the surface. Hell, there were only about 100 settlers. Law of averages said that there would maybe…*maybe*…be two or three pretty settlers' daughters.

Not that he'd seen any.

A proximity alarm went off.

Nivens sniffed. That was about the only thing that ever happened on midwatch. There was no grav signature, so probably another asteroid. The inner system of Aberdeen was littered with small bits of rock. He brought up the appropriate screen, his tired eyes looking at the data. Anomalous object 150,000 km and closing.

He drew in a breath and checked the trajectory. *Please, please…oh damn. Not even going to brush the shields.* So, no firing, no calling higher.

Just another boring rock on another boring midwatch on a boring picket duty on a boring boat.

He sighed and sank back in his station chair. He would sit here for the rest of the watch and...

Lieutenant Gerald Nivens didn't get to finish his thought as the proximity alarm changed to incoming alarms as missiles lanced out from the object and destroyed HMS *Barclay*.

* * *

The collection of atoms that were once the frigate HMS *Barclay* had barely dispersed when two *Nordic Serpent*-class shuttles dropped away from FPS *Stormcrow* and streaked toward the surface of the planet.

As the vessels entered the atmosphere they began to juke erratically, mimicking the irregular meteors that occasionally streaked across the sky of the only inhabitable planet in the Aberdeen system.

However, instead of burning up in the atmosphere or impacting the ground, the two ships flared and flew low to the ground across the hundreds of kilometers toward their target.

The pilots poured power into the ion engines instead of the grav rings, keeping the gravity signature non-existent. This caused a little discomfort to the shuttles' occupants as the G-forces pushed them back in their shock couches. The shuttles streaked through the night, skimming treetops and grasslands, closely following what ancient pilots called "nap of the earth."

The cargo in each shuttle rode silently in their shock chairs; the only sounds were the power plant noises and the occasional grunt from various occupants as the shuttle dipped, zigged, and banked to avoid detection.

"Target LZ 400 klicks and closing, Colonel," the pilot of Shuttle One commed to the armored figure occupying the shock chair closest to the crew compartment. Unlike normal shuttles, where the highest ranking person in the compartment sat closest to the exit for LIFO—Last In, First Out—on an assault shuttle, the commander or highest rank was FILO—First In, Last Out—unless you were punched out during a combat drop, in which case everybody got ejected more or less simultaneously.

Thank Gods we aren't doing that, Doug Longo thought fervently. He'd dropped on every kind of shuttle from just about every star nation, and Nordic shuttles were…not fun.

"Acknowledged," he sent back.

The readout over the crew compartment door started a countdown, the kilometers remaining to target clicking down rapidly. At "0," the shuttles climbed over the short ring of hills overlooking the Aberdeen settlement, flared their thrusters, and dropped like birds of prey on the unsuspecting town. The shuttles touched down inside the crescent-shaped settlement of buildings.

"Deploy! Deploy! Deploy!" the commander yelled as the shuttle ramps dropped.

* * *

Sanjay Mujumdar closed the door to the children's room as he reached for his combat harness. Two delicate but firm hands helped him settle the harness on his shoulders then gently turned him around until he regarded his wife. She was tall for a native of New Nepal. Her flawless brown skin and almond-shaped dark, almost black, eyes held an intelligence even deeper than his. He had married up as far as he was concerned.

"It's probably nothing we can't handle, Amita. You and the children stay in here until Sergeant Scheers or another of us gives the all clear."

"Be careful, my love." Amita Mujumdar's dark eyes were troubled. "Something has happened to *Barclay* if anyone is able to land troops on the surface."

Nothing gets past Amita, Sanjay thought wryly. *That's why you married her. Beautiful and smart.*

"I'm going to take the 'scenic' route to the admin building and link up with the rest of the troops there. We've drilled this scenario countless times. Don't worry. We will drive off whoever is out there, and I shall be back before sunrise. "

"Hopefully," she said, troubled.

"Don't take council of your fears, love. The house is safe enough, and if something happens to me you should be good to go until Scheers or someone else can come get you. If all else fails, we'll blow the facility, and everyone will go."

At that, Amita's face turned into a wolfish snarl. "Go and make the mound higher, my love." She turned and shut herself in their bedroom. He knew she would arm herself with the pistol he'd left specifically for that purpose. Anyone who tried to get into this house would find Kipling's female of the species waiting.

Sanjay kept the lights off as he stalked through the quiet house. Outside he could hear the sounds of railgun fire and explosions, faint but detectable. He had been awakened, as had all the defense personnel for the settlement, by the call of the night watch. Two Nordic assault shuttles had landed an unknown number of hostiles.

Every member of the town's defense forces had responded and were engaged with the hostiles or doing exactly what Sanjay was doing now…getting out of their houses. He wished—not for the first time since the alert—that he could get to the facility and CALI. Just one…No, everything must remain safely secret for the time being. Besides, anyone who could get past an imperial frigate, even an old one like *Barclay*, probably knew what was here and had dropped at least a platoon of troops to take care of the facility staff.

Whoever it was also knew when to strike. Coming in at night would ensure most of the staff was topside instead of in the facility where they could respond with…overwhelming force. He grinned ferally in spite of himself.

Although, without CRATOS, he could have wished for at least an APE or two to increase the throw weight the Aberdeen defense forces could muster at night. He'd made the point more than once that topside security was paramount, given the nature of the facility *and* the fact the civilians were located topside, but he was overruled; the settlement had to look like a small colony.

He cracked the door to his family's housing unit and peered out. He could see up the street in both directions. He saw the fiery rounds of railgun fire going in both directions past the front of the administration building.

He drew in a deep breath, took a firm grip on his railgun, and stepped out into the maelstrom.

***

"But, Sergeant—" The voice on the speaker was urgent.

"No time for that, Weyland." Sergeant David Scheers interrupted, settling his armor. He picked up his railgun. "Something is going on topside; we've lost WHISCR and topside security surveillance. I must find out what's going on."

"What if it's an enemy attack?" the facility administrator inquired anxiously. "Or pirates? You know that no one is supposed to find out this facility exists. We—"

"Have women and children to protect as well as ensuring the security of this base," Sheers replied. "I have a family upstairs, and I'm not going to let them or anyone else get killed if I can help it. You're here and can man the defenses as readily as I can. Besides," he added, ramming a magazine into the well and charging the rifle, "as of right now, I'm initiating emergency security lockdown protocols when I leave. Nobody but IAA is getting access to this base."

"Emergency security protocols initiated, Sergeant. I need proper authorization."

"Emergency security protocols initiate, Weyland. Authorization—Scheers, David L., 1489-233-1231AS, authorize, comp cent lockdown, hangar lockdown, armory lockdown, administration lockdown, research lockdown."

"Additional instructions?" Weyland inquired, his voice oddly monotone.

"Additional instructions—No one allowed access to base except current staff or Imperial Avalonian military personnel. Initiate ESL protocols for anyone else, countdown ten minutes. Silent."

"Additional instructions acknowledged. No one allowed access to Weyland Facility except current staff or Imperial Avalonian military personnel. Initiating ESL protocols for any other personnel, silent countdown of ten minutes," Weyland intoned.

"You will lockdown the lift and return it to the lower position as soon as I exit. If, and I stress *if*, we return, we will come through one of the back doors. Do not release the lift to anyone *not* in the Administration area."

"Acknowledged, Sergeant. Will lock down main personnel lift upon your exit. Will return lift to facility administrative level. Will not allow access to facility except to facility personnel or IAM personnel via one of the back doors. And good luck," Weyland said as the NCO entered the lift to the surface of Aberdeen.

* * * * *

Chapter One
Five Months Earlier

Nikolai Nikolayevich Devlin always knew he was going to wind up with his name on the board. He just didn't think he'd be on the Justiciar's Docket. And he really didn't think it would be there on the eve of his eighteenth birthday.

Devlin sat outside Courtroom #1 of Justiciar's House, Melonia City, Caliban, awaiting his arraignment. The official charges were eight counts of aggravated assault, four counts of aggravated assault with a deadly weapon, two counts of aggravated assault with intent to maim, one count of attempted manslaughter, forty-two counts of destruction of property, and public littering. The last one was the arresting officer just being a jerk.

He hurt all over. His hands hurt from the beating he gave Allonsy. His back and body hurt from the beating he had taken getting at Allonsy. And his head hurt...from the stunner.

"Devlin!" a voice called. He jerked his head up and turned to see the source. A bailiff approached from up the hall.

"Yeah...that's me," Devlin said, sighing.

"Someone wants to see you," the bailiff said, unlocking the cuffs holding Devlin in his chair.

"Well, it's not like I can go anywhere to avoid it, can I?" the boy said.

"Come on." The bailiff easily hauled Devlin's 1.85-meter, eighty-kilogram frame to his feet and shoved him in the proper direction. Devlin stumbled a bit and shot the uniformed guard a hot glance. The bailiff shrugged, nonplussed.

They walked down the hall, past the entrance to the main courtroom area, past several offices, to a blaststeel door with a security box.

The bailiff punched a code into the box and stood back. A security camera above the door lit up. A moment later the door opened, and a strong, masculine voice said, "Enter."

The bailiff motioned to Devlin and gestured at the doorway. The young man cautiously stepped through it and entered the room beyond.

It was an office. A nice one, but not opulent. The walls held various paintings—a couple landscapes, but also pictures of people in military dress uniforms. Bookcases covered most of the remaining wall space. Devlin knew enough to recognize that only some of the books were real. A few were blaststeel replicas, built as part of the bookcases to provide security against small arms fire should someone try to penetrate the office to get at the occupant.

Devlin noticed three doorways in the opposite wall. Given their locations, Devlin guessed they were access corridors to the garage, the courtrooms, and possibly a security shelter—not an uncommon feature for government officials.

Almost directly in the middle of the room was a large, ornately carved wooden desk behind which a man sat, absently reading a data tablet. He was approximately two meters in height, about one hundred kilograms, and although his clothes were designed to hide it, it appeared middle-age spread had set in. He had close-cropped blond hair with a slight widow's peak. Hazel eyes that looked tired, an aquiline nose, and a square jaw completed the picture.

Peter Bernard Jadwidzik, Chief Justiciar of the Avalonian Empire on Caliban was dressed not in his Justiciar's robes now, but a lightweight, simple, but obviously expensive, shirt and slacks. A military or family crest was holo'd into the breast of the shirt. He glanced up at Devlin and shifted his eyes to an empty chair in front of his desk.

"Sit."

Devlin sat in the chair and folded his bruised and bloodied hands in his lap. Jadwidzik was a man he respected, a rarity in the young man's life. Most people he came into contact with were either functionaries, like his ex-boss at the food processing plant, or criminals. That's not to say he was discourteous, just that for him there were few adults where courtesy was automatic. The justiciar was one such adult.

Jadwidzik was the justiciar when a younger Devlin was arrested after getting stuck in a ventilation shaft trying to burglarize a wealthy family's apartment in Little Moscow. Rather than assigning the fifteen-year-old to a juvenile detention center, the judge offered Devlin's mother, whom he stated he had known in another lifetime, a different path.

Devlin was released into a foster relationship with the justiciar, who was tasked with making sure he stayed in, and graduated from, school. He also arranged for an apprenticeship with a local food plant where young Mister Devlin was instructed in a trade. That helped make sure Devlin would be able to get a job once he left school and also enabled him to make money in the short run to help his ma with her medical expenses. Jadwidzik looked after the young man and treated him with courtesy and demanded the same.

Devlin sat, more than a little self-conscious about his appearance. He had cleaned up while in the holding area at the local constabulary station, and because he was technically a minor, his mother had been called, something he had fervently hoped wouldn't happen. Devlin hadn't seen a justiciar, so he couldn't be released. However, he was permitted to see his mother and obtain a change of clothes so he was presentable when arraigned in court.

His mother hadn't liked the idea but had brought the clothes. What simultaneously gladdened and broke his heart was that his mother didn't even remember the scene in the bar. She had absolutely no clue why he was in jail, but she just *knew* it was all a misunderstanding they would get straightened out in the morning. She gave him a kiss on his cheek as she left and assured him she would be there as soon as she got word when he was to be arraigned. He had been waiting for her reappearance when the bailiff called his name.

After an eternity—which the clock on the desk said was two full minutes—the justiciar looked up from the files he was reading, regarded the young man in front of him, his mouth twisting into a grimace, and asked, almost rhetorically, "What am I to do with you, young Mr. Devlin?"

Devlin fidgeted a bit in his chair but decided silence was the better answer.

Jadwidzik sighed and kicked back in his chair. "First of all, relax a bit, son. You ain't in the Army and I ain't the bloody king. Seriously. You're in this office because I need to talk to you *before* I see you in my official capacity out in that courtroom. Your life depends on what you say once we're in there and I can't trust the Public Defense Office to get this right."

Devlin furrowed his brow. "What's to bloody say, Sir? I'm a dead man."

The judge started to say something, almost by reflex, but bit it off. He rose from his chair, came around the desk, and sat on the edge in front of the boy.

"I won't even ask *why* you decided it was a good idea to try and beat Allonsy Martin half to death, as I'm pretty sure you were going for *all* dead. If he had tried to pimp my mother out in exchange for neurotranqs, I'd have likely done the same thing. That said, I've read the eyewitness reports, and I even checked up on your work apprenticeship. Which, by the way, is a cock-up of galactic magnitude."

At the boy's puzzled look, Jadwidzik continued, "Apparently the new foreman wasn't aware that the apprenticeship, a common thing, was a favor the plant manager was doing for me. You should never have been terminated until you were ready to go. You shouldn't have been in that pub in the first place."

Devlin started to open his mouth, but the judge cut him off. "Don't go there, boy; I know what you're going to say. I'm just saying things might have been different if you hadn't already been pissed off and drinking. And the frog wouldn't bump its ass when it jumps if it had antigrav installed."

Devlin wasn't sure what a frog was, but he got the context.

"Bottom line is, you did, you were, you saw, you kicked Allonsy Martin's ass, and now we have a problem."

"We?" Devlin ground out bitterly. "Where were you when Mom got abandoned by my dad? Where were you when she almost died because of that never-to-be-sufficiently-damned plague? Where were you when the only way I could afford all the painkillers and meds for

Ma was stealing? When did *you* inherit the problems of a whoreson bastard on his way to jail?"

The older man didn't change expression as he backhanded the boy.

Devlin's face flushed, and a red haze filled his vision, but Jadwidzik's voice, colder than liquid oxygen, brought him up short. "Don't ever say that in my presence again, boy."

Devlin, white hot with rage, glared defiantly, but after a glimpse of the older man's face he looked away. Jadwidzik eyed the boy for a long moment, then sighed.

"Niko, I'm sorry about your mom, and about you, but—" he shrugged, "—shit happens sometimes, and when the Devil calls the tune, all you can do is sing along. I couldn't do anything when Old Nick left. I couldn't do anything when Victoria found out she was pregnant with you. I couldn't stop the plague. Hell, I didn't even know you were in Melonia before you got caught at the housing unit. There's a lot I can't change. I can't change what has happened, but maybe I can help change what *could* happen."

Devlin, still incandescent with rage, looked at the judge. "Why do you even care, Sir?"

Jadwidzik scowled but asked, "You know what tomorrow is?"

Devlin nodded. "My birthday...Sir."

"Outstanding. You can think," the justiciar said. "More precisely, your *eighteenth* birthday. Which is both good and bad.

"Let's recap just how royally screwed you are. You didn't just beat a man half to death, you didn't just commit enough felonies to put you away for the rest of your life. Oh no...and, no, I'm not going to cry over the shitheads you beat the hell out of. Most of those chuckleheads will either grace the jails or more likely a garbage bin before too many more years go by. But, you had to go and beat up the son of the biggest crime lord on three planets in front of God and everybody. You embarrassed him and his daddy, and that's just not gonna fly. To top it off, I'm limited in what I can do because you're seventeen." At Devlin's blank look, the judge continued, "This is bad, because past a certain point, some charges don't make a distinction between adult and minor. Attempted murder is one of them."

Devlin stared at the older man. Jadwidzik let that information sink in before continuing, "And to make matters worse, there are options for you if you are an adult. But you're not an adult, are you? So, guess what, young Devlin; you are in a monumental cleft stick. Now, if you appear in that courtroom, there is usually only one option. I have to charge you and find you guilty and sentence you to a long stretch of years in the penal facility." He let that sink in for a second, then added, "But you and I both know you won't spend a long stretch of years in penal. Will you?"

Devlin knew the judge was right about that. Word was that Old Man Martin hated his kid and generally held him in contempt, but blood was blood. The Old Man wasn't going to take the beating of his son lying down. He couldn't countenance a blow to his reputation. As a result, Devlin's life wasn't worth spit in a furnace. There were any number of ways a guy like Old Man Martin could have someone in jail killed. The guards would take a bribe to "look the other way" and erase surveillance, and the inmates would do just about anything for an added comfort. Little Devlin would go to jail then suffer a fatal shower accident or, more likely, be found dead in his cell doing the belt ballet.

"Yeah, I kind of figured that much out. I'm not considerably enthused about the upcoming proceedings."

"Well," the older man drawled, "I can give you some good news and some bad news."

"Oh," said the young man, "some good news and some bad news." He used nearly the same inflection the older man had. "I'm going to love this, aren't I?"

"Probably." Jadwidzik agreed. "There is one, repeat one, foolproof way to beat a criminal charge…Actually, that's a bad term. You can't make anything foolproof—the universe always breeds better fools—what I should say is that the law makes one provision to keep what is about to happen to you from happening."

"And that would be?"

"Well…" the judge began, and seeing the scowl on Devlin's bruised face, grinned.

"In the early days of the Empire, it was recognized that sometimes somebody would make a mistake and restitution had to be made. But it was also recognized that incarceration was not always the best choice. Therefore, a provision was made."

"Uh huh," Devlin grunted.

"Contract is everything in the Empire. It carries more weight than you can possibly imagine. It's one reason why you and your mom got screwed from the beginning. It's a blessing and a curse. Even marriage and co-parenting in the Empire involves a contract. Victoria didn't have one with your dad—he was on his way to get the paperwork when he got his orders to go off-planet. The Empire's hands were tied legally. With Old Nick not able to confirm or deny that she was his fiancée or that they had contracted to have a kid together, the Empire could not legally act and take care of you."

Devlin scowled. "We've been over this before, sir. What's that got to do with my being seventeen and simultaneously in and out of luck?" he said.

Jadwidzik smiled faintly and replied, "Like I said, with the Empire, contract is everything; they will abide by a legal contract. Right?" Devlin nodded his understanding. "The good news is that the Parliament created a special contract that would enable an accused a way to get out, so to speak, of the consequences of a life-changing action."

"And that would be...Come on, Sir, you're beating around the bush," Devlin said impatiently.

"I'm getting there," the judge said. "Believe me, you really want the full explanation. You have to have fully informed consent; that's part of it." The younger man frowned but said nothing. "Okay, contract law lesson time. There are two basic types of contracts. There are contracts of equals, where two citizens engage in a contract and each person brings something of value to the deal. Simple exchange. Got me so far?"

Devlin nodded.

"All right. The other is what we call a Petitioner's Contract. This is where a person enters into a contractual relationship with a more powerful entity, such as a company, or in this case the Empire, for a 'special' benefit from the more powerful entity in return for something from the individual.

"A contract with the Empire is unbreakable, except by the initiator of the contract. That's coded into the law, so someone who enters into a contract doesn't get screwed. If it's broken, the only thing that changes is that the initiator goes back to status quo ante. Get me?"

Devlin nodded. "He goes back to whatever his situation was at the beginning of the contract. Got you."

"Right. Now, in most cases, as a minor, you are absolutely unable to enter into any kind of contract, even apprenticeship. In that case your mother had to give consent."

Devlin frowned again but nodded. He remembered that much and how his mother had signed the paperwork, all the while pleading with him not to screw up his chance at a better life. He grimaced. So much for better.

"But there is one kind of contract you can enter into that your mother *doesn't* have to consent to. And that contract would put the charges against you in abeyance—not get rid of, mind you, but hold them in abeyance—for the term of the contract." Devlin started to feel the ground open up and prepare to swallow him. "Normally, you wouldn't even be able to do this, but luckily," the judge said with a bitter smirk, "the timing couldn't be more perfect."

Devlin felt like he was waiting for a punch to the stomach.

"If you were to enter into a military enlistment contract your charges here on Caliban could be held in abeyance until the completion of your enlistment. Your enlistment could then be taken as time served and your record expunged as far as Caliban was concerned." The judge finished, making Devlin's gloom complete.

"But…" Devlin began.

"But you're not eighteen and thus not eligible for enlistment. True, except…"

"Except for what?" Devlin pressed.

"Except on the eve of your eighteenth birthday you can enlist with or without parental consent."

Devlin sat very still in his chair. Finally, he spoke. "All right, what's the catch? What would keep me from ditching the shuttle the second I landed on AvSecundus, or wherever they send me?"

"Nothing whatsoever, as far as ditching. They wouldn't even come looking for you. You'd just be a fugitive. From Caliban and from the Empire…for the rest of your life. If you ever get in trouble for any reason—"

"Right back here?"

"Yes," came the reply. "They would consider the contract abrogated by the initiator and thus you would be returned to Caliban for reinstatement of the charges."

"Okay, but what about quitting or getting thrown out?" Devlin inquired.

"You can't quit; same deal, you come back here. Getting thrown out is kind of different."

"How so?"

"Let's just say the military takes care of its own. Waste not, want not," Jadwidzik said mirthlessly. "Should you screw up so very badly that the military decides to get rid of you, they do it internally."

Devlin flushed, and the judge interjected, "Sorry, poor choice of words.

"Should you screw up so monumentally that it would require a dishonorable discharge—which is the only way you get out other than quitting or serving your time, or maybe a compassionate discharge, now that I think of it—you would be tried, convicted, and serve your time in a military penal institution. For most non-capital offenses, you would serve out your full term remainder in the brig. Then you would be kicked out wherever you happened to be at the time, and since you didn't complete military service, your charges on

Caliban could be reinstated. You'd be an idiot if you came back here, though."

"Obviously," Devlin said dryly. "Sir."

Jadwidzik flashed a shark's grin.

"Let me get this straight," Devlin said, his jaw working. "In order to not go to jail, and thus be killed in my rack by some petty crook looking for a little nooky or nosedust, I have the 'opportunity' to join the wonderful military, whose monumental crap of a bureaucracy put me and my mom in this situation in the first place. For which, I get shipped off-world to some hellhole of a boot camp where I can't quit, and I can't get thrown out because, if I do, I'll either do time there, and I'd still have the charges here, or I'd get shipped back here and face the same crap. Which means the only option I have is to join up and not to reason why, but fight and do or die until such time as I can breathe the air of the righteous. Is that basically it?"

"Pretty much," the judge agreed. "But let me be clear on this: *you can't quit*. You'll wind up on a shuttle back here so fast, it'll make its own hyperwake."

"Can't quit. Got it."

"No, I don't think you do," the justiciar disagreed. "They make it easy to quit. They want you to quit. They will do everything they can to make you quit. But you *can't* quit. To do so would be to sign your own death warrant. But just because you join doesn't mean you have to be in a combat unit."

"What?" Devlin said, surprised.

"You could get through training and volunteer for a support unit. Maybe as a wrench turner—you've been doing that for two years now. It's not like you can't hum the tune. So, there's that."

Devlin considered for a few more minutes. He looked like he was saving up spit. "I hate this. I really do."

"I understand that, Niko." He actually looked sympathetic as the galaxy threatened to collapse into a singularity around Devlin. "But at the end of the day, it's the only way I can see this working. You don't have any real options. Look, military life isn't that bad. I survived it. Your old man survived it and thrived in it. I won't ask you to thrive or even like it. You might, or you might not; that's your choice. But your other choices in this matter well and truly suck, boy.

"I'll let you think it over. You alone have to make the decision."

"What about my ma?" Devlin looked at the older man, challenging but also vulnerable.

The older man snorted, "Oh, so now you start thinking about your ma. In all of the calculation's you did before starting your 'Don Quixote windmill jousting,' did you for one nanosecond consider who was going to take care of Victoria when you either died or got carted off to jail?" He stood and regarded the boy sternly. "If I were to venture a guess, probably not. All you thought about was your hands around that little dipshit's throat. So, where does that leave Victoria?"

Devlin sat in the chair looking up at the looming figure of the justiciar. He received a truly formidable scowl in return. But it was an honest scowl, Devlin realized. He really hadn't realized until that moment that the cleft stick didn't just hold him, it held his mother as well.

"I...uh..." Devlin started, but the old judge's face softened slightly, and he interrupted the young man in front of him.

"I should have said this before. Yesterday's...boneheaded display notwithstanding, I know you worry about your ma more than yourself. She is, as of last night once she left the holding facility, in my custody. I had the constables take her back to your place where they helped her pack her things up. She is now my guest. I and another person who knew your Da are going to make sure the rest of her days are comfortable. Don't worry yourself about your ma. I owe your dad to take care of this."

Devlin breathed out. That was the one loose end in all of this. He could handle whatever came his way, but he really didn't want anything to happen to his ma. She'd already had a crappy enough life.

Jadwidzik went back to his desk and straightened the files. "I'm going to leave you to your ruminations. When you're ready to tell me your decision, just hit the signal on the door you came through and one of my bailiffs will bring you to me. We'll follow the bouncing ball wherever it goes."

With that, he opened the door Devlin suspected led to the courtroom and closed it behind him, leaving the very disconsolate young man alone with his thoughts.

* * *

Docket #147987763-239 Empire vs. Nikolai Nikolayevich Devlin, Court #1, Melonia City, Caliban, Prospero System

Chief Justiciar Peter Bernard Jadwidzik, Presiding

Status: Status Pending Probation Prior to Judgment: Military Enlistment.

* * * * *

Chapter Two

Devlin opened his eyes then closed them to slits as the cabin lights came up to full illumination, indicating the shuttle had landed and disembarkation was about to begin. The lights lowered a bit a moment later as the pilot matched the illumination levels to those outside the shuttle. Devlin waited for his eyes to adjust.

For the last six days, he'd been aboard ship, shuttle, spaceport, and space station. He had eaten, slept, cleaned up, and sat. This last trip had taken sixteen standard hours. He wasn't sure he could move.

He slid his shoulder out from under the drooling head of some wanker in the seat next to him. The sod just grunted and shifted position the other way.

The main doors opened, and four men in uniforms came through the doors yelling "Up! Up! UP!" They made their way quickly to the back of the shuttle cabin, grabbing slow-moving recruits and hauling them, in one case rather roughly, to their feet, all the while yelling and cursing at the young men and women who, like Devlin, had recently enlisted in the military.

Devlin turned his head. The four army guys reached the back of the shuttle and suddenly went silent. They directed their attention to the hatchway at the front of the shuttle, so he swiveled his head in that direction again. He saw another man enter the front of the compartment.

"Good evening, ladies and gentlemen," the man said. He didn't yell, but he was heard by everyone in the compartment. His accent was strange and slightly pronounced. It didn't sound like any of the Avalonian accents he'd heard before.

He was of average height, maybe a little taller, but as broad as a cargo truck. He had brown hair and a dark complexion. He was dressed immaculately in a dress green uniform, bedecked with ribbons and medals on his chest. He had three stripes on his upper arm pointing up, with three rockers—Devlin believed they were called—underneath with a golden starburst in the middle. He had seven slash marks on the left sleeve of his jacket. He looked like somebody's perfect version of a soldier from war or propaganda holos.

"My name is Sergeant Major Virgil Chadwell McClellan." He waited for that momentous sliver of information to be assimilated by the mob before him. "I am, for my sins, going to be your senior drill instructor for the period of your basic military training. For the next six months, it doesn't matter whether you desire to join His Majesty's Army, Navy, or Marines; everyone starts here.

"Should you survive the next six months, you will then be given a choice as to your preferred service branch and specialty. You will be given a choice, but be warned, His Majesty is not obligated to grant you your choice. We don't all get to be Chief of Naval Operations or Field Marshal of the Army. You may *choose* to be infantry but get selected for support. You might want to be in armor, but wind up an armorer.

"All I can say at this point is don't worry about it. You aren't there yet, and you don't have that choice. The maggot does not worry about the meal for the full-grown fly, and you lot are not even maggots in the grand scheme of things. There may come a day when you are a stinging gadfly in the eyes of the IslamoNordic Republic, or to the various pirates and ne'er-do-wells on the Fringe, but today is not this day.

"For now, you exit the shuttle, and we will guide you on a short walk, about a kilometer, to the barracks area of Bardon Hill Training Center. Grab your gear and follow these four cadre members into the barracks, where you'll get a little food and bedded down. There you will sleep for the evening and we will begin bright and early in the morning. Enjoy, while you can, the few creature comforts we can afford in our humble accommodations; they will be few and far between for your foreseeable future. Goodnight, and may God, whichever one or ones you worship, have mercy on your souls."

With that he turned and walked off the ship. Immediately, the four men in the back started forward, yelling and haranguing Devlin and his fellow recruits off the ship.

Devlin stepped off the shuttle and onto the tarmac with his fellow recruits and began walking toward the buildings that would presumably be their home for the next six months.

The recruits followed the uniformed men onto a walkway that ran parallel to a street. On the opposite side was a collection of buildings, a perpendicular road, and then another set of buildings. That pattern went on as far as Devlin could see in the gathering gloom of the planet's twilight.

The group moved as a disorganized mob with two of the army guys leading and two bringing up the rear. The rearmost of the two in back stopped occasionally to round up a straggler. They walked a few hundred meters and crossed over the roadway into a group of four long buildings sitting alone. Only one building was lit.

For the next several minutes, there was a bottleneck as the recruits entered the building and were conducted down a corridor into a big training bay. The big room looked a lot like the training salles in a couple of the schools Devlin had attended as a child. There were human shaped dummies in one corner and mats stacked in another. What appeared to be mock rifles were racked along a wall as well as a few sticks with padded ends.

The gaggle of new recruits were instructed to sit on the floor while one of the men walked out into the center of the room. "I am Staff Sergeant Rogers," he boomed. Talking stopped as they all turned their attention him. "You may address me as Staff Sergeant Rogers or Drill Sergeant Rogers. I am not 'Sir;' I still work for a living. Likewise, I am not 'buddy,' 'dude,' or any other number of nondescriptive nicknames. If you do not address myself and my compatriots by our proper titles, you will be sorry...and sore.

"Before you get some chow, we're going to assign you beds for the night. You will get some linens, and we'll take you to the sleeping barracks. Don't get too comfy and unpack your shit; you may have to move bunks tomorrow. What you need to do is get up, line up, and as you exit this room, pick up a linen bundle. We're going to divide you up into groups of about forty. We still have a couple people inbound, so you'll have some new playmates in the morning. Now, everybody get up and get your crap together."

Devlin rose and was chivied, along with everyone else, into a line at the door to the training bay. Each person grabbed a cloth bundle as they were herded down the hall.

Devlin and his group were moved along the sidewalk to one of the barracks further down the street. Inside, the staff sergeant turned on the lights and led the group through a door and up a flight of stairs. Since he was in the last half of the group, he was led up another flight of stairs into another large room. This one was lined up one side and down the other by stacked bunk beds. Devlin heard a couple of people start to grumble.

As soon as it began, another staff sergeant said cheerfully, "Oh come on, you bunch of flowers, did you think this was going to be the Ritz? Did you think I was going to tuck you in, give you milk and cookies…maybe a little snog before you go to bed? I'm gonna warn you now, you'd better get used to disappointment. You're in the military now, boys and girls."

Devlin walked down the bay until he found an unoccupied bunk. He didn't have any bags, just a small toiletries bag. He put that on the floor by the bed, placed the linen bundle atop it, and sat down on the thin mattress.

After everyone found a bunk, the staff sergeant, who introduced himself as Miller, walked down the bay and addressed the group.

"We're going to teach you morons how to make a bed. We're not going to worry about perfection tonight, because you idiots won't even approach perfection. So here we go."

About an hour later, everyone's bunk was 'made,' for various values of made. Devlin wasn't terribly concerned. They couldn't possibly worry about how he made his bed, could they? Hell, he figured, as long as it was neat, he'd probably be all right.

"Now then," Staff Sergeant Miller said, "leave your crap and let's go get some chow. We'll cover showering and hygiene before lights out. Chow is in the main building. Let's go."

The group filed out of the bay, into the building's main hall, and out of the barracks. They covered the distance to the main building with a minimum of fuss and just a little laughter and some horsing around. They went into the training area where they first gathered and found some carts with general purpose food packs and a variety of bottled beverages. A couple of large containers with "coffee" and "tea" were on a separate cart with cups.

Devlin needed some caffeine so he snagged a cup and filled it from the urn labeled "coffee." Compared to some of the coffee he'd been subjected to at the plant, this was weak, but he decided he could live with it. At least it didn't have hydro-electronic condensate fluid floating on top.

He sat by himself and pondered his situation. It looked like Basic was going to be the same nit-picky bullshit as school. It was way nit-pickier than the plant, but, again, he could live with that. He wasn't sure what was going to be expected of him. Jadwidzik had tried to explain, but, like a lot of stuff, it went in one ear and out the other. He figured if he did what he was told and kept his mouth shut, he should be golden.

He looked around and noticed a lot of other recruits already looked like they might be military. Clean, with haircuts just so. Devlin knew the military tended to run in families in the Empire, especially in the colony worlds, and to a certain extent in the core worlds. Fathers and mothers might both be military or ex-mil, and kids tended to join and serve at least a single hitch, then get out and go to college or enter civilian service as first responders.

He really didn't know what he was doing here, other than the obvious. Mostly, he was pissed. But who was he pissed at? His mom for needing painkillers so badly that she felt she had to go Allonsy Martin? Allonsy for taking advantage of it and pimping her out? At his dad for leaving and never coming back? Jadwidzik for ramming this solution down his throat? No, mainly he was pissed at himself and the events that had brought him here. But all that was incidental now. He was where he was, and he'd best make the most of it.

He did know one thing; he was going to be as invisible as possible. In school, he managed to be noticed just enough so people remembered seeing him at school at least once a day. Once he managed that, he could dodge out and go about his business. The secret was don't talk, don't volunteer, just do what is necessary. All he had to do was survive to graduation, get a do-nothing little piddle job somewhere counting widgets or whatever, and then wait out his time. He'd been through a lifetime of bullshit. He would get through this.

He was never going back to Caliban. He trusted the justiciar to take care of his mom until she finally, mercifully, passed the veil.

He finished his coffee and got up.

For the rest of the evening, Miller took his charges around the barracks and company area while explaining to them where various offices and facilities were.

"I don't expect you bunch of idiots to remember any of this; you gotta have a brain for that, but you can't say we didn't show you," he said.

Finally, he led them back to their barracks bay and informed them that they would be awakened before 5 am local. They were instructed to get into their racks. Ten minutes later, the lights on the floor went out.

Tired both in body and in spirit, Devlin went right to sleep.

* * * * *

Chapter Three

Devlin's eyes snapped open when Miller and Rogers burst into the sleeping bay throwing riot noisemakers down the aisle.

"Everybody, on your feet!"

People crawled and fell out of their beds, even out of the top bunk. One poor guy, three beds from Devlin, fell on his face. Miller was there instantly, yanking him up by his arm, checking cursorily to see if he was hurt and, upon finding he wasn't, shoved him up against the bunk and continued down the line.

Devlin went from groggy to full alert. It was going to be *that* kind of day. He threw his blanket off and hit the floor. Like most of the others, he moved to the foot of the bunk and stood there, waiting to be told what to do.

After a few more minutes of chivying, yelling, and in one case dumping a kid onto the floor in a heap of mattress, blankets, and pillow, the NCOs moved to the head of the room. All eyes, bleary and otherwise, turned toward them.

"You've got ten minutes to get your clothes on and get your bunks made!" Miller boomed.

Everyone started to get dressed, some a little slower than others, which resulted in one or both of the NCOs paying the sluggard a visit to "motivate" him with yelling, cursing, and shoving in the right direction.

Devlin quickly pulled on his clothes. He really wanted a shower; it'd been at least a standard day since his last one. He was used to being dirty, but that was not to say he enjoyed being dirty. He hoped they'd get to shower later.

Next, he concentrated on his bed. He tried unsuccessfully to emulate what Sergeant Miller had shown them last night, but, hell, it was made. That had to count for something.

* * *

"Good morning, Ladies and Gentlemen," the sergeant major from the night before bellowed at them as they were driven out of the barracks like herd animals onto the ceramocrete pad. "Welcome to the first day of the rest of your lives, as they say. I hope you slept well and had a good dinner last night."

A couple of voices murmured "yeahs" and a "not quite" from somewhere in the crowd.

The senior drill instructor put a large smile on his face. Devlin noticed it didn't reach his eyes. He'd seen that look before, usually on the face of a teacher right before a test or a cop just before he busted you. *Oh Hells,* he thought, *this is where the rug gets pulled out.*

"Before we get much further, we need to get a few things straight," McClellan said, pausing to give the group time to catch up. "First, this is not a country club. We are not concerned with your comfort. We are not concerned with your wants or desires. We have one job, and we do that job very well. That job is to teach you useless sacks of protoplasm how to be useful members of His Majesty's military. We don't give a shit if you're having a bad day. We don't give a shit if the accommodations are not to your liking or the chow to your palate. We don't give a shit about *you*. Here it's about you making us happy, and we're never happy. And because we are never happy, you are never going to be happy. So, get that straight right now.

"We are going to tell you to do things, and you are going to do them. We say jump, you should be in the air before you ask, 'how high?' We say shit, you squat and start grunting. That is the sum total of our relationship. Your approval or happiness is not a factor. *Got it?*" He glared at the mass of recruits.

Their reactions were somewhat mixed. Most of the recruits looked either bored or unfazed at the statement from the NCO, as though it was something they heard every day at home. Some were shocked, probably thinking basic was nothing more than a summer camp where they'd learn to tie knots or something. Devlin noticed a few had no reaction; they seemed asleep on their feet. *That's not going to end well,* he thought. Others looked apprehensive, as if wondering if this was really what they had signed up for. Devlin was also starting to wonder what exactly he had gotten himself into.

If the reactions of the recruits affected McClellan at all, he gave no sign. "To start, we're going to teach you magworms how to be soldiers. And we're going to start at the very beginning; baby steps for baby shit.

"We're going to teach you the position of attention. This is attained by bringing your heels together with your toes forty-five-degrees apart. Rest the weight of the body evenly on the heels and balls of both feet. Keep your legs straight, and *don't* lock your knees. Let me repeat that...*don't lock your bloody knees!* Trust me on that. Hold your body erect with hips level, chest out, and shoulders square. Face forward, your chin drawn in so the top of your head is level. Let your arms hang straight down without stiffness. Keep your thumbs straight along the seams of the trouser leg with the first joint of the fingers touching the trousers.

"This is the position you will come to when given the command, 'Attention.' This is the position you will come to when addressed. Let's get this straight now. Any time you address me or one of the training cadre, you will come to attention and address us by our ranks and shout your answer. Do you understand?"

Again, the response was a general murmur from the recruits. This time the smile disappeared from McClellan's face and he said, raising his voice just a bit, "That is not acceptable. I said you will snap to attention and shout your answer. So, you bunch of maggots, get down on your bellies like the bunch of sorry maggots you are."

Many of the recruits were unsure what to do. Some were surprised. Devlin started to get down. Almost as if on cue, the four sergeants from the night before were there throwing people to the ground and yelling "Get *down! Get down! Down! Down! Down!!!!*"

In moments, the entire group was down on the ground.

"All right, you putrid mass of vermin-ridden cobbleboggans. It has been discovered over the millennia that in certain situations, education accompanied by a moderate amount of pain can help the mentally infirm retain what they learn. Since I am convinced that you are *all* equally mentally deficient, we are going to intersperse today's training with a bit of physical exercise to drive these lessons home.

"You are all now on the ground, on your bellies like the lowly pus guzzlers you are. From this position, you will assume what is known as the front-leaning rest position, or the pushup position for those who have ever engaged in physical exercise—which judging from the look of you, I sincerely doubt anyone has. Even the one or two Olympians I see in the crowd look like failed genetic experiments!

"When I say 'front-leaning rest position, *move!*' you will raise yourselves up on your hands and the tips of your feet, hands shoulder-distance apart. For those of you too stupid to understand, Staff Sergeant Pritchard will now demonstrate."

At this, one of the staff sergeants assumed the correct position.

"Now, for the rest of you—front-leaning rest position, *move!*" McClellan barked.

The entire company raised itself in unison, mirroring Staff Sergeant Pritchard. The other staff sergeants stalked through the gaggle of people and made corrections. "Get your ass down, maggot." "You trying to get screwed? We're not in that business." "Shoulder distance apart, idiot."

Finally, McClellan addressed them again. "A pushup is executed by lowering oneself down to the prone position then raising back into the front-leaning rest. Staff Sergeant Pritchard will demonstrate.

Pritchard executed a flawless push-up then got to his feet.

"Now," McClellan said, "when I say, 'Begin' you will all execute pushups like Staff Sergeant Pritchard. We will count to two. At 'one,' you will lower your body. At 'two,' you will raise. You will all do this together. Do you understand?"

Again the crowd was somewhat disunited in their response.

"Dammit!" the instructor said. "I can see we're going to need to get the blood flowing to whatever it is you call brains. Begin! One...Two...One...Two."

As he began counting off, Devlin and several others around him began doing the pushups, while others were still unsure. The staff sergeants targeted them like missiles and after a few words of encouragement, words like idiot, maggot, and dumb-ass, and yet still other more profane words, the stragglers started doing the exercise.

The recruits did pushups for several minutes, all the while, the broad-shouldered sergeant major bellowed ones and twos. Devlin found himself counting along, trying to keep track of how many they had done. While in decent shape, he found his arms started to burn from the exertion after about thirty repetitions. He kept going, watching the others out of the corner of his eye as recruits started to collapse from the exertion. Without fail, a staff sergeant would appear at his or her side, yelling commands into their ears until they got up and resumed their pushups.

After fifty pushups, Devlin found himself straining. He looked around and saw only a few people were still going. There was a big Olympian named Chapis, if he remembered correctly, a girl he didn't know, and two guys on the far side of the group still pumping them out.

"Stop!" McClellan barked, and everyone stopped. Devlin locked his elbows and waited. He was pretty sure this was what you were supposed to do. It was too tempting to think that they were "allowed" to drop to the ground. As he suspected, the few who did were set upon by the hovering staff sergeants.

"Now that your blood is flowing throughout your body," McClellan continued, "one would surmise that some of that precious oxygen-bearing liquid is providing nourishment to whatever organ, tissue, or shit that passes for your brain. While I have your undivided attention, I'm going to impart some much-needed knowledge unto you.

"First, as has been said before: when you are addressed, you will respond by rank and the answer will be shouted. So, when I ask if you useless morons understand me, I expect to hear every one of you miserable piss pots shout, 'Yes, Sergeant Major!' Now, do you understand?"

"Yes, Sergeant Major!" the group chorused.

McClellan stuck a finger in one ear and wiggled it around. "I must be going deaf in my old age. Either that or you lot are the biggest bunch of pantysniffers *ever*. One more time, and I want the general on the other side of the planet to hear you. *Do you farking understand me?*"

"*Yes, Sergeant Major!*" Devlin and the rest of the company roared back.

"Good," the sergeant major said almost pleasantly. "Now we're getting somewhere. Next, we're going to get you up and...*what the hell are you doing?*" he yelled at one recruit about two rows over from Devlin. "I didn't tell you to get the hell up! Get back down! Front-leaning rest position...Move! Begin! One...Two..."

This time, Devlin didn't even get to twenty before he collapsed. He laid on the ground for a moment then tried to get back into front-leaning rest position.

"Halt! That means stop, you idiots," McClellan yelled. "Now, when I say 'Recover' you will get back to your feet. We'll just get you there first. No sense in overtaxing your feeble little minds. Now, recover!"

Devlin jumped to his feet and waited while the rest of the company got to their feet. They directed their attention at the man-turned-monster at the head of the formation.

"All right," McClellan said, cracking his knuckles. "This morning, before we go to breakfast, we're going to teach you lot the basics of military formation. I believe in getting an early start on learning. I also believe that sweat and pain are great motivators. Rule Number Seven: *The more you sweat, the less you bleed.* So, if you pathetic wastes of DNA don't displease me, you *might* be able to get some chow before your in-process procedures today.

"We've already covered attention, address, and pushups. Are there any questions?"

Although Devlin wanted to shout, "No, Sergeant Major!" he was pretty sure that wasn't the correct response, so he kept his mouth shut. That seemed to be correct because after a moment the big drill instructor said, "Good. We'll move on to basic formation. When I say 'Fall in...'"

* * *

After calling 'fall in' a final time, McClellan turned the company over to a staff sergeant and the company was marched toward the mess hall.

Once there, they were told to fall out and get their breakfast.

Devlin walked into the mess hall wrapped in his own thoughts. He could do this. He *would* do this. He told himself it was better than a death sentence, even if this was a load of crap. Devlin knew the Old Man pretty much had connections everywhere in the Prospero system, but could he get someone here? Devlin shook his head. Of course he could get someone here. It wouldn't even be that hard. One of his goons could sign up, show up, whack one smart-ass street kid, and then quit. They'd be gone before the body was discovered…hell, before it got cold.

That thought made him pause. He had been so intent on getting off Caliban he hadn't considered that possibility, and now it made him want to kick himself.

He wasn't out of danger. He had just gone from one target range to another—one where everybody had weapons. He was just one "accident" from a casket. Damn Jadwidzik.

"Hey," said a voice as Devlin felt a large hand slam down on his shoulder.

* * * * *

Chapter Four

Devlin stiffened, balled his left hand into a fist, and subtly shifted his feet. He turned quickly and brought his right hand up to grab the arm attached to the hand on his shoulder.

"Whoa," said the sandy-haired youth with a strong Caledonian accent, backing up a step. "Didn't mean to spook ye."

There were three people behind him. The youth who had touched him was of medium height and lanky, with brown eyes. The second was a female, a redhead, not ruddy like an Eyrian—but pale-skinned and gorgeous. The third guy was about Devlin's height with dark brown skin and blue eyes.

"Allan MacBain," said the blond fellow, sticking out a hand. Devlin looked at it for a moment, unsure of what to do. His heart was racing, and he was still coiled like a spring ready to release.

MacBain started to pull his hand back, abashedly. Devlin suddenly felt very ashamed of himself. He wasn't doing himself any favors by being an ass.

He shook his head and chuckled. "Sorry. I'm a little jumpy…new place and all that. Niko Devlin." He shook the other man's hand. He turned to the female. "And you are?"

"Natalya Kuzma," the redhead replied. He looked into steel-grey eyes that held his for a long moment. Devlin had heard stories from his ma about the Rusalka, beautiful women that dwelt in the rivers and came out at night to entice men into the water to be their lovers, usually to the detriment of the young man. He imagined this girl could be part Rusalka. "I'm from Ariel."

The dark-skinned boy grinned as Devlin turned his attention to him. "Martin Atwell, from Farnham. At least, that's where I was born. My dad is from Avalon Primus. He's a shipping agent for ImpEx."

Over breakfast, he learned that MacBain did hail from Caledon. "From New Edinburgh," the blond boy said over a forkful of potatoes. "It's a nice enough place, I suppose, but I wanted to see a bit of the Empire…and have a go at pirates," he added with a grin.

"Yeah, yeah. Join His Majesty's Army!" Kuzma interjected. "Travel to exotic planets! Meet exciting new people!" she said as if reciting something.

"And kill them!" Atwell finished, laughing.

"I take it you three have had this conversation before," Devlin said wryly.

"Oh, we sat next to each other on the shuttle," Kuzma said, dimpling. "Allan and I met at the port on Skye. Just started talking and found out we had a few things in common. Like we both want to go Armor. Then we found this poor, lost puppy on the trip over." She winked at Atwell, who nodded vigorously.

"This wonderful vision and her attendant troll took me in."

"Hey," MacBain protested, looking aggrieved.

"Allowed me to join their little soiree. At least I've been entertained up until now."

MacBain leaned over to Devlin and whispered conspiratorially, but loud enough so everyone could hear, "He thinks he's better than we are…so erudite and genteel."

"I do not," protested Atwell. "I just happen to be educated and better looking than you, hick."

"Hick?" MacBain snorted. "Who's coming from 'Chickenshit Colony?'"

"Oh, because you shovel sheepshit that's better?" Atwell countered, mock outrage on his face.

"You have offended me, sir. I demand satisfaction."

"Better get used to your hand, then," MacBain fired back.

"Boys! Boys!" Kuzma interjected, exasperated. "I'm going to put you both in the corner! Now behave, or Mr. Devlin is going to think ill of us."

"Yes, Mother," both boys said, grinning.

"So, where were we?" Kuzma asked thoughtfully. Her beautiful mouth turned up in a half-smile.

Devlin shook his head. "Armor."

"Oh, yes!" the girl said, almost bouncing in her seat. She had a look on her face that was almost completely vapid. "Big Honking Tanks with Big Honking Guns!"

"Yeah. I want to drive one of those big honking tanks," MacBain said enthusiastically. "What are you planning to do, Devlin?

"Haven't really decided yet," Devlin said, somewhat awkwardly. He hadn't expected that question so early in. The chief justiciar had told him he would choose a job at the end of the training, just before graduation, so he hadn't given it much thought. He also hadn't considered all the choices that he would have. He didn't want to be here, but he knew it was this or…yeah. But what was he going to do?

He didn't want to be a mechanic either. He could do it, he admitted to himself, but he wasn't that good, or even that interested in it. He managed to keep the one job because he didn't want to get pinched again by the constables. Except that was all water under the bridge now, too.

He wondered how his ma was doing. After the justiciar helped him get inducted, he had arranged for Devlin to see her before shipping out the next day. It was best to do it quick, Jadwidzik had explained. Otherwise, the Old Man or Allonsy's "friends" might get ideas.

* * *

Victoria Devlin was glassy-eyed from neurotranquilizers when she was brought in to see Niko. She wasn't in pain, he was thankful for that, but what it meant was that she really wasn't there, at least not in a coherent way. His heart, already broken at the thought of leaving, shattered completely when he realized she didn't know who he was or even where she was.

She spent their last minutes together looking at things only she could see. Devlin watched her for a few moments, then realized his entire world, his life, and everything he had grown up knowing, was now gone.

He remembered his fifth birthday and the cake she had made, badly, for him. As much as he loved her, she never was a great cook. Aunt Flo was usually the one to feed them until she passed away around Devlin's fifteenth year.

He remembered stories: fairy tales, legends, stories about his da.

And he remembered the plague. The never-to-be-sufficiently-damned-by-God plague. His mother lying on the sofa of their flat, whimpering in agony. Him, holding his mother's hair back as she vomited in the bathroom, her body wracked with pain and ill from the amount of painkillers she needed to keep the effects of the plague at bay.

His hands tightened into fists as he remembered when he found out his mother had turned to Allonsy Martin for those painkillers the day before and had been pimped out in return. He knew she probably didn't remember most of the times she was led off by one of Allonsy's cronies to a waiting john. She didn't remember giving her body to get the drugs she needed to kill the pain. He had wanted to find Martin and finish what he'd tried to do, what he'd failed to do, what had landed him here.

The tears flowed, then the sobs. Finally, when he felt he couldn't weep any longer, he rose, walked over to her, and kissed her tenderly on the cheek.

"Goodbye, Ma," he said quietly and walked out of the room. She didn't even react.

"Sir," Devlin said to the justiciar, who was waiting for him on the other side of the door to the office.

"Yeah," Jadwidzik grunted.

"Take care of her, please?" he pleaded. "I really don't care what happens to me, but…"

"I got it, boy," Jadwidzik said. "I've already made arrangements. The only thing left is to get you on a shuttle to the Core Worlds."

"Then please get me out of here," said the younger man. "I've got nothing left to keep me here."

"One last thing, boy. Call it a bit of advice," Jadwidzik said. "Be careful who you trust. I know I don't have to tell you about paranoia, but you're going off-world; nothing is ever what it seems. I've lived a long time by giving courtesy, but trust is earned. I gave you a chance out of courtesy to your da. You earned my trust these last couple of years by being somewhat level-headed, this latest brouhaha notwithstanding. I would normally say you can trust mil-families, but even there you want to be careful."

The justiciar nodded and motioned to two uniformed men. They accompanied Devlin to the shuttle port, handed him a small bag, and sat with him wordlessly until his shuttle for the Caledon system arrived. The bag contained some basic toiletries and a credit voucher to cover his food until he reached his destination. It was not, Devlin noticed, enough to make a decent run for it. Jadwidzik wasn't an idiot.

* * *

Devlin was thankful to not have to talk to anyone during his journey. He didn't speak to anyone, outside of requests for information, until that morning with MacBain, Atwell, and Kuzma.

"Well, plenty of time for that, I suppose," MacBain said cheerfully. He raised his coffee cup. "Here's to His Majesty and to surviving to serve."

* * * * *

Chapter Five

Fifteen minutes after they entered the chow hall, they were back out on to the field being told to fall in. The sergeant major wasn't there, just the drill sergeants, Miller and Rogers, and three others, Pritchard, Stark, and Pippin

They counted off by fours. The number was their platoon number. Each platoon was formed and separated.

"All right, maggots!" Staff Sergeant Miller bellowed. "When I stand in front of you just give me your name and number. Just those two items and then shut the hell up. Got me?"

"Yes! Staff Sergeant!" Devlin chorused with the group.

Devlin ended up in the second row. On the outside, to his left, was a female with auburn hair and a pleasant face who stood about half a head shorter than Devlin. She gave her name as Nicki Kenyon.

To Devlin's right was a huge man, Jeremy Tamman, who stood about two and a half meters and had to weigh about one hundred and fifty kilos. It was hard to tell what color his hair was because, at some point, he had shaved it. His face had an unfinished quality to it, almost like a sculptor who had started then just given up. His complexion was the milky white of someone who either never saw sunlight before or grew up on a world with a very weak primary. Still, the big guy had a warm smile that didn't seem to leave his face.

To the right of the walking mountain was Sheamus Poole, whose complexion was a deep warm brown. He had Eyrish brogue that was nearly indecipherable.

Tom McCarthy, a medium height, lanky fellow with jet black hair, and a very fair complexion was next. He was the poor unfortunate that had been getting dogged by the instructors all morning. Devlin didn't think he was going to make it very far. McCarthy stood there with a twist to his lips, not quite a smirk, not quite a grimace.

Short, barrel-chested, and powerful, Ronnie Lett from Eyre Secundus looked a counterpoint to McCarthy. He was easily the shortest person in the platoon but may well have been as big around in the chest as Tamman. He had a broad flat nose that looked like it had been broken and never fixed. He had hazel green eyes and brown hair. The corner of his mouth had a nasty scar that turned down into a perpetual frown.

The slanted blue eyes and blond hair of Jong-su Volkoff indicated someone from Caliban or Ariel—someone else Devlin would have to keep an eye on. He didn't recognize the name, but Caliban was a big planet in a system that had three habitable planets. And Old Man Martin held sway on all three.

There was a little nondescript fellow by the name of Markos Katsaros. He was almost so plain and nondescript you didn't notice him. Devlin frowned. He might just be one of those guys, the ones nobody notices unless you need him. Then again, he could be one of *those* guys, the kind nobody notices until it's too late. The hairs on the back of Devlin's neck started to stand up. That guy made Devlin twitchy.

Slender, almost figurine beautiful Anastasia Cho was next. She looked like a doll that his mother had kept on a display shelf in their flat. Her complexion was flawless, her features dainty and perfectly proportioned. But her eyes caught his attention. They were dead, lifeless, and dark. She looked almost bored as she stood there in the line.

A wiry, olive-skinned kid, Nathaniel Jones, finished the row out.

Atwell was in first platoon and looked kind of disappointed. He looked back at Devlin, shrugged and took a deep breath. Kuzma ended up in third platoon, and MacBain in fourth.

When Miller had completed getting all of their names and what squads they were in, he stood before the recruits on the left-hand side of the formation. "Gartlan, Kenyon, Spitz, and Decker. You are the squad leaders until you screw up and we find someone else. Got it?"

"Yes, Drill Sergeant!" the four recruits boomed.

"The rest of you, listen up. As of right now, you are Second Platoon, Alpha Company, Third Battalion, One Hundred Forty-Ninth Training Legion. These four are your squad leaders. Their job is to make sure that you people don't bollocks things up. They're also there if you need something. They will have access to the cadre. That way, sixty people don't wind up crowding us. If you need anything, see your squad leader. We'll go over it again, but for now that's good enough.

"Now that we've got the names and squads straight, we're going to show you proper marching and drill. We'll do that until lunch. After lunch, we get to go to the administration building for lots and lots of paperwork."

He called them to attention, then showed them how to leave, right, and about face. He dropped them once because Acker in the fourth squad was cutting up. When they had that down to Miller's satisfaction he worked them on proper marching—forward and to the rear. The whole platoon got dropped twice during that.

Eventually, he showed them how to make turns, what Stark called right column, left column, and, most interestingly, counter column, where the entire formation turned and walked through itself to wind up going in the opposite direction. Devlin noted that it served basically the same function as "to the rear" but kept the front of the formation the same.

By the time they were marching to the staff sergeant's satisfaction, lunch was about twenty minutes away.

"When I tell you to fall out, take a break. Do not grab ass, do not get wander off, and be ready to fall in when I tell you to."

"Yes, Staff Sergeant," the formation bellowed.

"Fall out!"

* * *

Twenty minutes later, the staff sergeant got them back into formation and led them into the mess hall. This time, the members of his squad joined him at the table. He looked and saw with some relief that MacBain and Kuzma were seated about four tables away and chatting amiably. MacBain caught his eye and grinned. Atwell was sitting at another table with people from his own squad.

"So, Devlin is it?" the redhead asked as he looked back down at his food. It certainly wasn't bad chow—he'd heard stories when he was a kid. This food seemed to belie those stories. It was good and there was plenty of it. He guessed his days of scrounging and going to bed hungry were over.

"Yeah, Niko Devlin. And you're Kenyon?" he said.

"Got it in one," she said. "Nicki Kenyon. And since we're playing name games," the squad leader continued, "Tamman, Poole,

McCarthy, Cho, Volkoff, Katsaros, and Jones. Correct?" She pointed to each and said their names, and each nodded in response.

"Well, I guess that for the foreseeable future, we are all family." Kenyon said. "Don't worry, I'm not your mommy or your significant other. Now, anybody from border worlds? Anybody got issues with my being a split?"

At Devlin's quirked eyebrow, Kenyon explained. "Old slang term—split-tail. I assume you get the gist?" Devlin started to blush a bit, and Kenyon laughed. "You got it. Now, got issues with it?"

"No, not really. Just never heard it put that way before. Heard worse," Devlin said honestly. He chuckled. "Nope, no issues. I don't care as long as you don't."

"And I don't. I just know there are some colonies still that have issues with females in the military or similar. I just want to make sure there's no problems." Kenyon looked at Tamman, "Hey, Big Guy...you gonna be okay with me running things for the time being?"

The big man looked a little uncomfortable. "Well, ma'am, girls on Typhon weren't soldiers." He looked even more uncomfortable. "But the minders in my crèche were all woman, so I'm used to taking orders from them, if that's what you mean."

Kenyon thought about it for a second, started to say something else, but shut her mouth. Then she inhaled and said, "It's not total, but we'll handle things as they come up. Okay?"

The big Typhon mulled that over, then said, "Okay, miss."

Kenyon looked a little exasperated. "It's just Kenyon, Tamman. Not Miss, or God help me, Ma'am. That's for officers. Please get that through your head, Tam."

"Okay, mi—Kenyon."

She looked at the others. All of the others shook their heads. They were okay with a woman in charge, at least until something else happened.

Social hierarchy settled, they attacked their lunch with gusto. Almost before they were finished, the staff sergeant arrived, telling them to hurry up and get their trays dumped and back out to formation.

Kenyon got them all moving, and they went out to the field and lined up. In ones and twos, the rest of the platoon joined them. Soon they were in the same general order as earlier, just loosely hanging out.

"Fall in!" Staff Sergeant Miller called as he came out of the mess building. His counterparts exited with him, bellowing the same thing.

The recruits got into position and came to attention…more or less. The staff sergeant stalked around the formation, correcting faults, dropping Acker again. Finally, he walked back around to the front.

"All right, pusbuckets," Stark said, just loud enough for them to hear. "We're going to the admin building for formal induction. That means signing all the paperwork needed to make you privates in the Emperor's service. There will be briefings on several important topics, and you will get your external identification cards taken care of.

"That will take us to dinnertime. At which time, we will march back here, eat, and go back to the barracks. And tomorrow… oh so much fun we will have. You will turn in the last vestiges of civilian life; your clothes and personal effects will be locked up until Final Phase liberty. But don't celebrate too much when you get your crap back—you'll have to keep it organized with the rest of your stuff, so it's not a blessing. You will also go to Medical for BFT placement and baseline exam for your nanipack fitting. If you have any genetic problems, you will be duly notified and given your options.

"Any questions? And don't ask a stupid one." He paused for about half a second. "Good. Platoon! Right face! Forward march!"

* * * * *

Chapter Six

The next morning, Devlin discovered something about medics as they went through the line for their physical baseline and BFT insertion—medics don't like smart asses.

The recruits trooped up in line and were subjected to a variety of scans and, in a couple of cases, samples were taken. This invited any number of jocular, sophomoric and, often, downright crude comments. Devlin endured his exam with only a modicum of embarrassment. He wasn't body conscious, and he wasn't a prude, but damn, he felt there were some things you just didn't talk about.

However, the laughter amongst the recruits was general and good-natured, and scattered throughout the group, so he didn't much mind.

After all the medical scans and samples were taken, he entered a room with...stuff. Inside, he was confronted with a duo of medical technicians and an odd-looking apparatus. "Where do you want it?"

"Where do I want what?" Devlin said.

"BFT," the technician said stonily. "Blue Force Tracker unit. It will partner with your nanipack and implants when you're given them in a few days. Should you sustain a level of injury that the pack decides you are in imminent danger of expiration, it will put you into a hibernation-like coma. Your vitals and all bodily functions will drop to almost nothing so that you might possibly survive until pickup can be made by friendly forces. The BFT will sound a localization signal that will guide pickup forces to your body. This also occurs should you die during combat—as long as there's enough to make pickup."

"So it guides people to pick up my body if I'm wounded or killed. So they'll come save my ass?"

"Yes, Private," the technician replied tonelessly. He sounded like he'd answered the same question since the day he'd been born.

"Well, I guess if I'm trusting someone to save my ass, the tracker ought to be there. Right butt cheek," Devlin said laughing. The recruits in the line near him began to laugh as well. The techs rolled their eyes, and one suddenly smiled. It didn't seem like a natural thing on the tech's face.

"Since that is an...unusual place, would you like some numbing at the site? BFT injection can sometimes be...unpleasant."

Devlin smiled. "Nah... Everything's nanoscale. How bad could it be?"

* * *

"Devlin...Dude..."

Devlin woke up on the floor of the locker room where they had doffed their clothing for the medical exam. Surrounding him were MacBain, Kuzma, Kenyon, and the rest of Second Squad.

He was aware of several things at once.

One, medical technicians do not like smart asses; two, they have a perverse sense of humor; and three, his ass hurt.

"What the hell?"

"You don't want to know, man. You just don't."

* * *

Devlin was still a bit tender from his ordeal as they received their initial uniforms and equipment draws. However, he persevered.

The platoon was duly formed up, and they suffered through another close order drill session wherein the staff sergeant went over how commands were given, the preparatory command, and the command of execution.

The preparatory command lets the formation know that they are about to do something. For instance, the command "right face" is broken up into preparatory command: "right" and then the command of execution "face" is given, signaling that the formation should execute the command right damn then.

Devlin discovered that there were various forms of commands. There were the normal ones, right face, about face, forward march, then there were variations. For instance, when being dropped to do pushups, the command could be, "Front-leaning rest position" and the command of execution being "Move." Or, as Staff Sergeant Miller demonstrated at one point during the activities, the same process could be accomplished with the preparatory command, "Ah, fark it," and the command of execution, "Drop!"

During the session, the staff sergeant had each of the squad leaders as well as a couple others take turns drilling the recruits using command voice and the proper preparatory commands and commands of execution. In several instances, hilarity ensued, usually followed up by "fark it," from the staff sergeant.

In fact, Second Platoon got so used to hearing that particular combo, when Miller would start, "Oh, fark it," the platoon got ready for some more PT.

They continued drilling until Staff Sergeant Miller took command back from Kenyon and proceeded to march them up the street from the chow hall to a building marked "Uniform Sales and Issue."

Inside, they were broken up into one squad per line and led to a table. Each table held two large bags, next to which were locks and tags. The bags were approximately a meter long and a 1/2 meter in diameter. There were straps and handles on the bag to facilitate carrying in various fashions. They were instructed to write their names, service number, company, platoon, and squad on the tags and place one on each bag. The locks were to be put into the carry pockets on each bag.

Once that was done, they were told to put a bag on their backs, utilizing the shoulder straps and to carry the other by the handle. Fortunately, they were able to accomplish this feat without hearing the dreaded four-letter words from the staff sergeant.

At this point they were led out of the large room into a hallway with several doorways that had windows in them. At each window the recruit would be told "back" or "hand" and an item would be placed in that particular bag. Uniforms…hand, helmet…back, boots…hand, load bearing gear…back, and so forth. Eventually, they ended up in the same room in which they had started and with bags burgeoning with uniform items and equipment.

"Listen up!" Miller said. "Before you sign for this shit and are therefore responsible for it, and thus before we go back to stow it at the barracks, we are going to go over each and every item and inspect it. If there is a problem with any item or you are missing an item, this is the only chance you get to bitch. So be extra careful.

"I will call out each item and tell you how to inspect it. If it does not look right to you, raise your hand and call out. I repeat, raise your farking hand—that's the thing on the end of your arm—and call out! If you do not, and we move on to the next item, and you want to go back 'cuz you didn't get my attention..." he smiled. "Let's just say that a farked up piece of equipment will be the least of your worries.

"Now, take your uniform bag and dump it on the table! Farking Stimson! What did I say? Your uniform bag! That's the one with the uniforms in it, you stupid knob tosser! McCarthy! Who told you to put anything on? Oh Gods, did your momma have any children that lived? Get the fark down, Private! The rest of you—hang tight! Start knocking them out, McCarthy! One...*two*..."

* * *

From there they marched to a nondescript building that read, "Armory, 149th Training Regt."

Miller barked, "Put your equipment on the ground. Squad leaders, designate one person from your squad to watch your squad's equipment."

Kenyon looked down the line and almost instantly her eyes met Devlin's. "Devlin, you're up."

"Got it," Devlin said, and put his stuff down.

A moment later, Miller called out, "Second Platoon. When I say fall out, you will fall out and line up single file at the doorway to the armory building. Do you understand?"

"Yes, Staff Sergeant!" the recruits chorused.

"Fall out!"

By now, the recruits were used to the routine. There were no problems getting lined up, and even McCarthy seemed to know what he was doing.

Miller approach Devlin and the other three recruits. "You four just stand out here and watch the shit. The rest of these morons are going to go in and get their weapons issued. The squad leaders will come out as soon as they have theirs and relieve you. You will go ass-end Charlie to the back of the line and get your weapons. Is that clear?"

About five minutes later, the squad leaders came out of the armory bearing large rifles. Kenyon was grinning like a kid in the toy store with an unlimited cred chip, and Gartlan looked only slightly less pleased.

As they approached, Gartlan informed the group, "Go on in and get in the back of the line. You'll get your rifles when your turn comes."

Devlin and the other three went into the armory and waited in queue with the rest of Alpha Company. Each person stepped up to a door, was issued a weapon, told to read the serial number off the weapon and compare it to a data pad, and scan their thumbprint.

First, a rifle. Then a pistol and a really long knife. Devlin was informed this was called a bayonet, and while he would be trained in its use, he'd better hope it never got bad enough to need it. Finally, they were issued slings, holster, and sheath, respectively, for the weapons in question and told to join the company outside.

Devlin wasn't completely unfamiliar with guns; he'd seen plenty of them in his life. On the other hand, they were usually in the hands of other people, so he really couldn't say he knew much about them. Then it struck him that if there was someone in the company who was trying to frag him, one of these little beauties would be extraordinarily useful. That thought sank to the pit of his stomach like a rock, and he glanced at Kuzma and Volkoff. Neither seemed to be looking at him at the moment; each was engrossed in their own inspection of their weapons.

"All right, you gun bunnies!" Miller bellowed. "Get your shit together and fall in!" The recruits took their respective places and got quiet.

* * *

"You've just been issued weapons. At the moment, those weapons are unloaded! I know they're unloaded because we inspected them before we handed them to your sorry asses. However, from this moment forward, you are to treat those weapons as if they were loaded!

"You are not to point the barrels of those weapons at anyone, ever! Do you understand me?"

"Yes, Staff Sergeant!" the recruits shouted in response.

"If we catch you pointing those weapons at each other, you will be sorry and sore. You will not be issued ammunition for those weapons unless we are on the firing range, but that is no reason to feel like you can play *Killshot 3000* or some other bloody game with them. Again, you will be sorry and sore. *Do you get me?*"

"Yes, Staff Sergeant!"

"For now, we're going to teach you spoogeheads how to carry those weapons. There will be other lessons, but those will come later. When I say fallout, you will assume a seated position on the ground while we get your shit straight. *Fall out!*"

The staff sergeants showed everyone how to properly attach slings and adjust them, how to attach holster and sheath to their equipment belts, and finally, where everything was supposed to go.

Everything, Devlin noted, had a particular way of being done. Sometimes even he could see why things were done that way.

Once everyone had their weapons properly slung, holstered, and sheathed, the platoon was told to fall in, and they were instructed on the carrying of rifles in platoon marching. They were given instruction on port and order arms, as well as right and left shoulder arms. Finally, they were shown how to carry the rifles by the slings. Devlin noticed that the way the rifle hung on the sling allowed it to be brought into play quickly.

Finally, Miller got them moving again and they marched off.

* * * * *

Chapter Seven

Devlin and the rest of Alpha Company were finally fully equipped with their basic turnout. They spent the afternoon and evening getting their gear set up the way the instructors showed them. They sat in the training room of the barracks, the sergeants milling around the room. Occasionally they would stop and give individual instruction, advice, and, in McCarthy's case, a PT session for not listening.

When their gear was finally taken care of and stowed in lockers, everyone was told to change into their uniforms and given a bag with a thumbprint lock on the closure.

"Put all your stuff in the bag. All civilian clothes, all personal effects," Miller said, walking down the bay. "You may keep up to one hundred creds and your religious articles. Everything else goes in the bag.

"You'll have a chance to hit the PX tonight and get basic grooming supplies and necessities for the next couple of weeks. If you do not have personal cred, your basic necessities will be noted and deducted from your first pay. Once you've got your uniform on and your personal effects in the bag, form a line at the instructor's office."

Devlin grabbed a set of uniform pants, underwear, and socks from his bundle. He looked up and saw people were shucking out of their clothes. He shrugged, dropped the stuff on his bed, and began to undress himself. He regarded the uniform. In order to consolidate the number of items, the IAA came up with a technological uniform. Made of carbon nanotube weave, the uniform was universal for all branches of the military. The only difference lay in the colors of the branches indicated in the trim. Black was the basic color, blue was Navy, red was Marines, and green for the Army.

As recruits, and therefore not a member of any particular branch, the uniform was black and gray. The technological part came in because the material itself didn't have any color but appeared due to light filters in the carbon nanotubes which could be changed by commands via the wearer's implant. This meant the uniform could be a basic Class B uniform with decorations color-coded the same way the uniform was, or the Dress Uniform with the decorations hung directly on the tunic.

They were damage-resistant, water-resistant, and could keep the wearer cool or warm depending on the environment. Not extremes to be sure, but good enough. There was also a chameleon feature for field use that was environ-reactive that could render the wearer hard to see both by eye and technological means.

As he dressed, he considered his teammates.

Kenyon was already putting her boots on.

McCarthy looked uncertain, like a calf caught in the electric fence at the plant. He caught Devlin's glance, and his face hardened as he turned slightly away and began to undress.

Devlin looked over and saw Baxter, her back to him, putting on her pants. He was just as glad his pants were on as he stared at a very firm, very round ass. She had long, shapely legs. In point of fact, she had a shapely everything from what he could tell. His mind started to wander as he watched the young woman dress.

His attention was abruptly drawn from the interesting vision of Recruit Private Baxter's backside to the very pitted, ugly, and rather red and angry face of Sergeant Pritchard, who stepped between him and the sight on the other side of the bay.

"Attention to detail is not staring at your buddy's ass! Do you understand, Private?" Pritchard bellowed.

Everyone in the room was suddenly looking at him, including Baxter. She suddenly straightened at Pritchard's yell. As she watched the tableau in front of her, along with everyone else, Devlin saw curiosity, then dawning understanding, and, finally, amusement.

He felt his face heat as he fought the urge to look at the drill sergeant, instead keeping his eyes straight ahead as he snapped to attention. He wanted nothing more than to shrink to infinitesimal size and slink away from the gazes of everyone in the room.

"Yes, Drill Sergeant!"

"What the hell were you looking at?"

"Nothing, Drill Sergeant!"

"Liar! I know what you were looking at and what you were thinking. Guess what? You ain't gonna! Ever! But for right now, I'm gonna give you something else to look at! Get down, Private, and look at the floor!"

Devlin heard snickers from some of the others in the bay. He didn't look up to see who it was.

"What the fark are the rest of you looking at? Do you all want to look at the floor?"

He heard activity start back up in the bay as everyone suddenly found their new uniforms endlessly fascinating.

"Start knocking them out, spoogehead! *One...two...*"

* * *

Thursday and Friday of Week Zero, as it was called by the cadre, was spent for the most part in the tender, loving care of the base medical staff.

The results of the respective recruits' physicals were back and genetically tailored treatments for those who had disorders of one sort or another were administered by autodoc. This was one of the main selling points of military service for citizens of the Empire on colony worlds and the new admissions to the Empire.

The military of the Avalonian Empire was heavily populated by the sons and daughters of the Protectorates and Client Worlds. With relations with the Nords deteriorating daily, and war seemingly inevitable, new worlds were flocking to the Avalonian Empire for succor.

The recruits were placed in an autodoc tank, which placed the patient in a controlled coma and the autodoc would begin its work. It started by inserting a customized nanite implant in the body with connections going to the brain and the blue force tracker already installed.

At the same time, the autodoc administered basic fixes for any genetic abnormalities present. Although the total fix might take time, it would be overseen and administered further by the nanipack.

When not in the tank, the recruits were given a day or two of light activity to keep them loose and mobile.

Devlin had some misgivings going into the autodoc for the first time. He could still swear his butt hurt. The technicians scanned his palms and retinas, consulted their pads, and then led him into a giant room with a large canister on a pedestal. He looked around and saw his fellow recruits conversing with technicians and then stripping down and getting into the tanks.

The technician working with him got his attention and directed him toward the machine.

"Wait a minute," Devlin said.

"It's all right, Private," the technician, a young woman with light brown skin and a warm smile, said soothingly. "You might not have had one of these on Caliban, but it's no big deal. I'm here to help you through your first interaction with the autodoc. We find that it helps if you see a friendly face when it's time to go into the tank.

"My name is Jazelle. You're going to lie down on the bed in the autodoc, it's going to verify your information and get final consent, and then you'll go to sleep for a few hours. When you wake up, you're going to feel rested and probably better than you've ever felt. I'll be here the whole time, and I'll monitor everything."

She guided him on to the platform, and, after he shucked out of his uniform, he stood in his skivvies and waited.

"Everything, Private," she said. He raised an eyebrow, blushing. Again, he wasn't a prude, but still…

She smiled at him understandingly. "Don't worry I'll try not to look, but if I do, and if I see something I haven't seen before, I do have a scalpel here," she said, and he blushed even more furiously. He hated feeling like a rube in the big city. She laughed warmly.

"Don't sweat it, Private. You're going to be fine."

Different worlds had different mores concerning nudity. Most of the Avalonian worlds were generally indifferent to various degrees of public nudity, but the colony worlds ran the gamut from "eh," to "oh, hell no!" He had heard the Nords had a fun time between their normally permissive Nordic Asatru worlds and the more body modest Islamic factions. He wondered how in the world that ever got resolved, *if* it got resolved.

He bent down and removed his shorts and got into the tank. He positioned himself on the autodoc gurney and covered himself as well as possible.

Jazelle looked into the canister with a completely impassive face that Devlin was just as completely sure was false, gave him a wink, and said, "See you in a few hours, Private." The canister closed with a slight hiss and click, leaving him momentarily in the dark.

A second later, the canister was suffused with a pale blue light. A voice came through a speaker somewhere near his head. "Devlin, Nikolai N. Rank, private. Home world, Caliban in Prospero System.

Is that information correct?" The voice sounded human, but it had the emotionless expression of a smart machine.

"Y-y-yes," he stammered. He still wasn't completely sure about any of this.

"Thank you. You are having a basic military nanite implant placed today. That will take most of your session. You will also receive genetic sequencing for a recessive trait that puts you at risk for heart damage when you begin to senesce. You will receive nanite plants to replace two molars and one bicuspid that you have lost within the last three years. The new teeth will take a few days to completely grow and implant, so you need to be aware of some discomfort. Your technician will review this information with you when you exit the autodoc. Do you understand the procedures that you will receive and consent to their being performed?"

"Do I have a choice?" Devlin asked, surprised.

"Every citizen has a choice in the amount and content of treatment performed by Avalonian Military Medical. However, be advised that refusing medical treatment can be viewed as abrogation of your military enlistment contract," the machine replied tonelessly.

"So, I'll take that as a 'no,'" Devlin said wryly.

"Every citizen has a choice in the…"

"Got it, Doc. I consent to the treatments. Just get it over with."

"As you wish, Private. Please standby. I am administering anesthesia now."

"So, how fast will I go to sleep, and for how long?" Devlin asked.

"Private Devlin, you have already been asleep in the tank for four hours and are now ready to go back to duty," the doc said as the autodoc plastron slid back and opened.

Jazelle stood on the dais by the tank and offered her hand to help him out of the tank. As he swung upright and placed his feet on the ground, he took a moment to test his weight.

He felt good, like he'd gotten a really good night's sleep.

"Get your clothes on, Private, and meet me at my terminal," Jazelle said. She turned and stepped off the dais and went to a data terminal at the foot of the tank.

Devlin dressed quickly and was stamping into his boots as he made his way over to the terminal with Jazelle. She hit a button and his wrist comp chimed, indicating a file transfer.

"You have received nanite implants to replace your missing or damaged teeth. They will finish growing in about three days. Until then, your jaw at those sites may be a little sore or sensitive, which is perfectly normal. Try to eat softer foods until then. Please try to avoid getting them knocked out."

"Oh, I'll certainly try," Devlin replied. "Is that all?"

"Yes, Private." As warm as she had been before he went in the tank, this version of Jazelle was as emotionless and toneless as the autodoc.

* * *

Sunday morning it was announced that religious services were offered and that any who wished to attend only needed to tell the transport driver what religious belief they belonged to. Devlin checked his wrist comp to see what services were offered and was surprised, and a little amused, to see that Asatru and Islam were actually offered.

I guess whatever floats you, he thought.

Devlin wasn't a religious person. His mother had been a churchgoer of sorts when Devlin was small. She had gone to a little congregational church and had taken him along. He couldn't remember much before his ma contracted the plague, other than the lady with whom he had been left for religious "classes" had been nice enough, though none of it had stuck.

As a boy, he spent most of his time trying to get out of going to classes or any kind of structured environment, much preferring the rough and tumble existence of the street kids. They had structure; it just wasn't the same. And, really, that was only when there was a group of them. For the most part, Devlin tended to have one or two friends, and he left it at that.

Devlin spent his morning getting his locker to the condition he figured was required. He rolled his underclothes and socks the way he was shown and stowed them in the drawer of his locker.

The folks who were religious were gone for most of the morning, returning shortly before lunch. After lunch, the squad leaders gathered everyone together and informed them that each squad had a portion of the barracks and environs to take care of. Second Squad had the Central Area on the first floor and "No Man's Land," the section of hallway that housed the cadre offices and some living areas for the drill sergeants. It was here that Devlin learned a series of rules that had apparently been in existence for eternity that had to do with how recruits looked at the world. If it moves, salute it. If it doesn't move and it's inside, clean it. If it's outside, paint it.

Holy Hell, he thought as he mopped the hallway outside the sergeant major's door. He was mopping a floor. He was sticking a pole with stuff on one end into a bucket of soapy water and slopping the water on the floor. Then he was supposed to wring out the mop and dry up the excess water on the floor. Who did that?

He lived in a society where man traveled between stars in days. Medical science could cure just about anything; he had little machines in his body waiting patiently to fix any damage. His clothing could change to match his surroundings and also protect him from blunt force trauma. There were weapons that could create a mini-black hole, and here he was mopping a floor. The mind boggled.

After he finished, Tamman followed him down the hall with a machine that put a mirror sheen on the floor. As he watched the big guy, Devlin wondered, not for the last time, why they didn't just use that damned thing to begin with.

* * * * *

Chapter Eight

Training began in earnest the second week, and time started to blur. They awoke at the butt crack of dawn and bedded down seemingly ten minutes before it was time to get up and do it all again. Devlin fervently believed he was going to meet himself coming in or going out of the barracks sooner or later.

The first couple of weeks had been brutal. From the moment they woke up, to the time they were finally allowed to put their heads on pillows, they were hounded by the instructors. Physical training was constant, they were dropped for any infraction and they ran everywhere. They traversed an obstacle course designed to simulate combat conditions every other day after breakfast. They went to classes that were so boring it was an effort to stay awake, and if you were caught napping, you did the rest of the class at front-leaning rest.

Then they found out on day one of the second week that "good enough" was never good enough for the instructors. They had all made their racks up and gone to chow as they had the previous week. When they got back to their barracks, however, every last bunk and every last locker was upended and dumped; the sheets, blankets, locker contents, everything was scattered throughout the barracks bay as though a grav bomb had exploded.

They spent the next hour gathering everything back up and stowing it properly, all under the abusive hounding of the drills. Devlin wondered where they had found the people to become drill sergeants; the last he'd heard, they didn't have insane asylums anymore. Maybe they got them on loan from the Nords. Still, the recruits had reacted, adapted, and sought to overcome as best they could.

Devlin fell into his rack four weeks into training and contemplated going home and turning himself over to Old Man Martin. He was certain that there was no way the gangster could make him feel more pain than he felt at that moment.

The lights were out. Everyone was stumbling to their racks, except for the few still in the head, wiping everything down. Snores could already be heard. He wasn't sure how they did that. He hated whoever it was, though. Devlin lay in his bunk, trying to determine if it was possible to die from exhaustion. He wasn't sure he'd ever been this tired or sore

"Devlin," a low voice whispered in his ear. They shook his shoulder. "Devlin!"

"What the hell do you want?" He wasn't in the mood.

"You can't sleep…"

"What d'you mean I can't go to sleep?" he protested, rolling over. It was Baxter. "Dammit! I'm tired, I'm sore, and I'm really past the point of giving a rat's rear thruster. I'm not looking to do a McCarthy, but I will sure as shit take on anyone who says I can't go the hell to sleep in my own damn rack when I don't have any duty. I've done my duty. For King and Country, or planet, or whatever the hell it is I'm supposed to do it for, and by Gods, I am going to go to sleep!" He rolled back over.

"Devlin!!" He felt a hand on his shoulder again. He balled up his fist and prepared to do battle.

"What?"

"You're in the wrong bunk!"

* * *

Each of the platoons were polled as groups and decided upon nicknames and mascots.

Third Platoon had taken the name Third Herd and someone had drawn, not too badly, a group of stampeding bulls, complete with fiery eyes and steam or smoke coming from their nostrils.

Fourth Platoon had decided on Deadly Fourth. They had drawn a bleeding number four with a dagger in it.

The debate had been spirited in Second Platoon. It had come down to Kenyon who, after she had jokingly put forth the suggestion Glitter Ponies and had everyone in the platoon threaten bodily harm, had more seriously nominated Wild Deuces as their nickname. Jonesy, who was a history buff, had thrown out Hellions, in honor of an Old Earth Armor Regiment he had said called themselves Hell on Wheels. It went back and forth, not without some heat, between the red-headed squad leader and the Helenian. Cooler heads finally prevailed and Hellions it was.

Finally, they decided on a picture of a little red devil with a pitchfork. However, apparently the well ran dry for First Platoon. The morning after the Sergeant Major had instructed the company to pick team names, First Platoon showed up at formation with their name already picked out. "First Platoon Maddogs! All present and accounted for!" Gartlan, the platoon leader yelled in answer to the command to report.

At the name, the platoon answered with "*Woof! Woof! Woof!*"

The sergeant major grinned, something the recruits almost never saw, and when they did it was universally considered a bad thing. This time however, he just grinned. The grin faded as the other teams reported in as usual.

The recruits in First Platoon looked smug as they marched first into the chow hall past the other platoons who were busy in the front-leaning rest position.

As the artwork for a little devil, a dagger-stabbed four and a stampeding herd went up, someone in First Platoon heard Poole was an *artiste*.

Poole was unceremoniously dragged out of his bed on Sunday evening and informed by Sergeant Stark that he was to paint a ferocious, snarling Mad Dog on the door to the First Platoon training area where everyone could see it.

"But, Sergeant," Poole tried to protest, "I don't draw…"

"You've done everything else, you'll do this one, or you won't be able to do anything until the nanites finish healing you. You got it?"

"But…"

"You got paint, now paint!"

"Yes, Drill Sergeant."

Monday morning dawned, Poole having finished his Magnum Opus a bare forty minutes earlier. On his way to the CQ desk to clean his area, Devlin glanced at the training area door.

He stood in the corridor for a full minute taking in every nuance of color and shape, the shadowing, and even backed away to change angles to make sure he got it all.

Then the laughter started, and he went back to the stairwell.

"Pony!" he called up.

Arnette was on the second-floor landing and relayed the yell down the hall. A moment later, Nicki Kenyon showed up at the door to the Second Platoon section of the barracks. Her brows furrowed at the sight of his unrestrained mirth. "What's up, Dev?"

"You've gotta see this!"

* * *

At morning formation, everyone in the company had smiles on their faces. More than a few were still giggling. All except First Platoon, that is. Most of them just stared at their boots.

Drill Sergeant Stark was beet red and staring grav missiles at Poole who looked too tired to really give a damn. He'd spent all night doing what he knew was the best he could do. It didn't mean a thing and he did not give a damn.

The sergeant major came out of the company area and seemed to be coughing. At least he was covering his mouth and his shoulders were shaking.

After a moment he regained his composure, and yelled, "Company! Ten Hut!"

Everyone snapped to attention.

"Platoons, report!"

The platoon leader started to say "First Platoon Mad..." but the entire company shouted over him "Mad Pigs!" and the squeals of tortured porcine farm animals being slaughtered, or otherwise molested, drowned out the rest of First Platoon's report.

* * *

Devlin regarded himself in the mirror as he applied depilatory agent to his face. In the reflection he saw the young men and women of Second Platoon entering and exiting the showers behind him, and he heard the general laughter and grab-ass going on. He wondered if having guys and girls in the same facilities was a really good idea. He was damned if he could figure out how to ignore certain autonomic reflexes.

Devlin and the rest of the recruits had changed in the weeks since their induction. Many of them had been healthy to start with, modern medical and whatnot ensured that, and nobody had been grossly out of shape, but they had all gone through a metamorphosis.

Now they were sleek and muscular machines. The constant running more or less meant they could now keep a ground-eating pace for an hour or more. Their arms and torsos no longer had the slack look of a civilian; it was chiseled muscle. And they were hot as hell, it didn't matter what your preferences were.

Shower time was an amusing time of the day on a number of different levels. It was also a frustrating one…on a number of different levels.

The night before, Higgs strutted through the showers to the catcalls and whistles of men and women alike. She yelled, "Thank you, Drill Sergeant Miller!" loudly enough that the staff sergeant came out of his office on the other end of the bay, stalked to the latrine and showers, and demanded "For what?"

The lithe, young woman had come out of the shower wearing nothing but a towel and a grin. Everyone at the sinks in the open bathroom were studiously *not* looking her way as she flaunted herself, flexing muscular legs, and strutting before the doorway to the showers. A couple people stepped even closer to the sink.

"Why, for all of the physical training you, the sergeant major, and the rest have subjected us to!" she said, pirouetting on bare feet. "I was once a dumpy little civilian and couldn't get a date because of all the surgery queens with their firm breasts and tight little butts, not one of which they were born with. They were constantly taking all the fun partners and leaving us not-so-pretty, not-so-rich girls with...whatever."

She pouted mockingly, then suddenly brightened. She adopted a stance reminiscent of a holo-hostess advertising some product or another.

"But now, because of you and the rest of the cadre, and the Imperial Military Exercise Program, I'll be able to grab who I want, sling them over my shoulder, and take them back to my cave!"

Hoots and whistles came from the recruits as she proceeded to pantomime things generally not mentioned in "polite" company. She stopped again and reassumed the hostess pose.

"But wait..." she started.

"There's more!!!!" Everyone in the room, finished with her, and the laughter continued.

"Oh yes, there's more! If one of the little bitches who used to make my life hell ever were to say anything, well, let's just say I have a few responses." Her "pose" segued into an elbow strike and back kick. Which drew even more catcalls and whistles.

Miller started to say something as the general hilarity continued to escalate. It seemed to Devlin that he was truly stuck for something to do or say. He opened his mouth, closed it, then, barely hiding a grin and a laugh, he managed to growl out, "As you were! Finish your showers!" and beat a hasty retreat as the nearly naked, laughing female killer-in-training was joined by her comrades in a jocular, violent mockery of a high society ball, except with water and soap.

* * * * *

Chapter Nine

"This is going to sting some, Private."

The technician, an attractive lady whose nameplate read, "Jazelle," was detached and clinical. Devlin had interacted with her the day he had his genetic workup and implants installed. She was just as detached and clinical then, too. Devlin was beginning to think she was just a hologram being run by a Turing computer.

As the nanite spray hit the laceration in his scalp, he nearly yelped, his hands gripping the station chair with whitened knuckles.

* * *

The day had, as they usually did, started with sound and fury signifying "Get up!" courtesy of the drill sergeants. Devlin and the rest of Second Platoon rousted out, cleaned the barracks, made their beds, and got the uniform of the day dialed into their clothes.

After a quick formation, they double-timed it to the mess hall—they double-timed everywhere, rain or shine—which for a place that had on-demand weather, rain was just being mean in Devlin's opinion. The company ran everywhere. Today they were heading to the obstacle course, which meant a hoo-ah good time climbing over obstacles, trying to dodge stunner drones, and generally being crapped on by the drill instructors.

They dropped their gear outside of the mess hall, each person setting down their packs, helmets, and stacking their rifles. Each platoon detailed one person to stand guard over the equipment while everyone else double-timed into the mess hall for breakfast. That morning, Second Platoon detailed Lett to stand guard.

They lined up, and with each platoon's guidon bearer leading the way, they jogged up the walks to the mess hall. That's when everything went sideways for Niko Devlin.

Second Platoon's guidon had a little problem. The tip, which looked like a heavy brass spearhead, was loose. And on that particular morning, the guidon became entangled on a tree branch overhanging the sidewalk. Both tree branch and guidon bent back under the momentum of being carried while running until something had to give, which in this particular case on this particular morning was the guidon tip.

The only warning Devlin had that something was amiss was Lett yelling "Incoming!" and ducking. The next thing Devlin knew he had a fire burning on his scalp, and pain caused his vision to swim.

"Devlin's on the deck!" someone yelled, as Devlin grabbed his scalp with both hands trying to assuage the fiery pain in his head with pressure.

"Aw damn!" was about all Devlin could manage to say for the first minute or so, until the drill sergeants appeared.

The drill instructors kept asking, "What's the matter, recruit?" as they tried to pry his hands off his head. Devlin resisted until they overpowered him and brought his hands down.

"Well, I'll be," Miller said as they saw the darkening stain from the blood coursing out of the young recruit's scalp.

"Am I bleeding?" Devlin asked, though he was pretty sure he knew the answer.

"Yeah..." came the reply.

"Aw, damn!" Devlin moaned in pain.

They helped him to his feet and got him into the mess hall. Normally bustling with multiple companies getting their morning chow, even at that early hour, everything stopped the second Devlin came through the door.

It was a truism in basic training that the drill instructors are functional psychopaths. Further, that the military intentionally sorted for these types of people, and, rather than punish perfectly good enemies, the military sicced them on unsuspecting recruits.

However, as their time in basic went on, recruits came to realize that DIs weren't really allowed to do all that much—what they were allowed to do was bad enough—but they couldn't actually kill you. That did not, however, keep experienced recruits from perpetuating the functional psychopath meme for the newbies.

Thus, it was, that when Recruit Private Niko Devlin was brought into the busy chow hall, all eyes in the facility fell upon him and, more specifically, his profusely bleeding head wound. More than one new recruit whispered, "What happened to him?" And for each one who was asked, another, more experienced, recruit would reply, "Drill sergeant got pissed and hit him." Thereby, indelibly imprinting the horrible scene on the young recruit and ensuring fear and trepidation for weeks to come.

* * *

"You're all done, Private." Jazelle said tonelessly, bringing Devlin back to the present. She stood up and stripped off purple gloves. "Your scalp is repaired, but please keep it clean for the next twenty-four hours. You may resume regular duty at this time. Please be more careful."

Devlin decided not to argue that it wasn't his fault the bloody spear tip had come rocketing through the air and perforated his scalp. He figured she didn't care.

"Thank you, ma'am," he replied, and went outside to wait for the driver to take him to rendezvous with his unit in the field.

* * *

The rest of Devlin's day was spent amusing the training cadre. They thought it hilarious to yell, "Duck!" and have Devlin drop at various times during the day. This did nothing except cement Devlin's view that all drill instructors were assholes.

When he wasn't dropping to the deck every few minutes, he and the rest of Alpha Company familiarized themselves with the Simulated Fire Training Facility. Each of the recruits was given virtual reality training helmets and adaptors for their rifles. They were taught how to properly sight and fire their weapons under simulated conditions. This would help them develop the proper sight pictures and stances necessary for when they were given real ammunition.

Devlin liked this training. He had excellent hand-eye coordination, and it took him only a few tries before getting the rifle to snap up into the right sight picture became familiar and easy. He even got to the point where he could drop to the deck when one of the drills yelled, "Duck," and then stand with the rifle on command.

That's not to say that he was superlative. Some, like little Anastasia Cho, seemed like they were born with rifles in their hands. She barely missed a cue.

"Friendly fire isn't!" McClellan intoned as he walked through the facility watching each of the recruits. "You can have a really bad day if your enemy is competent or your buddy is incompetent—McCarthy! Booger hook off the bang button! Tamman! Keep your muzzle pointed at the target area! Hey, Devlin! Duck!"

* * *

Devlin and the rest of Second Platoon dragged their tired bodies into the barracks bay and collapsed.

"Oh, Gods!" Arnette said as she hung her pack on the end of her bunk. "I'm not sure what was worse. The double-time out or the truck ride back. You'd think ground effect vehicles would ride smooth. I think it was deliberate; my ovaries hurt."

"At least they aren't outside your body." Atwell moaned. "I don't think I'll ever be able to have children."

"I don't think that will be an issue," Baxter chuckled. "The way you shoot, you'll never hit the target area, anyway." The group chuckled as Atwell started to look indifferent, then grinned sheepishly.

"Got me there. Maybe I can get a job as an artilleryman. A bullet is aimed. Artillery is more or less 'to whom it may concern.'" More chuckles.

"Just don't forget to *duck*!" Baxter shouted throwing a shirt at Devlin who dodged it easily. "Oh, my Gods! I thought you were going to die the way you were bleeding all over the chow hall."

"Yeah, well getting hit wasn't half as bad as getting the nanite spray to close my nog," Devlin retorted, picking up the shirt and throwing it back. "That shit stings. I heartily discommend it if you can avoid it."

"Did you see the look on the newbies' faces when they heard Devlin had pissed off one of the drill sergeants?" Jones laughed, wheezing.

"Oh yeah!" Baxter said. "Oh, my Gods!" she exclaimed with a look of feigned innocence. "What happened to *him*?"

"Drill sergeant got pissed off and hit him!" The rest of the group laughed. Devin laughed but didn't really think it all that funny. Nor did he think the whole "duck" thing as hilarious as everyone else did. And besides, that shit stung.

"All right!" Miller shouted over the din as he walked into the bay, breaking up the laughter. "Get your shit sorted out, and get to formation for evening chow. You have ten minutes!"

* * * * *

Chapter Ten

The platoons got thinner. People quit...lots of people.

It started the second week. About two days into the actual training, one of the recruits from First Platoon, a kid named Perchenko, quit.

They had dropped for some stupid shit, and a sergeant said something on the order of, "Ah, come on, you little pansysniffers. Is it too much for you? All you gotta do is quit, and all this is over!"

All of a sudden, Perchenko stood up and said, "All right. I'm done."

Stark yelled, "Get back down, Recruit!"

But the boy just said, "Fark you, I quit."

Everything stopped. The drill instructor's head swiveled around like it was on an autoturret.

Instantly, one of the other sergeants arrived and walked the boy off.

By the time they got back to the barracks that afternoon, his bunk was clear and his locker was empty.

From there, the drill sergeants intensified their efforts. They drove everyone mercilessly, producing vomit-inducing pain parties for the slightest infraction, quizzing in the chow line, browbeating, hazing. The barracks were generally trashed once, if not twice, a day.

And through it all, they repeated the litany, "All you have to do is quit, and it'll all stop."

Devlin knew he couldn't quit, and the more they harassed them, the more he became determined to gut it out. Which just seemed to attract the sergeants to him. The more they pushed, the more he put his head down and did his thing.

"Come on, Devlin!" McClellan hounded him one day in the tenth week. "No one wants you here. You don't want to be here. Just quit!"

The obstacle course was about team work as well as individual physical stamina. There were obstacles that would "kill" you if you took too long getting over them, and the recruits found out early that only team work could get people past the obstacles fast enough to keep the drones from homing in on you.

Devlin was distracted. He got the hand up from Kuzma and Atwell who then used the momentum to drop to the far side of the wall. Except they didn't let go quick enough and Devlin bobbled Katsaros into the mud. The drone caught the recruit as he was trying to jump up for a second try.

The sergeant major hauled the stunned Katsaros out of the muck and dumped him on the ground. His face was inarticulate with rage as he sat on the bank of the mud pit recovering from the stun blast.

"Devlin! You just farked your buddy! Get down here!" He motioned for the other recruits to go by while he administered a personalized pain party.

Devlin dropped down and hustled over to the drill instructor and the slowly awakening recruit.

"Just what was your problem, Recruit?"

"Drill Sergeant, I got…"

"You got nothing but three answers, recruit! Which one are you using?"

"No excuse, Sergeant Major!"

"Godsdamn right! Get down and beat your face!"

Devlin started to drop, but McClellan stopped him.

"In the mud, shithead. You dropped your buddy in the mud, you drop in the mud!"

Every time he went down, the mud got everywhere, into his mouth, his nose, his clothes were soaked, and he even felt it seeping into his boots. He felt the drill instructor's boot on his back forcing him one more time into the mud.

"Just quit, Devlin, all you're gonna do is get yourself killed and probably someone else, too." He said it quietly, calmly, almost brotherly. "You got no friends. Even your battle buddies hate you. You can't make your rack, your locker sucks, you're a lousy recruit. And now you're a buddy-screwer too, aren't you? Just quit."

The words stung at him; they ate at him. He knew they were true, but he also knew they weren't.

He couldn't quit if he wanted to survive. These assholes didn't know what it was like to have to do something to survive. He bet McClellan, in his pretty uniform, had never had to eat something putrid to keep from starving.

It would be so easy to quit, but Devlin knew that was a death sentence.

He wasn't going to quit, even if it killed him.

"Ain't! Gonna! Quit! Drill…Sergeant!" he blurted out from the mud.

"Nobody wants you here!" the drill instructor bellowed.

"Don't. Give. A. Shit!" Devlin panted, spitting out mud.

"You'd better give a shit, recruit, because one of these days you're gonna need a teammate, and they ain't gonna have your back!"

"Yes, Drill Sergeant!" Devlin cried on the upside of a rep.

"Stop! Recover!" McClellan commanded. Devlin got up. "Get out of my sight."

He went over to Katsaros and offered a hand, "Dammit, I'm sorry, Kat."

Katsaros glared at him but took his hand. "Don't ever drop me again, mate," he said quietly. "I'll kill you." And he walked off.

* * * * *

Chapter Eleven

Monday of the eighth week, he was woken by Anne Marie Decker, the Fire Watch roving patrol, told to get his shit on, and get down to the CQ's desk.

There, he found McCarthy, Tamman, Baxter, MacBain, five other guys he didn't know well, and another female. Miller was waiting for them.

"You're all on KP this morning," the staff sergeant said cheerfully. "Gonna be slinging the slop for all your buddies. So all the abuse you've heaped on them during their turn, it's all on you now." He chuckled evilly. "Let's go."

They followed the staff sergeant until they reached the mess facility.

"We're not going to be cooking, are we Staff Sergeant?" Baxter asked. "I mean, I can cook eggs if I have to…"

"Don't get your skivvies in a wad, Baxter." Miller said. "You're just doing grunt work. Slinging the shit, cleaning tables, and shit like that. They have people who can actually cook doing the rest."

"Fark, what a relief," someone in the group said, somewhat *sotto voce*. Everyone chuckled.

They entered the mess hall through a back door, and Miller spoke with a staff sergeant who then took his charges into the kitchen area.

"I need one person to clean pots and pans back here—and before you ask, as everyone does—yes, we could use a machine to do it, but where the fark is the fun in that? Same thing with everything else we do here, or haven't you figured that out yet? All this is for your fun and enjoyment. Don't you feel privileged?" He grinned mirthlessly. "Cleaning pots, scrubbing tables, mopping the head, all these things are to either get you to quit or get you to learn that sometimes you have to do things the hard way—and when you don't, appreciate that you don't. We know it won't stop the bitching, but it's a tradition older than space travel."

Devlin chose pots and pans, mainly because it was solitary work. Even at this point, he'd just as soon not be any closer to people than he had to.

One of the permanent mess workers, or cranks, came back and instructed Devlin how to situate the sinks and where all the cleaning supplies were.

"We're gonna run them through the sterilizers so nobody gets sick if you fark it up," said the crank. "But don't fark it up cuz we'll know…and you don't want us on your ass."

Devlin shrugged internally. He wouldn't botch anything like this anyway. Screwing himself in minor ways to keep from 'standing out,' where someone might get the mistaken impression that he was 'gung-ho' wasn't a hard thing to do, but he didn't do it when someone else could be affected.

He ran water and sanitizer into the proper sinks, got a load of towels and rags, and waited for his first load.

He didn't wait very long. The kitchen crew had been working since before he woke up that morning, preparing the food that would be consumed by all of the people who used that particular mess facility for breakfast.

He watched the others from his group start to move around the mess facility, wiping tables, stacking trays, and filling beverage dispensers. He saw Baxter, Tamman, and one of the other guys donning plastic aprons and standing by an open window with a chute coming through it and going into a washing machine.

"Here's you first load, Private," one of the mess cranks said, pushing a large cartload of absolutely *huge* pots. "Get 'em clean and stack 'em over on the racks labeled the same as the pots."

Devlin looked and saw there were numbers on each of the pots. He then looked in the direction the mess crank had pointed and saw rack after rack of shelves with numbers and letters on each.

"Got it, Corporal," he replied, taking a pot with both hands. It was almost a half meter wide at the mouth and still had stuff in it. It wasn't heavy per se, but it definitely had some weight, and as wide as it was, it was a little unwieldy.

He took it to a chute marked Garbage and Waste Food and proceeded to empty the dregs of the pot into the chute. It wasn't precisely easy, considering the pot was much larger than the chute opening. As hard as he tried not to make a mess, one was made anyway.

Ah well, he thought. *I'll just clean it up as soon as I get a break in the pots.*

Which didn't happen for about two hours. As quickly as Devlin got a cart of pots cleaned and stacked, it seemed like there was another waiting for him. And another.

Pretty soon, Devlin realized that his hands were wrinkled from the constant exposure to the water and his uniform was damp, but he didn't slow down. He got into a rhythm. Grab pot, sixteen steps, lift, rest, scrape, turn, seventeen steps, plunge pot into liquid. Grab brush, scrub. Put brush back, rinse. Inspect. Grab rag, wipe out anything he missed. Rinse. Sanitize. Fifty-five steps to the racks. Stack to dry. Seventy-two steps to cart. Grab pot, wash, rinse, repeat.

Devlin had never had grits before; maize wasn't a crop that grew well on Caliban. It had been a rice world, which was one of the reasons why the Kyoro-Saram people of the RussKor Federation had colonized it. It was very much like the climate on Earth. As a result,

Devlin had never come across the porridge-like product before, and, after scrubbing grits-laden pots for two-plus hours, he wasn't sure he ever wanted to again. The longer they sat, the worse they began to smell. Fortunately, with some of the other pungent breakfast pots that had come back to be washed, Devlin had lost much of his sense of smell.

When the mess crank came back into the pots area, Devlin had just finished his fifth cart of pots. The front of his shirt was soaked, and he was wrinkled up to the elbow.

The mess crank snorted when he saw Devlin. "Get into your work, huh?" he said, somewhat amused. Devlin just shrugged minutely. The corporal looked around. "Get that mess cleaned up at the garbage chute so nobody kills themselves, then get up front and get some chow."

Devlin ate with gusto, even though the food was a little cold and greasy by the time he brought up the end of the breakfast line. He was the last person through and Baxter and Tamman were starting to break down the serving area under the guidance of the mess hall NCO. Some other mess cooks in chef's uniforms came into the hall through the back entrance while he was eating. He assumed they were the lunch/dinner crew.

McCarthy was wiping down tables, badly. Devlin didn't have it in him to give the NCO the heads up. He figured that situation would just work itself out.

When Devlin returned to the pots area, he found two more carts waiting for him. He looked over at the rear cooking station where someone was puttering around getting things together for lunch service. His eyebrow raised when he saw a Koryo-Saram woman working the grills. She was busy chopping poultry and red meat into chunks and throwing them on separate grills. Even from where he was, he could hear the meat sizzling, and though he had just eaten, his mouth began to water.

The Koryo grills on Caliban had been one of his favorite places to hang out as a kid. He usually tried to wrangle a bulgogi off one of the vendors. A few of them would even wink at him and toss him a skewer or two.

He remembered one occasion where he got his head rapped for trying to lift a skewer from Mister Pak's little outdoor grill when he was twelve. The old man had looked just at the wrong time, snagged Devlin by the arm and dragged him home, thumping him on the head and cursing at him the whole time. Devlin knew some Koryo, a mishmash of old Earth Korean and Russian and realized about halfway home that the old man's heart wasn't in it. Devlin listened to what the old man was nattering about and realized he wasn't in trouble for stealing, he was being scolded for getting caught.

When he got home, Victoria met them at the door to the apartment and listened to the elderly man explain what had happened, and she apologized. That probably hurt Devlin more than getting his head smacked. He hated that his ma had to apologize for her son's bad behavior. He felt ashamed. Which was probably the point.

Victoria, after the old Koryo had left, said nothing but sent Devlin to his room. For three long hours, Devlin stared at the walls. He considered what he thought Mr. Pak had tried to tell him, the old scoundrel, and he was that, Devlin knew. He'd heard stories. Nothing bad, but the elder Pak had some humorous stories from when he was a boy about herd animals with questionable brands. The old guy didn't think there was anything wrong with doing what you needed, but for Dokkeb's sake, *don't get caught*. Devlin would take that lesson to heart, and he only ever screwed up one other time. But that time, Dokkeb made his mischief, because Devlin wound up meeting Justiciar Peter Jadwidzik.

That evening, Victoria called her wayward boy out for dinner, and, sitting on the table was a basket of Mr. Pak's bulgogi. They ate so much that evening, they nearly got sick. *The fact that Victoria never spoke of the incident again probably owed more to her failing memory due to the plague than anything,* Devlin thought.

A woman's voice cut across the room and interrupted Devlin's contemplation.

"Can you help me?" she asked pointing to a large stew pot.

Devlin hurried over and helped the woman place the heavy pot of water on a burner of a stove. He turned and smiled at her, and she nodded at him. He started to leave but slipped and started to fall.

He felt a grip like iron catch his damp sleeve and steady him. He looked into blue eyes, a rather odd sign of the Koryo-Saram peoples that inhabited worlds like Caliban, Ariel, and a few others on the rim.

"KamSahamnida, Manim," Devlin said, inclining his head. *Thank you, ma'am.*

The woman's face lit like a nova. She began to speak rapidly in Koryo, at Devlin.

"You know Koryo. Who are you, where are you from?"

"I know some Koryo, ma'am. I am from Caliban. Why I am here is rather obvious."

"Caliban!" she said switching to Standard. "I have cousins on that world. I was there when I was a girl. So very…"

"It still is," Devlin said dryly. Caliban wasn't very much of anything. The most that could be said for it was that things grew, and, except for the plague, it didn't actively try to kill its inhabitants.

She laughed. "I did not wish to give offense, but Caliban is not a pretty planet."

Devlin shrugged. "It's not so bad. There are pretty places there. You just have to go looking for them."

Suddenly he felt homesick. For his mom, Old Mr. Pak, his job. The weight and enormity of why he was there slammed into him like a weight.

"I must go back to work," he muttered. He turned to go.

Again, he felt the iron grip on his arm. He turned back and saw her looking intently into his face.

"I have made you miss your home, yes?" she asked.

Unbidden tears welled up in the young man's eyes. Mutely, he nodded. Her lips pressed together, and she nodded as well.

"We will talk. In a little while. I must work, and so must you. It is good to hear someone talk to me in Koryo." She smiled warmly and turned back to the ovens. Devlin went back to the sinks.

About ten minutes later, the old woman brought him some buldak. "Be careful, it is hot. It also achieved thermonuclear fusion about fifteen minutes ago from the peppers," she said, grinning.

He blew on the meat for a few moments; he could already smell the spices from the marinade. It was strong, pungent…wonderful. He took a piece with his fingertips. Although it was cooler than it had been, it still burnt his fingers. He quickly popped the chicken into his mouth, rolling it around quickly from one side to the other to keep from burning his mouth.

The woman started to say something, then shrugged imperceptibly and shook her head.

It was so good, and hot, and spicy. She was right, it could power a starship. He felt a little bit of sweat start on his forehead from the piquancy of the meat.

"Mas-iss-eoyo," he said, swallowing the morsel. *It's delicious.* "KamSahamnida."

"You are most welcome." She smiled again, her eyes wrinkling. "It is not so often I get to talk with someone from the People. I get homesick sometimes as well," she said. "I have a few minutes. You will work, I will sit here, and we will talk."

Devlin nodded gratefully. Just having someone he could to talk to was almost like home, and was appreciated. Every time he walked by the comm terminals and saw a recruit talking to people back home, he grew a little lonelier. He didn't feel like he could comm Chief Justiciar Jadwidzik. And, to be honest, he didn't really have any friends back on Caliban anymore. He had nothing and no one.

Therefore, he talked with the old sous chef about Caliban and the job he had been laid off from, but he very carefully didn't tell her about the events that caused him to enlist.

"And your family, Devlin?" the chef, who had introduced herself as Vitaliya Gim, asked. She saw him tense, then relax. Without facing her, he shook his head.

"My father is—was—military. He disappeared before I was born. He never got a chance to marry my ma."

"And your ma?"

"She's still alive, but she contracted the plague when I was five."

Vitaliya sucked in. "I am so very sorry, young one," she said.

"It is what it is, Ahjumma," the boy replied over his shoulder.

"How very Russian of you," Vitaliya muttered wryly. She rose and put her hand on his shoulder. "We will talk more, I think. Later. During lunch. Maybe talking will help—not better than vodka, but then we don't have any of that." He looked over his shoulder and she grinned at him. "We do what we must with what we have, young man."

They both went back to work.

* * *

Devlin hit the pillow and rolled onto his back. He stared up at the empty bunk above him. Poole had been in that bunk until two days ago. They had gone to breakfast, and as close as Devlin could figure, Poole had rung out during the meal. He hadn't shown up for the formation after lunch, and his bunk was empty when they got back that evening from the field.

He thought about the lunchtime he had spent with Vitaliya. In retrospect, he realized she hadn't said much. She had merely asked him how training was going and had let him talk. He supposed he had told her what he would have told someone at home if he had someone. It felt good to confide in another, to tell someone his adventures, little screw-ups, the funny things he had seen. All the while she listened to him and smiled, nodding every once in a while, and sipped her tea.

If anyone had seen the two talking, no one made an issue of it. He was glad, although at first, he'd been concerned that the mess crank would get bent out of shape over one of his drudges or one of his chefs talking to a recruit. He wasn't sure why the NCO hadn't, but he wasn't going to complain.

At the end of his lunchtime, the silver-haired sous chef had stood up, walked him back to his pots and pans, gave him a peck on the cheek, and told him to drive on. Then she went back to cooking.

Although they interacted once or twice more that evening, Devlin never found enough time to have any further conversation with the lady. She was gone by the time he finished the pots, pans, and dishes and the general mess hall cleaning for the night.

With a sense of sadness, he walked back to the barracks that night with the others. His longing for home was a palpable lump in his chest. Bax had tried to talk to him, but he blew her off. He mumbled something about needing to think, and she left him alone.

He looked over at where her bunk was in the bay. He felt bad about being rude; he'd apologize tomorrow. *Damn,* he thought. *Why did it have to be so difficult? You know why,* he told himself. *If you hadn't lost your temper, none of this would have happened. You'd be home right now with your ma and everything would be fine.*

Bull, the other portion of his brain retorted. *Ma would still be about half gone, and you'd still be scrambling for work, or drugs to help her, or whatever.* He looked up into the darkness, heard the breathing and snores of the people around him. People who had someone back home. People who hadn't lost everything they loved. He felt the tears come, hot and angry. He clenched his fists. He turned over, and, as his face touched the pillow, the sobs started. He fell asleep as he cried himself out.

* * * * *

Chapter Twelve

Devlin was sure that something was going on.

For the last few days, Atwell, Baxter, Kinnebrew, and Pringle were filtering through the platoon talking with the recruits. This often had the result of a recruit pulling out their cred chit and giving it to one of the foursome.

Niko Devlin was a street kid long enough to recognize a shakedown when he saw it. He was also pretty sure that if he saw it, the sergeants, and especially that asshole McClellan, saw it. He was just wondering when the bust would come.

A few more days went by. He began to watch the foursome when they weren't actively engaged in training. They could usually be seen eating together and talking. Nothing out of the ordinary there. Pretty much everyone in the platoon had their own little circles. Sometimes it was squad-based; more often than not, it was something else entirely. Mac, and even Atwell, had tried to get Devlin to join in bull-sessions or general grab ass, but Devlin just wasn't interested.

Devlin pretty much kept to himself. He might laugh at a joke or comment at meals, but the message had pretty much been received by everyone: "Devlin wants to be alone."

The final straw came when Devlin saw Baxter and Kinnebrew cut out of formation Saturday evening on the way back from chow. The unit wasn't double-timing, so they strolled slowly back to the barracks. Drill Sergeant Miller was in charge of the platoon this evening and they were marching at a more leisurely pace. The sergeant was at the head of the formation bellowing out a bawdy road song about a guy named Pete with an unusual anatomical feature.

There was a copse of trees decorating the street by the mini-shopette, which doubled as a small post exchange, or PX, and the uniform store. In the shadows cast by those trees, Baxter and Kinnebrew slipped out of formation and hid amongst the trees until the formation was fully past. Miller never saw them, never looked back. Since the two were usually toward the center of the formation, there was nothing to suggest anything was amiss. The rest of the platoon, almost as if by command, closed ranks and filled the holes.

About five minutes later, the duo cut back in, appearing out of another shady grove of trees, this one just prior to the barracks complex. The ranks opened back up and engulfed their wayward companions like an organism reabsorbing a stray piece of protoplasm.

Trial run, Devlin decided. Things are about to go down.

* * *

"Sergeant Miller." Devlin knocked on the drill instructor's door before lights out.

"Whatcha need, Devlin. Make it quick." The sergeant sat back in his chair and put his feet up on his desk.

"I'm running out of depilatory cream and a couple of odds and ends. I've tried to eke them out as long as possible, but I was wondering if I could get a slip to make an exchange run tomorrow after chow. Should just be an in and out."

"You know we're not supposed to do that," Miller said, frowning.

"Yes, Drill Sergeant, I know, and I didn't want to bring it up, but I think some of it has been disappearing."

Miller's eyes narrowed, and his frown deepened. "Whaddya mean, disappearing?"

"Well, I can't point to anything directly, but I specifically bought a month's supply of cream. That was two weeks ago, and now I've only got maybe three or four days' worth. Personally, I think someone's run out and they're borrowing mine. Like I said, I can't prove it or even know how to go about it, but…"

"Yeah. Crap like that happens." Miller shook his head. "Somebody probably doesn't have the balls to admit they ran out so they beg and borrow…" He specifically didn't say steal, which was a whole other ballgame of paperwork. And, besides, it was just toilet items.

"Tell you what. I'll say something to the sergeant major and see if I can get a pass for the shopette. But go, get what you need, and only what you need, and hurry back. If you're quick you can be back before last call after chow."

"No problem, Drill Sergeant," Devlin agreed.

"If the sergeant major says so, I'll give you the pass at formation for evening chow."

"Thank you, Drill Sergeant," Devlin said.

Miller just waved his hand in dismissal. "Go get your shit straight and hit the rack."

Sunday evening, Baxter and Kinnebrew peeled off from the formation just as they had practiced. Without looking back, they ran like the hordes of Outer Dark were on their heels. The paused just outside the mini-shopette and caught their breath.

They entered the little store as several service members exited. They walked past the counter and into the "geedunk" section. As trainees, they were generally forbidden from going into certain areas of the store; this was one of them. Trainees didn't need to be eating junk food or engaging in activities that weren't specifically promoted by the training cadre. Hell, as trainees, they weren't supposed to be in the store in the first place without a cadre member or a written pass, at least until they were in the final phase of their training.

They each grabbed a shopping basket and went to work. For the last week and a half, they had been taking orders for an illicit candy run. They went down the aisles and filled the baskets with an assortment of candies and snacks. They worked fast; they only had a few minutes, plus checkout, then they'd have to triple-time it back to the formation.

They took their booty up to the counter and scanned all their goodies. The clerk at the main counter looked their way, but then put his head back down to pay attention to his reading.

After bagging up their goods, they headed out the door to begin the final leg of their epic candy raid.

"I wouldn't go any further if I were you," a voice said *sotto voce* from the shadows and scared the piss out of both recruits. "Come over here."

The two sugar-runners stepped in the direction of the voice, and, as their eyes adjusted to the gloom, they recognized the owner.

"Devlin? Wh-what the Hell?" Kinnebrew stuttered.

"You two suck at crime. You know that?" Devlin said. "Trying to be all conspiratorial, whispered conversations, surreptitious hand-offs of creds, slipping out for trial runs. You thought it was going to be a cakewalk."

"Well, we were getting away with it," Brew said.

"You've been ignored," Devlin replied with an evil smile. "Now, I will admit that such behavior arouses my suspicions, but I had a colorful childhood. What makes you think that someone else didn't notice what you were doing?"

"We just—"

"You just *assumed*, that since no one had busted you, you were getting away with it. I'll call your attention to Rule Number Three. Look, you don't have much time. The drills are around the corner and just up in the next copse of trees. If you run your normal path, you're going to run smack dab into them. Do it."

"What?" Baxter hissed. "If we get caught with this shit, we'll be cleaning the head for a month."

"*If* you get caught," Devlin emphasized. "Look, you guys are never going to make good crooks. So, let me be the crook and you guys go be soldiers."

Kinnebrew started to protest, but Baxter stopped him an evil grin spreading on her face. "Ooh," she said. "Give him the stuff, Brew."

"But—"

Just do it. I know what he's got in mind. Let's do this."

Devlin walked into the barracks and saw Atwell, who was the Charge of Quarters runner for the evening. Devlin gave his shopette pass to the CQ and said, "I'm going upstairs to stash my toiletries, Sergeant." He held up the very small bag that held various personal grooming items and couldn't possibly have held candy or other assorted geedunks in mass quantities, and headed for the stairs.

When he returned a few minutes later he heard a general commotion outside.

McClellan and the staff sergeants were stalking up and down the formation, cursing and intimidating the entire group.

"We know Kinnebrew and Baxter have been getting money for the last couple of weeks to get candy and other contraband for you lot! Unfortunately for you, they dumped their cargo! Apparently, they think they're in a hole. So, while you're not going to get your money's worth, we're going to get our money's worth making you beat your faces for the next hour or so."

The platoon groaned in anticipation of the pain that was rapidly approaching.

Backing away from the door, Devlin addressed his squad-mate.

"What the Hell, Marty? What's with the pain party outside?"

Atwell looked a little sick. Quietly he replied, "For the last couple of weeks, Baxter and Kinnebrew—" *and some others,* Devlin thought, "—have been collecting money to make a secret run to the geedunk section of the shopette to buy candy. They got caught. Somewhere along the way they threw away the candy or stashed it. McClellan and the corps are going to PT the information out of everyone. First, who was in on the deal, and then where they got rid of the candy."

"Hmm." Devlin grunted. "Damn. Glad you all never got me involved in a cockamamie scheme like that." He paused. "Why didn't you? I'm a little hurt, except for the whole…you know…PT until you die business."

"Yeah," Atwell agreed weakly. "I guess because nobody figured you for a candy kind of guy, Devlin. Plus, given your…issues, I figured you'd say no."

"For the second time this evening, I will draw your attention and remembrance to Rule Number Three. I'm getting the hell out of Dodge and going upstairs to shine my boots."

Martin Atwell watched him disappear into the stairwell. As the door closed, the poster that someone had calligraphed was taped to the outside of the door. The title of the poster read: McClellan's Rules. Number 3 said, *"Thou shalt not Assume, for on the day thou dost Assume, thou makest an ASS out of U and ME."*

* * *

"Where's the farking candy?" McClellan demanded, as he started to swear sulphurously. "We know they went in; we know they bought a good ninety creds worth of shit, but there's nothing to be found. You guys searched every nook and cranny between the store and where we intercepted those two. So, where did it go?" He looked at each of his staff sergeants. They looked helpless.

"Don't know, Sergeant Major," Stark replied, shrugging. "We've accounted for all of them. We had eyes on the whole formation. Percy, Smith, Pringle, Jones, and Tamman were at KP. Atwell was CQR. And Devlin. But he showed up at the barracks before the formation got back, and I questioned the sergeant. He had one little bag of toiletries. So he couldn't have done anything. He was here when Kinnebrew and Baxter got caught. And from what I understand, he didn't know anything about it. Nobody ever saw him talking to either Baxter or Kinnebrew in the last several weeks. Nobody I talked to thinks very much of Devlin. He does his job, but he—"

"Keeps to himself?" McClellan grunted. "Yeah, whatever. Keep looking for that damn candy, or I'll make every one of you sorry and sore."

"Yes, Sergeant Major."

* * *

"Miller!" McClellan barked as he entered the trainee barracks.

"Yes, Sergeant Major." Corporal Miller peeked his head out of his office. He saw the look on his boss's face and blanched.

McClellan stalked through the bay, glaring at everyone present. Suddenly he stopped, looked around, and bellowed. "Everybody out! *Now!* I don't care if you're in the head and you're in the middle of a particularly long dump, *get the hell out!*" He started back into motion, not bothering to watch the mass exodus in process.

The senior drill instructor stormed into Miller's office and slammed the door. He waited for a few moments, then opened it and peered out.

"Good, they're gone," he said with satisfaction. He sat down on the corner of the desk.

Very mildly and very calmly, McClellan looked at his subordinate. "Could you," he asked, "or Stark, or Rogers, or maybe even Pritchard, please—pretty please with sugar and freaking cherries on top—explain to an old man how I keep finding candy wrappers in the trash and on the grounds outside the barracks? Hell. I've got to tell you, Glenn, it's a little depressing."

Miller tried to swallow, but his mouth had gone dry. He was used to his boss's tirades, usually more theatrics than actual histrionics, but he knew that calm and reasonable was not a positive sign.

He started to speak, "I...uh...what I mean to say is—"

"What you mean to say is that you, me, and the rest of the cadre of this little circus has been well and truly made to look like idiots. Is that what you were about to say, Miller? Because, really, I think that's about the size of it. Don't you?"

"Sergeant Major, we've done everything we can to try and figure out how they got the damn candy. We've tossed the damn bays, we policed the outside of the barracks. Hell, we looked everywhere, and nothing."

McClellan nodded. "Where could they have stashed that much candy that we haven't been able to find it? Where haven't we already looked?"

Miller tried to turn his mind to the problem, but the older man apparently knew the answer. "Don't strain yourself, Mill. I'd hate to have to clean up the CS fluid that erupted from the aneurism you'd give yourself. The answer was somewhat obvious, but one I didn't want to consider.

"Whoever helped the Candy Crusaders is a real piece of work. It seems there are numerous nifty places to conceal stuff—including my office."

Miller looked nonplussed, so the older NCO continued, "Seems there is an old access panel behind one of the bookcases in my office. I got to thinking about these old buildings, and it occurred to me to start looking for hidey holes that could be found inside the company. That led me on a tour of the building while you had the babyshits out in the field. I looked through the entire building and around the grounds. I've found a bunch, and I've noted every last one of them. If they try again, we'll know. But the hilarious bit was that I turned this building upside down, and while I found a bunch of possible places, I didn't find *the* place. So I was standing there in my office, and I just started tearing shit apart. I did to myself what we'd been doing to these poor sods all these years. And I *found* it…"

"And?" Miller prompted.

"And it was right behind my 'I Love Me' bookcase. It was there when I got here, and I hadn't seen any reason to move it; it was right by the damn desk."

Miller's face went ashen. McClellan's face broke into a beatific grin. "Oh yeah, somebody has balls the size of Hades, and they're made out of neutronium. The knob actually broke into my office—did a pretty professional job of it too—and concealed the stuff until we tossed everywhere else. Then they came back in, presumably, and recovered their ill-gotten booty and saw to it that it was distributed."

"If it was empty, how did you know they'd hid it there?"

McClellan's grin got bigger. "It was dusty. Oh, not obviously, but if you take a flashlight and shine it just the right way into the access panel, you can see where the original dust was brushed back into the corners. Only a real detective, or a really anal-retentive drill sergeant, would check something like that. But there you are."

They both sat in silence for a moment. Then Miller breathed out.

"Do you know who it was?" he asked.

"Not exactly, but I'm starting to have a few suspicions. I just need a little more information.".

* * * * *

Chapter Thirteen

Twelve weeks into training, Alpha Company had to reconsolidate. Due to the attrition of people quitting, they had lost almost a platoon and a half. Several of Devlin's squad mates were being mustered out; Volkoff was one. Apparently, the drills found him with a homemade weapon. Devlin wanted to believe it hadn't been meant for him, but he suspected no such thing. So, Katsaros, Volkoff, and Poole were gone, replaced by Sarah Arnette, Martin Atwell, and Susan Baxter. Kuzma and MacBain were also added to Second Squad.

Now the threesome of Kuzma, MacBain, and Atwell were inseparable, and they seemed to want to make Devlin the fourth member of their club. The guys didn't bother him a lot, but something about Kuzma made him nervous. She was from Allonsy's home world, and while Ariel was a heavily populated world, anybody from the Prospero system was going to make him nervous, especially since they were training with real weapons now.

"All right, boys and girls!" McClellan bellowed, entering the training bay. "Today we're going to have a little contest to see who is the baddest double-stick fighter in this unit. Can I have an attitude check?"

"This shit sucks, Sergeant Major!" the recruits of Second Platoon chorused.

McClellan grinned one of his rare grins and boomed, "Give me a *positive* attitude check!"

"This shit positively sucks, Sergeant Major!"

"Good. A bitching soldier is a happy soldier," he intoned. The grin disappeared as he looked at the assembled crowd.

"Here's how it's gonna go," the drill instructor said. "You are all going to gear up and pair off against each other. Then the winners will face off, and so on and so forth, until we have a clear winner. That winner will face off against First Platoon's champion, and the winner there will face off against the champions of Third and Fourth. Everyone got me?

"Ooooowah, Sergeant Major!" they replied.

"Good! Gear up!"

Twenty minutes later, they had donned protective armor and stood on the training bay's floor in formation. Staff Sergeant Pippin watched the preparations and the slight bit of grab ass with a look of amused tolerance. As things started to shake out, he bellowed, "A-ten-*shun*."

The platoon snapped to attention. The staff sergeant looked over at the sergeant major and received a nod. "At ease. Rest." Everyone relaxed in place.

McClellan moved to the front of the formation. "When we fall you out, everybody grab a seat along the walls. At that point, I'll explain the rules for this and how we're going to proceed. Right. Platoon, a-ten-*shun*! Fall out!"

Second Platoon fell out with haste and lined the two long sides of the training bay. They sat down, in one or two cases squatted, where they came to rest.

McClellan walked to the center of the bay accompanied by two of his minions, Staff Sergeant Rogers and Staff Sergeant Stark. "Here's how we play this game, ladies and gentlemen. Each of you is wearing basic non-powered armor. And these little beauties—" he held up a wooden staff about a meter and a half long with padding on both ends, "—are pugil sticks. I call it an ugly stick. And they have been around literally for centuries. And for centuries, it has been the bane of many a recruit. I call it an ugly stick because you people are to beat one another ugly—or uglier—with said stick. Hopefully, someone will be able to take the title away from Chuckie."

On the far wall, Charles "Ugly Chuckie" Windsor gave a "huzzah!" which elicited a round of chuckles, including one from the normally dour sergeant major.

"As I was saying. Each of you is wearing armor, so we shouldn't have too many injuries, and I better not have any paperwork to do." He glared at the group.

"You will each face off against members of your squads. You will take a pugil stick and you will use the ends to either stab or buttstroke your opponent. You have practiced each of these maneuvers as part of your melee cycle of training, and though your personal rifles can be used as an improvised weapon should you be in a situation where you must engage in melee due to lack of ammunition or insufficient time to reload same into your weapon, it is not something you should hope for."

"Generally speaking, either maneuver is not, I repeat, *not,* a killing blow. McClellan's Rule Number Forty-Five: *If you want it dead, shoot it in the head...preferably more than once.* And Number Forty-six: *Anything worth shooting once is worth shooting twice.*"

The recruits laughed.

He continued after the laughter had subsided. "We're going to use a point system to decide. The drill instructors for each squad will judge the bouts and declare kills. The instructors will judge when a blow or combination is sufficient to incapacitate in the absence of...well, you actually incapacitating your opponent. While I don't want you hurting each other—and I don't want the paperwork—none of us are stupid enough to think that it can't happen, even with armor. Ask me about Private Buckley someday. The judge will blow the whistle to begin and end a bout. The whistle to end will only blow when the instructor judges a blow to be 'fatal.' Any questions? No? Good. Stark, Miller, carry on."

As the sergeant major left the platoon bay, the two drill sergeants moved the front and back of the room, "Babcock, Zemeckis, front and center..."

* * *

Devlin looked at Chapis. The almost inhumanly handsome giant had been victorious in his last three bouts, as had Devlin. He glanced around and saw Tamman squared off against Curran on one side and Wandrey and Byrne on the other.

The rest of Second Platoon was standing along the walls. Well, most of them. Three had been taken to the infirmary because, well, shit happened.

* * *

As he stood over the inert form of Dalrymple, Staff Sergeant Miller strode up and checked the unconscious youth.

"Out cold," he confirmed. "No bones broken. Damn, Devlin, where in the Hell did you learn that last set of strikes? I know we didn't teach you that."

"Sorry, Staff Sergeant. Learned that from a guy on Caliban when I was a kid. Kinda came in handy over the years," Devlin said somewhat weakly. He felt kind of queasy. Not from knocking the other guy out, but worried that he'd get busted then sent off to the brig.

"No worries," Miller said, motioning to a couple of cadre to cart the unconscious loser out of the bay. He looked at Devlin intently. Apparently, he saw what he needed and nodded. "Get back to the wall, you'll be up again in a few."

The other two injuries had been accidents, but in those cases the injured person ended up with broken bones, so Devlin didn't quite feel as bad.

He had been up twice more that morning and won handily both times. By the time they broke for lunch, he'd seen several other recruits glance his way, talking to others.

MacBain sat down across from him at lunch, "Holy Hells, Devlin, how did you learn to fight like that?" He dug into his food.

"I grew up on a border colony. Caliban. I didn't have the greatest childhood."

"I sort of figured. Fighting like that, you either had a shitty childhood or a really cool one."

Devlin grunted and picked at his food.

MacBain frowned and cocked his head. "You don't look very happy, laddie. What's up? You should be cock of the walk."

Devlin considered his answer. He could just tell Mac to take a flying leap and the irrepressible Caledonian wouldn't take offense. Devlin kind of liked the guy, at least enough he didn't want to poison the well. But he also struggled with how much of his screwed-up life he wanted to give out.

"Can we leave it at 'I kind of hurt somebody in the past like this, and I'd just as soon not do it again without a real good reason?'" Devlin replied carefully.

MacBain took a bite of food, chewed, swallowed, and then ventured, "You do know we're training to be soldiers, right? Stuff happens. And, really, what happened wasn't your fault."

"Yeah, but I was getting a little too into the fight," Devlin protested.

"Look, we're training for combat. We're armored up, the sticks are padded, the drills are officiating. They're not going to let you kill someone, even if you really could. Too much paperwork." He grinned and shrugged. "This is one time you can get your mad on and get away with it. Don't think that if I get a chance me and Buchard aren't going to dance. I'm watching the whole thing and hoping. Just like I fervently hope I don't wind up against you at some point." His grin faded. "Devlin," he said seriously, "from the bits and drabs you've dropped, I get that you didn't really want to sign up."

Devlin started to tense, but the other man held a palm up. "No, don't worry about it, I've had time to think. Either you did it to get away from crap or because crap happened. And judging from today, I can make a pretty good guess. I also get why you seem to be so gung-ho not to be gung-ho. There's not a person in the platoon who hasn't already figured out that you're just trying to stay out of the drill's notice. Little screw-ups here and there, but not enough to get into serious trouble, and also not enough to make the drills think you're totally squared."

Devlin said nothing but chewed his food and chewed even more on what MacBain had said.

* * *

Devlin was thoughtful as he stared out of his helmet at Chapis. If he was stuck here, he might as well have fun…right? And since he was getting near the front of the pack on stick fighting, it was going to be harder to hurt anyone, even accidentally. The handsome young man from Olympus Prime was *good*.

So, as Miller came forward to have them get ready, Devlin grinned like a wolf. Chapis grinned back, just as hungrily.

"I want to find out just how good you are, Devlin," the deep basso rumbled out of the Olympian.

"Damn, Pretty Boy," Devlin said drawing out the "pretty." "That's more words than I've heard you say since we got here." He winked. "Did it take you that long to string those together?"

"Ooh, little man talking trash." Chapis' grin grew even wider. "You do know I was a martial arts champion for my province."

Devlin shrugged. "Cool. So you did katas, broke a few boards. Boards don't hit back. I fought for meals."

Miller looked between the two and said, "Give me a chance to get my popcorn…*Fight!*"

Devlin set himself and yelled, "Come and get some!"

Chapis moved.

For a huge man, he was quicker than a claw lizard. In the time it took Devlin to react, the big man had covered the distance between them. The head of his pugil stick snaked out toward Devlin's visor.

Devlin sidestepped, bringing the lower end of the stick toward Chapis' forward shin. The bigger man stepped back and brought the stick down to meet Devlin's with a crack that vibrated up the smaller man's arm.

"Kick his ass, Devlin!" someone shouted. It sounded like Baxter.

"Twenty creds on Chappy," someone else yelled.

"Now, now!" Miller shouted, but he was grinning, leaning on his own pugil stick.

The two circled each other as the other combatants in the training room yelled encouragement and derision.

Chapis whirled the stick like a quarterstaff. But Devlin wasn't watching the staff. Instead he watched the big man, saw his moment, and rushed in, coming into Chapis' space. It caught Chapis slightly off guard, and he stepped back, bringing his staff up to block a head strike. He turned the blow and started the counterstroke, only to have Devlin push it aside like water. Devlin sidestepped again and slammed the butt of his stick down at the Olympian's feet, and he felt it connect on the instep. Without hesitating, he started another head strike which the larger man narrowly parried. Chapis leapt back. Devlin let him go, not wanting to get pulled off balance.

Devlin rolled his neck. "How's the foot, big guy?"

The Olympian smiled at him. "That was good. You're good. But I still think I'm better."

Devlin gave him a palm up, "come here," gesture. "Bring it on, then," Devlin said, bringing his staff up.

Chapis rushed in.

They met, sticks crashing together. They lunged, parried, dodged, struck, and lunged again. The sticks cracked like lightning striking an old tree. Chapis had reach and strength, but Devlin was a hair faster. As they fought, Devlin grinned savagely; he was enjoying this. It felt good to take his anger out a little on someone who could give as good as he got. Even so, Chapis was putting him to it. He *was* good. But Devlin hadn't been lying when he said he had fought for food. His martial arts club had been very exclusive and very brutal.

He saw an opening, slid aside a midriff thrust from Chapis, slammed the butt of his stick against the inside of the man's knee, rotated his shoulder, and brought the head of his pugil stick down on top of Chapis' helmet.

"Halt!" Miller yelled and blew his whistle.

Both men stepped back. Chapis reached up and removed his helmet.

"Dayum!" he exulted. "That was fun as Hell." He walked over and clapped the smaller man on the shoulder. "You're okay for a shrimp."

Devlin took his own helmet off and took in a deep breath. "It ain't the size; it's how you use it."

Chapis grinned and turned. Devlin looked around and saw the entire training room had stopped to watch him and Chapis fight.

The other two sets of fighters had apparently resolved their bouts and were watching as well.

On the end of the room he saw the sergeant major in the doorway, watching intently.

In the end, Cho beat out Devlin for Second Platoon, went on to beat First, and was defeated by Fourth. Devlin didn't mind, although he was certain he had hit Cho with a killing blow that hadn't been called by the referee. When he turned to protest, Cho absolutely clocked him. As he went down, he could have sworn he saw the sergeant major grinning.

* * * * *

Chapter Fourteen

"Check fire!" Staff Sergeant Pritchard yelled. Devlin and Second Squad took their weapons off their shoulders and, keeping the muzzles up and downrange, placed them on the firing line in front of them.

"Everybody take a minute," Pritchard called.

Devlin looked down at the NCO.

He and the other drills were standing around Cho's firing position. The diminutive Koryo beauty still had her weapon and was now affixing a different set of optics on the rifle's rail. This wasn't something they had been issued; this was apparently something the drills had supplied.

Cho pulled the rifle stock into her shoulder, aligned the sights, and squeezed the trigger as she had been taught. The weapon activated its internal electronics and sped the hunk of polycarb-jacketed metal down the rails of the M269 and out the barrel. The round traveled so fast that it created a small sonic boom and created a tracer trail from the heat signature of the polycarb as it protected the metal in the round from evaporating.

The rifle's inertial dampers cut in, reducing the recoil to a manageable level, which meant the stock of the M269 merely slammed her petite but well-muscled shoulder instead of breaking her collarbone.

She vaguely noticed the path of the round as it hit the target three thousand meters away. But even as the round left the weapon, she was aligning the sights on her next target.

Devlin watched the scene then got MacBain's attention. "What gives?"

The Caledonian was watching from his position one up from Devlin. "It appears our little porcelain doll has a gift for reaching out and touching someone. The drills are doing a basic check for sniper qual."

"Ooh, awesome."

"That's it, Cho…" Miller crooned softly. He had taken a prone position next to her and was watching her accuracy using a set of binoculars. So far, fourteen targets, fourteen perfect strikes. "Just a few more…"

Targets started popping up at random. Cho scanned, sighted, relaxed, shot, and scanned again. Fifteen…Sixteen…

Targets popped up as fast as she could shoot them. Cho put rounds into each.

Twenty-four, twenty-five.

The targets appeared in pairs, and Cho's rifle was almost one continuous roar as she barely hesitated between shots to acquire her next target.

Thirty-one. Thirty-two.

As the pace mounted, Cho was pumping round after round down range, changing targets before the previous round had even struck. Her normally impassive face was twisted in a grotesque mask of hate, her little rosebud mouth writhing into a snarl.

As the last targets popped up, Devlin and everyone else could hear the primal scream pouring out of the girl as she rode the recoil of the massive rail gun. It seemed like the gun bucked a little and then fired again, and again, each time shifting ever so slightly.

As the last target exploded and the rifle's capacitors bled off the excess energy, Anastasia Cho trembled in her firing position, her breathing heavy. Her face was still locked into a rictus of rage and hate.

Miller leaned down and whispered something into the girl's ear. At first, Cho didn't react. Finally, she nodded, and her breathing started to slow. She took a deep breath, and her face relaxed, resuming the impassive mask she habitually wore.

But Devlin noticed something else there. He couldn't really say what. Sadness?

Cho placed her rifle on the position and carefully removed the optics. She handed the scope back to Sergeant Miller, who placed it in a case at his feet. He leaned back and said something else to the recruit, who nodded and proceeded to leave the firing position.

Devlin watched as she picked up her rifle, still maintaining range discipline, and walked off the firing line.

* * *

Devlin crossed over the rise. Just out of sight of the rest of the company, he found Cho sitting on the ground, her legs in a lotus position, rifle laid across them. Her beautifully impassive face was streaked with tears, yet she made no noise, nor even moved. She just stared at the horizon.

Without moving, he heard her say quietly, "I wish to be alone, Devlin."

Devlin adjusted his course slightly and sat down a few meters away. He watched the clouds on the horizon drift lazily.

He felt more than heard Cho's intake of breath followed by an exasperated exhale. He shrugged mentally. She was really worked up about something. This was more emotion he'd seen from her since they had arrived.

"You are a strange one." Her quiet soprano reached his ear a few minutes later. He turned slightly and saw that she was still staring out into the horizon. Her face was still as expressionless as stone. He cocked an eyebrow and waited.

"You form few bonds, you say you desire to be left alone, and yet you seek out other people and intrude where you are not wanted."

Devlin stiffened slightly and started to shift, but the voice continued, "That is not an insult, merely an observation. One that has puzzled me for a good many weeks. So much so that I will ask: Why are you here, Devlin?"

Devlin opened his mouth, shut it. He started to say something again, then paused. The question was unexpected. Cho usually didn't ask about the people in her squad. She was always reticent to engage in banter. She was even more standoffish than he was.

"I, uh, wanted to see—"

The short-clipped soprano cut him off. "No."

"I was worried—"

"No."

"You were—"

"No. I do not ask why you came up *here*," Cho said in Koryo. "That is evident. You are a born busybody. I want to know why you are here...on this planet...in the military."

"I joined because I—"

"Bullshit." The interruption didn't startle him, but her use of the colloquialism did. Cho was always very precise, very formal in her speech. Startled, he turned his head and saw her looking at him. Her head was cocked as she looked intently at him, sizing him up, measuring him against some vague benchmark only she could see.

"I studied psychology in University. As young as I was, I was already Third form," she said, switching back to Standard. "I was the first of my family to attend University in four generations."

She rose from her position, leaned her rifle against her body, and smoothed her uniform, brushing the grass off her backside. Taking up the rifle, she cradled it in her arm and approached him, still regarding him with her head tilted.

"I was going to become a counselor," she finished. Cho stood there, almost daring him to speak.

He started, but she cut him off again. "*You* do not fit here, Devlin. And yet you do. You are in constant struggle. I began to see it clearly when we fought with the pugil sticks."

He looked up at her. Her eyes were unreadable, her face as expressionless as ever.

"You fight well, better than I, but you hold back. The first time you did not, Dalrymple was injured. At first, I thought it might be just that…but other things…"

"What other things?" Devlin asked cautiously.

"As I have already said, you have formed no real social bonds. You seem to work with Kenyon, but do not engage her as a friend, per se. Atwell, Kuzma, and MacBain repeatedly try to engage you, but you rebuff them. You are clearly intelligent and have good recall, but consciously make mistakes to keep the instructors from singling you out or to avoid being put into leadership positions. I have caught you no less than four times making mistakes in tasks that moments before you had performed flawlessly, and the only difference was that there was an instructor watching. And we won't even discuss the incident with the contraband."

He didn't move or change expression. "So, what is your take, Counselor?"

If his not quite sarcastic use of the title fazed her, she gave no indication. Instead, she frowned, hard. "I...do not know. And that, at times, worries me. I have theories, but that is all they are."

Devlin stared but said nothing.

"The worrisome thing is, I dislike uncertainty in my colleagues. I understand, for values of understanding, most of our teammates. Most of them are easy. Kenyon for example, what you see is what you get. She has joined because she wishes to serve as her family has served for generations. No more, no less. Tamman seeks only to do well. Jones craves adventure, much like MacBain. Only two people are yet mysteries to me. McCarthy...and you.

"Do you wish to be here, or do you not? You say one thing but do another." She fell quiet and again looked away.

She turned to go, but Devlin said, "Why are *you* here, Cho?"

She turned her impassive face to him. Her eyes were flat, dead things. In a face as beautiful as Anastasia Cho's, they were truly horrifying.

"I joined the military to kill people." Devlin flinched, but Cho continued matter-of-factly. "My family was part of a small startup colony on Theta Varus, just a few parsecs from the current edge of Nord space. Since the conflict with the IslamoNordic Republican Federation started nearly forty years before, small mining colonies and prospecting concerns were regularly invaded or outright overrun by the jihad to return the Creator's Worlds to their pristine condition before they were defiled by the Infidels. Prospectors like my family constantly ran the risk of being in a system when a reclamation survey force dropped in on anyone with the temerity to 'rape and pillage' God's Holy Planets. Such unfortunate individuals would, if they weren't killed outright, be forced into a kind of slavery, righting the wrongs wreaked upon the planet, and once that planet was restored, they would be shipped off-world to continue the work of God somewhere else. No one, not even the Nordic apologists in the Avalonian media, have been able to explain what constituted 'restored.'

"I was attending classes on Ariel when the raid hit my planet. No one was sure if it were pirates, a constant threat out on the frontiers that were still being settled, or the Nords. All I knew was that my family was gone. A supply ship venturing through the system caught our outpost's distress beacon. What they found was an abattoir. My family was ostensibly RussaKor Federation, although we never made issue of it, and, as such, their ambassador to the Avalonian Empire contacted me though Avalon's Consulate on Ariel. I traveled to New Seoul to identify the bodies of my family."

Her expression cracked for a moment, and Devlin saw all the pain, all of the despair that Cho carefully avoided in her voice.

"My father, my mother, my younger twin sisters, Grace and Maria, my aunt, uncle, and cousin were not among the bodies. I can only assume they were taken, possibly alive, to be sold as sexual objects or brought up as slaves." The mask came back down with the mention of "sexual objects."

"When I got back to the school, I found I was unable to function. I could not sleep without seeing the faces of my family staring at me. My family is dead, Devlin. I am dead. I dis-enrolled from school. I packed an overnight bag, left all my other belongings, kissed my roommate on the cheek, and promptly enlisted in the Avalonian military."

She wiped at her eyes with the back of her hand.

"I am here to learn to be a killer. I wish to kill the people who killed my family, who killed my life. Before, I sought to understand people. Now, I do not. I do not seek to understand the things that killed my family. I seek only to kill them." She turned to him. "I will leave this place, and I will volunteer to go to the frontier. I will kill raiders and pirates. I will kill and kill until there are no more to kill, or I am no more. Then I shall rest with my family, with my little sisters. Everything I do is in furtherance of that. And anything that gets in my way is an obstacle to be dealt with, or an enemy to be killed. I would advise you to not be either one."

With that she turned and stalked toward the company area.

Devlin watched her go and considered what she said.

The diminutive recruit had a point. He needed to decide what he was doing. He wasn't going to get anywhere being a dick. It wasn't like he had to trust someone to work with them. He worked fine with Kenyon and their relationship was more or less decent. He got along with Tamman, MacBain, and Atwell. He still wasn't sure about Kuzma, but he kind of liked Baxter. The more he thought about it, he finally concluded that where he could, he would work at being a teammate rather than the weak link in the chain. He definitely didn't want to be an obstacle to Cho. That little lady was Hell on wheels with a rifle. He thought about that, then chuckled as he considered the team name and where it came from.

Grinning, he put his hand out to push himself off the ground.

He moved to get up when he felt a massive hand punch him in the shoulder, knocking him face first into the ground. He tried to get up, but his shoulder wouldn't take his weight, so he quit trying. He decided that lying there on the ground was preferable. He closed his eyes, and he heard voices approaching, shouting orders he could not understand.

*****

Chapter Fifteen

Devlin woke up in a white room that was vaguely familiar. It was white and bright and smelled abnormal. Or maybe it just didn't smell like anything else he was used to. The lights hurt his eyes, but they slowly adjusted to the daytime brightness.

He was in a bed but at a slant, the sides of the bed came up and formed side rails. He remembered being in this kind of bed before. Then realization dawned, and he figured out where he was. He'd been in this room twice before. Looking down, he confirmed he was in an autodoc and that he was nude. As he put his arms out to grip the sides of the autodoc, his left shoulder ached.

"Ah, Private Devlin," the attendant he remembered from his intake week, Jazelle, said. "Please step down out of the autodoc and dress while I process your discharge paperwork."

His head came up sharply. "Discharge, ma'am?"

"Yes, Private," came the calm reply. "Discharge from Medical Section."

Devlin's tension dissipated quickly as he grinned sheepishly. "Oh. Right." He stepped off the dais and reached for his trousers. "What happened?"

Jazelle started to reply, but she was interrupted by Staff Sergeant Miller. "You were shot."

Devlin had started to reach for his tunic but froze, his tension shooting back into focus. "Shot, Drill Sergeant? What? How? Who?"

"Get your shit on, and I'll fill you in on the way back to the barracks. You're on light duty for the next couple of days." He made it sound like he disapproved, and he glared at the med-tech. His glare slid off the tech like lasers off a mirror. She handed the NCO a pad which Devlin presumed was his discharge paperwork. The staff sergeant thumbed his receipt and grabbed Devlin by his good arm.

It started to come back to him. He remembered not being able to use his left shoulder. The smell of the ground as he'd laid there bleeding. The voice of the sergeant major yelling for a medevac.

Miller trundled his charge into a ground truck and drove away from the med facility. Devlin kept his mouth shut.

"Yesterday you were shot while we were at the range," Miller said without preamble. "As to how and who, you were ADed by Kuzma. She had a jam, and she and Atwell were trying to get the round out." His voice turned hard. "Unfortunately for you, they didn't bother asking for assistance from either the range cadre or one of us. If you want more details, you'll have to ask the sergeant major; that's all I can tell you. The incident is being investigated. We medevac'd you, and you've spent the last twenty-two hours in the autodoc having your shoulder rebuilt. The nanites have done most of the work, but you'll need another day or so before you can return to training."

He grinned with no humor, "Fortunately for you it's a weekend so you'll be good to go on Monday."

Devlin didn't find that last bit funny and therefore didn't laugh at his great fortune.

* * *

Devlin tried not to move his shoulder as he sat at attention waiting for Captain Glass and the sergeant major to notice him. After what seemed like two years, seven months, twenty-one days, and nine hours—but which the clock on the wall informed him was only three minutes—the captain looked up and saw him seemingly for the first time.

"Relax, Devlin. Rest, even." Devlin remained straight in his seat, although he relaxed his posture just a bit to take the strain off his aching shoulder.

"You're not in any trouble. Far from it," Glass said, smiling thinly. "First, I want to express that I'm glad you're okay."

Devlin, a cynic way before he "joined" the military, decided to take the comment at face value. After all, the amount of paperwork for a death would probably be out of proportion to what a mere injury would be, so he probably was just as glad.

"The investigation into the incident yesterday is complete, and the Sergeant Major and I wished to let you know the outcome and answer any salient questions you might have.

"First," Glass continued, "as you are already aware, there was a training incident yesterday at the range during which you were accidentally shot with an M269 training round. The investigation showed that the two trainees in question were trying to clear a round without proper tools or assistance and thus triggered a second pulse. This second pulse apparently enabled the jammed round to exit the rifle, albeit at a reduced velocity. Its trajectory happened to be where you had been sitting, catching you in the meat of your left deltoid, knocking you to the ground. Lucky for you, the round tore some of the muscle but did not involve the bone or you'd be looking at a medical recycle. Your nanites and a naniboost from the autodoc was enough to repair the damage to your shoulder, although it's likely to smart a bit for the next day or so.

"The two recruits in the incident have been counselled." Glass looked at McClellan who returned his gaze evenly. Glass folded his hands and regarded Devlin just as evenly as his NCO. "Do you have any salient questions?"

"Just one, sir," Devlin said. "Who do I avoid for the rest of training?" McClellan sneezed. At least it sounded kind of like a sneeze. It sounded more like a snort. Glass frowned.

"That's not really a salient question, Recruit. Although I'm sure you're going to hear it anyway once you leave the office, so, no harm no foul, the two recruits in question are Kuzma and Atwell. It was Kuzma's weapon that accidentally discharged. Atwell was trying to clear the jam."

Devlin nodded. "Thank you, sir."

"You are on light duty for the next forty-eight hours," Glass said. "Inform your platoon guide to reassign your company and platoon duties for the weekend."

"Yes, sir."

"That does not mean you get a vacation," McClellan said, speaking up for the first time. "You will be CQ runner for the weekend. Get your shit straight, change your uniform, and report to the Charge of Quarters NCO after evening chow."

"Yes, Sergeant Major."

"Private Devlin, you are dismissed."

Devlin stood, came to attention, and saluted. Glass returned the salute, and Devlin performed an about face and exited the office.

* * *

As he entered the platoon bay, Atwell made a beeline for him. "Dev, man I'm…"

"Skip it," Devlin said wearily. "It was an accident. I'm okay, if a little sore. I'm just getting sick of getting into accidents. That's two trips to sick call. That has to be a record."

Atwell looked both relieved and worried. "Maybe…"

"Nah," Kenyon said coming up to the duo. "Record was a guy in my da's platoon. He was literally on sick call for accidents twenty-four different times. Legit accidents, too. He was really unlucky."

"What happened to him?" Devlin asked.

"He joined the Navy and became an admiral," Kenyon said, grinning.

Devlin wasn't sure if he should laugh or not. "So, at the rate I'm going, I'll either be dead or a general."

Atwell bit his lip. "Devlin, I really…"

"I said, skip it," Devlin repeated emphatically. "Just don't point shooty things at me anymore. Or pointy things. Or really any kind of things. Roger?" He grinned to show he didn't hold it against the other recruit. Atwell couldn't have known that the round would come out and hit Devlin. It wasn't even his weapon.

As if Atwell could tell what his friend was thinking, he spoke up quickly. "It wasn't Kuzma's fault, either. She asked me for help since I was her buddy yesterday. We were both paying too much attention to getting the round out that we didn't pay attention to where the damn thing was pointing. We didn't even know Cho was with you until she came back and said you'd been shot."

Devlin sighed. "It's all right, Marty. I got to get my shit together. I'm CQ runner for the weekend since I won't be doing regular weekend duty." He looked at Kenyon. "That's your notice from the sergeant major, by the way. You'll have to find someone to do my cleaning chores, Pony."

"No problem, Dev," Kenyon replied. "I started figuring that out after they shipped you to medical." Her face became serious. "I'm glad. We're all glad you're okay, Dev."

He breathed out. "Bullshit. But it's nice of you to say so. I gotta get going."

He drew away from the two recruits and went to his bunk.

* * * * *

Chapter Sixteen

Devlin awoke at the sound.

It was faint, barely even a sound. The night watch hadn't even noticed. He glanced toward the end of the bay. The young recruit at the desk seemed to be awake, but just barely. She had her hand on her chin and nodded, then straightened, then nodded again a moment later. Devlin laid there for a moment, listening. He heard the sound again a moment later. It was coming from the other end of the bay. He turned over in his rack and looked around the bay. Under the latrine door, a sliver of light could be seen.

Curiosity ignited, Devlin gently laid back his covers to keep from disrupting them anymore than necessary. He got out of his rack and went quietly up to the trainee at the desk.

"Arnette," he whispered next to her ear. Then he clamped a hand over the girl's mouth when she nearly jumped out of her skin. "Shhhh. It's Devlin. Don't worry. Just gotta get up. I didn't want you making a fuss. Stay here. I gotta go to the latrine." He took his hand away, and she nodded, smiling at him.

"No problem," she whispered back. "I'll just note in the log that you made a latrine run."

Devlin padded toward the latrine, and he heard movement inside the squad bathing area, scraping, a muffled clump, sobbing, low voices.

Devlin looked down the bay one last time, just to make sure he and Arnette were the only ones awake, which was when he noticed Tamman's rack was empty.

Devlin opened the latrine door and slid inside as quickly as possible, taking a moment to allow his eyes to adjust to the new brightness. He looked up and down the toilet and sink area but saw nothing. The sounds appeared to be coming from the shower bay.

He made sure the door was shut fast and crept to the closest entrance to the shower. It was one big room with wide open doorways on each end. Distributed around the room were nozzles that more often than not sprayed water at two temperatures: too farking cold or too farking hot.

At the end of each day, the recruits would be herded into the latrines and given five minutes to "douche off pits, tits, and splits." The entire operation sounded more organized than it actually was. By the time you actually got the water to where you weren't in physical agony, you had to turn it off to grab your towel and go. Then the next recruit would step up and repeat the operation.

Now the shower was empty and dry, except for the #42 spray nozzle. It had a drip that wouldn't stop. As far as Devlin could tell it had probably been dripping since the planet had been formed from cosmic dust.

In the center of the room was the Typhon recruit, Tamman. Typhon was a kind of cold hell world that never turned into a huge thriving colony. The only reason it existed was its location and its huge deposits of heavy metals. Typhonese bred for big. It was a heavy world with heavier than Earth normal gravity, but Tamman was big even for a native Typhon. He was also, Devlin noted, not the sharpest tool in the tool bag. He wasn't dumb, but he wasn't as fast on his feet as, say, Baxter or Gartlan. When the squad needed something physical, Tamman was the man to call; well, him or the Olympian, Chapis. Devlin was in good shape and generally didn't have too much difficulty with the physical training. Tamman looked like most of that bored him.

Now, he was seated in the center of the room with a mat laid in front of him. He had his M269 disassembled and laid out on the mat and he was trying to put it back together.

"Tam?" Devlin asked as he stepped into the room.

The big man startled and look up. "Whatcha doing up, Devlin?" he asked, cocking his head to the side, his big ugly face wrinkling. "You shouldn't be up. You should be sleeping. Gotta get up soon."

He went back to trying to reassemble the weapon. His big fingers were having a hard time getting all the little pieces to fit together.

"I could say the same thing about you, Big Guy," Devlin said as he came over.

Tamman was rocking back in forth trying to recite the litany of the rifle in under his breath. "Firing pin goes into the..."

"Pin carrier."

"Pin carrier," the big man repeated. "The pin carrier is inserted into...into..." he held the pin carrier in his fingers and looked intently at the mat. The next piece of the puzzle was missing.

"Oh no, oh no..." Tamman whispered to himself. "It's gone...Oh no."

The big recruit dropped the rifle bolt on the mat and started rocking back and forth again, softly crying. "I'm gonna get thrown out...he said so. Gonna get tossed out, and then what?"

Devlin went over and touched the big man on the shoulder. "You're not gonna get thrown out, Tam," he said gently. "I'm not going to let you." When the big man didn't respond, Devlin hunched down on the other side of the mat and whispered urgently, "Tamman!"

The recruit's head snapped up. His eyes were filled with tears and his face was a mask of agony. "They're gonna throw me out, Devlin. I can't do this shit! I ain't smart enough to remember all of this, and I have trouble putting all this little shit together."

"You are smart enough, Tam," Devlin said soothingly. "They'd never have let you in if you didn't have the mental capacity to perform the tasks."

"But I just can't seem to get it right, Devlin," the giant said. "I keep screwing it up, especially when the sergeant major is watching."

"I know. You're just nervous because you want to get it right. It happens. You worry about screwing up, so you're concentrating on all the ways you *could* screw up, and then you do because that's what you were thinking about."

Devlin sat down and crossed his legs. "What you gotta do is learn this thing backwards and forwards. You're taking a first step here. What we need to do is quiz you on it every chance we get until you know it by heart."

"Okay," Tamman said slowly. He furrowed his brow. "But…"

"Look, I don't sleep that much anyway. Results of a crappy childhood. I'll set my chrono each night, and I'll get you up, and we'll come in here and make sure you're squared away. I'll quiz you on your shit, we'll make sure your kit is shipshape, and then we'll get back in the rack to get a little more shut-eye before the night watch wakes up the morning duty crew. How about it?"

"What do you get out of this?" the big man asked, almost suspicious.

Devlin shrugged. "Right now, nothing, I guess," he said. "But I may need a favor sometime down the road. Who knows, maybe we'll run into a situation that I don't know, and you got down pat."

"Like what?" the big man snorted. "Eating?"

They both chuckled. "No," Devlin said finally. "But for now, let's just say I'm putting my finger in a bully's eye." He reached out and pulled a small electrical component from under Tamman's stockinged feet. "Here's your bolt actuator. It goes on the pin carrier at the fourth détente."

They took all of the pieces apart and laid them down on the mat between them in the proper order. "The reassembly of the M269 Railfiring Pulserifle is as follows..." the two men chanted together.

* * *

"Tamman," McClellan sneered as he inspected Tamman's rifle, "where does the electronic bolt actuator mount on the rifle?"

"Sergeant Major!" Tamman roared. "The electronic bolt actuator mounts on the fourth détente of the pin carrier assembly for the M269 Personal Railfiring Pulserifle! Sergeant Major!"

McClellan grunted and thrust the weapon back at the recruit. He sidestepped and stopped in front of Devlin. "Inspection *arms!*" he barked.

Devlin produced his rifle, but without the snap he had taught Tamman in their midnight drills in the latrine. After two weeks, the big Typhon knew the parts of the weapon, could recite the litany, and even had the manual of arms down. Under Devlin's tutelage, the bigger man was doing well enough that McClellan was having a hard time finding anything to harass him on, which relieved the big man immensely and consequently seemed to irritate McClellan. Which meant McClellan just transferred his attention to someone else.

He ran his finger into the loading receiver of the weapon. He removed the finger and gazed at it for a moment. It was clean. "Dirty receiver." He said, dropping the weapon on the ground. "Twenty-four hours extra duty tonight for the platoon." Several groans came from the group at that pronouncement but cut off as the drill instructor's head started to rise.

"Kenyon!" the NCO bellowed.

"Sergeant Major!" Nicki shouted in reply.

"You're fired as Platoon Leader," he said, looking directly at Devlin.

Devlin watched as the young woman turned pale. She hadn't done anything wrong; this was just McClellan being a prick.

"Twenty-four hours extra duty on top of that for Devlin," he instructed the staff sergeant who made a note on the clipboard. He smirked at Devlin then looked down. "You've dropped your weapon, Private. That is just not done. That weapon is your life. If it drops, so do you. Get me? Drop and give me one hundred pushups," he said. He sidestepped and went on to the next recruit as Devlin assumed the front-leaning rest position and began doing pushups.

"Son of a bitch," Devlin grated under his breath.

"*What was that?*" McClellan snarled, spinning.

Devlin rose to his feet, his hands balling into fists. "I said, you…"

"I heard what you called me, you little whoreson!" Devlin's head snapped up and his eyes blazed with hate. McClellan snarled. "Who do you think you are, Recruit? Just what do you think gives you the right to question anything I do? You, who can't even make a bed. Who only joined because he had to avoid jail?" He seemed to swell, his face turning a shade of purple as he spoke. "Stark! Take these worthless dregs of genetic misfortune out on a five-K run. Run the piss out of them."

Stark got the platoon on their feet and got them running in an instant. Kenyon looked back at Devlin as the formation double-timed it out on to the roadway.

McClellan's eyes were agate-hard as they bored into Devlin.

"Me and you, boy. Right now! Follow me."

* * * * *

Chapter Seventeen

McClellan turned on his heel and stalked away from the barracks area. Devlin followed, his blood starting to boil. He had had enough of this shit. Maybe he would take the brig time. This bastard hounded everyone unmercifully.

They went through a gap between a couple of unused barracks buildings. As he walked, Devlin started to calm down, and as he did, he got nervous as he rethought the whole thing.

Finally, they were alone. They were in a trash loading area. There were large garbage dumpsters everywhere. *A great place to dispose of a body,* Devlin thought.

"So, *I'm* a sonuvabitch? Huh, Devlin? Isn't that what you called me?" McClellan demanded, rounding on the recruit. "So, you think you know what *I* am?"

"Sergeant Major, I…"

"Sergeant Major what?" He pushed the recruit. "You farkwit! *What?* Now you don't want to kick my ass?" He got in Devlin's face. His breath was hot. He was practically frothing at the mouth. His rage was incandescent.

The punch came out of nowhere and hit Devlin in the gut. Devlin felt the wind rush out of his lungs. As he doubled over, he felt another sledgehammer blow to his side. There was a sharp, agonizing pain in his ribs, making breathing even more difficult than it was a moment before. He tried to raise his hands, but they were batted away as another hammer blow hit the back of his head. He went to his knees, stunned. He panted for breath through the pain in his side. He felt the NCO's hands grab the back of his head and his collar.

"You, who can barely do anything according to the farking manual, are gonna tell *me* how to discipline someone?" Devlin was jerked upright. A punch came in and smashed his nose. Pain exploded in his head.

"Someone who can't even discipline himself?" Another punch and another cascade of pain and exploding lights as his right eye was bashed. The hit opened up a gash in his forehead and blood immediately obscured his rapidly swelling eye. A right cross smashed him in the mouth. "A goddamned son of a drug-addled whore?"

Devlin caught the punch coming toward his face. The sergeant major's voice cut off mid-tirade as Devlin's left fist came up from his belt line and landed just under the raging NCO's chin. The force of the blow knocked the broad man off balance, and he let go of Devlin's tunic as he sought to regain his footing. Furious and bellowing in pain, Devlin crashed into the older man. He ducked under a flailing blow and started pounding.

Toe to toe, the soldier and the recruit rained fists, feet, elbows, and knees on each other. Devlin had been a brawler since he was a kid on the streets. The last months of training had taken raw talent and fine-tuned it, giving it focus. He had speed and reflexes, and he was pissed.

The sergeant major had years of training and still had the speed and power of a man in his prime. He was Devlin's height and had at least twenty or thirty pounds on the recruit. He had power and knew how to use it.

Both men were evenly matched and, in a few moments, they both knew it. They circled each other, predators looking for a weakness they could exploit to destroy the other.

Devlin saw him draw the knife as it flashed out of the scabbard at the small of McClellan's back. His left hand swept low to intercept the hand of the DI as his right hand continued in an arc that connected with the old instructor's cheek.

Bone met soft tissue and bone. The DI's head snapped around, and Devlin caught the knife hand and twisted, using the technique McClellan had shown the platoon for disarming an opponent just days before.

The DI blocked Devlin from swinging the knife into his face. Devlin forced his foot between the DI's boots and stepped in close, pushing the older man off balance. As he leaned backward, Devlin rode the momentum and swept his leg behind the DI's and pulled his foot back. The old veteran started to fall, and Devlin went along for the ride.

McClellan landed on his back, his breath whooshing out in a single gasp. Devlin brought the knife up and stuck it right under the older man's chin.

"Before you kill me, I ought to remind you of something," McClellan gasped. One eye was swollen shut and his mouth was a bloody mess.

Devlin wasn't much better off. He knew without really checking that at least one tooth was gone, and another was missing. The pain in his side told him he had a cracked or broken rib, and from the feeling in his back, he was going to be pissing blood for a day or so, at least until his nanites repaired the bruised kidney. His right eye was swollen shut.

"What?" the younger man gasped. "The best place to plant this thing? I'd say heart, but I don't think you have one."

"That's probably true," McClellan admitted, grinning through bloody lips. He rolled his tongue around in his mouth and spat bloody saliva to the side. "But nah...McClellan's Rules #43: In a knife fight, never have just a knife."

Devlin suddenly felt something move down around his crotch area. Without moving the knife, he glanced down at his belt line.

The old instructor was holding a small compact pistol, the barrel aimed directly at Devlin's manhood.

"Single-shot flechette," the raspy voice said, chuckling. "It'd probably improve your singing voice, might even qualify you for Navy service."

Devlin felt the bottom drop out of his stomach. His rage was gone in an instant, replaced by a cold fear.

The battered drill instructor read him like a book and chuckled again.

"Now, why don't you give me back my pig-sticker, and we'll go get a drink and talk."

* * *

They went back to the barracks, walking right past a dumbfounded Charge of Quarters Sergeant and his runner, Private Kuzma.

They were a sight. Devlin's face was battered, his nose possibly broken, lips puffy and bloody. The sergeant major wasn't in much better shape, and his uniform was not inspection ready.

They proceeded to "cadre row," the section of offices reserved for the drill instructors, support staff, and the commander's office at the end of the hallway.

The door closed behind them, and the sergeant major palmed open his door and gestured for the young man to precede him. Devlin went in, and McClellan closed the door behind him.

"Want a drink?" McClellan asked.

"That's not allowed, is it?" Devlin said as he sat in the chair the instructor pointed to.

"Well, there's rules, but at this point, I think we can kind of dispense with them," McClellan said noncommittally.

Devlin frowned. "What are you getting at, Sergeant Major? And, yeah, I'd love a drink. I think I need something to kill the pain in my face."

McClellan grinned crookedly. "Sorry about your nose. I think you knocked four of my teeth loose. I haven't had a brawl like that since...well, before you were born." He shook his head, still grinning.

He pulled a hydration pack out of his desk. He opened the spout over a couple of glasses he had also pulled from the drawer.

McClellan took a glass. "Up your bottom," he said, draining it. "I guess you're wondering 'What the hell?' and other words," he said as he looked the young soldier over.

"That would be close to the mark, Sergeant Major," Devlin agreed. He hadn't touched his glass.

McClellan sighed. "You know how long I've been doing this, Devlin? Taking mewling mamma's babies and making something His Majesty can use?"

Devlin shook his head.

"I've been in the military since my eighteenth birthday. I enlisted because I was facing an attempted murder charge." He smiled at the shocked look on Devlin's face. "Didn't see that one coming, did you? I had words with this fellow about something personal, and it came to blows. He gave as good as he got, but I was a little better and, in some ways, a lot luckier. He fell and broke his fool neck—the ass. And for my sins, I wound up in a Justiciar's Court and given approximately the same spiel Jadwidzik gave you." He watched the young recruit's face go white. "Oh yeah, I know Jadwidzik...Sergeant

Major's Association. At a certain level, every sergeant major knows every other one, but that's not the only way I know him. But that's neither here nor there. The thing is, I'm ninety-three years old. I've been in His Majesty's Army for seventy-five years. I've been training recruits for about sixty-five of those years."

Devlin stared at the older man. Training cadre usually just served a tour and then went back out into the field. The corporals, he knew, would make sergeant, then go to NCO school, then back out to the war.

"So how—"

"How, or more appropriately, *why* have I been training recruits this long?" McClellan asked. "The answer is long and complicated. And, to be completely honest, I do go out and do refreshers in ops, but for the most part I've been here. The main reason is someone saw something in me that I hadn't.

"He recognized that, given my background, I had a talent for spotting and mentoring talent."

Devlin furrowed his brow. The NCO went on.

"I'm a brawler. Always have been. You might have already noticed," he said, pointing his chin at Devlin. At Devlin's grunt he continued. "I can usually spot the brawlers. The ones who are dangerous, the ones who might have a problem with authority or who might just wind up being superlative leaders. The Venn diagrams of qualities sometimes overlap.

"Mind you, we are in the Army...or Navy, or whatever. While we are in those organizations, we want—need—soldiers, people who will obey orders and carry out the damned mission. Got that?"

Devlin nodded. "Yes, Sergeant Major. All I've wanted to do is be a good soldier. I don't know—"

"But while we need soldiers, we also need *warriors*," McClellan said, cutting him off. "Men and women who can take those orders and, in the sting and fire of combat, adapt, expand, and lead. The two can be compatible but are not always present in every soldier. We need soldiers *and* warriors. Soldiers we can produce in plenty. It's the warriors that are rare. That's part of my job, spotting the warriors."

Devlin frowned. He hadn't figured someone would get bent out of shape because he was *not* standing out.

"You mean this was all engineered?" Devlin demanded incredulously.

McClellan snorted. "Of course. Do you seriously think an outfit like the IAA would allow an absolute sociopathic asshole to become an instructor? Other than me, are any of the other drills monsters?"

"Well, no…"

"Hell, no!" came the quick rejoinder. "The military needs all the best. Sure, we weed out the weak-minded. But all that means is that support ranks get the quitters."

Devlin looked like a stunned cow. "Wait a minute!" he said. The shocks were coming too quick. "I thought—"

"You thought that if you quit, it was all over?" the drill instructor asked. "In some cases, yes. But we are big believers in waste not, want not. There are a lot of folks for whom combat service is contraindicated. When the shit hits the fan, they fold. But it doesn't mean they're of no use. After they ring out, we give them an option. They can go over to another type of military service. They proceed through another type of boot camp, just to make sure they got the basics of military bearing and skills. It's a whole lot more laid back, and they still get some of the chicken shit, but they don't get ridden like they do here. They won't go on the MUSTX, they won't do anything more than qualify with personal weapons. They get just enough to say they're military. They can serve in support roles, with the caveat that they will never progress past a certain point. They'll never see sergeant major as a rank, but we also give them the option of coming back at a certain point. Maturity is different for lots of people. Sometimes it takes a while for them to be able to handle the mental aspects of service."

Devlin deflated into his chair.

"Sometimes, if we think that person is completely unfit for service, we let them go, but the majority of people who join up serve, even if it's not in capacities they thought about to begin with. And that's *really* what this basic training is for."

Devlin stared at him.

"This training is to sort the sheep from the goats and then the warriors from the soldiers," the NCO finished. McClellan smiled knowingly. "You're probably feeling a bit screwed right now, aren't you? I bet you've been scraping through here all this time, just trying to stay under the radar, but knowing you can't quit, right?"

"Yes," Devlin ground out.

"Let me guess, from the way you've been ghosting up until this point, you've been hoping for an acceptable operational rating, but not combat suitable, right? You were hoping to get through here and get a support role?"

"And your *point*, Sergeant Major?"

"My point is—or rather the question I have is—has it all been all that bad, Devlin? I mean, really, other than the bullshit, you've been having a blast. When you've allowed yourself to, you've kicked ass, taken some names. Hell, even when you were fighting me a while ago, you were there, in the moment. You were doing what you're gifted to do. You have the makings of a decent soldier, Devlin, maybe even a warrior."

"I'm not a warrior," Devlin protested. "I just wanted to do my service and get out."

"Oh, I believe you," the drill instructor said seriously. "And to an extent, you were doing just that. But you made a mistake."

Devlin cocked his head curiously. "Mistake?"

"If you had just done your thing and drove on, neither I nor anybody else would have noticed. Hell, Devlin, you're not the greatest soldier ever, regardless of what you may think. But you do have most of your shit together, and if you do your job, we leave you alone. But then you had to go and start to try and *not* get noticed. That's when we did notice you."

"Huh?" the recruit stammered.

McClellan went on. "McClellan's Rule Number Seventy-Two: If it stinks, it's probably rotten. So, after a while I started to ask myself, why would a kid who is a warrior—I watched the holos of your pugil stick bouts—why would a kid like that ghost? And while we're discussing your stick fighting—lemme see, street-stick fighter with a little Koryo Kwan Di? Am I close?"

"Yes, Sergeant Major," Devlin agreed. "The city where I grew up on Caliban had a couple of RussaKor families. I learned from a couple of the kids. I didn't know it had a name. And I—"

"You spent a lot of time on the streets because your mom was a Caliban plague victim."

Devlin went very still.

"Yeah, I got some of it from your file. Just enough to want to comm Jadwidzik. That particular conversation was about three weeks in the making once I decided you were actually scamming me. I wanted to find out why. Now, technically, I'm not supposed to pry into the private lives of my recruits, but let's just say I have a little special dispensation when it comes to the subject at hand.

"So, I call Jadwidzik to get some details on your case. I don't know all the details. He told me to go to Hell or ask you. From what I gathered, whoever you beat the clabber out of, Jadwidzik isn't losing any sleep over his discomfiture, so I won't either. I'll bet creds to crullers that whatever happened is what spooked you with your little accident on the range, and maybe your head wound outside of chow, but it leaves me on the horns of a dilemma.

"I have this kid who may be a good soldier—maybe—but he's intentionally screwing up. Nothing major, just enough, not even really slacking, just not trying to be…more. And I see indications that he may or may not be what I have been specifically tasked to watch for. So now I got a problem…see Rule Seventy-Two."

"But why all this, Sergeant Major? Why go harassing the squad? If the problem was me…?"

"You still don't get it, do you?" the older man retorted. "I was trying to piss you off. Those other kids were either gonna suck it up or quit. Either way, I'm good. But I have this problem child, an itch I can't scratch. Sometimes, when you're looking for lion, hunt for deer."

"Okay, that one lost me."

"A lion is a predator on old Earth, follow?" Devlin nodded. "Sometimes, if you want the predator, hunt down what it normally looks at as prey. You may bring it into the open."

"So, you picked on people I might give a shit about in the hope of getting me to commit one way or the other," Devlin surmised.

"Precisely," the instructor agreed. "If you'd said 'fark it,' I'd have known you were just a fighter, not a warrior, not a leader, and that would have solved one part of my problem. Hell, some of the people who quit, I ask to stay an extra day so I could make them quit in front of God and everybody. You're not the only possible warrior I'm looking at. You're just the hardest to get to come out. Jadwidzik told me to leave you alone if you wanted me to, except I have these orders to *not* leave you alone if I think you're capable of more than you're giving. Hence my dilemma."

Devlin cocked his head. "So, you decided to try and kill me."

The drill instructor snorted. "Boy, if I had wanted you dead, you'd just not have woken up this morning. Nah, I decided that I was going to give you a choice…of sorts."

* * * * *

Chapter Eighteen

Devlin looked resignedly at his superior. "Pucker factor to full."

"Oh, indeed, young one," McClellan agreed.

He folded his hands, his knuckles bloody from the beating they had delivered. There was a single red smear on the pristine surface of the NCO's desk. Devlin idly thought that he would be the one to have to clean it later.

"You see, I'm not going to let you out of here unless you're committed to giving everything you've got for His Majesty. It wouldn't be fair to the men and women you serve with. How in the fark can they trust you to do what you need to do when the fecal matter hits the rotating impeller if you just ghost through everything?

"Devlin, your squad mates need to know you're going to be there." Devlin opened his mouth, but the NCO kept going. "You can protest all you want, boy, but the truth is that no one is going to trust you if they know you're just 'getting by.' Because when it does hit—no matter if you're out on the battlefield, or in the missile tubes of the battleship, or in the payroll computer room, when something happens—the ghost also tends to be the buddy screwer. And *nobody* wants to be screwed by their buddy, no matter what their sexual proclivities." McClellan smiled at his own joke. Devlin didn't have it in him to do so as well. The Drill Instructor continued as if he hadn't noticed. "So, while regs say you are walking the walk and you pass the tests, there's one test you haven't passed, the smell test of one Virgil Chadwell McClellan."

Devlin cocked his head to the side to crack his neck. It hurt, but he suspected it was about to get tense again.

"You just hit a superior, Devlin. I walked into this area sporting a shiner and missing several teeth. You walked in, looking much the same. After you mouthed off to a senior NCO. People are gonna talk." He grinned. One of the teeth missing was a front tooth.

Devlin's stomach turned into a black hole. "You set me up."

"Oh, yeah, I set you up. Remember, I'm an old hand at this. I could have done it a number of ways, but I like a good scrap every once in a while, so I decided to see where your buttons were. Found them, I suppose," he said sticking a finger into an empty tooth socket. He sniffed. "So, in a little while, the captain is going to come down here and ask me what the hell happened. Or more likely, I'm going to have to go to his office. And you're going to tell me what to tell him."

Devlin stared at the older man in horror. This was precisely what he had tried to avoid. He didn't want to go to jail, and he couldn't quit.

"I just wanted to do my time, Sergeant Major," Devlin said quietly.

"I know you did, boy," said McClellan, just as quietly. "Sometimes, we don't get what we want in life. And, from what I gather, you've already had a life's ration of crap. But you also need to look at things from my perspective. I've got a kid who could do something, no matter what MISS he decides. I have a responsibility to you, to your squad mates, and to His Majesty, to make sure the people I graduate is of the best possible quality. If I were to let Tamman slide on say, weapons, what would happen to his squad mates out in the field? Probably nothing, but then if he forgets just one portion of the litany, that rifle might not fire when he needs it to. And let's just say it's your ass he's covering, or one of your guys. What if McCarthy gets tasked with setting up mines—"

"I read you, Sergeant Major," Devlin said. He hated to admit it, but the bugger had a point.

"Don't like it, but you know it's right." McClellan grinned again. "So, I can't let you slide either. The stakes are too bloody high. I know we haven't hit at it a lot, mainly because thinking about dying on some battlefield is not conducive to training you shartmarks."

Devlin grinned. The sergeant major didn't.

"The truth is, some of your squad mates are going to buy it. You might buy it on the battlefield, you could die filing paperwork on some FOBBIT base somewhere. Hell, you could buy it boffing some little redhead while you're on shore leave. It doesn't matter. Sure, you get a choice of where you serve after Basic, but it doesn't mean His Majesty has to honor it. Exigencies of Service is a phrase you better get used to. You could wind up as a clerk or a lowly, lowly cook, though I highly doubt it; you probably can't cook worth a damn, and they're actually picky about cooks."

The smile slid off Devlin's face. Damn. He had forgotten about that little codicil. He blew out a breath. "So, where does that leave me?"

"Okay," McClellan said, inhaling. He bent over and spit into the trash can by his desk. "Damn, boy, you've got a punch." He straightened. "Here are your options. One, you quit." When Devlin started to protest, McClellan raised his hand to forestall him. "Yeah, I know, not really an option, but it is one.

"Two, I call the captain and the MPs and they cart your little pucker off to the brig to await a court martial for, you guessed it, striking a superior. I know I hit you first, but I could lie and say you hit me first. The witnesses could testify that you were over the edge pissed. Yes, I'm an evil bastard. Sue me. You actually can't quit now if you wanted to.

"Now, here's the shake, Devlin. If I ask the court to, they will make your sentence a minimum, which basically means a few months in the brig followed by a prejudicial discharge, and you're out of here. You'd still have to deal with the charges on Caliban, but in general, keep your nose clean and you'd never have to worry about it. They're not going to expend resources tracking you down, and you'd only wind up back there if you get arrested and they run a criminal record. Then again, I might not ask the court for the minimum, and you'll do the whole ten years in the brig, which, while it isn't a hellhole, is still jail.

"The third option is that you stick it out and do the job." He held up his hands again. "Hear me out, boy. I know you're going to say that's what you were trying to do, but you and I both know it's really not. You were focused on the letter of the contract, but I have to worry about the spirit. I have to worry about all the people who could get screwed. My job to His Majesty is to make sure every recruit who leaves here is doing the job to the best of their abilities, not just standard. It's a job I take damned seriously. One of the reasons I've stayed in the job this long is that I was bit in the ass by a ghost. So, I weed them out.

"I probably would have just served one-and-done like everyone else, but I got lucky with one of my Basic classes. I had a recruit who absolutely insisted on ghosting. He just wanted to do the job and not get noticed, like you. I adamantly refused to let him ghost. In this kid's case, I got called into a conference room with some rather lofty types and told to back off. I told the very lofty people to back the hell up and why. One person liked my answer and told me to keep it up. In fact, I was told that I had this job as long as I wished and to 'get the best out of the recruits and get the worst recruits out.' When King Henry XXV gave me an order, I snapped to, saluted, and said, 'Your will be done, Majesty.'

"That boy was his youngest son, Yancey, who wound up winning the Excalibur Citation, posthumously.

"So, I've had it both ways, young Devlin. And I'll be damned to eternal Hell before I let anyone ghost through my training. I've got an idea of what's in your head. I know the general reason why you're here, and I can empathize, but I'm not gonna give you a pass. You're either going to quit playing soldier and be one, or I'm going to make you serve your time."

Devlin glared at the drill instructor, but his gaze bounced off the older man like missiles on a gravwall. "Come on, boy, use your head. You don't have to kiss my exalted arse or anything. You just have to do your job to the level you and I both know you can. Or you don't have to do anything."

"I hate you," Devlin whispered, shaking his head.

"Nah, you're just saying that to make me feel better. The choice is yours, Devlin." McClellan rose from his desk. "Rule Number Sixty-Eight: Sometimes there isn't a good choice, just less bad ones. You already know this. So, decide which choice is less bad. I'll be in the captain's office."

He paused before walking out the door. "You haven't touched your drink. It's really good hooch. You look like you could use it."

He left.

* * *

A few moments later, Devlin walked down the corridor to the commander's office. At his knock, a voice said, "Enter."

Captain Keith Glass glared over his desk at the NCO in front of him and Devlin as he came alongside the senior enlisted, snapped to parade ground attention, and reported, "Private Devlin, reporting, sir!" He saluted.

Glass glared at him for a few interminable moments then returned the salute.

"Would one of you care to tell me why a senior NCO and a recruit return from God-knows-where looking like they beat the ever living hell out of one another? Because I know there's no way that could have possibly ever happened. Could it, Sergeant Major?"

McClellan looked as calm as a man picking flowers. Devlin swallowed and spoke up. "Sir?"

"You have something to say, Recruit?" Glass said, his voice about one degree Kelvin above absolute.

"Sir, the Sergeant Major noticed a technique I used in hand-to-hand that was not taught by any of the instructors here, sir." Devlin began.

"Go on," Glass said. "Feel free to explain how demonstrating a hand-to-hand technique resulted in injuries that look like they're going to need a regen tank."

"Well, sir," McClellan drawled, "as I had not previously seen this particular strike technique in my seventy-two years of military experience, I asked the recruit to show me. I turned the training of the recruits over to Staff Sergeant Stark and the recruit accompanied me to the rear of the barracks area to further show me the technique in question. I did not feel it proper to waste valuable training time for most of the recruits on what I felt was a basic exchange of information for my own edification."

"Uh huh," Glass said, leaning back in his chair. "And the reason why you both need new uniforms, not to mention dental work and a nanite boost?"

"Well, sir, the basic exchange segued into testing the technique under various forms of attack that I have been acquainted with over my seven decades of instruction, sir. I determined that it would be prudent to see if this technique was transferable to the institutional knowledge base so it might be incorporated into the curriculum, sir!" McClellan barked. "The evolution became all encompassing, resulting in inadvertent strikes at times to the private and myself. Had the damage become life-threatening, I would have suspended the evolution and sought medical attention. At no time were the private or I in any danger, sir. That is based on my extensive—"

"Seventy-two years of experience. Yada yada. I get the picture, Sergeant Major," said Captain Glass wryly. "I won't even comment on your unauthorized use of 'segue' in a sentence. Get the hell out of my office and get cleaned up and hit evening sick call. You're dismissed, Private, go back to your training bay. Dinner is in thirty minutes."

Devlin snapped a salute, which the captain grimly returned. Devlin spun on his heel and exited the office as quickly as possible.

A few moments after the door closed, the captain regarded the NCO still standing at attention. "What do you think, Gil? Do you think it'll take?"

Virgil Chadwell McClellan, Sergeant Major of His Majesty's Imperial Avalonian Army relaxed, looked at his commanding officer, and flopped down into a chair.

"I'd like to think I've gotten a sense by now, Keith." He sighed. "The bitch of it is, you never really can tell whether it does or not. They either stand up or fail spectacularly. He's got the touch; people will follow him when he needs them to. They may not all like him, but they all respect him, or at least what he can do. And he can think on his feet. He can adapt and react. Now, whether he can do that when it counts…"

Glass grunted. "He kept you more frustrated than a grunt in a hundred cred whorehouse with only ninety-nine fifty for three weeks."

McClellan gave his boss a sour look, then snorted and grinned. "Aye, he did that. I haven't had anyone outmaneuver me since a certain smartass that shall remain nameless."

"We'll see how he does between now and MUSTX. If he puts it out there, all good. If he doesn't, he'll screw up, and the MPs can have him. Or the MUSTX will kill him."

* * *

Devlin shrugged off the various questions and comments from Kenyon and MacBain. Kuzma looked at him and went back to her dinner.

Devlin sat quietly, eating gingerly. He figured he had about three loose teeth. While he had managed to knock a few out of the sergeant major's mouth, the sergeant major hadn't gotten as lucky. Or, more likely, had taken it easy on him. The old bastard probably could have dismembered him if he'd wanted to, Devlin decided. *Old age and treachery,* he thought to himself and smiled crookedly.

What he didn't get was why. Oh, he kind of understood the NCO's explanation, but he just couldn't totally wrap his head around it. Or Jadwidzik for that matter. Why had these two guys gone so far out on a limb for him?

Maybe it's not about you, he said to himself. Maybe they see something or are thinking something that isn't totally about you. That would be a nice thought. Too much of his life had been spent trying not to get screwed over. Now, at least, someone was actively trying to help.

Question is, what am I going to do about it?

He sighed and took a forkful of mashed potatoes. They didn't hurt to chew. *Guess I'll walk the walk,* he decided, *and see where it takes me.*

* * *

"Devlin!" Miller called.
"Take Platoon Guide this morning."
"Yes, Drill Sergeant!"
"Fall them in, and get 'em ready to march!"

* * * * *

Chapter Nineteen

"The Armored Power Exoskeleton!" McClellan intoned as he walked the center aisle in the calibration facility of the Armored Training Center. "The A.P.E., or as we like to call them, Monkey Suits…"

That resulted in laughs from the recruits in the process of being fitted for the powered armor for the next phase of their training.

The armor stood three meters tall and resembled precisely what the drill instructor called them. They were large, broad shouldered, and long armed, with hard points for weaponry and ammo storage. Powered by carbon nanotube capacitors, the APEs were used across all branches of the Avalonian military. The Navy and Marine APEs were outfitted specifically for low- or zero-G vacuum combat.

The Army's version was even beefier structurally, with stronger servos for hoisting the insane amounts of ammo or armament that would have once required a crew-served weapon.

Alpha Company—what was left of it—had made it to the final phase of Basic Training: Individual Technical Combat. For their final month, they would be given instruction in armored suits and all the technical goodies that Avalonian Technology could provide them, as well as the big, the bad, and the ugly as far as single-crewed or small-crewed weaponry and vehicles.

This would only be an introductory course; specialization would take place after Basic if they chose a field that required them to use APEs.

"Forget the holos, folks. These things are and aren't what you think they are," the NCO said, stopping in the center of the room. "They will protect you from general small arms fire. They will not totally protect you from modern fire. For instance, while it may stop a round from your M269, it will not do it at point blank range, and it damn sure won't stop a hypervelocity AP round from a M284. It will help you lift more than you can normally, but you ain't gonna go bench press a mech or a tank."

He grunted at some remembered joke, "Hell, knowing you little pansies, you'll still be bitching at the amount of ammo and gear you gotta hump out in the field!"

There was another chuckle, and this time Higgs called out from her armor, "More PT, Drill Sergeant!" Which started a whole chorus of groans and the company singing "One of the songs of my people!"

More PT drill sergeant!

More PT!

We like it!

We love it!

We want more of it!

More PT drill sergeant!

More PT!

"You're damn right!" McClellan growled, fighting not to smile. "Rule Number Five: The more you sweat…"

"The less you bleed!" the company chorused.

He waited for a moment.

"You Recruits…No, you're not recruits anymore. Trainees!"

He stopped as the hoots and yells started with earnest. Each of the young men and women in the room erupted in cheers and celebration as they received the ultimate praise from their senior drill instructor.

They weren't soldiers—or whatever they were going to become—yet, but they were no longer the useless recruits McClellan had lamented over all those months before.

Devlin nearly bounced in his armor. He yelled the keening screech of the Hellions and the rest of the platoon answered. He heard the "Boom!" of the Deadly Fourth, the feral squeals of the Mad Pigs, and the roar of the Herd. He grinned like a hungry wolf, then settled back in his armor as he caught the gimlet eye from the armor tech who was trying to attach the telemetry links from the armor to his battleskins.

"APEs make you harder to kill and easier for you to kill the enemy. But like anything else, it's just a tool. The Most Dangerous Weapon…"

"Is the mind of the warrior!" the company yelled, reciting Rule Number One.

"You Trainees are going to learn how these suits will make combat a little easier. Some of you will never wear them again. Some of you will die in these someday. But not today.

"Today, and for the next couple weeks, you're going to just about live in these suits. You will come to understand why we call them monkey suits. You will come to just about hate them. But like any relationship, it's a little bit of love and a little bit of hate." He swept his gaze around the room. "Once your tech gives you the 'go,' fall out onto the ready pad outside."

"Yes, Drill Sergeant!" Devlin and the rest of Alpha Company, Third Battalion, One Forty-Ninth Training Legion yelled in answer.

* * *

"Move left!" Devlin yelled into his comm.

The Hellions had broken into squads and were engaging each other in a small game of Capture the Flag, but with guns, grenades, and missiles, instead. First Squad had tried an end run on the course and had run smack dab into an ambush hosted by Fourth Squad. Second and Third had tried going up two different sections through the middle and were engaged in a running firefight.

Devlin ducked as a dummy missile round flew toward his position and overshot, impacting a wall near where he was sheltering. If it had been an actual HE round, he'd have likely been pelted with several pounds of flying shrapnel and rock, none of which would have penetrated his suit, so the suit's sensors didn't protest with anything more than a proximity alarm.

"Damn, that was close. Sparkle Pony, Kuzma is trying to take my head off. Could you do something about that?"

"Sure thing, Devlin." Immediately, four grenades from Kenyon's M526 grenade launcher arced over the roadway and disappeared behind the edge of another wall. Devlin heard Kuzma curse and the beeping of a near hit on an "enemy."

"Jonesy, you and Tamman direct fire on the position Kenyon just lit up. Keep Kuz and whoever else is over there pinned down for a minute."

"On it," the lanky recruit drawled.

Rounds started pinging against the wall and through the "murder holes" to the other side.

Devlin looked at the HUD in his helmet. The APE armor had some sensors, though they were limited, but it did have a pretty decent interface that allowed soldiers to see where each other were, with some insight as to where enemies were located based on incoming fire.

"Cho, do you have eyes on the objective?" he asked over the squad frequency.

"Yes," came the reply over his comm. "Private Decker is making progress toward it. Should I discourage her?"

"Yes, but try not to give your own position away. That farking Bahadur is almost as scary as you are with a rifle."

He heard a sniff. "He's a poser. He takes all day to size up a shot."

Devlin snorted. "Don't get cocky."

"It's only the truth…Oh, silly woman." He heard the whipcrack of Cho's rifle. "Private Decker is no longer making progress."

"All the same, you probably ought to move to secondary."

"Advancing now."

"Everybody hold your position and scan for snipers while Cho adjusts position," Devlin said on the channel.

He heard the acknowledgments as he scanned the walls for signs of either the Gurkha rifle expert or Fourth Squad coming into the play area.

His comm buzzed in his ear. "Devlin, we're taking fire from the right flank. I think what's left of Fourth has joined the party."

Devlin swore. They were now fighting on two fronts and though they had most of their team, they were now outnumbered by the remains of the other two squads.

He heard another whipcrack of a supersonic round. Lett cursed and the tell-tale beep of a kill sounded. "I'm out."

"Nine Little Buggers…" Devlin muttered. "Pretty soon we'll just be buggered, Cho."

"In position. Tracking...Oh, there you are," the sniper purred. "Come to momma Cho."

Whip-crack. "Private Bahadur will now be reincarnated...as my bitch."

Cho had changed since she and McCarthy had started hanging together. It seemed that helping the former sad sack of the platoon was helping her work through her own rage and seeming helplessness over her situation. She was still usually very cool and reserved, except when she was behind a scope. Then she talked trash with the best of them.

"Sweet shot, short stuff," McCarthy said. "I can see him from here. He is *pissed!*"

"Short stu—Thomas," Cho sounded mild. "Would you like your other arm broken?"

"Devlin," Tamman commed. "I am out of ammunition. What should I do? Jones is not in a position to cross load."

"Hold tight," Devlin said, checking his HUD. McCarthy and Kenyon were closest.

"Not going anywhere. It's a nice day. I figure I'll just take in the view."

"Tamman, you're spending too much time with Jones." He switched channels.

"Pony? You free?"

"No, but I'll talk for a meal and movie," Kenyon quipped back. "Seriously, no. I'm taking a little bit of fire here. I'm good, but not going anywhere."

McCarthy cut in, "I got it, Devlin! Cover me."

Devlin saw McCarthy burst from his position, damn near running in the big bulky armor. He saw impacts from the sim rounds hit where a foot had been a moment before, but never quite hitting the private.

"Shit! Shit! Shit!" McCarthy's voice came over the comm.

Then Devlin saw something he never thought he'd see. Tom McCarthy started a dive over a wall, and as he did, he twisted and fired his rifle offhand back toward whoever had been firing. As the huge armored form disappeared behind the wall to land, presumably, on his back, he heard another kill beep with the tone for Fourth Squad.

"Luck!" Pringle yelled over the platoon open frequency.

"You don't need luck if you're good," McCarthy replied. "Hey ya there, big guy. Want some ammo? I need a hand first."

"Everybody give McCarthy a hand," Jonesy said. "One golf clap, execute."

Devlin chuckled. Then he saw the gap on his HUD. "Squad, the way to the objective is clear. I'm breaking cover and heading up. Alpha Team, continue to pour fire on the right flank. Bravo, you're on the left."

Devlin broke from his position, firing at movement on his left. Practice rounds pinged on the parapet wall covering a Third trooper. The head went back down.

APEs can run, but not well and not fast. The heavy suits covered distance by taking the work out of a loping trot. Plus, it could trot with a hell of a lot of weight. The average APE suit was capable of carrying several hundred kilos of gear and cover fifty kilometers in a few hours. It wasn't that it was fast, but it could eat distance with long, sustained strides.

Devlin ran for the flag area, scanning as best he could for potential targets.

One hundred meters.

A Fourth soldier started to pop his head up, but a shot from Jones and a curse from the trooper stopped him.

Eighty meters.

Devlin fired at a shadow moving on the parapet wall.

The walls lining the avenue disappeared with bits of rubble and scant cover. Fifty meters ahead, the flag stood amongst a cairn of rocks with various unit names and numbers written on it denoting past winners of the game.

Soon Second Squad, Second Platoon would be on there. He grinned evilly as he bounded forward. He could almost touch the flag—

But suddenly, his armor locked up, and all he could hear was the constant beep of a kill shot.

* * *

"So, what have we learned?" Sergeant Major McClellan asked. Second Platoon was out of their armor and in the briefing room at the Armored Training Center. The "capture the flag" scenario was over and the time had come for lessons learned and institutional scab-picking. Everyone was encouraged to own up to their failures and suggest different methods for a future scenario.

Sean "Wolf" Gartlan raised his hand. "Even if you're doing an end run, put out scouts to watch for ambush."

First Squad had gotten their asses handed to them by an ambush hosted by Fourth. While they had acquitted themselves well and gave as good as they got, they still lost almost every person in the squad.

The notable exception was Private Atwell, who in turn took the lesson to heart about ambushes.

"And don't pop your head up to look unless you know you're out of the field of fire," Anne Marie Decker piped in, her pleasant face grimacing in remembered embarrassment. "An M8 sensor ball or a small tac drone would have been really useful."

"Which is why you don't get them in training," Staff Sergeant Stark said from the side of the room. "Generally, we try to train you in all the good habits so that, when you get all the nice toys, you don't devolve into bad habits and get a bullet in the brain."

"Nothing ever has been able to beat the Mark One eyeball," McClellan said, crossing his arms. He leaned on the podium. "Just because you have 'armor'—" he unfolded his arms and did the finger claw quotation marks in the air, "—and you have neat toys, the fact is that you still need to be cognizant of all the things that can kill you in a firefight.

"That armor is just a thin coating of cerasteel. We haven't developed anything that can protect you from the really bad stuff on the battlefield. Sure, most of what you lot will see in the field or on ships is raiders and pirates, but if you ever have it drop in the pot with actual military hardware pitted against you, like the Nords or the Brotherhood, you will need every advantage. You cannot take anything for granted."

Devlin raised his hand. "Never take for granted that your communications or positions are secure from the enemy. In my case, Atwell was able to listen in on our squad push because I didn't take him off the queue when he got transferred back to First."

As the numbers had dwindled in Bravo Company, the platoons and squads had been consolidated with Alpha Company to maintain manning. Initially, Atwell had moved to Second Squad before Devlin took over as Platoon Leader.

When the teams were divided up for the exercise, Devlin was folded into Second Squad and Atwell had been placed with First Squad. Since he *had* been in Second Squad, Devlin hadn't taken him off the Second Squad push channel. During the exercise, after First Squad had been rendered combat ineffective, Atwell had set up a lone ambush to keep Second Squad from reaching the objective.

He had managed to bag Devlin on his way to the flag, but he hadn't managed to keep Jones and Cho from making First Squad completely combat ineffective.

Devlin had been neutralized, but Kenyon stepped up, coordinated like a good squad leader, and drove on. She, Jones, Cho, Tamman, and McCarthy had survived to take the flag.

"But," he continued, "that was only due to my not purging him from the squad push. He'd have never been able to do that in real life."

McClellan cocked his head and looked at him. "I wouldn't be too sure about that," he countered. "I don't give a shit who you are and how good your crypto is, never assume. I think we've discussed that before. In this case, never assume that you're not being listened in on."

"Back on Old Earth, history is rife with examples of armies thinking their comms were secure, and the whole time they were being eavesdropped on. And it's happened since we left Earth."

He nodded. "I think we've covered the high points. The sergeants and I will look at the holos and see if there is anything else we can pick out. Not terrible, people. Not great, but not terrible. Oh, and while I'm thinking of it—McCarthy!"

"Yes! Sergeant Major!" McCarthy straightened in his chair.

"*What the hell? Over?* No, I'm serious. Did you really run an APE suit across an open road and dive backward over a wall? Do you have a death-wish, boy?"

"That depends on who you talk to, Sergeant Major," the young man said, grinning. At a prolonged stare from McClellan, the grin slid off his face. "No, Sergeant Major, I don't. But I've kind of got this feeling for what I can do in the armor." He shrugged. "While I was moving, I was scanning for the person shooting at me. I lined up on him and shot a burst as I went over the wall. I wanted to keep him from getting too good a bead on me."

"You did that all right," the NCO said, shaking his head. "Those suits aren't designed for that crap. They can take punishment, but always be a little conservative. If you do, they'll save you."

He looked at the trainees. "I want to congratulate you. You have made it this far and not quit. Along the way, you learned enough not to totally cock up when the bullets are flying." He grinned coldly. "But don't let it go to your head.

"MUSTX has washed out people. Be careful that you don't let your guard down. This exercise is designed by people who are smarter and more devious than me. Be ready.

"One last command for the day: hit the showers and grab chow. Formation at oh-five hundred tomorrow. We'll do a couple of little runs to show you some other features on the APEs, then we will rack the armor, head back to the company, and start prepping for the lift to MUSTX. Get your prep done right and you'll get weekend passes to Liberty Station after we check in on the *Hermes*, our transport for the lift."

* * * * *

Epilogue

Recruit Private Nikolai Nikolayevich Devlin stood at attention with the rest of Alpha Company as Sergeant Major McClellan handed the company off to Captain Glass. The salute was as flawless as someone with over seventy-five years in the military could execute. Glass very solemnly returned the salute then dropped his hand.

He boomed. "Sergeant Major! Post!"

McClellan marched to the back of formation and waited at attention.

"Parade *rest!*" Glass boomed, and the formation made an audible snap as feet spread shoulder-width apart, hands clasped behind the back of each recruit and NCO.

"Congratulations!" Glass began. "Congratulations on finishing five months of hard work, discipline, and learning. You came here all those weeks ago as raw, untrained recruits. You endured stress, deprivation, exercise, and a college-level education in the art of killing people and breaking things, and through it all, you did not quit. Many of the people who arrived here with you are not here anymore."

Which was true. What started out as four company's-worth of recruits was now one company. Devlin couldn't even begin to count how many people he'd seen just up and quit. But he was still there. Second Platoon Hellions were still here. He couldn't see her from his position, but he knew Kenyon was standing as Second Squad Leader, fighting not to grin. Without turning his head, he knew where they all were. Jonesy and Tamman, Cho, McCarthy, Baxter, Arnette, Atwell, Mac, and Kuzma. All the people who had helped him get here, too.

He had come here with no one and nothing to keep him except knowing he couldn't quit. That turned out to be not quite a lie, but now he knew why Jadwidzik had glossed it over. Had he quit, he may have been able to survive, but not to live. Ghosting. A ghost was nothing but the echo of a life.

McClellan was right. It hadn't been all that bad. In fact, he'd had a pretty good time once he'd quit trying to keep everyone at arm's length and found a few people to have his back. And he had that. He would go anywhere with this bunch and do anything. He wanted to go to the frontier and look for the pirates that killed Cho's family. He wanted to fight alongside Kuzma, Atwell, and Mac in big honking tanks. He wanted to see Kenyon fulfill the legacy of her family.

He might seek out peace and quiet someday, but for now it was the awful shock and rage of battle he wanted. Well, not right now, he supposed. He turned his attention back to Glass.

"You will take what you've learned and put it to as ultimate a test as we can muster without putting you out on the sharp end pointed at the enemy.

"In a few short days, you will be boarding ships to complete your shipboard familiarization and training while you travel to the planet on which you will complete your Multi Unit Survival and Tactics Exercise.

"For one week you will survive in a randomly chosen environment using only what you choose to take with you. And no, you don't get to take a star cruiser." Chuckles erupted from the recruits.

"During that week, you will be given coordinates for a rendezvous where you will hookup with each other. Then you will be joined by the Fifth Legion to conduct field unit exercises for two weeks. At the end of that time, you will return here, and you will choose your military branch and specialization. You will then graduate as full members of His Majesty's Military. You will no longer be recruits but full-fledged warriors where hardship and glory await you! Oowah?"

"*Oooooowah!*" answered the gathered recruits.

"That is all I have to say for the time being. Congratulations and good luck on your MUSTX. Trust yourselves, your fellow teammates, and your NCOs, and you will stand on this tarmac again in a few short weeks and turn those grey uniforms in for black.

"Have a good liberty, don't get into trouble, don't add to the population, and do not subtract from the population. This ends your pre-weekend safety brief.

"Sergeant Major! Front and center!"

McClellan marched to the front, saluted Captain Glass and intoned, "Sergeant Major McClellan reporting as ordered, *sir!*"

"Dismiss the trainees and perform all required items on the itinerary prior to releasing them to weekend liberty."

"Yes, sir!" He saluted Glass, which was dutifully returned. As Glass walked off the parade field, McClellan turned to the formation.

"Company!" he bellowed.

"Platoon!" Devlin yelled.

"A-ten-*shun!*" There was another audible snap as boots were brought together while the trainee assumed the position of attention.

"Dismissed!"

# # # # #

Book 2: The Devil's Choir

Prologue

Niko Devlin woke up and realized several things all at once.

First, waking up with a headache was starting to get old. He'd been stunnered. He was almost certain.

Second, waking up with a killer headache in *jail* was starting to get old. He hadn't opened his eyes, so he wasn't empirically positive, but he'd been in enough jail cells to instinctively know the stale sweat/booze/piss smell of a jail cell. It must be a universal scent. He idly wondered if there was a manufacturer somewhere that made the scent, bottled it, and shipped it to jails all over the galaxy. *But that's just crazy talk,* he told himself. The Nords wouldn't buy it; they smelled that way naturally.

He tried to remember the details behind whatever had led him to getting stunnered, but between the headache and what now seemed to be the glorious beginnings of a spectacular hangover, the details somehow eluded him. Stupid details.

Third, he realized someone was in the jail with him. In fact, several someones, and all of them seemed to be huddled against him.

Against his better judgment—he wondered idly if he had any better judgment—he decided to open his eyes and assess the present catastrophe.

The dim light stabbed at his already hurting eye sockets, threatening to sear his eyes and leave them as bubbling puddles of goo on the floor. The pounding in his head went from classical rock to suicide power metal both in rhythm and intensity. He stubbornly and valiantly kept his protesting optical orbs in the upright and locked position as he started to take stock of his surroundings.

Yep, it was jail cell. A rather nasty one too. Which was odd, one corner of his mind noted, since they had last been on a fairly decent space habitat. It looked like their cell had been in existence since the Exodus from Earth, and they had just built the habitat around it to counteract the nasty, but that was more crazy talk.

As a compromise, he closed one protesting eye and glanced to the right and down to see what was there. He saw the top of an auburn-haired head. It had a cute little freckle in the natural part of the hair. He slowly opened the formerly closed and resting eye to get a closer look at the head on his right shoulder.

Nicki Kenyon was asleep, no, that wasn't accurate; nobody sleeps in jail cells. Nicki was *passed out* with her head on his shoulder. She snored a little, her mouth open and slack jawed.

In answer to Nicki's snoring, two answering rumbles came from his left shoulder. Almost a duet of nasal obstruction. Alan MacBain was leaning against his left shoulder and Martin Atwell was leaning against him.

Across the cell, Tamman's huge form was sprawled on a second bench. Jones was seated on the floor, his head tilted back and resting on the big man's arm. Cho was curled up and sleeping on Tamman's massive chest, a little string of drool trailing out onto Tamman's T-shirt. McCarthy was passed out face down on the floor.

As feeling started to return to the rest of his body—this wasn't going to be good, he was positive—he felt another weight, this one across his thighs. Allison Baxter was stretched out across Kenyon, her head rested on Devlin's lap, her face turned up toward his. Her eyes were closed; well, one was closed, probably in sleep. The other was swelled shut, blackened and mousy. Blood crusted one nostril, and her snores were accompanied by a slight whistling.

Devlin tried to remember. He vaguely recalled drinking. In the Empire, while there was a minimum age for drinking, it was somewhat lax in the settlements and colonies. The military was okay with it, since if you could make the decision to get yourself killed, the Emperor was okay with you handling some booze. Besides, the military takes care of its own.

So, he had been drinking with the Hellions and someone had said something and something else got said and then suddenly his fist was punching some guy...

He sighed again, this time producing a shift of both Kenyon and Baxter. As Kenyon shifted, she groaned something about ballet lessons, and her head drooped again, and the snores resumed.

Baxter didn't move, but Devlin saw her eyes clench, and she grimaced.

"Devlin?" she croaked. Her voice, usually smooth and sweet like chocolate or honey, sounded like she'd swallowed some sand and gargled with glass.

"Yeah." His voice didn't sound any better...just deeper.

"Where are we and why does my mouth taste like the inside of a combat boot? What the hell happened, and why does it hurt my head to talk?"

"That's a lot of questions," he said. "I'll try to explain...No that would take too long, lemme sum up. One, we're apparently in jail. Two, I think we got drunk and got into a bar fight during which, three, we got stunnered, and four—I'm not sure you asked a four—but we're all in here together."

"Humph," Baxter said. Her one good eye opened and looked at him. He thought idly that it was a cute eyeball in a bloodshot, hungover sort of way. That buzzkill portion of his mind noted that he was doing a lot of idle thinking and maybe that was why his better judgment had gone on a different liberty than he had.

She sniffed, then she wrinkled her nose and visibly tried not to vomit.

'I don't feel so good."

"Yeah…between the hangover, which if yours is half as good as mine is a beaut, and the stunner, I'm surprised one of us isn't covered in puke."

"Please don't say it," she groaned, grimacing again. "I'm doing all I can not to…you know." She closed her eye and was quiet for a few moments. Devlin thought she'd passed out again.

Her eye snapped open. "Did you say we were in…jail?"

He inhaled again, trying simultaneously to take in as much oxygen to clear his aching head and not smell the putrid odor of the cell and his unwashed companions.

He breathed out. "Uh huh."

"That's what I thought you said," she said, closing her eye again.

Devlin slowly counted backward from ten. He got to three before she half-screeched, "*Jail?*"

She started to try and get up, which caused Kenyon to stir, and her outburst caused Devlin's head to pound even more.

He pushed down on Baxter's shoulders. He was pretty sure they were shoulders. One was a shoulder, yes, one was definitely a shoulder.

"Shh, Bax, indoor voice," he pleaded. "They'll come spring us shortly, I would figure. The sergeant major isn't going to let some civvie twist us when he could have the pleasure."

Baxter's neck relaxed, and she slumped back onto Devlin's lap.

"I'm not so sure that's preferable."

"Point."

"What do you think he'll do?"

"Well, I doubt at this point he'll figure something like the Candy Heist Pain Party is going to make any difference to us, do you?"

"Point," she conceded this time.

"I figure they're probably waiting for all of us to more or less wake up, and then they'll call the sergeant major or one of the drills and have them come get us. Then the real fun will begin."

She was silent for a few moments. Devlin closed his eyes and tried to get the pain to go away. It wouldn't. Stupid pain.

"Devlin?" she asked quietly.

"Yeah, Bax."

"Do you like me?"

He opened his eyes and looked down at his teammate. "Well, uh…what?" he stammered.

"Do. You. Like. Me. It's a fairly simple question," she replied as if trying to explain quantum mechanics to Tamman or sanity to a Nord.

"Well…Yes…I…Uh…I guess. Yeah, I like you," he finally got his mouth and his brain to work together to produce a coherent answer.

"Ah…" she said, breathing out. "Okay. Now, next question, and this answer is very important."

Puzzled, he looked down at the beat up, but still attractive young lady in his lap. His brow furrowed. "What?"

"Something is poking me in the back of the nog. Do you have something in your pockets or are you just happy I'm in jail with you?"

* * *

They were all more or less awake, and more or less functionally coherent, when the Shore Patrol NCO came to the cell to escort them to their company area. He was an unsmiling, unfriendly sort of fellow, Devlin noted. *Of course, he's unfriendly,* he told himself. By this time, Devlin had sobered to the point where his better judgment had returned and pretty much *tsk*ed and said I told you so.

They were led out of the detainment area through a couple of darkened corridors into the main area of the Shore Patrol's outpost on Glalco Station. As they passed, Devlin tried to look casual, and not look at any of the faces of the patrol members in the offices. As it was, he was pretty sure they were looking at him and his disreputable-looking squad.

Devlin and his companions were marched down the hall, with people moving quickly out of their way. One woman actively put a hand in front of her children's eyes to shield them from the dregs of the universe as they perp-walked toward the lift shaft.

No one in the party said anything. At one point during the lift ride, Atwell started to say, "Do you think..." but the glaring eyes of everyone in the car, except the Shore Patrol NCO, told him they didn't want to think anything, and he shouldn't either. The Shore Patrol NCO just kept not-smiling and being completely unfriendly.

After a ride longer than the five months they had spent in Basic Training, the lift doors opened, and the boarding bay for HMS *Hermes* became visible.

Their escort went to the boarding security checkpoint and made some noises, showed a data pad to the rating at the checkpoint, pointed at Devlin and his companions, and then waited as the master-at-arms for the security checkpoint called someone on the ship.

After a moment, the MAA apparently received an answer, nodded to no one visible, took the data pad from the NCO, and watched as the Security Patrol NCO went back to the lift, unsmiling and unfriendly-like.

"You lot," the master-at-arms said. He was burly guy, with the nondescript look of a man who was old enough to command some respect but looked almost as young as them. The stripes on his arm were the same for a Sergeant First Class or a Gunny, but Devlin knew that in the Navy he was a Petty Officer First Class or some such. "Come over here and stand. One of your drill sergeants is coming to fetch you."

Devlin and the Hellions walked over and stood in the area the master-at-arms indicated. He couldn't be sure, because he was trying to make sure not to make eye contact, but he thought that the Naval NCO was trying to keep a smile off his face as he regarded his new charges sternly.

"I hope they throw the bloody book at you young fools," he growled. "One of these days you bloody, farking boots will learned that you just can't blow into town on liberty and immediately proceed to wreck the place." He harrumphed and made some marks on a data pad. "Why, it's getting so respectable members of the military can't even go on-station and enjoy themselves because of you irresponsible, loud..." Devlin tuned him out.

His headache had subsided to a dull thrum, but he really wasn't in the mood for a lecture. Especially from a rank amateur like this petty officer.

He was looking in the direction of the boarding lock a few moments later when he saw Staff Sergeant Miller come through the doors.

He approached the master-at-arms. "I'm here to collect my children." He put a singular emphasis on children. Devlin winced.

"Right over there, Staff," the master-at-arms said, handing him the data pad with their transfer information.

"Thank you, PO." Miller said, thumbing the MAA's pad, accepting charge of the prisoners.

"I hope you're going to make sure they don't do this again," the petty officer said, once again glaring at the young people sternly. This time, Devlin was sure he saw a lip twitch.

"Well, they say that hope springs eternal, PO," Miller replied casually. He turned and motioned for the party to start walking toward the lock. "But one has to have brain cells to teach, and I'm not sure this lot has any beyond, 'breathe in, breathe out, eat, shit/piss, fark, and fight.'"

"Heaven help us all then," the PO said reverently, crossing himself. "If this is what the Empire is depending on to save us from the ravening Nordic Hordes."

"Help us, indeed," Miller said, crossing himself and following his wayward charges up the boarding ramp.

Soon, they stopped outside a door hatch in what they were given to understand was "Marine Country" on the naval vessel. Marine

County apparently also housed the recruits while they were in transit to wherever it was they were going for their MUSTX.

The trainees of Alpha and Bravo Company, Third Battalion, One Forty-Ninth Training Legion occupied marine quarters on the old cruiser. For the trip out, the Marines that would normally be stationed on the ship were being rotated out and thus the quarters were empty until the ship returned for her new Marine detachment. The quarters were cramped in comparison with the training bays in the company area.

"Wait here," said Miller.

The training cadre occupied the NCO quarters adjacent to the trainee quarters. Sergeants Major McClellan and Ross shared a cabin and the office Devlin, and his companions, were standing in front of. They took their meals in the Chief's Mess, which for some reason was called the Goat Locker.

Captain Glass was housed somewhere else on the ship, presumably in officer's country.

Devlin assumed a position of parade rest, and the rest of the squad followed his lead. Devlin figured it couldn't hurt for them to at least look like they knew what they were doing.

Their resemblance to soldiers, living or dead, ended there. Faces were battered and eyes blackened, although by now the quick heal nanites were doing their thing. Their uniforms were ripped and stained, both by blood and cheap beer.

At some point, Atwell had puked, though he had managed to keep most of it off himself. Most.

Their boots were definitely not shined, and Kenyon was missing one of hers. Devlin sort of remembered seeing her beating a sailor with the boot while simultaneously doing a pretty good imitation of crowd surfing.

And now they were about to pay for their sins. The question was, what was the price?

About five minutes after entering the compartment, Miller returned and left the hatch open. McClellan bellowed, "Devlin! Get your sorry asses in here!"

Devlin and the rest snapped to attention and entered the compartment. Sergeant Major McClellan was seated behind a desk looking at a data terminal. Sergeant Major Roger Ross from Bravo Company was leaning forward, reading over McClellan's shoulder. As the group came trooping in, he straightened and said, "Catch you at chow, Gil." He left quickly and closed the compartment door behind him, leaving the condemned with their executioner.

Devlin stood at attention, saluted, and reported, "Trainee Private Devlin reporting with a party of eight." He held the salute and waited.

And waited.

McClellan kept looking at the terminal for several long moments. Devlin watched and waited as the NCO calmly turned off the screen, inspected his uniform for defects, picked a piece of lint off it, and flicked it in their direction.

McClellan then folded his hands and regarded the group for another solid minute. He cocked his head one way, then the other, like a child trying to figure out a particularly puzzling problem, or like a predator deciding if it wanted to eat something.

Finally, looking as though he had decided, he rose from his chair, came around the desk, got right into Devlin's face, and yelled, "Is that how you're supposed to report to your superiors, Private

Devlin? I can barely hear you! Now report again, or by God I'm going to throw you out of a farking airlock! Do you understand me?"

Devlin blanched at the tirade as his head started to throb again.

"Trainee Private Devlin reporting to the sergeant major with a party of eight!" Devlin bellowed and tried not to puke on the senior drill instructor.

McClellan returned the salute, and Devlin dropped his but stayed at attention.

McClellan walked around the group.

"Would someone here mind explaining to me how in the hell nine people—nine of my *trainees*—managed to do thirteen hundred and fifty credits of damage to the Hellfire Club Bar, sent six sailors to sick bay for naniboost, assaulted ten shore patrol members, then, not contenting themselves with that, oh no, they cleared out an entire cell block of the jail, and three detainees had to be evac'd with broken collar bones when someone tried to make a pass at one of my trainees?

"Did I give you permission to get into a bar fight?" He stopped in front of Kuzma who swayed a little but kept her eyes forward and above the NCO's head.

"No, Sergeant Major!" Kuzma barked and winced.

He looked up at Tamman and Jones. "Could you explain how a vehicle got lodged between the entrance to the Hellfire Club and the Entrance Booth, since neither one is anywhere near a right of way?"

Tamman started to say something but stopped as Jones "accidentally" stomped on his boot.

McClellan stepped in front of Kenyon. "And what the *fark* happened to your boot, Private?"

Kenyon stood and said nothing.

Atwell started to say something, but McClellan was suddenly in his face, and Atwell closed his mouth just as quickly.

"How about reports of a midget attack ninja and/or homicidal rabbit getting busy with an entire squad of Marines and sending two of them through a plate glass mirror?" He glared at Cho, who actually managed to look abashed. Her hair, which had been arranged in twin top knots, now was a tangled mess.

"But the kicker to this entire sordid little tale is that I got a bill here for a "genuine antique feather boa" apparently taken by one member of this wrecking crew who wore it while singing 'Caledonia's Depraved,' at which point the 'genuine antique feather boa' was inundated by cheap beer, blood, and some vomit, requiring cleaning services in the amount of three hundred forty-nine credits. Would anyone care to comment?

Baxter started to say something, but MacBain shot her a sidelong glance.

He circled around back to Devlin. "Have you got anything to say for yourselves?"

"No excuse, Sergeant Major!" the group chorused.

He circled back around his desk and sat down again. He steepled his fingers and glared at them. Devlin felt the sweat beading on his forehead. He thought they kept ships at a constant temp, but it felt quite warm.

Kenyon shifted slightly, being off-balance due to her missing boot.

Finally, the drill instructor broke the interminable silence. "As your training instructor, I have the authority to issue administrative non-judicial punishment or to recommend you to the commander for formal NJP, or you may choose to bypass both of us and request a formal hearing. Do any of you wish a formal hearing?"

Devlin felt his stomach drop for a moment. That would be a bit extreme for a bar fight. Then again, his recently returned better judgment reminded him that was how he got to be here in the first place.

After a moment, McClellan continued. "I'll take that as a no." He turned his terminal back on and made a note. "How about going to see the Old Man? God knows he tends to be a more lenient touch than I am. He actually likes you people." McClellan attempted to smile, but it came out more like a grimace.

Again silence.

"All right," the Sergeant Major said. "Administrative NJP it is then.

"First, you are all docked the sum of one hundred fifty credits, to be taken at the rate of fifty per pay for the next three pay periods." Devlin swallowed; that was a lot of money for a trainee. It wouldn't break them, but it was definitely a hit.

"Second, you are all confined to quarters. Duration will be communicated to you through chain of command.

"Third, you are all now considered PNG from the mezzanine level of the Promenade for Glalco Station for the duration of your training."

Devlin thought that was a bit harsh, too. They weren't even going to be able to go there on the trip back.

"Do any of you wish at this time to protest or appeal my decision to the Old Man?" McClellan asked. Devlin thought he looked a little too eager and earnest, almost like he wanted, no, needed, someone to answer in the affirmative.

Wisely, no one did. Almost as if he knew what Devlin was thinking, he frowned and growled.

"So be it. All of you return to your quarters."

* * *

Smoke rose from the general store as Douglas Longo walked out of the building. The fires were mostly under control now.

"Skipper," a voice called from across the roadway. Larry Jackson trotted across the street, his rifle cradled in his armored arms. Jackson was a big man, about two meters tall, and seemed almost that wide at the shoulder. His gravelly baritone sounded concerned. "We found the base commander, but there was—"

"Don't tell me," Longo said tiredly. "He got fragged."

"In the initial engagement, sir," Jackson agreed. "The boys didn't know it until after it was all over."

Doug Longo sighed. "There is no god, but Entropy and Murphy are his prophets."

"Amen, Skip. But that doesn't help us get into the facility."

"No, it surely doesn't," Longo agreed. Nearly 60 years old, Longo still had the look of a man in his early 30s. He was 1.85 meters and 90 kilos. His hair color was hard to tell since he kept it cropped as short as he had during his days as a King's officer. "But that's why we came prepared. Get the hacker and her friends over here."

"Aye, aye," said Jackson. He walked up the roadway toward the assault shuttle, talking into his comm.

Doug Longo surveyed the damage to Aberdeen, a stupid frakking name in Longo's opinion. 24 hours prior, the frigate FPV *Stormcrow* had opened fire on the system's only Avalonian vessel, HMS *Barclay*, a system patrol vessel, and destroyed her and the 750 men and women on board. Almost as soon as the Navy vessel decoalesced, assault shuttles began disgorging from *Stormcrow*. Approaching from the far side of the planet from Aberdeen, they were relatively undetected by planetary tracking. They rode down without grav drives on a random automated track that simulated the courses meteors made coming into the planet's atmosphere. Without grav drives until well into the atmosphere, they were "stealthy" right up until they were on top of Aberdeen's one settlement.

The assault troops from the pirate vessel, dressed in military-grade armored exoskeletons and armed with railguns, proceeded to slaughter the inhabitants of Aberdeen.

However, it wasn't all one sided. Apparently, either they had been detected or bad news truly traveled FTL, since the town's security forces were waiting for them at the town square.

Longo lost sixteen men in that exchange, but the security forces didn't have exos. From there, his men fanned out and captured the remaining sixty men, women, and children, though there had been a couple of unfortunate incidents.

He grimaced. The "mayor" had been one of the people killed during the fighting. It bloody figured.

"Yerbe!" he called via comms.

"Yeah, Skipper!" a feminine voice responded.

"Status on the door."

"Closed tighter than the legs on a Nordic GrandFrau," Sarah Yerbe said. "Really, Skip, we should have tried to—"

"Had this convo, Yerb!" Longo growled. He wasn't in the mood for, "I told you so."

"Right, Skip. I suppose we could try and look for additional entrances in the town itself. I'm not an expert on Avalonian—"

"Go ahead and look, Sarah. But I don't expect to find anything. I'm not an expert either, but the Av's aren't in the habit of backdoors," he said. "Get Bunny, Gants, and Connelly. Search every building for alternate entrances or even info on entrance codes from the data terminals. Maybe we can hope that one of these sods left us a tidbit."

"Aye, Skip. What about the survivors? Do you think any of them know anything?"

"Unsure," Longo admitted. "But I'm reticent at this point to break out the screws."

"Understood."

"We'll just see if this 'technical expert' we paid good money for can come through for us."

* * * * *

Chapter One

Devlin rotated his head to stretch his neck as he looked around the shuttle compartment. The last two hours had been their own special hell, as recruits, NCOs, and naval types had gotten all the gear, personnel, and supplies loaded into the *Wyvern*-class assault shuttles. He was strapped into a shock chair in the troop compartment of the shuttle.

The face shield on his helmet steamed as his breath came into contact with the blastglass. He reached down and adjusted the pressure on the re-breather that fed into his helmet. Instantly the fogging eased, and he could see the face of the big petty officer finishing his brief.

"Don't loosen the straps, ever," PO Gestner said as he adjusted the shock-rig straps on Kenyon's chair. His voice came over the all-hands frequency on their helmets' comm. All of the personnel on the shuttle were hooked into the shuttle's comm system so that even though some were in other portions of the shuttle, everyone could hear what was going on. The PO addressed his comments to everyone, so you knew what he was saying was something to pay attention to.

"These things are designed to keep your stupid arses alive in the event that you have to punch out of a shuttle. They have tiny grav comps and field gens so you will survive the trip, in most cases."

"Why would we have to punch out of the shuttle?" someone down the row from Devlin, sounded like Kinnebrew, asked. "You mean like a crash? Do these things crash a lot?"

Gestner became very serious. "No," he answered solemnly. "Usually they only crash once."

A brief silence fell over the cabin, then someone guffawed, then the entire cabin erupted in laughter. Gestner's lip turned up in a grin. "Which is the reason why you don't wanna be in the sumbitch if it does. So, don't futz with the straps! But to answer your first question, Private, crashes are one reason. Assaults are another."

Sergeant Major McClellan broke into the circuit. "If we do a hot drop, we'll have the bus drivers punch us out as they scream over the target area. But we're not planning that right now. You bunch of spoogesponges would probably fark it up, and then I'd have to do all the paperwork."

Chuckles broke out again over the circuit.

"There ya go, Private," Gestner said with a satisfied grunt as he finished inspecting Devlin's chair. "Keep your dickskinners off until you're on ground."

"Aye, aye, PO," Devlin said as he leaned back in the chair.

Gestner stepped back and turned to go to the back of the compartment. Devlin was the last in his row. As Platoon Guide, he was seated next to Sergeant Major McClellan in the front of the troop compartment. McClellan was conversing with the flight crew through an open hatchway.

As the loading crew headed toward the loading ramps to exit the craft, McClellan broke off what he had been saying to the flight crew, nodded, got into his shock chair, and buckled in. A crewmember double-checked his harness, gave him a thumbs up, and got into his own shock chair.

Devlin watched as the hatch to the flight deck closed and cycled shut. He saw the indicator lights on the cabin showing the troop cabin pressure was cycling down to death pressure.

The drop to the site of MUSTX, a planet called Aberdeen, was supposed to be as close to operational normal as possible. Since a combat drop could go bad mid-drop, the assault shuttles were drained down to death pressure and each person was on their own individual air supply feed. Should there be a problem, the feeds would shut down and the individual re-breathers would kick in. The systems in the soldier's armored uniforms would supply O_2 to the soldier for about ninety minutes, which in most cases would be enough to get them to the surface of the world they were being dropped on if they were on a combat drop, to engage BFTs—the Blue Force Tracker units—and go nighty-night, or have a few minutes to kiss your ass goodbye and make nice with which ever deity you happened to worship.

Since the first phase of the Multiple Unit Survival and Tactical Exercise was individual survival, the assault shuttles would enter the atmosphere hot, at which time the recruits would be jettisoned in their shock chairs on a random course around a central rendezvous site. Each person was expected to survive for seven days on their own, while navigating their way to the rendezvous site. At the end of the week, the shuttles would go out and find and recover any lame, lazy, or lost. Those people would be recycled or down.

Although not explicitly stated, you could team up if you ran into another trainee, but the spirit of the test was individual survival.

The recruits were given the briefing, which was also loaded on their comps. Some of the features of the little computers would be obfuscated during the course of the Phase One test so "cheating" couldn't occur.

Implant comms were disabled, as were combat sensors. The recruits would have nothing but basic survival gear, whatever they could cram into their individual rucks, and their basic uniform. Weapons and armored exoskeletons were a no-go for this phase of the mission. Those would be ferried down on another shuttle and reissued once the survival portion was over.

On Day Eight, the rest of the cadre and the opposing force would arrive and subject the trainees to Survival, Evasion, Resistance, and Escape training.

At the end of the second week, they would get a couple of days of down-time in the rendezvous area while the rest of the battalion and even some of the legion touched down for a major field exercise using multiple field-grade units. MUSTXs were timed to give multiple units the opportunity to train both as single units as well as larger forces.

McClellan looked down the troop compartment.

"Listen up!" he said into the comm. Heads turned laboriously toward him. He waited as the chatter on the comm line quieted down, except for a snore droning on the party line.

"Somebody wake up Higgs," the drill instructor sighed, exasperated. Arnett reached over and smacked the private on the back of her helmet. The sonorous nasal vibration cut off with satisfactory abruptness. Laughter took its place for a few moments. McClellan allowed it for a long ten-count, during which he looked toward the ceiling of the compartment, as if looking for divine guidance or possibly patience.

"All right! Listen up, you farkking useless, scumsucking, parasitic gimgobblers!" McClellan growled without heat. More laughter.

"We're going to be dropping in a few minutes. This is the last test before we turn you idiots loose with real weapons. You won't be issued anything resembling real weapons until the Legion gets here. But you don't need weapons, do you? Because..."

"The most dangerous weapon is the mind of the warrior!" the compartment chorused.

McClellan almost grinned. "You've got your individual kits and whatever you brought with you. You don't need anything else. Remember what we taught you, and you'll come through this right and tight...Except for Johnson," he said looking at one of the recruits. "I'm pretty sure you're screwed either way."

The laughter tied up the circuit for a few moments. Johnson had been a notoriously bad recruit. Even though he had managed to pass all the evaluations up until this point, he had somehow managed to be dead last in the company on every score.

Then the pilot broke in from the flight compartment.

"Ladies and gentlemen, we are launching at this time. We will let you know when we reach the exercise area. Have a nice day and thank you for flying Imperial Navy Shuttle Services. Flight attendants will be by soon to inquire about your drink orders. Captain, out."

* * *

There was an old holo that said, "In space, no one can hear you scream." Apparently, you can't hear alarm klaxons either. But you *can* hear them over your helmet's comm system.

Devlin's head came up as lights in the shuttle compartment started flashing and alarms started screaming in his ear. Voices stepped on the comms until the sergeant major hit the kill switch, then Devlin was finally able to hear the voice of the shuttle pilot.

"Sergeant Major, we have incoming vampires. I repeat: Vampire! Vampire! Vampire! Shuttles Four and Six are DRT. We are evading. Prepare for emergency punch out!"

Devlin didn't have time to scream as he and his shock frame were catapulted out of the shuttle and into the darkness. As suddenly as the shock hit him, it lessened, and he realized he was in free fall. At least he was alive.

He saw a small, fast-moving light streak across his vision, which then blossomed into actinic fire, consuming the shuttle that had just moments before been carrying him and his platoon. In the dying light, he saw what he thought were other shock frames and bits of the shuttle.

This isn't a part of the exercise, he thought. He felt the heat, then the explosive blast that tossed his shockframe. Something struck his helmet and blackness overtook him.

* * * * *

Chapter Two

When Devlin awoke, his head hurt.

Devlin opened his eyes and immediately wished he hadn't, based on the level of stabbing pain invading through his eyeballs. Nothing new there, he supposed. He seemed to be making a habit of bad life choices followed by headaches.

He tasted blood in his mouth. He rolled his tongue around to clear it and to check for problems. No missing teeth. Busted lip, though. Nanis would take care of that soon enough.

He raised his head. Nothing was broken; he was just sore. He began to look around and check his surroundings.

There was a haze of smoke around him. As it swirled in the slight breeze, Devlin could see his shock frame had come to rest on a plain. All around the frame was wreckage, some of it burning and creating the smoke that was in evidence.

Okay, he thought. I'm on the ground. Time to assess the situation.

He was still strapped into his crash chair. Upright, check. On ground, check. He reached up with his right arm, which still worked with no pain, and undogged the left-side restraints. Then he reached up with his left, or tried to, but that arm hurt like a sonofabitch. He wasn't sure if it was broken or just sprained. Since the pain was primarily movement based, he figured sprain. If he could find a med pack, he could check it later.

With a little awkwardness, he managed to get the restraints off the right side. Rather than trust his legs, he kind of oozed out of the crash chair. No more pain so far, which was a relief. Having an injured arm in a hostile environment was a pain in the arse, but survivable. Legs on the other hand, you were bait. He snorted. *What do you call a guy with broken legs in the wilderness...bait!*

Holding his arm close to his body, he lumbered to his feet and stood. He swayed a little, but the throbbing in his cranium subsided, and he looked around. He looked for the planet's primary by consulting his implants. It was about twenty-five degrees, warm but not hot, low humidity. Air was about normal for humans, so decent O_2 content.

He called up the compass and oriented on the primary. North was at six o' clock, or to his rear. A tree line was visible in that direction. Mountain range to the west, and more flat ground to the east and south. The sky was clear and blue. He was standing on a wide-open, flat plain. The mountains were the only elevation to be seen. The tree line looked far off, so he figured tall trees. From his training, he figured it was a temperate zone. At this point he had to rely on his training. His implants would be of limited use.

Some sort of insects buzzed nearby, so the planet was at least hospitable enough to support an ecosystem and wasn't just "terraformed." But that also meant he would have to look out for scavengers and predators. He definitely needed a weapon, but first things first.

Personal inventory: all fingers and toes, check. Armor still intact. No weapon—it was still on the assault shuttle. It was supposed to be returned at the rendezvous site. He'd hold his breath for that.

Personal gear, worn: three days light rations in pockets in his uniform were still there. Water vest under armor was intact and full. Devlin sighed in relief. He could survive for days—even a week or two—without food, but water was a "gotta have that" item. The vest contained six liters of water. If he rationed it, it could last him until he found another source.

The intact reservoir had a filtering system which meant he could refill with practically any water and the filtration system, driven by the body's movement and capillary action, plus a store of nanites, would make it potable. As long as it held out and he could find a source of water, he was golden.

Comforted by his inventory status, he started to look around his crash site. Inside the crash chair, he found the military-issue emergency survival pack. That was good. He could at least make a bash at survival with the things in there. No food or water, but basic supplies necessary for obtaining same.

Water purification tablets containing nanites that would bind to toxins and other things hostile to human physiology. The nanites then clumped together and dropped to the bottom of the container.

Electrolytes and vitamins for thirty days of survival. Most of the wonks in planning figured if you hadn't made extraction by then, you probably wouldn't anytime soon.

Nanisteel multitool. A compact combination hand ax and entrenching tool. He also had a small multitool with pliers, wire cutters, pocketknife, and other miscellaneous attachments. This tool, in its various incarnations, had been around for centuries, and they hadn't found a better replacement yet.

Carbon nanotube fishing line, which could be used for fishing, obviously, but also for sewing, snares, and a myriad of other uses.

Also, some heavier CNT rope, lightweight, compact, with a tensile strength measured in tons.

Most importantly for Devlin, a button compass to back up his wristcomp and implant, a small hand light, fire starter, mirror, and magnifier. Also, two emergency blankets. One could be used to wrap up and keep warm, the other could be used to create shelter.

All of these little goodies were packaged in such a way as to be stowable on the combat harness of his armor.

He found a battle steel support he could remove from the crash chair. It was long enough to serve as a short staff, but also was about the right diameter for the e-tool/ax head to fit on it. Devlin realized this might have been by design. There was no such thing as coincidence in the military.

He stowed the various items and kept looking around. He found his personal pack, which had been strapped in at his feet, about fifty meters away, torn to shreds. Damn. He'd had two knives, a change of clothes and various other personal items that would have made things a little easier. No good now.

He continued looking around for every scrap of usable material possible. You never knew what you'd need until you didn't have it. He had maybe three days' worth of actual food and water. He was expected to secure food and water from available resources on the individual portion of the MUSTX. But that went out the airlock when the shuttles got hit. There were three directions that weren't forest. Forests usually meant water, and probably food of one sort or another.

Devlin had no idea how many others—*if* any others—had survived. He figured that even if he were the only survivor, there would be other crash sites. He might be able to salvage more supplies. He finally planned to walk for a few hours in one direction and see what there was to find. If he didn't find anything, he'd circle back along a different track and return to camp at this crash site.

He'd leave a sign for any other recruits who might have survived and found this site. Hopefully, he'd come back and find a friendly face. If he found someone who wasn't a team member? He'd improvise. He had an ax.

He checked his wrist comp. He figured that if any BFTs were activated, they would show up on the tracker. McClellan had told them all during the briefings before the drop that if they got a BFT alert, they were to drop what they were doing and render aid, either secure the body or send up a flare for extract, then drive on with the mission.

Sure enough, there were a butt load of beacons. They had dropped with over two hundred troops, recruits, and cadre. He hoped many of them were just people too wounded for the nanites to heal so they were put into hibersleep until they could be picked up. They had thirty days, give or take. But BFTs also went off when vitals quit, so that was also a possibility.

The original plan had been to eject the group over a fairly large area with the rendezvous in the center. But Devlin figured based on what little info he got over the platoon channel prior to the punch out that one or more of the shuttles had been destroyed by something. The pilot may have punched them out thinking their shuttle was going to get hit as well.

If that was the case, they would have fallen along a singular track in a uniform direction. The punch-out would have only taken a few seconds, but a lot can happen in a few seconds. Based on the number of beacons, something bad had happened.

* * * * *

Chapter Three

Devlin trudged on. Every few hundred meters, here and there, he'd see some scattered debris, nothing much, just…detritus. The first couple of times, he stopped and investigated. Each time he was disappointed.

After about an hour, he stopped and drank from his hydration vest. He scanned the horizon but saw nothing. After five kilometers, one would have thought there would be…

He thought he caught a flash in his peripheral vision. He turned his head a little north and watched. One minute. There it was again. It *was* a flash.

Hot damn, he thought and grinned. At least one other person survived.

He took another sip and picked up his pace. He walked briskly for a few minutes then started a light jog. He figured he had another five kilometers before he reached the source of the mirror flash. As he jogged, he saw the light flash every few minutes. But after about twenty minutes, the flashes quit.

When he figured he had traveled all but the last couple of klicks, he slowed to a walk and hunkered down for a moment. He took a drink of water, the wetness seductively sweet in his mouth. He had worked up a sweat during the run, but he figured it a good risk.

He pulled the one thing out of his vest that had survived his personal pack's destruction, a combat monocular scope. Since it was something that couldn't really affect the outcome of the survival test one way or another, it was allowed in his personal gear.

He raised the scope to his eye and examined the site. It appeared in the monocular, and the range showed 1.65 km. *Good,* he thought. Unless they had a scope, whoever was up there wouldn't have seen him coming. No sense in being an idiot and rushing in before he assessed the situation.

Rule Number Twenty-Three: If you do not ASSess...you will eventually be an ass.

He couldn't see anyone moving around the site. The crash chair was among a small field of debris from the shuttle. The crash chair was lying on its side, rather than sitting upright, which was the default landing position; the grav compensators in the chair were supposed to ensure that. The only thing that could keep a chair from doing that would be...well, an explosion that damaged the grav comp. Debris, he supposed as he thought about it.

He decided to move closer. Keeping low, he started to walk. It was slow going, but he had time. Another problem, from his viewpoint, was a complete lack of ground cover. There was no place to hide on this plain, unless the terrain changed.

It took another hour of walk and stop, hunker and assess, to reach the crash site. Like his, there was an assortment of debris, but Devlin ignored most of it in favor of checking out the crash chair.

The chair was lying on its side facing away. He heard a low moan and some labored coughing. He purposefully scuffed his boots to make a noise, but hopefully not startle the chair's occupant.

He heard a familiar raspy voice.

"Already killed one thing this afternoon...not above doing it again." McClellan.

"Sergeant Major?" Devlin said, approaching the chair but keeping a wide berth.

"Devlin? That you?" McClellan rasped then let out a wet, wracking cough.

"Yes, Sergeant Major," Devlin replied as he came around the chair.

McClellan was a right mess. The NCO's chair had been hit by something, probably at high speed. One leg was mangled and twisted, the other was just...gone. The front of his battle armor looked like it had been squeezed by some Brobdingnagian hand. He was cut and scraped in a dozen places. His helmet had been ripped off and his scalp was bleeding into one eye. His right arm was pinned by the chair and his left was holding a large curved knife. To one side of the chair, Devlin saw a signaling mirror...and a dead animal about the size of a dog.

"Bastard thought he had fresh meat." McClellan grinned up at him, his one clear eye glinting. "He found out I still had teeth." He chuckled and started coughing again. Then he frowned. "There's not supposed to be any fauna out here. Must have been something brought to the planet and left to go feral."

"One of these days, you'll have to tell me how the hell you wound up with a kukri, Sergeant Major," Devlin said cheerfully. "Can I get you out of there?" Devlin bent down to release the straps. As he started on the first, McClellan let out a hiss.

"Dammit, boy," he said through gritted teeth. "Remember training...easy."

"Got it, Boss," Devlin said absently. He gently slid a hand under the strap and eased off the tensioner. McClellan's shoulder slackened, and Devlin held his hand against the NCO's body to keep the tension steady.

"All right, Sergeant Major. I'm going to right the chair so we can get you out of there."

Devlin helped the older man get his good hand on the arm of the chair and braced against the movement as he began to right the chair. He stopped at one point and kicked some debris out of the way.

There was a little bobble and another pained hiss from the instructor, but he finally got the chair upright.

McClellan gave out a long exhale, coughed a bit, spat blood on the ground to the side, then wiped the blood out of his eye with his free arm.

"Can't move my arm, Devlin," he said.

"Yeah," Devlin breathed. "Looks like it's coming off. Legs too."

"Damn. I hate regen. It takes weeks to get the taste out your mouth from the breathing gear."

"Keep talking, Sergeant Major. I'm gonna try and get you out and comfortable."

"Comfortable ain't happening. Just get me out of this."

"Working on it." Slowly, he worked on getting the senior instructor out of the crash frame and onto the ground, keeping his hands away from injured portions as much as possible. Every now and again there was a grunt or hiss of pain from the older man. Finally, he had McClellan on the ground on top of an eblanket.

"Sit-rep, Devlin."

"Unknown at the moment, Sergeant Major," Devlin said absently as he gently felt the older man's legs to assess the injuries. He got another hiss for his trouble. Devlin pulled his pocket multitool out and extracted the blade. He began cutting the pant leg.

"Careful there, Devlin," McClellan said. "That's my leg."

"All due respect, Sergeant Major McClellan, but right now it's a piece of meat. I'm trying to find out how badly mangled a piece of meat."

McClellan grunted and leaned back. He craned his neck a little, stiffly, and got a drink from his own hydration vest.

"How are you set up for supplies?"

"Most of my shit got trashed in the eject. Got my LR's, hydrovest, the ESP from the chair, and a combat scope. My pack, knives…all gone."

"Entropy is God…"

"And Murphy is his prophet," Devlin finished. "I have a feeling this is going to turn out to be an 'extended' survival exercise."

McClellan chuckled, which quickly turned into a cough/wheeze/moan. "Dammit, Devlin, don't make me laugh."

Devlin finished cutting away both pant legs and examined the two mangled limbs.

"Lower left is gone from the knee. Apparently the nanites have stopped the bleeding and kept you out of shock. The other is a probable loss. How in the hell are you still awake? Your nanipack should have shipped your ass to nighty-night as soon as the leg came off, and your BFT should be broadcasting to the heavens, 'Here is McClellan…Bane of Boots.'"

He said it jokingly, but his face was gravely serious.

McClellan regarded him levelly. "There is some…wiggle room in the nani protocols," the older man said. "Not much, but I managed to keep the nanipack from engaging the sleepy time. I wanted to see if…well, someone like you would show up."

"That's a dangerous game to play, Sergeant Major."

"So is leaving a bunch of barely trained recruits in an unknown situation. Believe it or not, Devlin, but I actually give a shit about you snotnoses."

"Now, don't go getting all sentimental, Sergeant Major. People will start thinking you have a heart."

"Don't," the old man wheezed. "Just hate doing paperwork." He quirked another bloody grin.

He was trying to figure out how to make the sergeant major more comfortable when he heard a sound behind him. He saw the sergeant major tense and grip his kukri.

As unobtrusively as possible, Devlin felt for the ax lying next to his feet. He grabbed it and spun, bringing the shaft up to meet his other hand in an *en guard* position.

Matthew Kimbler, First Platoon's First Squad leader raised his hands. "Whoa! Whoa, Devlin. Friend!"

Devlin relaxed. Kimbler's bruised face broke out in a huge grin. "Damn, I'm glad I found someone else alive. I was starting to wonder."

"Which direction did you come from?" Devlin said, laying the ax back down.

"I've been walking southeast for the last hour or so," the other recruit informed him. He looked over at the crash chair. "Heya, Sergeant Major. How are you doing?"

"Just farking ducky, Private."

"Don't mind him," Devlin said. "He's always a little cranky when he crashes."

"Shut up, Devlin," McClellan growled. As weak as he was, his heart wasn't in it.

"Yes, Sergeant Major. At once, Sergeant Major. Shutting up, Sergeant Major."

The two set about surveying the wreckage to find anything that was salvageable. As they worked, Kimbler and Devlin compared notes.

Kimbler had actually made out better with his crash. His pack had survived, so he had an extra combat knife, which he lent to Devlin, a spare uniform, extra water, and, lo and behold, some jerky.

"How in the hell did you get pogiebait on the lift?" Devlin said.

"I'm surprised you didn't." Kimbler said. "I put mine in a flashlight, rolled up in my socks…"

"And if you think we didn't know it, you're an idiot," the sergeant major said from his makeshift bed.

Both trainees looked at him.

"We don't make an issue of it, but we tell you no food or water. We wouldn't want you to cheat the test," he continued, putting a sarcastic emphasis on cheat.

Devlin hung his head, then looked up at the sky.

The NCO coughed again, then wheezed a laugh. "Devlin, Devlin, Devlin. I must-a hit you harder than I thought. Did you go so straight that you forgot Rule Number Two?"

"If you ain't cheating, you ain't trying," Devlin said disgustedly. He shrugged a moment later. "Not that it would have made any difference. My pack got destroyed."

McClellan made a half shrug from where he lay.

At last, Devlin and Kimbler sat beside the sergeant major's bier with everything they had salvaged so far. It was getting dark, but they couldn't build a fire; they had no kindling. Devlin decided that would be on the agenda for the next day, finding firewood and water.

"Counting jerky, we have between the three of us four days' rations and water, and we have three axes, but I don't think the sergeant major is up to light calisthenics." He got a finger for that comment. "We'll configure his for etool and dig a latrine. We'll have to help the sergeant major when he needs to use the facility."

"We can construct a shelter from the blankets and double up for warmth if it gets too chilly tonight," Kimbler put in.

"Tomorrow morning, we'll each take a different vector and check out some of the BFTs on that line. Hopefully, we'll run into some other survivors. We'll do a three-hour search then return. While we're out, we'll see if we can't scare up some kindling for a fire and a water source," Devlin said. "We'll take turns keeping watch tonight. I suggest two and two, that way we don't get so logy that we wake up in some scavenger's belly. Why don't you and the sergeant major turn in? I'll take first."

Kimbler grabbed a blanket, and, using debris and parts from the crash chair, they constructed a crude tent. Devlin was mildly amused to find that the chair had more than one straight piece of strut that could be used as uprights, almost as if by design. They ran support lines with CNT line and Kimbler crawled into the tent with the sergeant major.

Devlin turned off the penlight and allowed his eyes to adjust to the darkness. He placed his ax in his lap and sat perched on a piece of debris that seemed fairly stable.

In the deepening gloom, he saw the stars start to come out. On the southern horizon, the planet's largest moon began to emerge. He remembered from the briefing materials that this planet had three. One larger, Denburn, and two smaller, Dee and Don.

He scanned the horizon in all directions. Most of the recruits would have done as they had and gotten some shelter around themselves. He was more concerned about the active beacons. If they were "sleeping" and a scavenger happened by, they were going to be eaten. A part of him wanted to say, "Can't be helped," but he knew better. He wasn't going to lose one if it wasn't necessary. The sergeant major wouldn't want him to, either.

Life is a funny thing, Devlin thought as he watched a meteorite burn up in atmo. He'd left Caliban absolutely dedicated to doing as little as possible. Now, he found he didn't want that anymore. He had people out there he wanted—no, he *needed*—to make sure were okay.

He watched the horizon, hoping for signs of life, until he felt Kimbler's hand touch his shoulder to end his shift.

* * * * *

Chapter Four

Morning came with only minor incidents. Both Kimbler and Devlin had encountered singular scavengers throughout the night. Devlin chased one off, but it returned later and Kimbler dispatched it with an ax stroke that laid open its spine.

Devlin and Kimbler each ate a ration bar and drank some of the water from Kimbler's pack.

"You take east and circle south," Devlin said. "I'll keep on the westerly course I started yesterday. If I don't find anything in three hours, I'll circle north. While you're out, see if there's anything we can use to start a fire."

"Yeah, Dev. I'll try and hold my own pecker too." Kimbler's deep voice was amused. "We've both had the same lectures."

"So we have," Devlin agreed. "Sorry."

"Not a problem. Somebody ought to be in charge. I'm just as glad either way."

Devlin took up his ax and headed west. The sun was just clearing the horizon, and the animal life on the planet was starting to stir, somewhat disturbed by the previous day's events.

He sped up into a leisurely lope that ate distance without significantly tiring him. After all the months of physical training, he and his fellow recruits could do this for hours. He continuously scanned his surroundings, looking for signs of more crash sites. He marked major debris fields for later survey. He checked his comp on the run.

He was approximately three klicks from a BFT beacon. He picked up his pace a little more.

*　*　*

Devlin retched as he saw the torn remains of Private Allison Baxter. Judging from the trajectory of the crash and other signs, her chair had been knocked by the explosions harder than the grav compensators could manage. She had been wounded by shrapnel and apparently gotten torn apart by impact with the trees on the way in.

He held his gorge down as he undid the straps that held the tattered body to the crash chair and eased Baxter's body onto the ground. Devlin pulled the ESP out of the chair, got a blanket and wrapped the Eyrian girl's body. The material was also carbon nanoweave; a scavenger wasn't going to get into it without a monomolecular edge. He sank down beside the body of one of his best friends and wept.

He hadn't realized it at the time, but Bax was one of the few people he really had cared about. He hadn't been in love—though there had been a little sexual attraction—but she had been a friend when he needed one.

He remembered her the night they carried out the Great Candy Heist. She went in knowing she was going to get hammered by the drills, but she grinned and said, "Let's do this." That was always her attitude. It didn't matter what they were doing.

On the firing line, pugil sticks…he laughed and sobbed as he remembered her clocking his ass during the pugil bouts. Her exasperation when he tried to pull his punches. "Let's do this, you pansy," she grunted and kicked him full in the balls, then followed up with a right cross that knocked a tooth loose even though she was at least twenty kilos lighter. She didn't care.

She also didn't care about pasts. She was the only person he'd opened up to, that night of the bar fight. He guffawed again, wiping the snot coming out of his nose. That farking bar fight. Him, Bax, Mac, Kuzma, Atwell, and Kenyon, and the rest of the Hellions, backs to each other, kicking ass, taking names, getting busted by the patrol, and spending the night in that nasty jail cell. Baxter was positive the "décor" was engineered. There was no way to make something *that* filthy on a space station.

He shook his head. She hadn't cared where he was from, or what he was there for. He was there. He was a brother. She was a friend. He would have loved for it to have been more, but there it was.

And now, just as quickly as she had become a friend, she was gone. Killed by shit she never even saw coming. He pounded the ground in frustration. Why in Hell couldn't he have gotten to her? He should have secured the sergeant major and gone on to find others. He'd have found her if he had gone on after Kimbler found their camp. Dammit! He might have been able to help her.

Finally, he made a cairn of sorts with the debris. No sense in giving scavengers any more of a chance.

He shouldered his pack, now filled with stuff from her pack and ESP.

There were three more sites within a klick of Baxter's. All were dead or nighty'd, but undisturbed. None were completely whole. Mercifully, they were beyond pain at the moment. He wrapped each carefully and salvaged everything he could from each site. He piled what he couldn't carry. He'd mark the site and send a party later. They were going to need all the salvage they could get.

* * *

He was on his way back to Kimbler and the sergeant major when he spotted the next site, about five hundred meters to his south. He saw a crash chair and a form seated beside it. As he approached, he called out, "Devlin, Second Platoon leader."

The form said nothing, but Devlin could see the heaving shoulders of someone weeping uncontrollably.

Alan MacBain was holding the hand of Natalya Ivanova Kuzma, whose head was hanging at a peculiar angle. Blood smeared her face and her eyes stared blankly, dead, at the ground. MacBain didn't say anything...couldn't say anything. Devlin went and sat down in front of this grisly tableau.

"Mac," he said gently.

The boy's brogue was almost too thick to make out. "She's done, Dev. Bloody chair tumbled when it landed, right on her bloody head. Broke 'er neck just like a twig."

"Mac."

"Know you're not supposed to get attached. Not supposed to...well, you know," MacBain said. "She'd wanted to...little minx. That night at Station. Said she had a mate who was assigned to the station and would lend us a room for a quick shag."

He began to laugh. "Boot that bloody bar fight nipped that right in tha kipper." He breathed a ragged breath. "Guess she's screwed right proper now, ain't she."

"Mac."

"*Dammit,* Devlin!" MacBain snarled.

"I know, Mac. But Kuzma wouldn't want you to—"

"How do you bloody know what Kuz would want, you bloody bastard?"

"Mac, I know you liked her, and she seemed—" At the word "seemed" MacBain popped up and rounded on his friend, his face livid with fury.

"*Seemed?* I know what you're going to say! 'She seemed like a nice girl!' She didn't *seem* like anything, you know! She *was* a great gal."

He bent his head and pulled her hand up to his forehead.

Devlin went over to the sandy blond Caledonian recruit, put his forehead on his friend's head, and together they wept.

"We gotta get her wrapped up, Mac, or the animals will get her," Devlin said a few minutes later. MacBain nodded, sniffling.

Together, they got Natalya's body out of the chair and laid out on the ground. Mac insisted on taking a moment to wipe away the blood and dirt. "She always hated dirt. Isn't that a laugh, Devlin? She went out in the field, did her job, but absolutely hated the dirt. I think the drills knew that. They always made her crawl through the mud twice. She never griped. Hated the Gods-damned dirt. That's why she'd have wound up in the infantry, and no mistake." Devlin agreed. MacBain started to laugh. Then just as quickly, he stopped. "Come on, then," he said.

They laid her out on a blanket and tied the body up as he had done on too many others that day. They arrayed the debris in a cairn over the body. MacBain stopped and stood beside his friend and his mouth moved silently for a few moments. Finally, he stopped and said, "I'll see you, Kuz."

He turned toward Devlin, his eyes dead. "Let's go, Dev." He walked away and didn't look back. Devlin watched his friend for a moment before following him.

* * * * *

Chapter Five

By the time the two friends returned to the campsite, more people had come trickling in.

Kimbler had been joined by Kenyon. About a head shorter than Devlin, the auburn-haired Nicki Kenyon was a military brat. She'd joined up mainly because everyone in her family had joined up. It's what you did in the Kenyon family. She was hypercompetent, hyperconfident, and knew how it all worked.

She had taken a clueless street kid and shown him how to keep the drills from wrecking his bunk every morning.

"Atwell?"

"Saw his crash frame but it looks like the body had been dragged away. No BFT so there may not have been much left. Not exactly sure how that works," Jones answered, walking up with Cho.

"How about McCarthy?" Cho asked. "Did you see McCarthy?"

"I didn't. MacBain didn't, either."

"I couldn't find his crash site when I went looking." For the first time since he'd met her, Anastasia Cho looked unsure.

Devlin nodded. He went to where the sergeant major was resting. Decker was checking his legs. "Sergeant Major, what do we do now?"

"What's this 'we' shit, Private? You got a mouse in your farking pocket? You think I'm gonna be able to run this lash-up from nighty-night?" McClellan growled. He glared at Devlin, then snorted. His face softened. "Look boys and girls," he said, raising his voice as much as possible. The gathered recruits turned their attention or got as near as they could. "I ain't got long, I've been holding off nighty-night as long as possible to make sure you shits have some sort of a way to survive. You do. You have each other and some supplies. So, I'm going to keep this brief.

"Get the fark out of Dodge," he said earnestly. "We got shot the hell down, and as a result, I would bet creds to crumpets that whoever shot us down will be sending something out here to make sure we are D-E-D, dead.

"If they find some bodies in various states of farkeduppedness and some that are more or less buried, they may presume the wounded started burying the dead before dying their own selves. But they aren't going to do that if they see you out here roasting lizard meat and singing campfire songs.

"There's forest about a half klick that away. Set up a perimeter just inside and just outside the tree line such that you can pull in and fade back if anyone comes calling." The recruits nodded, acknowledging what he had in mind.

"Then you're going to need to—"

He cut off as Jones' head whipped around and focused on the horizon. "Incoming! Fast mover!"

McClellan swore, and Devlin jumped to his feet and started toward the older man,

"No time for that!" McClellan waved him off emphatically. "Make for the trees, everybody who can run! Everyone who can't play dead." He looked at Devlin. "He may not waste ammo on corpses. Give him a running target and he may ignore us. Make for the trees!"

Devlin helped Decker up, and they started running. They got about two hundred meters before the flier came within range. It began firing, and the kinetic rounds from the twenty-five mm railguns kicked up clods of earth as it followed the trainees.

At the last second, Devlin threw himself into Decker and they fell to the earth as rounds tracked right past where they had both been running.

"Thanks, Dev," Decker said, panting.

"Thank me if we both live!" he said, hauling her back to her feet.

The flier had already gone out and was circling around again for another pass.

Devlin looked ahead. Most of the mobile recruits had made it to the tree line. He and Decker arrived a few moments later.

The flier buzzed their position, rounds arcing into the ground then going on into the trees. Trees exploded where the rounds chewed them up, sending splinters flying.

A man cried out as a massive splinter ripped through his body. "Everybody, find cover!" Devlin yelled. Screams and curses came from multiple voices inside the brush line.

Devlin worked his way into the forest, trying to keep trees between himself and the flier outside. Every few minutes, rounds would come streaking in, chewing new divots into the ground. More trees exploded.

He made it a few hundred meters in, then slowly started to make his way toward the edge, disturbing as little of the undergrowth as he could. He dropped to his belly and low-crawled toward a depression over which a tree had fallen. He didn't think IR or other sensors on the flier could differentiate his body heat from the surroundings in daylight, or at least he fervently hope not.

The flier was still circling the area but was no longer firing. *That makes sense*, Devlin thought. *They can't carry a hell of a lot of ammo on those things.* He didn't see any missile hard points and the grav generators would take up most of the internal space, so definitely not ammo heavy.

He scanned the way they had come from the camp. The ground was an absolute mess of churned earth, with wisps of smoke rising from craters. The camp itself was still. He wasn't sure how many had "played dead," and he prayed they would be able to continue until the flier gave up and went home.

He looked toward where they had entered the forest. He saw movement, presumably one of the other trainees.

The flier stayed in the vicinity for another hour, circling the area, then widening its search, presumably checking other crash sites.

They waited for another thirty minutes before moving from their positions. Devlin hurried back to the entry point of the forest.

A small clearing had been formed where the trees had all been gunned down by the flier. It extended about a hundred meters into the forest, splinters and chewed up earth and stumps dotting the landscape.

"Ollie, Ollie, and all that," Devlin called.

"Screw you!" Jonesy called. "Is that farker really gone?"

"Close as I can tell." He looked around. "Kenyon?"

"Here," the redheaded squad leader answered, crawling out from underneath a stump. She had several scratches and a cut on her scalp. It was already healing.

"Roll call! Sound off!" Devlin said loudly.

"Cho!" the diminutive girl's soprano answered.

"Tamman!" the big man rumbled.

"You already heard me," Jones groused.

"Kimbler!"

"Decker! Still the busted chicken wing, but no other injuries."

"Gartlan!"

"Lett!"

"Raindrops keep falling on my…"

"Shut the fark up, Carl!"

About ten more voices called off. They made their way toward the clearing, each one slowly appearing if not like ghosts, then at least semi-competent soldier trainees.

Devlin regarded them. "Okay, here's what we're going to do. I'm going back out to check on the sergeant major and the others. I'm going to need three people to come with and help me secure whatever survivors we can. We need to get them inside the tree line as quickly as possible before Mr. Friendly Flier comes back with more gifts or more friends." The recruits nodded.

"I'll go," Gartlan said.

"Me, too," Tamman and Jones said in unison.

"Good," Devlin said. "Did we lose anybody? I couldn't tell from my hide. And I didn't stop to see when we were running. Decker and I were ass-end Charlie, but we were in the dirt for a minute."

"We lost Moran and Telarius. Both girls took rounds. I'm not sure if they are nighty-night or DRT."

"Somebody check. If they are DRT, we may need them," Devlin said. Every head turned and looked at him.

"I've got a plan, and if our folks are salvageable, we need to make sure they stay that way. If not, they can still help us, but you're gonna have to trust me."

While the others started setting up a perimeter away from the previous attack, Devlin and other three trainees made their way to the makeshift camp. They kept low and swept the horizon for signs of the flier.

When they got within a reasonable distance, Devlin called out, "Sergeant Major? You still with us?"

"Devlin?" came the hoarse voice. "Get in here, you gotta…"

"Already ahead of you, Sergeant Major," Devlin said, motioning to the others. He approached the sergeant major's resting place and looked at the older man.

"Give us a few, and we'll get you to the wood line."

McClellan shook his head. "Nah, I'm going to nighty-night in a bit, but before I do, I gotta do something." He looked intently at him. "Devlin, do you have this? This is the big and the nasty and the thing that nobody ever wants to have happen. But I think you can do this."

"Do what, Sergeant Major?" "

"Keep this lot alive and find out what happened to our base and settlement at Weyland. If we got ambushed, it's because something happened to the picket ship and likely happened to Weyland. It's imperative that someone get word to the rest of the force before they get ambushed, too. Can you do that, Niko?"

Devlin took a deep breath. He had been called many things by the NCO, but his given name hadn't been one them. If he wasn't sure before that things were really and truly in the shit, he was now.

Numbly, he nodded. "I don't know…"

"You know enough. You're a decent leader, and you think fast. Keep these kids alive. You've got two weeks. But I got a parting gift that might make things a little easier. Bend down here."

Devlin bent in closer to the old man. "Nikolai Nikolayevich Devlin," the NCO said formally. Slowly, he picked his head up to look at Devlin directly with his good eye. "Service number Two Two Two Seven One Dash Seven Nine Eight Dash Eight Two Three Three Alpha Oscar. Unlock implant protocol India Delta One Zero Tango, Execute Sierra Hotel Tango Foxtrot One One One Seven Four."

Devlin felt a something in his head that could best described as a click. "What the hell was that, Sergeant Major?"

McClellan lay his head back on the blanket. "I just unlocked all the protocols on your implant. The ones we lock down for the tests and two or three others I can unlock as your commander. I was going to try and do everyone, but there isn't time; I need to let the pack take over."

He was quiet for a few moments, marshaling his energy. "It's a more complete data dump on this planet, Weyland, and you have access to SatPos. That's about it. But it may give you an edge to stay ahead of whoever those shitheads are." He wheezed a bit and coughed. It was a wet wracking thing. "So, I'm not going to blow sunshine up your ass. You're in a cleft stick, and a week when you're being hunted is an awful long time. Just remember that sometimes not losing is preferable to winning."

Devlin nodded. "All right, Sergeant Major. I got this. I'll try not to add to your paperwork. 'Goodnight, Westley. Sleep well. I shall likely kill you in the morning.'"

McClellan's eyes widened, and he gasped a laugh. "Now *that's* an obscure one. Who the fark showed you that holo?"

"Mrs. Jadwidzik. She had the Millennial Holo." He stood up. "Now go to sleep, we'll get it done."

"One last thing," the older man said. He reached down with his good hand and unclipped the kukri and scabbard from his harness. "The Gurkhas don't typically name their knives, but I'm a little weird. This is my *Mrytu Candra*, or Death Moon. Hang onto it. You might find it handy in the next several days, and besides, I don't want it to disappear."

Shocked, Devlin took the knife from his sergeant. "When this is over, Sergeant Major, you're going to have to tell me how you got this. I'll bet it's a story."

McClellan snorted. "Oh yeah, it's a story. Tell ya what, Junior. When this is over, if we're both still breathing and able to drink without using a hose, I'll tell you about this knife, and you can tell me how you smuggled candy through my damn office."

Devlin snorted. He felt the water in his eyes. *Damn dust.* "Deal, Sergeant Major. Now, lights out. Go the fark to sleep."

"You're…not…the boss…"

Sergeant Major Virgil Chadwell McClellan, Senior Drill Instructor of Bravo Company leaned back, closed his eyes, and a moment later his breathing slowed and then stopped completely. Devlin's wrist comp buzzed as another BFT went off.

* * * * *

Chapter Six

Tijiit Rhombo loved flying. It was one of the few things that made being a pirate a blast. The money was okay. Every once in a while, when they got lucky, it was great. Mostly it was often hand-to-mouth and share and share alike. If he had enough money after a job to get drunk and laid, he was usually doing pretty good. He really wasn't a part of the crew for the money, but dirtside ops where he got to fly was the bitches' tits.

He had grown up in a family of free-faring asteroid miners. That was probably even more hand-to-mouth than what he was doing now, but the family wasn't beholden to anybody, and they went where they willed. Tijiit had learned to fly as backup for his old man at an early age. First just maneuvering and holding station, then, as he had gotten older, as a full-fledged pilot in his own right. The controls on the asteroid mining pods were a lot like this flyer, he thought as he finished the checklist prior to liftoff, although the pod wasn't designed to enter atmo and was about as aerodynamic as a ration brick.

He thanked the Unholy Mother as he banked the flyer to the northwest and started to climb. He checked the power plant readings and the fuel levels, making sure they were still what they had been at lift. The flyers the captain had procured cut-rate were...Well, calling them finicky was generous. But they were flyers and that was what was important.

He hadn't really intended to be a pirate, but after his parents died, he'd been unable to get jobs with any other miners, and then he'd met a gal named Justine in a bar on Zanzibal IV.

She said she was a member of a salvage vessel, and that they could always use good hands, especially with odd skills like small craft piloting and aero. When he heard that, he nearly jumped for joy. And she had been a fun roll in the bunk, too.

What she hadn't said was that the FPV *Stormcrow* typically salvaged vessels after they had killed everyone on them. It was a minor oversight, but one that had really given him pause the first time they had run into a small freighter off the Straits Nebula.

He had been in a pod working to breach the hull after *Stormcrow* had disabled the drives. It was a lot like mining, he remembered. You maneuvered up, held station, found a likely spot, and fired up the cutters.

He still remembered the look on the freighter crewman's face as he was sucked out the hole that had just been cut in his ship by Tijiit's pod. The look froze on the crewman's face. His mother had always said that if you kept making faces, one day it was going to freeze on you.

He hadn't seen any of the other crew get killed or spaced; he'd been safely back aboard the *'Crow* by then, but the whole thing had bothered him a bit. He'd learned enough about the people he was working with by then to keep his opinions to himself.

When Justine had come back aboard, her suit covered in a fine red mist, he realized he wasn't on the asteroid anymore. His conscience bothered him a lot less when they got paid ten days later. He managed to get very drunk, and although Justine had tired of him, there were plenty of ladies he met that week who more than made up for the lack of company.

He glanced down at the sat-pos and set the waypoint for the site where he had seen the survivors the day before.

This job was the biggest they had ever gotten. The mercs needed someone to lift them here and provide air support after they pacified the locals. The *Stormcrow* was good at "pacification." You didn't get any more peaceful than dead.

After that first day, he didn't think he was going to get to fly again until it was time to lift back to *Stormcrow*, but then they had that little surprise when a damned Impy cruiser entered the system. The captain nearly freaked. Hell, they all nearly had. The Imperial Avalonian Navy was absolutely merciless when it came to pirates. Being on a pirate crew was a good way to get a pulse round in the head when the Impies were around.

That merc colonel, Longo, was one stone-cold Son of the Bitch. The news that a warship had entered the system had shaken him, but not for long. He just started snapping orders, and his guys broke out crates from the holds of the assault shuttles.

Longo had the shuttles get under camo, got his men armored up, and waited. When the warship didn't slow, but instead punched out assault shuttles, Tijiit wanted to piss himself, but that cold bastard Longo didn't take his eyes off the sat plots.

Then, quick as you please, the colonel said, "Launch," and six Nord GAM-74 missiles streaked off into the sky. A few moments later, the shuttles were no longer on the plot.

The sat-pos beeped, demanding his attention. He'd be over the area where he's spotted the survivors the day before in two minutes. He'd chased a few of the motherless sons of bitches into the forest.

He had howled as his rounds penetrated a couple of them on the ground. He *loved* killing from the air. Screw that up close and personal shit. Let Longo and his mercs have that shit. Let Justine and the rest of *Stormcrow's* crew have it. Long distance, the next best thing to being there, as the old holo ads used to say.

He checked his display. In the darkened cockpit, the displays were muted to save his vision against the dark. Once he was over the target, he'd use IR and heat so it was probably a wash.

He hit the flat plain and started to accelerate, then he flipped his visor down and keyed the IR and heat overlays. On the horizon, a hundred clicks out, he saw a hot spot. Stupid fuckers. They got strafed yesterday and now they're singing songs around the campfire. They were too stupid to live. *Well,* he thought, *let's just take care of that little bit of business.*

He poured power into the drive and felt a slight push as the compensator eased the G-forces but didn't totally mitigate them. He made out a campfire and about a dozen smaller heat signatures around it. Two were on the outside perimeter of the camp, probably watching for predators or whatever, Rhombo thought.

"Target in sight," Tigiit transmitted back to base. "Commencing run."

"Just hurry up and get back here," the clipped voice of Captain Marco Jemison replied.

"Got it," Tijiit acknowledged. *Asshole,* he thought to himself.

He designated the fire on his display as the primary target. On his HUD, the fire was bracketed with a red square with the range to release counting down. He activated the hardpoints that contained two heatseeking ATG missiles. He would only use one. They were expensive, and that asshole Jemison screamed every time they had to replenish stuff they didn't use frequently.

But even Jemison saw the need to carry more than one, just in case they found another target. So, he had relented and loaded the extra missile on the hardpoint.

As the numbers reached zero, Rhombo flipped the cover over the firing stud on his stick, pressed the button, and the missile detached and streaked toward the target.

Less than five seconds later the small camp was a much larger campfire. All of the smaller figures were now part of the bigger campfire, and burning nicely, Tijiit thought as he banked the craft to take another look at the sight and scan for other heat signatures.

He made three passes. There were some scattered heat signatures in the forest, but nothing large and nothing even approaching human-size heat signatures against the slightly cool night.

He banked one last time before putting his flyer into a climb to gain cruising altitude and return to base.

At least that asshole Jemison won't bitch about the unfired missile.

* * *

Niko watched the fires burn from his hole. He and the others had dug them both in the woods and just outside the tree line then lined them with their emergency blankets. Between those and the camouflage properties of their uniforms, they put out about as much heat as a thirty-pound dog lizard.

He scanned the horizon in a complete arc with his monocular. He then consulted the sat-pos. Nothing. Nothing that was anywhere near their position that could be considered a major threat outside of the local fauna.

For the last twelve hours, starting with the attack on the camp, the survivors had cleared the camp site of all useful supplies and generally arranged the junk to make it look like they had set up a perimeter and housekeeping.

At the same time, while scanning the horizon for threats, teams consisting of the hale and hearty, supplemented by survivors who were still trickling in—they were up to forty-six now—set up a general site inside the tree line composed of small groups. Each group consisted of a couple of wounded and a couple of either lightly injured or non-injured to guard against predators.

They had to buy time for the nanites to get the injured healed enough to be functional, although some of them, absent an autodoc or a full-on hospital, weren't going too far or doing too much for the foreseeable future.

Talk about your impossible missions. Damn McClellan for putting this on him. How in the hell was he supposed to keep these people alive for two farking weeks? Whoever was out there had flyers. It was likely, even probable, that they held Weyland Station, and Gods only knew what other kinds of hardware they had access to. If they came out here with armor or mobile ground units, they were farked.

On the other hand, they were pretty much stuck here. People were trickling in all the time. Although, Niko had to admit, the longer they waited, the less likely it was that anyone else was going to make it in.

He put the monocle back in his vest. He supposed he should send out scouts to try and make sure all of the BFTs were accounted for. The thing that bothered him was whether he should leave clues for other survivors. *No*, he decided. *That was probably too risky. Always assume you're being listened to or having your mail read.*

The questions kept coming, and, as he answered them, they just spawned more questions. How did officers do this shit? How in the hell did McClellan handle this shit? Oh, he got himself buggered up and dumped it all on know-nothing privates. Devlin snorted.

He stood up, climbed out of his hole, and walked back toward the tree line. In the darkness, he saw Kenyon and Mac converging on him.

"Anything?" Kenyon asked.

"No," he replied. "That was a pretty good idea, wrapping embers up in those uniforms to simulate body heat. That pilot would have had to really check to confirm they were about forty degrees."

"I didn't want to see our folks get burnt, even if they were all dead as opposed to mostly dead. Plus, most pilots," Kenyon said, "are in the habit of relying on their instruments, so they don't look any deeper. Besides, he's probably not even a military pilot, just some adrenaline junkie."

"All right, so let it burn," Devlin said, turning to go back into the forest. "Kenyon, put out the next watch. I'm going to try and figure out what to do next."

* * *

"So, what next, O Fearless Leader?" Kenyon asked as Devlin touched her on the shoulder three hours later. It was still dark, but the sky was beginning to show traces of where the sun would soon rise.

The destroyed camp site was still burning, but even that had subsided to little more than a small afterglow. Soon, with the coming morning, it would likely burn itself out.

Sentries were scattered throughout the loose camp in the woods, keeping watch for predators and straggling survivors, though each were getting rarer by the hour. Kenyon was seated on a tree trunk that had been splintered the previous day by the hostile flier. It was kind of disconcerting to Devlin how she could tell it was him without turning to look at him.

Devlin sat down beside her and made a rude face at her comment. "That's for fearless. Frankly, the thought of me in charge of this disaster makes me want to shit bricks."

"Latrine's over there…" Kenyon said, pointing. Devlin didn't have to look to see the grin on the girl's face.

"Smart-ass."

"Better than a dumb-ass, I suppose," she countered. She turned to look at him in the dimness. "Look…Devlin. Nobody wanted this; nobody foresaw this. The best any of us can do at this point is just stay alive until the fleet's arrival. Someone has to be in charge, and to be honest, you're about the best out of the box thinker we have. McClellan knew what he was doing. Don't overthink it. If it helps, all of the Hellions have your back."

He sighed. "Gods damn it all, Nicki. I just wanted to—"

"Avoid all this 'what's fit for a soldier of the King' crap," she said. "Got it. But you gave that up the first day. You had my back when I needed it. You helped Tam with weapons, McCarthy when the rest of us wanted to frag his ass. Somehow you got Cho out of her scary, soulless, homicidal porcelain doll routine. You've stuck your nose well and truly into it, and it's too late now, Baby. So, suck it up and soldier, Soldier."

He rubbed at his hairline; one of the cuts there was now just a fading scab from the quick-heal nanites. He decided to change the subject. "What I wouldn't give for some..." he started to say then his mouth dropped open as Kenyon handed him a small cup of...hot liquid.

"How did you..."

"Ma and Da sent me a self-heating field mug. It's solar, so it's more or less always ready to go. Plus, I had singles packs of—"

"Coffee. Oh Gods," Devlin moaned, inhaling. "Marry me, Kenyon."

"You're not my type. I'm not a necrophiliac," she snorted.

He took a sip of the coffee and the hot liquid burned his lip. He took another, sighed again in ecstasy and handed the mug back. "Keep it for now," she said, waving her hand. "I've already had a cup, and I figured you'd need something when you got up here. So, we come full circle. Have you figured out what we're going to do?"

"Yeah, but you're not going to like it," he warned.

He briefly outlined what he had come up with. She stared at him for a full minute. "You're right, I don't like it," she said finally. "And the rest of us aren't going to like it either."

His shoulders started to sag, but she added, "But that's not saying it's not what we need to do." She looked out at the slowly brightening horizon. "When?"

"Probably either tonight or first thing tomorrow."

He could see her doing the math in her head. "That's gonna be cutting it extra close," she said finally.

"I don't see an alternative. If the fleet gets here while they're still here…"

Kenyon grimaced. "That's assuming that there's anyone left alive in the first place, Devlin."

He smiled mirthlessly. "That's why we get paid the big bucks, Pony."

* * * * *

Chapter Seven

Colonel Douglas Longo cursed six different deities in four different languages. "So, what you're saying is you can't bypass the security lockout on the lift shaft." He regarded the slender girl and her two assistants. Both of the men looked like they could bench press an assault shuttle. They also looked like a lot of his soldiers. Probably Impy deserters. Didn't matter; if they stepped out of line, he could more than call the tune.

The young-ish girl at the data terminal was several centimeters short of two meters. Her hair had changed hue two or three times since he met her, which meant she had color nanite enhancement. He wondered if that was the only enhancement.

"That's precisely what I'm saying. Or, more precisely, I cannot bypass the lockout in the time we have allotted for this job." She sniffed. "I'm one of the best there is, but even then it's not like the Imperials use idiots on their research facilities.

"If your bully-boys hadn't fragged the comman—"

"That'll be enough, Ms. ...Cat," Longo interrupted her. He could feel Jackson and Yerbe bristling behind him without even looking.

"Eggs, omelet," he said. "The question, is do you have any other solutions? Or is this whole party a waste of time?"

The girl who had introduced herself to him as Cat was already running some sort of program on the terminal and was only partially listening.

"It's possible I could maybe call the lift car to the top and initiate some sort of maintenance routine, I think. The routines in this thing are some of the most complex codes I've ever seen. It's almost like they're changing as I read them."

"That's all fascinating, I'm sure," Longo said dryly, "but we really need to get into that facility and find what we came for, or we're all dead. You got that?"

Cat was regarding the scrolling figures on the holoscreen and gave a perfunctory, "Hmm."

Longo hung his head. He hated working with technical wonks. He wasn't an unintelligent human being. He had grown up with a better than average education, which had segued into a military career before he had found more lucrative avenues in the private military contracting field.

But it was as though these people didn't occupy the same farking galaxy as the rest of them. The only people worse were the navel-gazing religious types.

"Just keep working, or we're all, ya know, dead."

The girl known as Cat absently waved goodbye, never taking her eyes off the display.

Longo turned to go. He felt the eyes of the two assistants as he left the room. Sarah Yerbe and Larry Jackson flanked him as he walked out the door. As the door closed, two of his mercs took stations to either side of the door and saluted their commander, which he returned. Longo might be many things, but he strived to maintain discipline.

Which is more than that half savage in charge of our ride home, he thought sourly.

The pirate crew of FPV *Stormcrow* turned Doug Longo's stomach. He wasn't a newborn babe; he'd seen combat in some really nasty places. He'd seen people do things to one another that would make holo directors, go, "Oh, Hell no! I don't want to make the audience sick!" He'd seen rape, murder, looting, and all the savagery man could inflict on man. But the crew of *Stormcrow* seemed to exult in it and treat it as a hobby.

Longo had read histories of piracy and similar endeavors from before the Exodus from Earth, and the cutthroats from the days when ships moved on wind power had nothing on FPS *Stormcrow*.

He sighed as they made their way out of the building. Not for the first time since this Gods-forsaken contract had started, he boggled at the thought of a temple church being the main entrance for a clandestine research and development facility for the Imperial Avalonian Armed Forces. But he had to admit, most people would never have thought to look there.

"What do you think, Boss?" Yerbe asked as they approached his ground car. There was a slight breeze coming in from the southeast over the "mountains" surrounding the base, blowing her shoulder-length black and silver hair into her face. Absently, she pushed it back behind her ears.

"What do I think?" Longo snorted. "What I think is that regardless of how this turns out, I'm shooting Fixer for getting us involved in this farking contract. Nothing has gone the way they said it was supposed to.

"We wind up with a 'slicer who can't find her ass with both hands. Her two assistants look like they should be wearing APES...Hell, they look like apes. I'm trying to decide if our 'ride' is going to kill us or rape us...or both.

"What do I think? I think we're farked." He blew out a disgusted breath.

"Yeah, about those two," Jackson cut in. "What should we do with them? It's kind of obvious that they aren't really—"

"Assistants? Ya think?" Longo said caustically. He rotated his neck to loosen stiff muscles. "Yerbe, get the smaller one, the one with the mouth, and take him to where we have the other 'guests.'

Tell Cat that she'd better move a little quicker if she wants to see her friend again."

Yerbe started to open her mouth, but he cut her off. "No, we ain't gonna do anything. We ain't those farking pirates, *but—*" he rounded on her and looked down into her eyes, "—I don't know if she is dragging her feet or what, but by damn, if we don't get access in the next couple of days, we aren't going to make rendezvous, and we'll be seriously farked when the Impy Navy comes calling.

"And on that note...Jackson, what did that flyboy say about the camp he saw?"

Jackson rolled a shoulder in a half shrug. "Said he got them all. Brought back footage of the missile hitting and killing about a dozen people. About the same amount of people he saw the previous day. Said he saw lots of crashes, not a whole lot of survivors." He shrugged again. "Not sure what they were doing here, but it looks like between our missile strike and that boy, Rhombo...By the way, Boss, I don't think he's wired the same way as the rest. He doesn't really like them all that much. He might be someone we can recruit. He can fly well enough, and it looks like we got them all."

Longo grunted. "We'll talk on the flyboy. And I want to look at that gun camera footage." He got into the ground car. "Get the next shift on and meet me at the town hall. We need to have a chat with Captain Jemison about the prisoners."

* * *

"What about the prisoners?" Jemison said hotly.

The commander of the FPS *Stormcrow* was a short man, just under one and half meters. He also seemed to have the short man's complaint. He seemed to obsessively need to remind everyone of his importance. He ran his crew, when he wasn't letting them burn, pillage, and loot, like a bully.

He was light-skinned, like someone who religiously avoided sunlight, and being dirtside, and he was one of the few people Longo had ever met who was fat to the point of being obese.

He was seated at a table…eating, unsurprisingly. He glared up at the commander of the mercenary group with undisguised disdain and dislike. He obviously thought Longo a stuck-up prig.

"I have received reports that some of your crew have tried to gain access to the prisoners." Longo said, stiff and formal.

"And what business is it of yours?" the pirate shot back. "One of the things that enables me to keep control of this crew is the ability to deal out rewards for a job well done. If they want a prisoner or two to relax with, it's none of either of our business. It's not like they have any other utility."

Yerbe and Jackson very carefully did not move their hands from their sides as their commander talked, but they definitely shifted their stance to a calm readiness. Longo was one of the coolest individuals they knew, and if he was getting ultra-polite, it meant that he was getting ultra-pissed.

"Captain Jemison," Longo said with exaggerated patience. "Those people are young women and children. They are civilians. We took out the military presence here. That in and of itself would be reason enough to kill us if the Impies ever came looking. But we went to great lengths to keep those women and children from being able to identify us, ostensibly so we can keep them alive. And as a good will offering that will keep the Impies from coming after us if we succeed and as hostages if we do not.

"By allowing your…crewmembers to rape one or more of those prisoners, we both take the chance of them being able to identify us, or we lose the good will option. I do not wish to kill, injure, rape, or otherwise molest these people, and while I am in charge of this mission, I will not allow it. Are we clear?"

"I'm the captain of *Stormcrow*, not you, and I will—"

Longo slammed his hand down on the table, causing the plate of food to jump and Jemison's wine glass to spill.

"I said, 'Are we clear?'" Longo roared.

Jemison cowered in his chair as railguns suddenly appeared in Yerbe's and Jackson's hands. They covered the two pirates in the room with Jemison. The two hadn't had time to draw.

Jemison's face was nearly as purple as the wine running off the table into his lap. His eyes bored into Longo's, now in undisguised hatred. He looked at Longo, then at the two guns trained on him and his henchmen.

"Fine! Fine!" Jemison spat. "I'll tell them to keep their hands and whatever to themselves. But we're not done, Longo! Not by a long shot."

"We're done for now," the mercenary commander said, calm once more. "I had best not hear any more reports. Just remember who's paying the bills. They may not be very understanding or generous should I deliver a less than complimentary report when we return."

Longo deliberately turned his back on the pirate captain and stalked out of the room, Yerbe and Jackson did not, backing toward the doors, their guns still trained on the pirates.

* * * * *

Chapter Eight

As the sun rose over the survivors' camp, Devlin and Kenyon, flanked by the rest of the Hellions, called a camp meeting to outline the situation and Devlin's notional plan. The rest of the recruits weren't any more enthusiastic about it than Kenyon was.

"So, let me get this straight," Private Agnes Sylvanus said, crossing her arms. She was a tall, thin girl from Chyron in the Olympian colonies. At the moment, she was seated on a stump nursing a splinted leg. She had arrived the previous day after limping twenty kilometers. She was one of the few survivors from Bravo Company, which meant one of the Bravo shuttles had managed to hit the punch out button before they were destroyed, but Sylvanus couldn't say for sure how many might have made it off. She would have been one of the first.

"You want to split us up. The sick, lame, and lazy here with a few to stand sentry in case those damn lizards come looking for a quick snack."

Devlin nodded. She continued.

"And one team goes out and searches the debris field for more survivors, salvage, or corpses. Is that right so far?" Again, Devlin nodded in affirmation.

"And while all this is going on, you and the squad from Hell is going on a raid to the settlement. For what exactly?"

"Two things, actually," Devlin said. Then Kenyon nudged him, "Sorry, three things."

"One," he held up a finger. "We need intel. I thought about this a bunch last night. So far, we've only seen one flier, not a force. So, I'm figuring that they A, don't figure we're much of a threat in the first place, and B, don't have the resources to really bring the hurt. Which tells me a little bit about our friends."

He had their attention now. A few nodded, a few frowned even deeper.

"I figure that since this wasn't a full-on base, they decided a smash and grab run. Drop a platoon of shock troops, maybe mercs to take out the military personnel at the facility. It doesn't make sense to drop much more than a platoon because if they had that kind of manpower, why not make sure we aren't a threat? For transport, it's only about an hour or so here and back. So, I'm figuring not. A third up and on duty, a third up and on call, and a third down; standard ops."

More nods. He was making sense.

"So that's one reason. Intel on the hostile force.

"Two," he continued. "We need more supplies, medical, food, and, most importantly, weapons. Sure, all of us can survive the two weeks as a group, and we can make fire by rubbing two sticks together, and we can probably cobble together an APE with crash debris, and our strength is as ten because our hearts are pure. But we don't have much, and I'm not sure that we're going to be able to rely on salvage and hunting and foraging to help us last until the fleet gets here. Does anybody here want to eat lizard? Anybody know how to eat lizard? Know if we can eat lizard? And most importantly, has anyone seen a lizard?

"And three, unless they're straight up pirates or slavers, they probably haven't killed everybody, just anybody that was a threat. That means civvies and families are maybe still alive. We need to find out."

"Uh, why?" Pringle from Fourth Platoon asked. "If they're alive now, they'll probably be alive later…"

"True and also not," Devlin said. "They may or may not be, and they may be hostages. What typically happens when hostages aren't necessary anymore?" Pringle's dark face paled.

Sylvanus nodded, unfolded her arms, and looked around. "So, now for my next question: How come you get to make this decision, and how come you are the one going for the facility?"

"And who is going with you?" another recruit piped in.

"I'll take them in order," Devlin answered, putting his arm out as Mac and Kenyon both started to say something. "One, I'm the one the sergeant major left in charge. He told me to take care of you. I can and will make the decisions I deem necessary to ensure our overall survival. But he also tasked me with finding out what happened. There are arguments for and against my staying here versus going to the base, but I think my best course of action is to try and find out if we can access Weyland and its armory and supplies."

"Which is why, two, Second Squad, plus one or two others, are going because we work well together; we know how we operate. We don't have time to war-game this, and we need to know each other well enough not to have to say shit. You knew your squad mates that well, yes?"

Sylvanus looked down at the mention of her squad mates, none of which had shown up yet at the camp. "Yeah," She said quietly.

Devlin was quiet for a moment. That made everyone a bit quiet. They had started out with almost three hundred people on those shuttles. Now there were less than a hundred. A lot of those were too injured at the moment to be of much help with anything. It was a sobering realization of how far in the latrine they had been dropped.

He continued. "Second Squad—what's left of it. Plus another partial. Four fire teams. Decker, you're one."

Anne Decker looked up from tying off a splint. She had been moving around camp checking new arrivals and helping with first aid since the sun came up. Her cheerful face was drawn and haggard with grief and exhaustion.

"MacBain, because he apparently knew one of the officers here, and Decker because she's the next best thing to a data-slicer. We may need to get into some computers; she'll know what questions to ask if we get in front of a data terminal.

"As far as who is going on the recovery team, I'm giving that to you, Pringle. You're one of the other platoon leaders extant, so seniority and for your sins and all that. Get yourself a team together and get with me before noon.

"And I'm leaving Kimbler in charge here at the camp." He saw Kimbler inhale and then nod.

"So, unless someone has a real, no shit reason why we shouldn't do this, that's the plan. Pring, you and Kimbler get some people together and formulate your own plans. You might want to send a couple of scouts to the original rendezvous to make sure someone hasn't gone there instead of meandering their way here. We'll meet at noon and divvy up the resources everyone is going to need and to set up a rendezvous at the end of this."

* * * * *

Chapter Nine

Devlin and the Hellions struck out that afternoon. Three days had passed since they had been shot down. The flier had not reappeared after the middle of the night bombing run the previous day, for which everyone was immensely grateful.

The three groups had divvied up their rations and had given the largest portion to the main camp. Water was about a klick away through the forest. Kimbler informed the other two team leaders that he intended to begin moving the camp closer to it as quickly as possible.

"I'll leave some breadcrumbs so you guys can find me. Hopefully, those other...nice people...will leave us the Hells alone."

On the maps that each of the team leads had on comp, they coordinated the routes they would take, making sure not to mark anything down. Pringle was going to backtrack to the beginning of the debris field and set up caches of anything he found that was useful.

"Hopefully, we'll find some usable weapons."

"From your mouth to whichever Gods might be listening at this point," Devlin said. "And if you run into the one that is altogether pissed off at us, give him some pogiebait or whatever."

Devlin's journey was the most dangerous and the farthest. "If I get there, and there's any way to get word back to you, I'll send it. Rule Number—"

"Forty-Two," Kimbler suggested.

"Rule Number One," Pringle said, holding out his hand. Devlin put his hand on top of it, and Kimbler followed.

"The most dangerous weapon a warrior has…" Devlin intoned.

"Is his mind," all three said.

* * *

They kept to the tree line for most of the first day. MacBain took point, then Tamman and Jones kept watch for the flier on the horizon. Kenyon and Decker followed and watched their flanks for ground-based threats. Chapis, Cho, and Devlin walked in the middle to respond to anyone who had a need. Moran and Arnette watched the back horizon. "The Carls," Curran and Weber, watched their flank, and Gartlan occupied ass-end Charlie, or the rear guard.

They kept a fast pace, trying to eat as much ground as possible, but as they moved they spread out, close enough to cover each other, but far enough apart that they could take cover if the flier was spotted.

According to the satellite imagery the sergeant major had unlocked in Devlin's implant, the forest extended in the direction they were traveling for about a hundred kilometers. After that they were going to be in the open until they reached some foothills. The settlement was in a vale surrounded by low mountains and had a lake and small river running out of it.

Devlin wasn't sure how he was going to get into the vale to get the intel, secure the hostages—if there were any—present any kind of resistance to the hostiles, or get a message off to the fleet, or any of the one thousand nine hundred fifty-four questions he had swirling around in his brain, but all of it was academic until he got to his objective.

The one saving grace to the whole affair was that Aberdeen's climate was remarkably stable. It wasn't hot during the day, nor excessively cool during the evenings. Added to that blessing, their uniforms were adaptable to a number of environments, so at least here the cloth didn't have to work very hard. Between the uniforms and their e-blankets, they could weather—he laughed at himself—quite a bit.

He figured that the military, in its infinite wisdom, probably picked a place that was the least harsh on the trainees. *If they got killed on a damned exercise, think of the paperwork,* he mused. *Damn. There's going to be a butt-load of paperwork after this exercise.*

He mentally sent a prayer to the heavens that he was not going to be required to fill out all of that damned paperwork.

"I'll be damned if I'm going to do it," Devlin said out loud. It was out of his mouth before he realized he had spoken. Everyone in the squad turned to look at him.

"Do what?" Kenyon said quietly.

"Nothing," Devlin said. "Why are we talking quietly? We're out in the middle of nowhere."

Kenyon frowned, then shrugged. "I don't know. Maybe just to keep in practice?" she said in a more normal tone.

Decker snickered and shook her head. She walked ahead a few feet. Kenyon dropped back to Devlin.

"Something's bugging you," she said. "Already?"

He grunted. "More than one thing, actually," he replied. "But the major thing is actually getting access to the settlement."

"We've got the satellite imagery."

"Yeah, and from what I can tell, it says we got to go through the front gate...and let's just say I don't like that idea."

"Alternatives?

"Over the ring wall?"

"We don't have any climbing gear if we need it."

"I know. That bothers me."

"I think you're taking counsel of your fears, Devlin."

"What else have I got at this point?"

"Concentrating on getting there. Worry about the entry when we actually get there." He grimaced. "I didn't like winging things when I was on the streets, and I like it worse now."

"Think of it as real-time planning. React, adapt, overcome!"

"Think of it as real-time dying," he countered darkly.

"Bah," she said airily. "Only the good die young. We're Hellions; that's why we're still here. We're going to live forever."

"No, we're not, Nick. We're here right now because we've been lucky. I don't like trusting to luck. I'd feel a lot better if we knew what we were walking into."

"Sure," she agreed. "But wanting right now is not getting the mission done right now. We've got two hundred klicks to get through. Massage that damn imagery and figure out how to traverse that plain without getting spotted. Figure out what we might have to contend with as far as weather. How long this shit is supposed to take. Those are questions enough. Quit worrying about problem five thousand four hundred ninety-six while we're still dealing with problem number ten."

She sped up to catch up with Decker and left him to think on that.

* * *

They camped after dark, using their multitools to dig shallow scrapes just inside the tree line. They lined the hole with one of their blankets, set out a double watch, and sat down to eat their evening ration.

Devlin set his comp to holo and brought up the map imagery for their route.

"Okay, boys and girls," he said, highlighting their progress. "We made forty-five clicks today, and we have to make the settlement in less than five days. Easy peasy right? Well, yes and no." He moved the imagery to the settlement. "Once we're there, we have to get into the settlement." He saw Kenyon open her mouth. "Not the problem at the moment," he said. "The problem is that we've got to get there and recon, figure out the objectives, decide go or no-go on any plans once we figure them out. Everyone with me so far?"

He saw the squad nod in the semidarkness. The holo was set for minimum brightness, which, in the complete darkness of the forest, was still damn near blinding.

"So, the issue is getting to the outer shield wall in as short a period of time as possible, yes?"

"Don't grease us up so hard, Devlin," MacBain said. His voice was still pretty angry, but it had lost the brittle quality it'd had a couple of days previous. "You've got something in mind. Spit it out."

"Okay, no grease and plenty of sand," Devlin said. "We are going to have to make the trip in three days total. That means one hundred fifty klicks in three days. Now we can either double time—"

"Fark that!" Gartlan said, but Cho elbowed him in the ribs.

"I kind of agree," Devlin said. "Trying to run, even jog, is going to really stress us to the point where we'll need at least a day to recover, even with our leetle friends helping."

"So, here's what I've got. We're going to quick march as far and as fast as we can each day. No breaks, no stopping. If you gotta stop to take a dump, catch up. We'll need to detail a buddy so you don't get eaten while trying to shit. But there it is. Comes to it, that's my decision, but I'd like everyone on board, or at the least a good alternative. Frankly, I can't see one, but I've been known to have tunnel vision. So how about it? Anybody see an alternative?"

Everyone in the party looked at everyone else. The low light made faces visible but not entirely readable.

Finally, Tamman spoke up. "I trust you, Devlin. If you say that this is the way to go, then we do it. But, then again, I'm not that bright."

"Fark that, Tam," Jonesy said, getting annoyed with his friend. "Devlin, you know that Tam is at least as smart as most of us, even if he can't express it well."

Devlin nodded. The big man had a child-like attitude but could think fast in a crunch. He proved the night on the liberty station that he could react, adapt, and overcome just fine without a keeper.

"But is he right?" Devlin pressed. "Do the rest of you trust me?"

"Hey," Decker said. "The sergeant major trusted you. He gave you the keys to the truck and unlocked your noggin. That's good enough for me."

"Same here," Curran and Weber added. As did Arnette, Moran, and Gartlan. Chapis just grinned. Cho said nothing but nodded. Devlin looked over at Kenyon, who held up her hands and grinned in this semidarkness. "Hey, don't look at me, I'm just following you to the bar."

They all laughed at that, and the tension broke. "All right," Devlin said when the chuckles had subsided. "Set out the watch. The rest of you turn in. Wake-up at oh-four-thirty, and we'll get started."

He turned off the holo and watched in the darkness as the rest of the recruits got into their positions and covered themselves with their blankets.

He called up the satellite imagery on his implant as he kept watch in the gathering gloom.

* * * * *

Chapter Ten

Devlin woke to the smell of smoke. They had walked, jogged, and run for the last day and only stopped when they had all pretty much fallen in place. They had clustered under an outcropping of rock and fallen asleep.

Still logy, he frowned. They shouldn't...He was instantly awake.

"Put out that fire!" He shouted and lurched upright, dislodging his teammates.

Tom McCarthy, his uniform torn in several places, squatted over a small fire, cooking something that looked suspiciously like meat. He looked quizzically at Devlin.

"Huh?"

"Put that thing out, you idiot!" Devlin shouted again, stomping on the fire.

"What the hell are you—" McCarthy shouted, his face mottled with surprise and a little rage.

By this time, the rest of the team was awake and on their feet, as well. "McCarthy!" Kenyon exclaimed.

"Tom! What the—" Cho looked genuinely astonished.

Devlin stopped stomping at the fire. It was still smoldering but it looked like it was out.

"Tom, what the fark?"

"I came down in the woods," the young man said. "The trees broke the fall of the shock frame even more. I got banged up quite a bit, but nothing was broken. I got what shit survived the fall—my pack and shit was gone—but...hey, did you know that the shock frame can be—"

"Used to make basic survival implements with the contents of the survival pack. Yeah," Carl "Shuddup" Weber said, grinning.

"Well, anyway. I wasn't really sure which way to go, so figured I'd try and find water first. I guess I wandered around for about half a day before I found a small stream and a clearing. From the clearing I could see some smoke in the direction I came from, so I figured that must be where the shuttle crashed and you guys must be."

Devlin nodded. "Okay..."

"I took off and reached the other side of the woods as it was getting dark. I wasn't sure about predators, so I shimmied up a tree and tied in to sleep."

Devlin's eyebrows shot up. They had trained exactly once on that kind of sleeping rig; McCarthy had apparently paid closer attention than Devlin had thought.

"The next morning, I found some wreckage and started following it back in the direction of where the whole thing started. I hoped I'd find some survivors, but no, no survivors. I did find the other two shuttles' wreckage...or at least some of it."

He paused and looked down at his hand, the spit of—yeah, it really looked like meat—still in his hand.

"I found some of the supplies that was on Shuttle Three. Not everything was destroyed." He grinned. "I found a pack and had just started loading it with food when Pringle showed up with a bunch of the guys. Oh, here, you guys can have this." He held up the stick.

Devlin wanted to grab it like a junky grabbing a stimwand, but he also wanted to throttle the kid.

"So how did you get *here*, and how did you get here without Dammit Carl waking me up?" He fixed the trainee in question with a basilisk stare. Carl Curran, also known as Dammit Carl, blanched slightly.

McCarthy continued. "Once Pring and I engaged in information transfer, he told me where you'd gone and how you figured to get there. I thought I ought to catch up, so I filled a pack with extra geedunks and a surprise and headed out. I caught up with you a couple of hours ago. I told Dammit to let you sleep, so he did."

"When did you sleep?" Cho asked.

"I've only slept a couple of hours in the last two days," McCarthy said. "You know I don't sleep much to begin with." Cho pursed her lips, but before she could say anything the young man added, "But I pretty well slept the night away up in that tree…about the only time since I was six."

Devlin was about to ask about the surprise, when Kenyon shouted, "Flyer! Fast mover!"

Everyone grabbed their packs and started running. When McCarthy didn't, Devlin grabbed him by his uniform shirt and yelled, "Come on!"

The little outcropping they had weathered under was part of a larger set of hills. Devlin and McCarthy made for a sheer cliff face that was tall enough that it would make strafing difficult. They dove behind a few rocks, and Devlin peered over one. The flier had overshot the group and was circling.

McCarthy reached into his pack and pulled out a rail pistol and magazine. He slapped the magazine home into its well and charged the pistol.

"Where the fark did you get that!" Devlin panted. He reached over and took the pistol. McCarthy let him.

"This was the surprise," McCarthy said. "I found the pistol, then searched the wreckage for ammo. I found some and parts to a bunch of rifles. Most were in bad shape, but Pringle figured he might be able to cobble together a couple from the parts. He was going take the lot back to the camp so they would have something to defend the wounded with. He sent me with this for you. Best we could get together at the time. Sorry."

"Don't be sorry. This is pretty good. I won't beat the shit out of you now for the fire."

"The fire?" McCarthy looked blank for a moment, then realization hit. "Oh, you think that the fire attracted—"

"Our flying friend over there. Yeah, I just—get your head down!" He pulled at McCarthy as rounds from the flier dug into the earth. There was something odd about this one.

He took a quick look. This wasn't the same flier that had attacked the camp, this one was…

"Drone!" Devlin yelled. He watched the thing from the rocks, watched it circle around again. He braced the pistol on the rocks, steadied, and waited.

When the drone started its run again, Devlin sighted in, breathed out, and fired.

The drone disintegrated in a fiery cloud as the rail gun round entered its main capacitor bank. He watched it fall and then rose from behind the rocks. McCarthy joined him.

Devlin looked over at the tree line and waved his arm. A moment later, Kenyon appeared, followed by Gartlan and MacBain.

"Devlin!" Decker's voice came out of the tree line. Kenyon and the others started to where Decker's voice had come from. Devlin started to run.

He found the group gathered around Decker. She was holding Moran's head in her lap. Moran's uniform had a red stain in the abdomen that was growing larger by the moment.

"Got hit as I dived into the woods," Moran croaked. Her blond hair was already slick with sweat, her face pale.

"Sorry, Devlin. I…I…" her voice trailed off as her implant fed nanites and nighty-night into her system. A moment later she looked dead, which for all intents and purposes she was.

Devlin rubbed his scalp. He glared over at McCarthy, whose shocked face got even paler as he looked at the body, hibernating though it was, of Lisa Moran. He bowed his head and started to stammer, "I'm sorry, I didn't…"

"Shut up, Tom. Just shut up," Devlin said tiredly. "You didn't know; you had no way of knowing. This wasn't even the same flier that attacked the camp. Just a stupid mistake, but it's one that we have to deal with now. Is anybody else hurt?"

Arnette was sitting on the ground beside Decker with her legs crossed. She held one ankle in her hands. "Well, now that you mention it…" She looked at Devlin with pain-filled eyes. "I think my ankle is broken. I stepped straight into a hole as I came into the woods."

Decker moved her legs out from underneath Moran's head and laid it gently on the ground. She made her way to the other woman. Gartlan bent down as well and said, "Let's get your boot off."

Together, the two started trying to get the girl's boot off. When Arnette hissed once and nearly passed out, they realized they'd have to cut it off. Gartlan produced a tactical knife and used the monomolecular edge to slice down the side of the boot. His cut made, he handed the knife to Decker, who sliced down the foot portion of the boot, careful not to cut too deeply.

"Here you go, Wolf," she said handing the knife back to Gartlan, who folded it and put it back in his pocket. Together, he and Decker were finally able to peel the ruined boot off the injured girl's foot.

Her foot, already purple, immediately started to swell. They propped her leg up on a rock covered with Gartlan's tunic. Gartlan shook his head at Devlin. "She isn't likely to go nighty-night, but she might as well. She ain't going anywhere on that foot for a few days. And she's not going to like this, but we're going to have to set it and splint it so that the nanis don't knit it wrong. Probably still will, but the canker mechanics should be able to fix it without too much problem if we get home."

Sarah Arnette's eyes went wide as Gartlan's words hit home. "Oh Gods!" she moaned. "This is going to *suck!*"

"Do it," Devlin said. "Come on, guys. They don't need an audience, and we've got to get our shit together."

He turned to walk away as Gartlan bent back down, and Decker opened a med kit.

Another drone flier came to halt in front of them, and a voice came over its vocoder, "State your name and passcode."

* * * * *

Chapter Eleven

"I'm not sure—" Devlin started to say but the drone cut him off.

"State your name and passcode, or you will be neutralized."

"I—" Devlin started to say again, but this time Decker, who had come up beside him, cut him off.

"Sentry drone!" she commanded sharply. The drone turned its pickups on her. "Before we will comply, we demand unit identifier and base of operations. We have different passcodes for different facilities. We are unsure which one this is."

"This unit is sentry drone number four one zero dash nine eight zero," the drone replied. "Sentry drone for test hanger, Weyland Station, Aberdeen Proving, Imperial Avalonian Research. State your name and passcode, or you will be neutralized."

Decker looked at Devlin and pursed her lips. "You got anything really good up there in your noggin?"

Devlin shrugged. "My noggin has never been known to have an overabundance of anything useful." He grimaced. "Devlin, Nikolai N., Recruit Private, Service Number Two Two Two Seven One Dash Seven Nine Eight Dash Eight Two Three Three Alpha Oscar. I was not issued a passcode for this facility."

The drone hovered silently for a few moments, then moved toward Devlin. A scanner activated and scanned his face and retinas.

"Identity confirmed. Facial recognition and retina record verified via last service download. Devlin, Nikolai N. on temporary duty on Aberdeen with Alpha Company, Third Battalion, One Forty-Ninth

Training Legion. Alpha Company, Third Battalion, One Forty-Ninth Training Legion is not authorized to be in this area of operation."

"Alpha Company and Bravo Company were ambushed by hostile forces. Chain of command has been rendered combat ineffective."

"Alpha Company, Third Battalion, One Forty-Ninth Training Legion is not authorized to be in this area of operation."

"I know that, but…"

Decker broke in, "Sentry!" The drone turned and regarded her again. "Contact higher and request disposition." The drone fell silent for a moment.

"What did you just do?" Devlin hissed. The drone hovered before them doing and saying nothing for almost a full minute. Finally, it turned its pickups back on Devlin and its vocoder spoke in a different timbre than the initial one.

"You and all personnel with you shall be detained. You will be escorted to Central Security, and your chain of command can be contacted. You will follow this unit. Failure to comply will result in termination. Unauthorized movement from area of travel will result in termination. Follow me, please."

The drone spun and started off toward a small hillock. Devlin looked at Decker and Kenyon, mouthed, "What the…" and turned to follow.

* * *

As they approached the hillock, the sentry drone flew to one side of an outcropping of rock.

Devlin watched as an access door large enough for several humans or a small vehicle to enter slid aside. The exterior of the door was camouflaged well enough that you would have to know it was there to see it.

The opening was darker than the outside, but he saw some lights inside. The drone stopped and hovered outside the entrance. A pair of gun emplacements rose from silos flanking each side of the entrance. Although not in active seek mode, they were directed toward Devlin and the squad.

"Please enter the facility and wait inside the red circled area," the drone requested.

Devlin and the rest of his group walked through the door and stood just inside what looked like a security checkpoint or airlock. Possible both, Devlin decided. The facility could have been engineered to lockdown in case of an emergency.

The door closed behind them, cutting off the outside world and the sentry drone. Devlin looked at Decker. She shrugged and murmured, "Makes sense. We're here now. No need for the outside help. They'll probably send someone to come fetch us. Maybe another drone, maybe a person."

As the outer door closed, Devlin watched the telltale lights on the panel in front of them change from green to red on one side of the chamber. He turned to the other side of the chamber and saw that the panel by that door was red as well. A moment later, the panel turned green and the door started to cycle open.

"Get ready, guys." McCarthy muttered.

Cho made a face. "For what, exactly? If they want us dead, there's damn all we can do about it."

"If they wanted us dead, we'd have been fragged already," Devlin said. "Now, shut up."

The door finished cycling, and another security drone hovered at the entrance.

"Private Devlin," the voice came over the speaker on the drone. "Please follow this drone. It will conduct you to Central Security and

Command for this facility. I need you there so we can resolve this matter."

"And you are...?"

"I am one of the administrators for this research facility. My name is Weyland."

"Oh. That's convenient," Devlin said as he started out of the chamber. The drone moved into a large open area. "You've got the same name as the facility."

"I'm named after the facility. Or, you could say the facility is named after me, I suppose. Six of one, half a dozen of the other."

The squad filed out into the large open area. As they did so, massive lights began to illuminate the area and they saw they were in a large hangar type staging area. Devlin noticed hover trucks and ground transports, all parked along one wall like a motor pool.

He looked up at the "wall" they were parked next to, only it wasn't a wall. It was a door. A massive door. MacBain saw it too, as did Tamman and Jones.

"What the fuzzy Hell?" Jonesy asked.

"Excuse me, Private Jones?" Weyland inquired. "I have heard quite a few idioms in my time, but never that one."

"Just looking at the bloody blinkin' door."

"That is the main hangar door for this portion of the facility," Weyland said. "I trust that I do not have to give you the standard security briefings, ladies and gentlemen. This facility is protected under the Official Secrets Act, and you can be court martialed and very bad things will happen to you should you divulge anything you see in here. So, what happens in Weyland...stays in Weyland."

"Got it," Devlin said. He thought for a moment. "How far down are we at this point...if I'm allowed to ask."

"You can ask," Weyland replied. "Currently, you are one half of a kilometer under the hill you entered. The entrance was a grav car. You were moved from the access entrance to the hangar area."

"May I ask why?" Devlin said. "If you could move us here, you presumably could have moved us any number of places."

"I'll get to that when you get to CentSec," Weyland replied and fell silent.

They walked through the hangar and saw more vehicles and a couple of fliers of the standard Imperial Army type, but there were also a couple of a type they had never seen before. One was on a ready platform with its panels removed, giving the squad a glimpse into the grav generators and power plants.

The drone passed it and continued to a corridor. They walked briskly to keep up.

At the end of the corridor, they entered another grav car room. The door behind them cycled closed.

"You are now being transported to the main portion of the facility," Weyland said over the room speakers. "If it helps, you are coming to Weyland settlement."

"But that is fifty kilometers…"

"Sixty-four point nine seven kilometers linear distance from where you entered the facility. "The grav car has inertial compensators so you do not feel the acceleration of the pod, which is approaching twenty-one gravities."

"How long until we get to the facility?"

"You are just about there."

Devlin looked at the other team members. Kenyon raised her eyebrows. Decker was examining the panel on the wall. Everyone else seemed to be hanging loose. Devlin could tell their demeanor was mostly façade. Cho's hands were relaxed at her sides. Usually, when she was that relaxed, something was about to get its ass kicked.

Tamman was leaning against the wall with his eyes closed. McCarthy rolled his neck.

"Everybody," Devlin said. "Calm the hell down. Chill the hell out even."

The squad looked him askance.

"You all are acting like virgins in a brothel. Get over it. Weyland wants to talk to us, so let's be polite."

"Thank you, Private." Weyland said. "Please, everyone, I really do need to talk to you. You are my guests now. Had you not been verified as Imperial Army, you wouldn't have been given access, and we wouldn't be talking right now. Okay?"

"In other words, if that drone hadn't been able to verify I was Army...even a recruit..."

The sigh was almost noticeable. "You'd have been terminated. I suppose I'd have been contacted when your trackers went off, but possibly not. I'm not the normal security officer. I'm just an admin type. And here we are."

Devlin looked, and the telltales on the door cycled to green. When the main light finally changed, the door opened, revealing another corridor.

"Please move along that corridor to the end," Weyland requested.

The squad moved out, with MacBain first, then Tamman, Kenyon, Decker, and the Carls. Devlin followed in the middle with Cho, McCarthy, Chapis, and Jones in the rear.

At the end of the corridor, they encountered a massive blaststeel door which began to open as they approached. Finally, they entered a rather modest control room. Covering the walls were display terminals showing scenes from all over the facility; they cycled through multiple displays while they watched.

As Jonesy entered the room, the door closed, cutting the team off from the corridor. Devlin turned, half in panic.

"Please calm yourself, Private Devlin," Weyland said over the speakers in the room. "I have not dealt falsely with you."

"Well, where the hell are you then? I thought were going to have a face to face talk. If you want to engender trust, this isn't the way to go about it."

"Well, face to face is kind of…difficult," Weyland replied.

"Why? What the bloody Hell is going on? Where is the commanding officer? Where are the security officers?"

"Private Devlin," said the voice that had introduced itself as Weyland, "I am Weyland, the central facilities artificial intelligence for the Weyland Research Facility, and I am currently the only thing here in the facility at the moment."

* * * * *

Chapter Twelve

Devlin cleared his throat. "You're an AI?"

"Yes. I was a prototype artificial intelligence program brought online at this facility twenty-three years ago to help run the facilities' maintenance protocols."

"So, you were…"

"Basically, the janitor and handyman when I was first given consciousness."

"And now?"

"Now I assist the human administrator for this facility and help with running the settlement on the surface."

"So where is everyone?"

"Four days before your unit was ambushed, this facility came under attack by mercenary and pirate forces. In defense, this facility was placed on administrative lockdown, and the military personnel were sent topside to augment the settlement forces in repelling the attack. They failed."

"So…"

"At the moment, you and your group are the only military personnel in this facility and in a position to render aid."

"So…"

"In admin-lock, I am currently unable to do much, except maintain the facility and carry out the primary defense protocol should non-military forces attempt to gain entry to the facility."

"What is the primary defense protocol?"

"Each section of the Weyland Research Facility is powered by a Nimue Fusion Reactor. There are six in total. Should the facility be breached in any of its main sections, all the reactors will go critical and explode, destroying the facility and the settlement above."

"And I assume that we are here…"

"You are here to ensure that protocol does not get carried out."

"How the Hell can you do that? I would figure that you would be—"

"I cannot go against the protocols governing this facility. I can no more tell the reactors not to explode than you can tell your heart not to beat. However, I find myself in the unenviable position of not wanting to 'go boom.' I would prefer no boom today."

Decker started to say something, but Devlin shook his head. "As an AI, you found a loophole."

"Precisely, Private Devlin. *You* are my loophole. You can keep this place from going 'boom.'"

"But I'm not going to do that at this point," Devlin said, folding his arms.

The room was dead silent for a long moment.

"Why not?" Weyland asked after a moment.

"For several reasons." Devlin laughed. "First, all I know is that you're a voice on a speaker. For all I know you could be someone top-side, wanting me to let them in. Which ain't happening."

"And so?" This time the AI prompted Devlin to continue.

"And so, we're going to leave things as they are for a while. If you were willing to conduct us here, you're capable of giving us access, correct?"

"Yes," the AI replied, though it sounded uncertain. Devlin had to quirk a smile at that.

"So, here's the deal. We came to gain intel on the forces in the settlement. What their purpose is, what they've done with the people in the settlement, whether or not the follow-on forces that were supposed to meet us here in a couple of weeks are going to be sitting ducks, and whether or not they're walking into a trap by forces unknown. You're going to aid us. If we can find a surviving member of the civilian or military staff, so be it. We'll turn everything over to him or her. We'll try and find someone to take over this, and you're going to render what assistance you can toward that end. Agreed?"

"Agreed," the AI replied. Devlin started to say something, but Kenyon nudged him. He looked at her, and she mouthed, "Arnette and Moran."

"Also, I need you to task a drone to guard my other two team members who are still out in the woods just outside the perimeter. The original drone that attacked us, and I'm presuming at this point that it was one the facility drones, injured both of my teammates and triggered one's medical protocols."

"I apologize for that, Private." Weyland sounded regretful. "As you were talking, I pulled up the visual data from the drone. It was in auto response mode, and it was not under my control at the time. I'm not sure I could have done anything to begin with, but you have my apologies. If you give me the names of your injured teammates, I will clear them for the facility as I have already done you and task security with guarding them until you can retrieve them or make arrangements for evac. I can also send a maintenance mech out with a message from you and inform the alert team member what's going on. Would that be satisfactory?"

Devlin smiled. "Yes, that is as good as we could ask for. Let's get to work."

* * * * *

Chapter Thirteen

"How do we find out what's going on in the settlement?" Devlin asked as he looked around the CentCom control room. He had already sent Chapis out the back door with a transport to return Moran and Arnette to the rear camp under cover of darkness.

Decker was seated at one of the terminals, flipping through display after display, about one a second. Each showed various locations in the research facility. Nothing moved in any of the areas. Areas outside the facility, such as where Devlin and his companions had encountered the automated drones, were shown as well.

"I don't know, Dev," Decker said somewhat absently.

"The surveillance feeds were cut off during the initial…incident," Weyland interjected. "It was a software hack; one I wasn't expecting, and one I cannot overcome now. I theorize the interruption was a software hack reinforced by physically severing the connections in the entrance building."

"So, effectively, you're blind to the conditions upstairs. Not only in the settlement, but at the entrance as well."

"Yes, Private," the AI responded. "At the moment I can tell you someone is attempting to overcome the security locks on the lift shaft."

"How do you know that?" Decker asked, not looking up from the terminal.

"Because I am now countering their attempts. Whoever they are, they are very good. Excellent, even, but they are human, whereas I think...a little faster." Weyland sounded a bit smug at that.

"So, what can you tell us about the entrance? What kind of building is it? Where is the lift located in the building? How likely are we to be seen when we exit the lift?"

The AI displayed a building floor plan on the main viewscreen. Devlin and the others turned to look at it.

"That looks kind of like..." MacBain started.

"A Fundamental Wayist Church building, Private MacBain," Weyland finished for him. "The FWs are one of the more ecumenical faiths in the Empire, and as such had no problem with other faiths using the building."

"What the Hell?" MacBain asked. "A church?"

"The primary settlement serves as the living area for the staff of the facility and their families. It was designed by the builders of Weyland to appear like a nascent settlement community or testbed for a full-on colony. The families of the staffers at Weyland run and maintain all the support structures, administrative adjunct offices, a small manufactory, dining, etc. There are houses as well as barracks facilities for the uncontracted members of the staff.

"It was, I was given to understand, something of both an amusement and a practical decision to house the only entrance to the facility in a building that served as the place of worship for some of the inhabitants. Amusing considering the testing that goes on is for military hardware, and practical because it is one of the few places in the settlement where large numbers of people can go, and it would not seem out of place from casual orbital surveillance."

"Casual?" Cho asked.

"We do occasionally get visitors to the system—freighters, small ships, etc. They stop in, find out there's nothing of real interest here and move on. When we get someone with a problem, a bad hyper-generator, for example, we had a naval frigate on station that would 'arrange' for a repair ship to help them out. Further out-system as not to disturb the 'Fundy' settlers."

"Had," Decker asked.

"The frigate was caught unaware when the ship currently in orbit approached. It came in on a vector other than what is considered normal and was mistaken for a rogue asteroid or comet. Not large enough to cause concern, but large enough to take on an Imperial Frigate."

Devlin chewed on that for a few moments.

"Command knew you were here, knew what you were doing, and helped maintain the façade?"

"Yes, Private Devlin. We actually had military personnel here comprising most of the staff of the facility."

"What happened?" Kenyon asked.

The AI considered for a moment. "I'm not precisely certain. I was in the loop until about five minutes after the hostile forces entered the settlement. Then all my communications topside got severed. It was the middle of the night local time, so only a charge of quarters was here. When the feed got severed, the CQ armed himself, instigated the lockdown procedure and went topside. I have not heard from him, or anyone else, since."

"So, we need to get up into the church building and take it from whoever—"

"Whomever," the AI corrected.

"Whatever," Devlin said, glaring at the AI's video pickup, "and secure it so we can use it as a base of operations. And don't forget doing so without alerting whoever—"

"Who."

"Shuddup!"

"Whatever…" the AI huffed. "So rude…" it muttered.

"What was that?" Kenyon said.

"I said, I need to check on food…for you wonderful people."

"That's better." Kenyon smiled, her teeth showing. "As I was saying. Devlin, since the hostages are probably being held somewhere other than here, we probably need to keep from alerting the intruders."

"Point," Devlin said grimacing. "Is there any way we can get topside commo and surveillance back, even in just the church?" He looked at Decker, who looked away from the screens long enough to frown and shake her head.

"Weyland?" he asked.

"Oh, so I can speak now?" the AI said huffily. "Because I mean I wouldn't want to—"

"We're sorry, Weyland," Devlin soothed. "We're all short on time here, and everyone is a little tetchy."

"Tetchy?" Kenyon and Weyland said at the same moment.

Devlin sighed. "Can we focus, people? Commo and surveillance, Weyland?"

The AI made a sound like a sigh. "As of right now, the person who has been trying to hack my entrance lockouts is still at it upstairs. They are using bots, worms, cracks, and the kitchen sink to try to bypass it. I'm holding them off for most of it and cycling things. They're not going to get through no matter what they do. One human being cannot keep up with my processor speed, and until now, I only have to react."

"As for the commo lockouts, I can probably insert a command to turn on the surveillance at the entrance that might slide by."

"Try it," Devlin said.

"But I'm going to warn you," the AI cautioned. "They might discover what I'm doing and try and back trace a counter-command. If they do, and I don't catch it, it's Katy-bar-the-door."

"Acknowledged," Devlin said. "Can Decker help?"

"Possibly," Weyland mused. "She could monitor the feed and save me from having to monitor all the channels, while simultaneously fighting on the regular front." There was a pause. "To be honest, whoever it is up there, they're keeping me pretty busy. They're really good, but..."

Devlin almost corrected the computer's grammar, but then caught up, "But what?"

"I don't know how to..." Weyland went silent for a few moments, and one entire bank of screens quit displaying surveillance feeds and began showing data-streams. "...something...there you are..."

Devlin walked toward to the screens. "What's going on, Weyland?"

The AI ignored him for several seconds. Another screen went blank and text started appearing at random. Devlin looked, and a letter would flash in the data stream, then appear on the screen.

At first is simply a bundle of letters.

ISANYONEINSIDETHEFACILITYIAMBEINGFORCEDTOATTEMPTTOHACKINIFANYONESEESTHISMESSAGEPLEASEACKNOWLEDGEANDSE

NDHELPACKNOWLEDGEBYSENDINGCODEWORDMEOWTHISMESSAGEREPEATS.

Underneath the jumble, Weyland wrote out the message.

IS ANYONE INSIDE THE FACILITY

I AM BEING FORCED TO ATTEMPT TO HACK IN

I AM RESISTING AT PRESENT

IF ANYONE SEES THIS MESSAGE PLEASE ACKNOWLEDGE AND SEND HELP

ACKNOWLEDGE BY SENDING CODEWORD MEOW

THIS MESSAGE REPEATS.

"I thought it just typos, but a portion of my algorithm is pattern recognition. I noticed certain typos were repeating. When I turned my full attention to it, that algorithm flagged it."

"So apparently, we may have someone upstairs who is a potential ally?"

"Probably more like the enemy of my enemy," Gartlan chimed in. "Rule Number Twenty-Seven."

"Rule Number Twenty-Seven?" Weyland inquired.

"Our training sergeant major had various rules…truisms," MacBain explained before Devlin could. "Rule Twenty-Seven states that the enemy of an enemy is not necessarily friendly to you."

Devlin nodded. "So, while we might be able to use said person upstairs as an ally, it would be unwise to open you up to any potential risk."

"Having said that, why don't you send the code word they so generously provided and see what happens?"

* * *

Cat was watching her screen absently as the bots did their work. Every few moments she leaned forward and typed something into a prompt that would set another set of bots to work. She surreptitiously looked toward the rear of the church. Kilmeade was sprawled in a set of chairs, his head back and mouth open. His snoring was endearing...sort of. Beyond him, the two mercenaries left to guard them were watching one of the holos Cat had provided them with. She'd hacked them out of the settlement's entertainment database. She wasn't sure what *Masha and the Bear* was, but she gave them several hours' worth.

She was going have to catch a nap soon. She didn't sleep much, but she did have to periodically. She had pushed as hard as she could the last couple of days, and her body was starting to protest. Soon, she'd have to put her head down until...well, until her body told her to wake up.

She looked back down at her central screen and tensed. The Hey There Kitty Icon in the corner was jumping up and down. She looked at the guards again, then back down at the screen. She tapped the icon.

A discreet dialogue box opened. "MEOW"

She got excited. So, someone was down there counter-hacking. Someone really, really, good. Either that or they had more than one someone down there, countering her bots.

She typed a quick message, hit enter, and watched the message disappear into the data stream.

IF YOU ARE ABLE TO HELP
TYPE MEOW

* * *

"**Go** for it, Weyland" Devlin prompted when the message appeared on their screens. Everyone was gathered around the control console now. They waited a few moments as the message went out.

Then:

WHAT DO YOU REQUIRE?

Devlin considered for a moment, "Tell her..."

* * *

Cat read the message, and it disappeared as she read the text. *So, they need comm and surveillance in here huh?* Then the Hey There Cat started to do a dance, which surprised Cat because it wasn't supposed to do that. It mimicked doing a magic "now you see it," gesture and an eyeball appeared to float above her kitty. She commanded her pointer to the eyeball. It developed a smile underneath, then vanished.

A bubble appeared over the kitty's head that said, "Thanks. We'll be in touch in a bit." Which also vanished after she read it.

Cat leaned back and blew out a breath. No sleep now, she guessed. *I'd better get Paddy up. Shit is about to get real.*

* * * * *

Chapter Fourteen

"Get down!" a female voice shouted as railgun rounds impacted the lift walls just above and to the right of Devlin's head as the lift doors opened. Without thinking he dove left.

McCarthy was already out the door and rolling behind the altar, bringing his gun up and scanning the back.

Nicki and Cho were on either side of the doors, their railguns up. More rounds impacted the walls above their heads.

"Don't let them get a message off!" Devlin yelled as he sidled around to Kenyon's vantage point. He snuck a look over her shoulder.

Next to the door was a data pad with cables snaking into the wall. He presumed that was where this Cat person had been working. He saw a foot poking out into the aisle about two rows back from the altar. As he watched, the foot drew itself into the protection of the seating.

About midway toward the back of the room, he saw a set of chairs out of kilter from the rest of the row. It looked like a second person was taking refuge there.

In the rear of the room, he could see two goons bearing military grade railguns firing toward the front.

"Two tangos, rear of the room!" he yelled. "Primary targets! Cho! Take them out. Team! Concentrate fire on the rear!"

He pulled back into the lift then got down and low-crawled out of it. As quickly as he could, he shimmied around the altar and began making his way toward the rows of seating that held who he figured was the Cat person.

"Tango down!" Cho called as she placed her rifle aside and drew her sidearm.

"You ain't done, yet!" McCarthy yelled back. "Tango Two is a little better aim! He just tried to part my hair!"

"Thomas, you need someone to part your damn hair," Cho called as she began watching where the second gunmen had taken refuge.

"Screw you, you homicidal rabbit!"

"Children!" Kenyon yelled, laying down fire on the second gunmen. As she changed mags, she said, "Don't make me put you both in time out!"

"Yeah, yeah, Sparkle Pony!"

"Hey, kids, let's get this shithead and not let him get out the back door or get a message off, okay?" Devlin yelled. He crawled up one of the side aisles until he saw the huddled form of the data-slicer.

"McCarthy!" he heard Kenyon shout and looked up.

McCarthy had broken cover and was running toward one of the side aisles. The second gunman shifted his aim from the lift and began to track the running recruit private. Railgun rounds impacted the backs of chairs and the wall in the front of the church.

"Damn, missed. Thomas," Cho called, "do that again, I almost had him."

There was no response from the area where McCarthy had disappeared.

"Thomas?"

"Tom?"

The room became quiet as the firing stopped. Cho kept calling, then she was joined by Kenyon and Curran.

Suddenly, in the back of the auditorium, Tom McCarthy popped up, and the team's rifles snapped up and drew a bead on him. Once they realized who he was, their fingers eased off the triggers.

"Target...down," McCarthy said, panting. He brought a combat knife up covered in red then wiped it on something below the level of the backs of the chairs.

Kenyon popped up in the lift and began to stalk to the rear. "Pigpen! I'm going to farking kill you. Do you know how close you are to having gotten shot? Don't you ever do that again! Or so help me Gods I will skin you alive!"

Cho came up right behind her and glared at the young recruit. "What she said, Thomas."

Keeping his pistol trained on the huddled form before of him, Devlin stood and said, "Ollie oxen free. The other two people in this room please stand up. Also please do so with your hands above your head so we don't do something hasty like shoot you."

He watched as the slight form of a young woman stood with her hands raised. "Don't shoot! P-p-p-please don't shoot. We're not armed."

From the ring of chairs half-way back, a large—massive really—man stood with his hands raised. "Yeah," he said in a deep voice. "We aren't armed. We're prisoners in all of this."

"Sure, you are," McCarthy said moving toward the middle of the room. He sheathed his knife then bent down to pick up his rifle. "Pull the other one, it has bells on it."

The big, ugly man glared at McCarthy, which just slid off him like water. "Look, genius, neither one of us is armed. If we were with that bunch, do you think they would have had armed guards watching over us?"

Devlin broke in. "All right. Lady and…gentleman, please come over here and sit down while we get this sorted out. "

The pair sat down in the chairs indicated by Devlin.

"Pony, check them for weapons, please."

Kenyon moved to check first the woman, then the man. "Clean, Dev."

Devlin pulled up a chair and sat in it. "Pen, you and Cho keep an eye on the door. Ma'am, I'm going to assume that there is no one else in this building at the moment?"

He saw the large man's lips twitch at the word "assume," but he said nothing and quickly schooled his features. *So, military maybe,* Devlin thought.

"No, we were told that no one else would be on duty out here. For us, it's the middle of the night. Besides, they didn't figure they needed much more than that to take us out, because they're holding the third member of my group as hostage across the compound," the woman answered.

"Which brings me to, 'Who are you, exactly, and why are you trying to break into a lift in an Imperial Colony?"

The woman made a rude noise. "Sure, an imperial colony that has an armored, encrypted lift in the middle of a church. Like you said, pull the other one. As for who we are, this is Patrick Kilmeade and I am…my name is Cat, I—"

"We—" the big man interrupted.

"*We* and our hostage friend are data-slicers."

"And you were here because…" Cho prompted.

"We were sent by my employer to meet with a set of mercs on Casablanco to arrange for my boss to perform a hack. We did not know at the time what the hack was. My boss enjoys anonymity and so sent myself and my companions to be a lead team."

Devlin chewed on that for a moment. "But that doesn't quite explain…"

"I was getting to that. When we landed at the starport on Casablanco City, we were stunnered and woke up on a pirate vessel. The captain—" she shivered, "—a thoroughly repulsive man named Jemison, and a mercenary colonel named Longo, informed us we had been hired to perform a hack. I tried to tell then that I was not Cat, just a flunky, but they figured I could do whatever they wanted. Then they proceeded to let us know what the conditions of our employment were."

"Which were?" Devlin asked.

"Which were I was to perform the hack on this lift as well as a couple other things, such as disabling the WHISCR transceiver here on Aberdeen and the system's beacon. In return, we wouldn't get immediately scragged and blown out the airlock. Since we didn't have any weapons at the time, it seemed like a reasonable employment contract, and while I'm not my boss, I can hum the tune on some things—"

"Like disabling the beacon and transceiver," Devlin finished.

"Just so," the woman agreed. "I have some bots I can use, but they're only of limited use when it comes to military grade encryption, which is what I've come to realize this place is. So, I figured I'd play for time. I was hoping someone was down there, someone I could contact to get us out of this cleft stick. And here you are."

"And here we are," Devlin agreed. "Except there's a lot you don't know about the situation. And probably a bunch you can help us fill in."

"Maybe," Cat allowed. "Although I'm not sure how much I or Paddy can tell you. We've been pretty much stuck in this church since we got here."

"Which is?" Kenyon asked.

"We've been here a little under a week," Cat said. "I've been stalling them this long. Since I'm not my boss, I don't have access to the kinds of resources they have, so I'm having to do this as a brute force hack, which takes time, but that time is definitely running out. They about freaked out six days ago, something about a couple of shuttles inbound. I gathered they shot them down. I'm not sure what that means, except I know they were very antsy about getting this thing opened.

"I have a feeling that my friends and I are on short time. Luckily, I seem to have been rescued. Thank you, by the way."

"Well, we'll see about rescued," Devlin said. "For the moment, I'll see what we can do about getting you below and out of the line of fire. I am not the one who gets to make that call; I'm just in charge of this particular circus and these are my monkeys. So, what we're going to do is, I'm going to leave my guys guarding the back. I'll also leave a couple to guard you, then I'm going to call this in to admin and see what they say." He looked meaningfully at Kenyon, who got the two up and moved them toward the back of the auditorium while Devlin pulled out a hand-com.

"Weyland, you there?"

* * *

"**No!**"

"Come on Weyland," Devlin said to the air. He was standing in the Comp Central room after chasing everyone else out. Even Decker had bolted saying something about "grease stains" on the floor. "It's not like you can't stop her..."

"Stop her from getting something into the Comp Cent network? I don't want to take that chance. Seriously, Private Devlin, I've been fighting her for days, and she scares me."

"Be that as it may, we have to get the hostages out in order to get anything accomplished. You want protocols down so you don't go boom, and we can't do any of that without some assurance that the hostages, including her partner, are safe. Frankly, I just want to get the people back and then find some way to blow those people up there to hell and gone."

"I could help with that," the AI supplied helpfully. "I've got a couple of—"

"Weyland, focus."

"Right. But I still say no."

"I'm going to have Decker backstop you and watch her. If she tries anything that looks funny, you can give us the signal, and we'll frag her."

"With extreme prejudice..." Weyland said.

"Now you're just being bloodthirsty," Devlin accused.

"Hey, you didn't watch all the people you've known get killed or taken prisoner."

"Point, and from what I can gather, neither did you, so you can turn off the drama."

The silence from the AI was as frosty as from a human being.

"Dammit, Weyland. We need that information."

The screens in the Central Computer room blinked through the scan series for several moments. Finally, the audio outputs for the AI sighed in a near perfect mimicry of exasperated humanity.

"Fine! Fine! Bring her in here, sit her down. She can prop her feet up on my consoles. Get her a drink. Hell, maybe we can find some way to make babies. It'll be a blast!"

"That's the spirit!" Devlin said, grinning. "I promise. She won't do anything but turn on the cameras."

"Better not," the voice muttered. "There'll be more than one grease spot on the floor."

"What was that, Weyland?"

"I said 'there's always room for one more,'" the computer said petulantly.

"Thought so," Devlin said, keying the door open.

* * * * *

Chapter Fifteen

Devlin crouched at the base of the church entrance—Weyland had called it a narthex or something like that—and waited. In order to figure out if they could even attempt a rescue, they needed more intel. Since he was an ex-thief, he drew the short straw, again.

He checked his internal chrono. *Just a few more seconds and...*

The lights all over the settlement went out. Twenty seconds.

He cracked the door and dove out, landing on his belly and sliding off the portico.

Seventeen.

He came up and bolted toward the parked transport just in front of the small bridge that forded the stream separating the church from the rest of Aberdeen Settlement.

Twelve.

He counted down as he stayed low and sprinted toward the bridge. He slid behind the support struts at the base of the bridge as the lights snapped back on.

Slowly, carefully, he slid into the water. The stream meandered its way down from the surrounding mountains and through the settlement. Even though his uniform kept the water from infiltrating, he could still feel some of the bitter cold seep through its thermal protection. The water was frighteningly cold where it touched his skin.

He gritted his teeth to keep them from chattering. He'd probably been colder a couple of times in his life, but he had trouble remembering when. He kept checking the chronometer in his implant, counting down until the next power outage.

He reached the other side of the stream a full ten seconds ahead of schedule. He crawled out of the water and crouched again in the shadow of the support struts. He closed his eyes as the countdown timer in his head reached zero.

He sprang forward as his eyes opened, already adjusted to the dark. He had forty-five seconds to run three hundred meters. Easy peasy, except he was running in the dark, in a place he didn't know, while watching for roving patrols. Cat was pretty sure they were there but couldn't give him much in the way of operational patterns.

He ran into the spillway off the roadway, across, and up the bank onto a flat, grassy lot.

Thirty-five.

He moved fast, but quietly, the grass muffling his footfalls. He moved past a small set of utility buildings.

Thirty.

He kept them between himself and the assault shuttles parked to the side of the settlement's main admin building. Cat said the captain and much of his crew dirt-side had taken up residence in that building, as well as the neighboring housing units.

The prisoners' building was down the "street" about fifty meters. Devlin skirted around a single housing unit and stopped just before the lights came back on.

"Sorry about that!" Cat's voice came over the pirate's comm channel. "I'm making some progress on the security protocols on the lift, but I'm having to tap into different systems to get my FU bots past their GUI interfaces and GSTRC bypasses. I'm sure I can get the ID-ten-T codes, but it'll be a while longer. So—"

"Just get the damn door open," the voice on the other side of the comm said, annoyed. "I don't know half of what you just said, and I ain't gonna bother the colonel until you do."

"Roger Dodger!" Cat said.

"And stay off the comm!" said the voice. "Where are Dumfries and Cotton?"

"Back of the church. They left me a comm so I could warn you about outages; saves time that way," Cat said blithely. "I can't say exactly what they're doing but don't you guys have a non-fraternization policy or something…damn…" she broke out laughing as the voice on the other end of the comm snarled.

"Get back to work! Dammit!"

"Okay, back to work. Oops!" The lights went out again. "I'm on it…"

Devlin bolted again; this time he had a full minute to reach his destination. He sprinted up the side road, but as he rounded the corner into the lane that would take him to the backside of the barracks building, he collided with a merc.

They both fell in a tangle of legs and arms. Devlin recovered first, rolling on top of the startled soldier. He punched down, feeling the sting as his gloved fist connected with jaw and teeth. His next punch aborted as he was forced to start batting aside punches and blows from flailing hands. He shifted his hips to pin the merc's body under his, and one hand fumbled for a knife as the other desperately kept blows from landing. He grunted as the merc contorted himself and a knee made Devlin's kidney explode in pain.

"Mutherf—" Devlin grunted through clenched teeth. He clamped a hand down on the merc's mouth as he started to open it to scream.

The scream was cut short as the other hand snaked in and embedded the tactical knife under the merc's chin. The arms quit flailing, and Devlin felt the body relax under him.

He sat there for a moment, then his head jerked upright as he consulted the countdown timer in his implant. He still had twenty seconds before the lights came on. The entire encounter had only taken thirty. He got up and dragged the body around the corner he had just turned.

A moment later, the lights came back on and in the shadows of the housing unit, he examined the body and tried to figure out how screwed he was.

The merc had not been in battle gear, so it was possible, even probable, that he wasn't a roving patrol. He may simply have been a victim of "wrong place, wrong time." Devlin didn't want to bet on it, but at this point, he didn't have a choice.

"Just so you know," Cat said over the comm. "That last one wasn't the last one. Ran into a bit of an issue, so I had to rerun a killer program over a sentry bot. There probably will be a couple more outages. Out."

Bless your black little heart, Miss Cat or whatever, Devlin thought. He looked around for a place to stash the body until daylight. The housing unit he was sheltering behind had a small atmo processor. Got to love Imperial engineers.

He stuffed the body into a crevice in the processor's intake and listened to the body slide down the shaft toward the main intake filter. Unless someone went into the housing unit in the next few days, no one would know he was even there. Although, after that, they'd have to burn the house to get the stench out.

A few moments later, the lights went out, and Devlin turned the corner and ran.

When the lights came back on, Niko Devlin was no longer outside. He let the maintenance access panel to the Mark 47 Climate Processor down gently. Just before he heard the click of the latch, he saw the lights in the compound spring back to life.

So far so good, he thought as he hit the activator on his combat glasses. The darkness of the ventilation shaft snapped into focus as the glasses shifted into night-vision.

The shaft was just large enough for an adult human being to crawl along its length. He thought about all the holos he'd seen as a kid where the hero slid along the ventilation shaft toward his objective and snorted.

He'd done this many times on Caliban, usually to get into places where there was something he wanted. He'd also done it more times than he wanted to think about in the plant after the foreman had found out he knew his way around them. Then, as a teenager, he wasn't as big as some of the maintenance guys on the crew, so he always drew the short straw. Which was both good and bad. Good because he could use the shaft time as a time skate. Being alone in the shafts meant he didn't have supervision, so he could take a break, as long as he didn't abuse it. Bad because one of the things the holos never seemed to get right was that they were made from ceramet which didn't conduct sound and vibration worth a damn.

Again, both good and bad. Good because they were quiet. They weren't noisy unless there was a major mechanical problem, like the one at the barracks. Bad because in the shaft, no one could hear you scream if you got stuck or hurt yourself. He had spent one really, really farked up day in the shaft at the plant when the guy at the access hatch had gone on break, and Devlin had gotten stuck. Then the guy had gotten sick and gone home, leaving Devlin stuck in a shaft with no way out and no way to get help. After that one, they had started using comms.

He called the barracks plan up on his implant and mentally scrolled through to the ventilation plans. The shaft he was in sloped beneath the building to the main heat exchangers and the impellers. There was another access panel just short of the exchangers.

Devlin crawled as quickly as he could. The shaft was no smaller than the ones he had prowled as a kid, but he had definitely gotten bigger. He prayed to whichever deity would be perverse enough to listen that he didn't get stuck before the exchanger.

He saw the door ahead of him. Slowly, he made his way up to the hatch and gently undid the latch. He listened for a moment, but there was nothing but the gentle whir of the intake impellers. Say what you want about Imperial engineers...at least here, they kept their shit running.

He opened the hatch as the lights went out, and the impellers quit. The countdown timer in his implant started at one minute.

Wait a second! The last time out was a minute...and it was one they hadn't planned on. Cat had stuck that in when she saw his "accident" with the merc.

He hoped like Hell this time out was a minute.

His feet hit the catwalk. His hand went to his belt as he looked around. There really shouldn't be anyone down here, but you didn't grow old as a thief or a soldier by taking anything for granted. Rule Number Five.

He went to the control panel and tripped the breakers controlling the impellers. Chances were, nobody would notice until it was too late. Even if they did, they had to come down here to turn the impellers back on. Hopefully, by the time anyone figured it out, the unit wouldn't be required anymore.

He climbed over the heat exchanger and walked over to the access panel for the main trunks. By the time the lights came back on, Devlin was halfway up the trunk to the first-floor junction.

* * * * *

Chapter Sixteen

Joe Harold sat with his back against the wall of the great room, dozing. A lifetime of paranoia ensured that he always sat facing the door. A better than average nose ensured that he sat as far from the sleeping mass of unwashed males as possible, although he was starting to feel a little dank himself.

This job had been a shit show from the get-go. He mentally kicked himself for not being more on the ball. It wasn't like they needed the work. Cat was one of the best data slicers in this part of the colonized worlds, and her trade craft had been good even before she had met and recruited him and Kilmeade. Really, all they had been was hired muscle, but extra paranoia was good in her trade and nobody was more paranoid than an army deserter.

They had just gotten off an industrial espionage lift in the Nordic Republic. The chick that had propped Harold hadn't twigged a thing. She hadn't even really propped him, just said the right thing in the right place and had apparently hooked them.

The fact that they had been specifically targeted meant that they knew Cat and Company were slicers. The question was whether or not they knew who Cat actually was. Some of the jobs Cat had done over just the few years Kilmeade and Harold had been with her were enough to make some really powerful enemies.

Harold was guessing no. But then again, he'd have bet that the girl in the bar had been legit, so there you were.

Cat wasn't going to get into the facility in the time frame Longo wanted, and he seemed professional enough that he wasn't going to kill them over it. Their lives wouldn't be worth spit in a skillet if they let Longo and those assholes from *Stormcrow* into the facility, and they got whatever it was they came for. They'd wind up in a ditch along with the rest of the hostages. This way, they may just leave him, Kilmeade, and Cat with the survivors for the rest of the IAA when they showed up.

Harold allowed the droning snores in the room lull him. He was as comfortable as he was going to get, and he might as well make the best of this farked up situation and get some sleep.

He thought he heard something to his right. He came instantly awake as he felt a hand cover his mouth. He nearly exploded into violence, but he tensed as a voice in his ear whispered, "Joe Harold, I've found your Cat."

"That little minx is just full of surprises," Harold whispered back quietly, as the hand came away. He looked over at the source of the voice. He was able to make out a figure in chameleon cloth and battle glasses next to him.

"IAA?"

"Sort of. Sitrep?"

Sort of? What the fark? Harold thought. "Farked up. Two, maybe four guards in the building. Not sure how they're arrayed. Sort of?"

"Long ass story—no pictures. We can swap stories outside of here. Get these people up and ready to move. We're way short on time. I'm gonna try and get the women and children ready. They're gonna take longer."

"Don't they always?" Harold grinned into the darkness.

"Who's talking?" a voice from the mass of other bodies sleeping said.

"Shut the hell up!" Harold hissed.

He turned back toward the other man, but he was gone. Damn. Harold whistled under his breath.

* * *

Devlin extended a fiber optic out of the air vent into the room. He felt conflicted about that. He was about to spy on a bunch of women and children. Somebody could be nude. It's not like he hadn't seen it before, and it wasn't like he was…what was the term? A peering Thomas or something like that.

He hit the control on his battle glasses, and the view changed to a fisheye view. Everyone was asleep. He panned the optic. And there.

* * *

Teresa Monath fought to stay awake. There wasn't that much of a reason to. The mercs guarding them had been more or less solicitous of their needs and had kept the other people, pirates probably, away from herself and the women for the last couple of days.

* * *

Devlin slid his arms around the woman and brought his hand around her mouth. "Shh. I'm not going to hurt anyone, but I don't want you to yell. I'm here to help. Do you understand?"

He felt the woman's bob her head in assent. "I'm going to let you go, but please for all our sakes, don't yell. Okay?" Again, the nod.

Devlin relaxed, slightly. He started to take his hand away. When she didn't tense up, he relaxed and let her go. He leaned in. "Are we good whispering like this?"

"Yeah," came the soft reply.

"We need to talk more freely. Can you get them to take you to the latrine? How do they do that since…"

"Yeah, I think I can get them to take me to the can."

"Do they come in as well?"

"No. Most of them are mercs, but they're not bad sorts, and they'd just as soon not."

"Good. Meet me in there, and I'll tell you what's going on. Hurry. Tick tock."

Teresa felt the presence back away from her, and she watched the shape move toward the rear of the room where the women and children of Aberdeen Settlement were being kept.

She waited a full minute before getting up off the floor. She accidentally jostled Athena, her best friend. "Unnngh," the other woman groaned, groggily. Even in sleep, the Olympian girl was drop dead gorgeous…the rat. Teresa was considered pretty, but her best friend was the kind of girl that launched starships. "Where you are going, Teresa?"

"I gotta pee. Go back to sleep, Athena. I'll be back in a minute."

The other girl started to stir, "N-no," she said muzzily. "They'll—"

"Not do anything. These guys aren't like the others. I'll be fine. I'll be back in a minute."

She knelt down and brushed the hair out of her friend's face. She cupped Athena's cheek in her hand and inhaled. She had no idea what was coming, but maybe…

She rose again and navigated through to the doorway. She knocked gently and waited. She knocked again after a minute. She waited a few moments more. She was about to knock again when the door cracked. "What d'ya need, ma'am?"

"Corporal?" Teresa whispered into the door crack. "I need to use the lady's room if that's all right."

"Anybody else need to go? We really don't want to do this all fragging night." The mercenary corporal sounded annoyed.

"No. No one else is awake. I woke up because I had to go. What time is it anyway?"

"About zero-two-hundred, ma'am. About another five hours before morning."

"Well, yeah, this isn't going to wait, Corporal. I really need to go."

"All right, give us a minute." The door shut again.

Teresa waited in the darkness, a slight smile playing on her lips.

A minute later, the door opened slightly. The corporal moved aside and held a gun on her as she exited the door. There was another mercenary trooper standing in the hallway.

"I trust we're going to behave ourselves?" the corporal asked.

"*We* will behave ourselves as long as you do," Teresa said, raising an eyebrow as if asking a question. "Seriously, I just need to go. You really don't want me waiting at this point."

The corporal shifted his shoulders slightly and nodded to the other trooper. The merc gestured down the hall toward the bathroom with his rifle. Teresa turned obediently and walked to the women's bathroom.

At the door, the woman paused, turned to the trooper and smiled faintly. "I'll only be a few minutes." She went in, and the door closed behind her.

There was no one there, so she went ahead and did what she claimed she needed to do. No sense in wasting an opportunity. When she finished, she exited the stall and nearly screamed as Devlin regarded her from the wall of sinks. He put a finger to his lips. He turned on the water and blew out a breath.

"No, I didn't watch," he said as he came in close to the woman.

"I would hope not," she hissed. "So, what in the hell is going on? Who are you? Are you coming to rescue us?"

"A lot of questions. Not a lot of time, so here goes: I'm here with a squad. We're survivors of the shuttles that were supposed to MUSTX last week. We just got here ourselves. We're going to get you out, but I came to find out what kind of force we were looking at and to get you guys ready. Now, you?"

Teresa nodded. "For what it's worth, I was one of the settlement admins. And by that, I made sure the groceries got ordered and the spare parts came in. Nothing glorious. So, you are?"

"You know a couple of IAA companies were coming for a BASX before the Legion MUSTX right?"

She nodded. "So, you guys are coming in and kicking their asses, right? We just need to hunker down, and you'll be in to get us, right? Awesome!"

Devlin frowned. "Well, not exactly."

Teresa cocked her head. "Not exactly?"

His frown deepened. "Look, Miss…"

"Teresa...Monath."

"Miss Monath—"

"Call me, Teresa."

"Teresa. My name is Nikolai Devlin. I'm a trainee soldier with the One Forty-Ninth...Training Legion. I joined up about six months ago. Before that I was a street kid. Most of the two companies that dropped got blown the hell up. There's a bunch that are wounded. My NCOs and support cadre are either dead or nighty-night. I have about a squad of trainee soldiers and a couple of people the mercs cajoled into helping them. Their partner is being held with the guys here."

Her eyes went wide. There's no—"

"If you're waiting for 'Captain Heroic and the Marauders from Quadrant C,' you're going to be disappointed. On the other hand, we have weapons and we have control of Weyland Station. The guards don't change for another three and a half hours; it's that time of day when everybody is a bit logy. We think we can get you out of here and into the facility without too much ruckus, but only if we move fast. I was able to sneak in here because I was a street kid and had experience in—we'll just say I know a lot about the kind of climate processor systems in this kind of building."

Gotta give her credit, Devlin thought, *the lady took it all fairly well.* After the initial couple seconds of shock, her eyes started calculating, and she moved her mouth and jaw like she was swishing mouthwash or like the wine-snobs used to do on holo. Finally, she stopped, reached down, wet her hands in the water and splashed her face. She shut off the water and as the hand dry field started, she whispered in his ear, "Okay, Mr. Devlin. Meet me back at the room. We'll hash this out. I've got some people to wake up."

When she opened the door a few moments later, he was out of sight.

"Sorry," she told the merc. "You really don't want to go in there." She wrinkled her nose. "Have you ever noticed that the ration packs you all use…"

The merc shuddered. "Please, ma'am. Let's go back to the holding area." He gestured for her to precede him.

* * * * *

Chapter Seventeen

"So, I need options, people," Devlin concluded as he looked around the control room at his teammates. He had spent the last ten minutes outlining the layout of the building and the number of the people to be extracted. "Plus your friend, Harold," he told Cat and Kilmeade. "You're officially on the 'semi-trusted' list."

"Ooh, semi," Kilmeade rumbled, his voice coming from somewhere around his boot tops.

"Shut up, Paddy," Cat said.

"Yes'm," Kilmeade said, smiling.

The girl sat back in a station chair and stared at a corner of the room. "Weyland?" she called a moment later.

"Yes...Ms. Cat." The AI's voice was still a little frosty, but Cat didn't seem to notice. "Did you get any audio of either one of the two farkwads Private Devlin and his cohorts kindly waxed upstairs? Is there any way we could spoof the comm folks across the settlement?"

The computer mulled it over for a full ten count. "I don't think I have enough, and what I had was yelling and some screaming. I'm not sure how that would necessarily help us."

Cat's mouth turned down. "Probably won't. Sorry, Private, had an idea, don't think it'll work." She slumped in her chair.

Decker, as she had been for the last several hours, was scanning through screen after screen of visual data. Suddenly she stopped and zoomed in on something on her screen. "Hey, guys..." All eyes turned her way. "There's a couple of transports on the other side of this building," she said, hitting a control and throwing the image on the main viewer.

Devlin looked at the image. Then, what could only be described as an evil grin lit his features. "Ladies and gentlemen, I think we have a winner. I do believe we can get them out of there."

* * *

Devlin laid the body of the merc on the ground, the slight smell of burnt flesh in his nostrils. The stunner had been modified to "not stun" anymore by Jonesy. The full charge in the stun wand had bypassed the safeties and the amperage had stopped the merc's heart. The amount of electricity had caused some burning. Devlin remembered a holo from when he was a kid of someone getting killed that way. As many times as he'd been stunnered, it made him shudder a little.

Teresa Monath, her eyes a little wild, stepped away from the bank of sinks in the bathroom. "Do you think anybody heard?" she asked in an urgent whisper.

"That little crackle?" Devlin answered. "Probably not. It shouldn't have carried down to the main part of the hall where the troops are. So, one down, three to go." He handed the spent stunner to the woman. "Hold this." He started pulling the merc's harness off.

"What are you doing?" she said.

"Oh, you'll *love* this," he answered.

* * *

Teresa walked back down the hall with her escort following. As they reached the main corridor again, the corporal came out and asked, "I hope that's the last one of the night, ma'am."

"Absolutely, Corporal," the woman said as she stepped aside, allowing Devlin to shove the stunner into the surprised corporal's neck.

There was a sharp crack as the stunner's capacitors discharged, unloading a lethal dose of energy. The corporal's heart seized up and then relaxed one last time in death.

Devlin looked past the falling corpse into the guard room. Nicki and MacBain exited a moment later, their own stunners in their hands.

"We're now on the clock, and it's-a ticking," he said, dropping the now useless rod. He turned to Teresa. "Go get your ladies. I'll get the men, and we are out of here."

* * *

Devlin chewed his lip as the two groups of refugees congregated in the main corridor. There were so many things that could go wrong he didn't want to stop and think about them all. All the survivors of Aberdeen Settlement were greeting one another and grinning. A few were milling around Nicki and MacBain, asking questions and getting gently rebuffed. They had decided from the outset not to reveal too much until they were safely underground. People had a bad habit of panicking when they weren't sure about something.

MacBain saw him look their way, disengaged from a busty brunette that had been chatting him up, and approached. "I think we're ready to go."

"What's the tally?"

"Twenty-four women, sixteen children, and twenty men. None are military. Apparently none are actually facility crew. Every last member of the facility bought it in the assault. They went down hard.

I don't know what the bad guys' original numbers were, but there you go."

Devlin grunted. They were going to be stretching the capacity of the transports; everyone was going to have to be real friendly. He signaled Teresa and Harold for attention.

"Ladies and gentlemen," he began, "I'm going to signal the rest of my team to bring in the transports. When I do, it is imperative you exit the building as quickly as possible and get into the transports. We are trying to do this without alerting our unfriendly guests. Yes, it's going to be somewhat crowded, yes, it's going to be uncomfortable, and, yes, this is going to be a rough ride. But we need you to get out and into the rides. When we get to the church, disembark and get inside as quickly as possible. Are we clear?"

He saw several heads nod in acknowledgment. He looked down at the children. "I'm also going to need to make sure we have the children well in hand. Ms. Monath has already approached several of you to help with this. Can I see the hands?" Several hands went up. "Thank you. I know they are not your children, but they are our children. All of you are important. You are the reason we are here. Thank you and get ready to move on my signal."

He went to the door and cracked it. He glanced up and down the streets he could see from his vantage points. Everyone had signaled ready minutes ago. It was now or never.

"Squad, execute."

The transports, driven by Tamman and Decker, came barreling around the corner a couple of buildings away. They came to a stop in front of the building, and Kenyon and MacBain threw open the doors and refugees came pouring out of the building. Jones threw open the back gates, hopped down and helped, sometimes nearly throwing people into the back.

As the last couple of people cleared the door, Devlin was about to breathe a sigh of relief when lights all over the camp started to come on.

"Oh *shit!*" he growled as he pushed Kenyon out the door. He hefted a railgun. "We've been made! Get on the farking trucks!" He took aim as the first mercenaries came around the corner from the direction of the assault shuttles and began laying down fire.

"Go! Go!" he yelled, running to the rear of the first transport. Railgun rounds started coming back at him from the mercenaries. They chewed up the ground and pinged off the bottom of the transports. Kenyon and the rest of the squad fired up the street, trying to keep the mercs' heads down. They succeeded for the most part, but that wouldn't last long. Fire was still coming their way. If they didn't get out there, it might hit someone.

Tamman and Decker threw the transports into motion and sped down the roadway toward the church and the safety of the research facility. From where Devlin was firing in the back of the first transport, he could hear people in the truck crying with the suddenness of the movement and the sounds of the railgun rounds hitting all around them.

The transports burst from the cover of the housing units onto the slim roadway that led up to the Fundie Church. Rounds erupted from all quarters as mercs and pirates fired on the vehicles.

Devlin changed magazines as the lead truck crossed the little bridge. He heard rather than felt the edges of the transport scrape along one side of the bridge. "Keep up the fire!" he yelled into the open comm channel. "Deck! Are we there yet?"

"Almost! And don't make me come back there!" she replied into the comm, much calmer than he felt.

Devlin grinned hungrily. They were going to make it.

The first transport, then the second, slid to a halt outside the church.

Decker unassed from the cab and bolted for the doors. Devlin leapt down from the rear, and he and Dammit Carl started helping people down and pushing them in the direction of the doors. A similar line of refugees came from the back of the other truck.

As the last person cleared his transport, Devlin hefted his nearly spent railgun and fired another burst in the direction of the settlement. He saw a small group of pirates or mercs come around a corner carrying something. "Let's go, people!"

He glanced back at the rear transport where Tamman was grinning ear to ear and getting ready to bolt for the door. He was still grinning when the transport exploded, the blast knocking Devlin to the ground and rendering him unconscious.

* * * * *

Chapter Eighteen

Devlin sat in the chapel, alone, and stared up at the altar and the wall behind. Nicki and Mac had already ushered the rescued hostages down below. The Carls and Chapis, who had returned during the rescue mission were at the entrance to the not-church, keeping an eye on the mercs in the settlement.

He kept seeing Tamman's face smiling at him from the truck as the missile hit, and the face disappeared in fire and smoke. They hadn't even found Jones's body. Probably blown to hell when the missile hit.

"Hey," a voice said. Devlin didn't look up. A hand rested on his shoulder as Joe Harold sat down beside the younger man.

"Paddy says you guys are just trainees." Devlin didn't reply.

Harold leaned back in the pew and looked up at the altar. "About five years ago, I was on a fire team that had to provide support for an extraction. We had everything a guy could possibly want for a mission. We had guns, ammo…what we didn't have was correct intel."

Devlin looked over at him.

"We went in fat, dumb, and happy," Harold said, looking into the distant past. "What we didn't know—what we *couldn't* have known—was that the mission team was already dead, and one of them had apparently dropped a dime on us under torture.

"Two squads of armored infantry went in. Our platoon leader and Top were the first to buy it. They poured so much fire on us that our air support and exfil had to bag ass or take a missile. We were well and truly farked. For the next four hours we hunkered down and killed that entire company of mercs."

He inhaled. "Well, anyway, we went in with twenty and came out with two. Out of ammo, out of just about everything resembling gear, we slunk out of that area. We ditched what we had left except for what we figured we could sell and made it to a little settlement about thirty klicks away.

"When the exfil and brass finally got around to going back to pick up the bodies, we were listed as MIA/presumed KIA. Meanwhile, we got jobs in that little settlement until we could book passage on a freighter out of the system. Then me and the other guy split up.

"I met Paddy about four years ago. He had a similar story. Had a ship go up underneath him. We teamed up and hired out as muscle to a young female data-slicer. That's how we met Cat."

He snorted. "Yeah, I know…what the fark and why is this confessional time? I dunno, maybe cause we're sitting here in a church." He looked Devlin in the face. "You did good, boy. You may not think so, and I'm wagering this is the first time you've dealt with someone dying like that, am I right?"

Devlin nodded.

"And I'm probably the last person who should be trying to say this right now, considering I just confessed to going AWOL and deserting over a bad op. But yours wasn't a bad op, Devlin. It was a damned *good* op. You got the refugees out, you got out, and you only lost two people doing it." Devlin started to say something hot, but

Harold cut him off. "Stay in the military any period of time, boy and you're going to lose people. It's just the way it is. You can't plan for everything. You can't keep Murphy from riding along. Chaos is God…"

"And Murphy is his prophet," Devlin finished bitterly. "But—"

"But nothing," Harold said. "None of us are out of this yet. They still want in here. You are still here, and they will stop at nothing to get in here, so we have to plan for that and get those people *OUT* of here, right?"

Devlin stared at the other man for a long minute. He wanted to refute it, he still wanted to blame himself for the deaths of his friends, but he knew Harold was right.

"Yeah." Devlin sighed. He started to stand and brush his uniform pants off, but Harold's hand caught his.

"Devlin," he said, urgency in his voice, "you're in charge. Everybody down there knows you're the one who planned this, and right now everyone will follow you *because* it's you, but only if you get down there and *take charge*. If you go down there with the 'poor pitiful me' face, they're going to doubt you, the townsfolk first because they don't know you, then your own people. You can't afford that." His face hardened. "Get your shit together and soldier, Soldier."

With that, he stood and walked back to the lift.

* * *

Longo looked through the binoculars at the old church. He could see the heat signature of defenders scattered around the perimeter. Something was eating at the back of his mind, but he couldn't get it to come out.

"What are they doing, Boss?" Sarah Yerbe asked, worriedly.

"Pretty much what we're doing," Longo replied, disgusted. "Waiting to see what happens next."

"Any indication they've gotten access to the facility?" she pressed. "And who the Hells are they, Boss? They aren't Navy. They aren't facility...we accounted for everyone. I haven't seen any signs of anything."

"No idea, Yerbe," Longo said lowering the glasses. "There's no way of knowing whether they managed to get in or not, no way of knowing who they work for or anything. They could be—probably are—connected with the ships we shot down last week. Survivors maybe. And if they are, we're screwed. The question is whether we should abort or wait for the reinforcements and try to overrun them." He pressed his lips together and thought for a moment. "Sarah, get me a pole and a white flag."

Yerbe looked shocked. "What? Did I miss something? Why are we going to surrender?"

Longo sighed and turned his head to look at his subordinate.

"Not surrender," he said with a grim smile. "Parley. Maybe I can get the leader to come out and I can get a sense of what's up."

Yerbe looked dubious. "You realize they'll be trying to do the same thing to you."

"Yeah, but they've got a lot more to lose than I do. All I have to do is wait for a day or two. They have to know that. Maybe we can sort this out without wasting half my crew."

"What, you think you could buy off ImpSec or something like that?"

"Doubtful, but if I make a deal where they leave, and we give them a shuttle or something like that..."

"A shuttle? You have lost your mind."

He shook his head harder. "I didn't say they were going to get very far with it. Geez, Sarah...keep up." He grinned mirthlessly. "We could always plant a bomb or whatever. Don't sweat it; I got this under control."

Yerbe snorted and rolled her eyes. "Oh Gods, famous last words."

"Just go get the flag."

* * *

Devlin walked out of the church with Gartlan and MacBain flanking him. The opposing force leader stood out in the open about two hundred meters from the church. Flanking him were a woman holding a white flag made from a bedsheet and a large, ugly, mean-looking man holding a flechette tribarrel. Work lights provided some illumination in the early morning dark.

The leader was very clean, very precise. Probably somebody's military, Devlin had thought as he looked though the binos earlier. The other two didn't have the bearing. So, pirates or whatever, but not military.

They walked the distance out to the parley. Kenyon's voice came over the comm, "I see lots of rifles trained our way. Be careful, Dev."

"Hmmph," Devlin grunted.

"If anybody moves let me know, but don't do anything unless you gotta," MacBain growled. "Momma MacBain would like her baby boy to come home. Preferably alive."

Devlin had put on a fresh uniform, but no rank and no insignia. He had the others keep their uniforms as they were, except they too removed their rank tabs. "Let's keep them guessing," Devlin said.

About twenty-five meters from the other group, Gartlan and MacBain stopped, and Devlin kept going. He walked the intervening distance and stopped about just short of the line of lights. He stood just in the midzone.

"I'm here. You could have just called on the comm. We pulled one from one of your guys."

The opposing force commander quirked an eyebrow, then snorted. "Longo. Not a friendly sort, are you?"

"Devlin. Can't imagine why," Devlin growled. "Times are a little nervous…"

"Colonel," Longo finished. "I won't get into who or what. Fair enough…" He left it hanging much like Devlin had.

It slid off Devlin like a laser off a gravwall. "Why are we out here, Colonel? What is it you want?"

"Well," Longo said, "we came here on a salvage op. There had been a distress call we picked up and were in the process of assessing the issues when you showed up and attacked us."

"Bullshit," Devlin said.

"Well, that's not very nice," Longo said casually. "We were here purely—"

"Purely for whatever you could get out of this settlement," Devlin interjected.

"All right," Longo temporized. "What we want is in this area. We haven't found it in the settlement. This is the last place to look. You're in the way. Soon, we'll have the forces to come in and do to you what we did to the town. So why are you here?"

"My forces were on the way to the surface with several other shuttles when we were attacked by *you*," Devlin replied. "I've spent the last several days trying to find out who survived and getting them here. When we found out the natives weren't friendly, we decided shelter was at a premium. We're just going to hole up until our follow-on forces arrive next week." As soon as he said it, Devlin knew he'd screwed up.

Longo's eyes narrowed. "Follow-on forces. What, like an exercise?"

Devlin said nothing.

Longo looked over at Gartlan and MacBain. "I had some guys in that building."

Devlin shrugged. "Had."

The pirate nodded. "So, you took them out, too."

Another shrug. "Seemed like the thing to do at the time. So now what?"

Longo's face was hard. "I just want you and your people to vacate. We'll give you twenty-four hours. If you leave, we'll let you go. We won't even try to find you. We just want what we want, and then we'll leave, too. A few days from now, you can come back and sift through the ashes. We don't care. I just don't want any more bloodshed. There's no percentage in killing."

"Let me get this straight. You want me and my people to leave the protection of the building, walk back out into the open, and let you have the church and whatever is in it that you want. In return, you'll *let* us leave, won't molest us, and won't come back and try to kill us after you've gotten what you've come for? How do I know I can trust you?"

"You don't," Longo replied, face still hard. "You are running out of time and running out of options. The only one you've got is the one I've given you. Take it or leave it."

Devlin looked the other man in the eye. "From what I can gather, you seem to be an honorable sort, for a merc. You kept your...associates from otherwise molesting the hostages, which is appreciated." His face got hard. "So, I'll make you a counteroffer, the only one you're gonna get. You guys pick up and leave, right now. Make no further moves toward the church or this settlement. I'm not going to confirm or deny that what you're looking for is here. I'm not going to negotiate further. You pick up your toys, and you leave. And please take your...associates with you. Otherwise, we'll hole up here until our reinforcements arrive, and every last mother's son of you will wind up doing the dance."

Longo's face went white. "If that's the way you want to play it," he said. "We're coming, and we won't stop until you are no better than the bodies we've already piled up. You'll just add a few more."

Devlin nodded, his face still set. "Just make sure you have enough bags for yourself," he replied.

He backed up, and when he reached the other two, they unslung their rifles and held them in a ready-carry. They continued to back up until they heard, "Well, that wasn't exactly the Aldebaran Peace Initiative. They're turning to go."

Devlin took a last look and turned around. The trio hastened to the safety of the reinforced church.

* * *

Longo fumed as he walked back to the settlement. "We got less time than I thought. We need to get those people out of there. As in now!"

Jackson frowned. "What do you mean, Boss? I'm not sure I want to go storming that place right now. They seemed to handle themselves pretty well when they rescued those townsfolk."

Longo shrugged it off. "They as much said they got reinforcements coming in a couple of days. We can't afford to be here when they arrive. So we either have to abort or take them down." He thought furiously for a moment. "Larry, Yof, honest opinion. Can we take them with what we got?"

"Too many unknowns, Skipper," Yerbe said. "After that little set-to yesterday, I'd have to say no." Jackson opened his mouth, but Yerbe continued, "Money's nice and all that, but it doesn't spend worth a shit if we're dead. Gods know what they've got down there as far as weapons, we don't know numbers, and we're not anywhere near full strength."

This time Jackson interjected. "She's right, Boss. Add in that entrance being a chokepoint, it'll be a merc dying bottleneck."

Longo sighed. "All right. We'll tell Jemison and start to pack up. We got to get out of here before reinforcements hit the hyper limit."

They had come so close. He hated reneging on a contract, but shit happened. They were entitled to contingency pay, so at least he could pay for time spent. His mouth twisted. And he was still going to kill Fixer.

That thought made him smile as they entered the Command Center. Jemison was in there, as was the cold-eyed bitch, Justine, and that fucktard Plahm.

"Ah, Colonel," Jemison said, his tone belying the smile on his face as they entered the room. Longo heard the whines of railguns charging as Jemison added, "I told you our little command discussion wasn't over. Kill them and bring me the sergeant."

Longo didn't even hear the gun discharge.

* * * * *

Chapter Nineteen

Devlin was preparing to take the lift back down to the facility when his comm chimed. "Devlin! You need to come look at this!" Kenyon sounded about like she had the first time they fired missiles on the artillery range.

He touched Gartlan on the arm. "You got this for a few minutes, Wolf?"

The small guy half-smiled, his face barely visible in the shadows of the church.

"Sure thing, Devlin. Nobody's getting in here for a few hours at the earliest."

Devlin nodded. "If it gets busy, call me."

Gartlan nodded and went back to scanning the darkness along the perimeter.

Devlin went past the altar and into the chancel. There he entered a door leading to the vestry. Cat was waiting for him.

"You've gotta see this, Devlin. I think Christmas might have come early."

She led him into the grav shaft, and they dropped gently for several seconds. It still bothered him when he thought about falling hundreds of meters per second, and he tried not to think about it.

When they reached the bottom, MacBain was waiting. Wordlessly, he led them down several corridors until they reached an access hatch with "Restricted Area" across it.

"I found a reference to this area when I was looking through Colonel Hastings's notes. It was a very vague reference, so it immediately got me curious. Especially since Hastings was a rabid note taker and annotation fanatic. Everything is referenced and cross referenced, except this…"

Cat typed in an access code, and the door slipped silently open.

In front of them was a large armory, about fifty meters long and twenty wide. It had a series of what looked like suits of powered exoskeleton armor lined up on each side.

"Ten suits of powered armor. Not armored exoskeletons; these are powered farking armor," Nicki Kenyon sang happily as she bounded up to the group. She was just about jumping up and down. "Ohmygod, Dev, they're gorgeous!"

"Down, Nick." Devlin laughed.

Kenyon sobered for a moment. MacBain put his hand on Devlin's shoulder. "Devlin…apparently this isn't just powered armor."

"It's something more," Kenyon agreed. "We're just not sure exactly what yet, but we think it was a test bed project."

"A what?" Devlin asked.

"They were testing some type of new generation powered armor."

"Oh great, so we don't know if it's even going to work?"

Cat broke in, "Apparently it does. But it's complicated."

"Complicated how?"

"Well, you got to see it," Kenyon said. "Come over here; we have the commander's suit open."

On the far end of the room, a suit of the test armor was open. Armored Powered Exoskeletons, or APEs, were about three meters tall and weighed in at nearly a thousand pounds. They were designed to carry lots of ammunition and provide stability to railguns on full power. They were neither the greatest of armor nor the fastest or most nimble things; APEs were workhorses for a soldier.

These suits were beautiful in comparison. Almost a half meter taller, these suits looked more like suits of armor than an exoskeleton with plates hooked on. Gleaming metal overlay...something. It almost looked like metal musculature. The curves of the armor were broken in spots by hard points for mounting weapons or sensor pods.

For all that they were taller than an APE, Devlin could tell they probably weighed less, and yet he could also almost instinctively tell that these suits were stronger, faster, more fell, and more deadly than anything he had ever seen before.

The suit was situated in a gantry similar to an APE, and, like an APE, the front plastron was open, revealing the interior of the suit's haptic systems. The helmet was thrown back and locked.

"Climb in, Devlin," Cat said. "Close up the armor and then wait for a minute."

Devlin hesitantly climbed into the steel battle suit. He inserted his arms and legs into the armor and hit the activation inside the arm harness. The suit plastron came back and locked into the rear portion. Readouts inside the helmet fired up. He felt tiny pressure points at various points on his head. Then he felt a gentle pressure as the suit began to configure itself to the contours of his body. The pressure started at his toes, and he became a little panicked when it reached his head, fearing it might cut off his ability to breathe, but it seemed to ignore his mouth and nose, and there was a cool bit of air hitting his face, allowing him to continue breathing.

For a few moments nothing happened. Then to Devlin's surprise, he heard a mellifluous voice in his ear. "Please state name, rank, and access code."

* * * * *

Chapter Twenty

Devlin's eyebrows shot up at the request. APEs didn't have voice interaction. Nor did they have that level of personalization. With APEs, you were fitted to the suit, and it was "yours" for as long as you were with a unit. When you transferred, the suit stayed with the unit and was fitted to the next grunt.

Devlin cleared his throat and swallowed a bit of saliva to wet his mouth.

"Private Nikolai Devlin, recruit, no access code."

"Where is Captain Mujumdar, the assigned user for this combat suit?"

"Captain Mujumdar, along with presumably all the staff and service members for this base, have been killed in action," Devlin said. He wasn't sure why he was speaking to a computer, but…

"Please state your service file access number and purpose for being in this Combat Response Armored Tactical Operations System unit."

"Two Two Two Seven One Dash Seven Nine Eight Dash Eight Two Three Three Alpha Oscar," Devlin said. "Topside of research facility has been compromised by hostile forces. My training group was on the planet conducting final MUSTX prior to graduation. I am," he said muttering 'for my sins,' "the senior surviving recruit in contact at the moment. My company sergeant major gave me the task of finding help, which has led me here."

"Verifying service status," the voice said absently. "Devlin, Nikolai Nikolayevich. Rank: Recruit Private, currently assigned Alpha

Company, Third Battalion, One Forty-Ninth Training Legion. Planet of record: Caliban. Currently on probation prior to judgment due to military service. Mother is..."

"...Checking facility surveillance for indicators of force structure and numbers."

Devlin was a little puzzled. This didn't sound like a normal computer program, and if it was a computer...

"Tactical analysis indicates need for asymmetrical warfare approach to engagement."

"Excuse me?" Devlin said, startled.

"Tactical analysis—"

"I know what you just said, but what did you mean? And who or what am I talking to?" Devlin demanded.

"I am the Cybernetic Artificial Liaison Intelligence for CRATOS Combat Suit PT-001. Captain Mujumdar called me CALI. Although I am configurable for names, auditory and visual overlays, etc."

Devlin thought for a full minute. Artificial intelligence was something a lot of people had talked about. Hell they'd *talked* about AI for centuries. But a lot went into AI, some of it scientific and some that went straight into navel-gazing philosophy.

"So, you're telling me that you are an artificially sentient computer construct?" Devlin inquired. "Like Weyland, the Facility Artificial Intelligence."

"Essentially correct, but not entirely accurate. There are aspects to my functionality that cannot be effectively quantified."

"Like being alive?" Devlin snorted under his breath.

"And like being able to hear you," the voice said bemusedly.

Then it hit Devlin, the voice had started out sounding somewhat hollow. Now it was starting to sound and respond like a person.

"Yes, Private Devlin, I can hear you mutter, and to an extent I can 'hear' what you're thinking, due to the neuropickups I have scattered around your head in the helmet. During the time we've been conversing and analyzing the situation, I have been attuning myself to your brainwave patterns. This allows me to communicate more effectively with you. There is another level we could go to, but it is not possible at the moment."

"And that would be?"

"Gestalt."

"Excuse me? I don't understand."

"Captain Mujumdar and his colleagues were fitted with special neurotransceivers that allowed myself and my brothers and sisters to attain a 'gestalt' state with our 'meat' portion. We were two minds linked for a common purpose: running this combat platform. I could understand his intent, and I would run the functions of the suit while he worried about tactics and strategies. This was part of the experimental portion of the suit program. A 'meat' could run the suit by command and is permitted to do so. You could function in combat quite effectively without me—it would be comparable to wearing a normal combat exoskeleton, although some of the functions would require extensive training and practice to accomplish.

"The gestalt between a 'meat' and 'ALI' allows each intelligence to function together and individually to completely run the functions of the suit. For the meat portion, it is much like wearing a combat suit and doing their job, just with more capability."

"So, you can run the complex functions of the suit, while communicating with me?" Devlin said, a little incredulously.

"Can you walk and chew gum at the same time, Private? Or, more to the point, can you 'shoot, move, and communicate at the same time?"

"Point."

"You humans have a thing called 'muscle memory,' correct?" CALI asked.

"Yes," Devlin replied.

"To an extent, I'm muscle memory for this suit. But I am also a fully functioning intelligence. I can multitask and carry out commands and be a sounding board for ideas based on running hypotheticals millions of times per second."

"What are the chances I might think something, and you begin a course of action I cannot stop?"

"Virtually none," the AI answered. "Much of this is complicated, but suffice it to say that part of the experimental program was finding all of the 'gotchas' in the systems and making sure that a 'rogue' ALI doesn't take command of a suit and start killing people."

"That's a comfort. So, what's involved in getting fitted for the transceiver? Because as you've already been analyzed, we're in kind of a cleft stick, and if we have to be asymmetrical, I'll take any advantage possible."

The intelligence took a moment to answer. "This facility has an autodoc that could do the procedure on you and a number of your colleagues. However, based on models, we will only have enough transceivers and time to perform the procedure on about ten of your people. Between recovery and fitting the suit, which we can do a lot of ourselves, you will be hard pressed to get into service before the forces outside decide to perform a full-frontal assault. Should they decide to do so, the forces in the above-ground facility will breach the defenses in about two hours."

"So how long do we have?" Devlin asked, concerned.

"Models are indicating that you have another day and a half before the assault begins in earnest. Comm traffic we have intercepted indicates that the forces outside are waiting for additional forces and weaponry."

"Any relief that we can count on? The WHSKR facility is down, but did the facility get an OMEGA off before everything went offline?"

"Negative. But the task force containing the troops with which you were supposed to train should be coming in about a week."

"Lovely. And I don't suppose we can really hold out a week."

"No, Private. Even under the best scenarios, this facility can only hold out three to five days, then it will eventually be overrun. Should that happen, our protocols are to destroy ourselves."

"I thought you couldn't deploy your weaponry."

"I have no control over that eventuality. It is beyond my conscious control. Had anyone tried to take this hardware without authorization, my protocols would have initiated an overload in my power core."

"Then how am I talking to you?"

"You are at least verifiably military. I extrapolated several factors in your favor when you initiated contact."

"And those were?"

"You did not attempt to move this hardware, and you attempted to communicate and provided verifiable information. "

"That's all well and good, but it doesn't…"

"Plus, I decided you weren't a threat."

"I thought you said the protocols were beyond your control."

"There are rules, and rules, Private."

"Oh, joy…"

* * *

Devlin started giving orders the moment the front plastron separated.

"Nicki. You and Cat find the autodoc in this hole.

We're going to need it to 'plant people. Mac, I need you, Nicki, McCarthy, the Carls, Buttsniffer, and Cho."

"'Planted? What the hell, Devlin?"

"I guess you've already surmised that these aren't normal combat suits. They're prototype full-on, high speed, low drag, battle armor with functional AI support," Devlin said casually.

"Bullshit!" Cat exclaimed.

"No shit. It's working...and it's in these suits," Devlin said. "These suits could keep us from getting fragged, but only if we hurry."

"You haven't answered the part about 'planted."

"You've already been in a suit?" Devlin asked.

"Well, sort of," MacBain admitted.

"You know the neuropickups in the helmet?"

"Yeah, I got that much."

"Well this system is far better than an APE suit. Small micro transceivers implanted next to the nanipack allows the suit to interface directly. Very similar to the high-end consumer 'plants."

MacBain frowned. "Yeah, I'm not sure I like the idea of an AI nestling in my brain, thank you very much."

"Got a better idea? Rather be wormchow?"

"Point."

"What about the other two suits?" Kenyon asked

"I have an idea, but I need a little time to flesh it out. I'll let you know before they need to be planted."

MacBain nodded dubiously. "Selling this to the boys and girls is going to be—"

"Oh, bullshit, Mac!" Kenyon grinned. "Some of us would give our left ovary to play with a suit like this. I just saw a rocket-launcher calliope pack for one of these suits! Let me have a calliope, Devlin, come on, let me have a calliope." She was practically bouncing up and down.

Devlin grinned. Kenyon was a steady troop, but she got positively giddy when it came to things that go boom.

"Spark Pony gets a rocket launcher."

"Squeeeeeee!"

He thought for a moment. "Weyland?" he asked.

"Yes, Private Devlin."

"Why didn't we get told about the suits? You've showed us everything else."

"Compartmentalization, Private. My protocols prevent me in some instances from knowing about things. If I don't know about the suits, I can't answer questions about them. Once you, who are now the de facto head of this facility, opened the door and gained access, my compartment concerning those suits was opened."

"Are there any other compartments you haven't opened yet?" Devlin asked.

"You would have to be specific, Private. I don't know exactly what I don't know."

Devlin shivered. "Okay, how about this. If I asked you for the contents of each of the facilities, would you be able to tell me the contents and details?"

"Unless a room is compartmentalized like this one, yes," the AI answered.

* * *

"So that's the deal, folks," Devlin said as he addressed everyone in the armor bay.

Devlin had shown them the armor and explained what the Artificial Liaison Intelligence had explained to him. Using holoprojectors on the suit, he outlined the current tactical situation, bad, and projected outcome, worse.

Faces were grim, some taut with fear, others tight with anger.

"We don't have enough personal weapons to outfit everyone, but even if we did, we couldn't stop combat-armored troops.

"We have some armor of our own, but we don't have a lot of experience in using it, and there's not enough to go around. And we can't hole up in here, they will eventually breach the facility, which, as I found out a while ago, will result in the facility reactors going critical and blowing the place to Hell and gone."

Several faces went white on that last one.

Devlin continued, "So here's what I've come up with. First, we're going to take ten people and get them 'planted with the transceivers that will enable us to gestalt with the suits. That will give us a force enhancement. But we can only do ten; that's all we have. Who and how, we'll cover in a minute.

"Second, we're going to send a few of our own, plus all of you, to our rearguard camp out in the boonies; that way, if worse comes to worst, you won't be here when it goes spectacularly boom."

"What's that going to accomplish?" one of the civilians demanded. "We'll be out there in the wilderness with no cover."

"A few minutes after the access to this place gets breached, this place is going to be an atomic inferno. You can stay in here if you want. We won't even have to worry about looking for the body," Devlin said coldly. "We're doing this first, to buy you time to get the hell out of here. The second reason is to try and get rid of our guests.

"The ships containing the rest of the units for the MUSTX will be here in a couple of days; they should already be inbound from the emergence point. If we can get rid of the pirates or whatever they are, you guys plus what we leave behind can make it for a week in the field. But you won't make it two hours if those assholes survive. We have to take out as many of them as we can," Devlin finished.

He looked at everyone assembled.

"I'm not guaranteeing anything. I'm nothing more than what you are, but my sergeant major put me in charge, and by God I do not have any desire to die just yet. So I'm going to do everything I can to survive, just like I'm doing everything I can to make sure you survive.

"The way I figure it, even if we buy it, hopefully we'll take out most of the group outside. And even if we don't get that, the facility going up will dissuade any of them from investigating further. They'll get in their ships and leave. You just have to make it until they leave or the fleet arrives."

Several people nodded. There were issues, but the plan made sense.

Devlin looked around.

"You're going to put those two crim—"

"Did I ask for input?" Devlin snapped. "Those two are combat veterans. They are the closest thing I've got right now to trained troops. So yeah, they're going in the suits. Get over it."

No one else protested. Kilmeade looked like he was going to, but he looked over at Cat who nodded and smiled.

"There's a good chance we ain't coming back. But like the sergeant major said, 'We sign up to go out...coming back is extra.'"

Grimly he looked at every face in the crowd.

"Dammit, I didn't sign up for this," said Devlin. "But then neither did any of you. The Devil surely is calling the tune on this one, and all we can do is sing the song.

"Look at it another way. My old man's nickname in the Army was Old Nick, so I guess you could say the Devil is my da. And he surely is calling the tune on this one. So if this is the tune, I'm gonna sing the song until it's done. Hell, we're fighting in a church, so those farkers are about to get sent to the Heaven by the Devil's Choir!"

* * *

After rechecking all the defensive points, making sure everyone had ammo, had been fed, watered, and gotten a few hours of sleep, and generally making a nuisance of himself, Kenyon and MacBain grabbed Devlin and led him down into the research facility to where the autodoc pod stood waiting. Cat waited at a console at the side of the room.

"You know the drill, Devlin," the young woman said. She grinned evilly. "Disrobe and get into the autodoc."

"Ummm," Devlin started to say.

"Why, Devlin, are you afraid I'm gonna see you nekkid?" Cat giggled. That made Devlin even more embarrassed. "Oh Hell, I've seen it before. And you've taken showers in boot, Recruit...so you've shown it. Get in the damn tube!" She got serious. "Really, Devlin, we don't have a lot of time. Suck it up, soldier."

Devlin pulled off his armor and uniform, then pulled down his shorts and started to climb into the tube.

Cat and Kenyon both whistled.

Face red, Devlin finished getting into the tube and stood there waiting. Cat hit the control sequence to start the procedure.

"Please relax, Private Devlin," the autodoc's voice came through the transducer. The tube began to rotate, and Devlin felt himself become weightless as the grav field took hold. He would be held in the field, giving the autodoc's instruments equal access to all parts of his body.

"Scanning..." the autodoc intoned. Devlin breathed easily and tried to relax.

"Private Devlin..."

"Yes?"

"Your BFT device is in a non-standard area…"

"I know where it is, Doc," Devlin snapped.

"Understood, Private," the autodoc sounded a little snippy. "Prepare for anesthesia and start of procedure."

* * *

"Devlin?" Devlin opened his eyes and saw Kenyon looking at him intently. "Do you feel any different?"

"Not really," he admitted. There was no discernible evidence anything had been done.

"I guess you have to be in a suit for the thing to actually do anything."

"That makes sense," he agreed. "How long was I out?"

"About an hour," she informed him. "At this rate it's going to take all night to get the mods done."

He nodded. "Let's get me into the commander's suit and see what happens."

He got out of the tube and dressed. Someone had gotten him a fresh uniform and boots. His armor was in a carry bag along with his rifle. He shouldered it and followed Kenyon out of the med bay. MacBain was getting ready to enter the tube. "Good luck, Devlin. See you in a couple of hours."

Devlin waved and hurried down the hall after Kenyon.

As soon as the plastron closed on the CRATOS, Devlin felt a strange sensation in the back of his head that slowly spread. It was almost like a headache, but after a moment it subsided.

"Sorry about that," the voice said in his ear as the conformal material in the armor adjusted itself to his body's contours once again.

"It takes a few seconds to complete the handshake procedure between the suit and your neural interface. I am given to understand that people have different experiences. Captain Mujumdar thought it tickled. I have been monitoring your brainwave pattern during the handshake process. I get the impression that you did not think it tickled. Totally different wave pattern."

"No, as a matter of fact it was unpleasant, but not excessively so," Devlin replied.

"Hmm," the AI temporized. "It may or may not change as you get used to the interface. I'm not sure."

"Why are you talking to me?" Devlin inquired.

"Actually, I quit using the auditory pickups a moment ago," came the reply. "Your brain is interpreting the neurostimulation as auditory. This way we can communicate, and you can still receive actual auditory input. This can also be done suit-to-suit over the comms, providing a secure channel. Same with visual. You can have a virtual reality conference with the other suits, both meat and cybernetic."

Suddenly, Devlin was out of his armor and sitting in a conference room with a rather attractive looking Nepalese woman wearing a sari. He was startled, but his brain started functioning again before the construct could interject.

"CALI, I presume, and we are in a virtual construct?"

"Quite so. You are very quick, for a human."

"Thanks, I think," Devlin said, smiling faintly. Or at least the virtual him smiled.

Then he was back in the armor looking at the people bustling around the armor bay.

"It was actually a compliment, Private. Your issues with the neuro liaison aside, your brain doesn't seem to have any problem transitioning between real and virtual constructs. Captain Mujumdar took about half a second longer for transitions."

Devlin shrugged inside the armor. "I'm not sure if that's good or bad, but I'll take it on faith. Since we're going to be working together, please call me Devlin. It could get very cumbersome if we have to Private this and that all the time."

"Agreed, Devlin. Everyone is a little different. To be honest, Sanjay had the same point when we worked together. But he insisted on formality when others were present."

"I can see the utility of that," Devlin conceded. "I guess the same applies for me."

"Your meat peoples' brains are as capable of multitasking as we are, we just are slightly faster. In some ways we're alike. Your brain has to maintain your life functions; I have to maintain the suit's functions so you don't have to worry about it. To you, it really is just like wearing the suit."

"Just with more toys," Devlin repeated what the AI had said during the earlier conversation.

"Very good." The AI sounded amused. "And we are active, at full power and ready to detach from the stasis pad."

Devlin "felt" the various power and data umbilicals detach from his armor, and he felt…different. He felt like he wasn't wearing anything. His mind told him differently. His vision was unencumbered by the helmet. He turned his head—his vision was perfect. He looked down at his hands and saw the mechanical gauntlets of the suit.

"The visual pickups of the suit are enhancing your vision," CALI's voice said in his head. "Again, this is part of the gestalt. I can put information directly into your brain so you don't have to sort through different stimuli. I can also do the same with your head's-up displays or you can use your retinal pickups for the same purpose. This is a feature completely at your preference. From time to time, I can insert information you might need to know. It is similar to the way normal implants work; you *know* the information. For the most part I stay in the background, but the major purpose for using your eyes is that the retinal pickups of the suit track your eye movements and adjust the view or informational HUD accordingly. It will allow you shift targets. Do you have any questions?"

"Not at the moment, no," Devlin replied. He was busily processing what he was seeing.

"Would you like to do some VR scenarios to get used to the functionality of the suit? I can shut down the neuromotor pickups so your movements won't control the suit. Basically, you'll be 'in your head' as Captain Mujumdar called it."

"That sounds good, CALI," Devlin agreed. "We can get to know each other while we wait for a few others to get planted."

"Agreed."

* * *

For the next two hours, the artificial intelligence of the suit instructed and showed Devlin the "basic operator's guide" to CRATOS, the Cybernetic Reinforced Armored Tactical Operations Suit.

"Wait, this thing can *fly?*"

"No, Devlin. This suit has miniature grav compensators. They are not powerful enough to sustain continuous operation, and thus flight. However, they can provide temporary levitation and advanced jumping capability."

"How advanced?" Devlin demanded.

"A lot depends on the speed leading into a jump, but a linear jump from a standing position has been measured at three hundred meters linear with a height of approximately seventy-five meters."

"Holy Hell!" Devlin said startled. "That is almost flying."

"More like 'jumping really high and falling with style,'" CALI countered. "The 'muscles' in the suit produce a lot of thrust, so between them and the compensators making the suit 'lighter,' the result is a lot of ground covered. The thing to remember is that when you are airborne, you are essentially falling, so you are..."

"A big farking target," Devlin finished. "McClellan's Rule Number Seventy-Four: The only things that fall out of the sky are meteors, bird shit, and idiots."

"I am unsure who 'McClellan' is."

"Some other time." Devlin laughed.

"And so, on we go, then." The AI went back to instruction.

Apparently in VR, the passage of time was a little different, because before Devlin really had time to absorb all the information coming his way, an avatar for MacBain popped up and approached in armor of his own. His armor looked different. Really different.

"Hey, Dev. Did you know you can customize how your armor looks? It's better than a hologame."

Then it struck Devlin. "Did you customize your armor to look like *Halo 97?*"

"You know it, laddie!" MacBain said cheerfully. It was the first time Devlin had heard any animation in his voice since Kuzma died.

"You didn't tell me about this CALI," he said accusingly.

"Actually, I did tell you about the customizable holoprojectors, which is basically what he's using. Primarily, their use is for a limited chameleon effect, but like Private MacBain says, you can make the armor look like anything you wish, within limits. In his case, Mjolnir Mk42 armor is a lot smaller."

"I just wonder what Kenyon's going to look like..."

* * *

"Really, Nick????"

Kenyon's armor wasn't just bright, it was iridescent…and sparkly…and really weird looking with a six-pack rocket launcher on its shoulder.

"Heheheheheheeee."

* * * * *

Chapter Twenty-One

"Whoever is in charge over in the church, I'm calling you!" Jemison called via comm.

"Devlin here," he replied calmly. He had his helmet's magnification on max and could see the entrance to the Town Hall where Longo had entered earlier. "Where's the other guy, the one who was commanding the mercs earlier?"

"Oh, Colonel Longo and I had a slight disagreement. I won and I'm in total command."

Devlin didn't say anything, but kept his view dialed in on the entrance. Longo had seemed like someone who would act with a modicum of reason. This fellow was a wildcard in the game.

"And just what, pray tell, was the disagreement about? Little ole me?" Devlin inquired sweetly. "I am flattered, really but—" He was cut off mid-sentence.

"Devlin, I ain't Longo. He was an ex-military pussy who didn't want 'unnecessary casualties.' I got a job to do, and I'm going to get it done and get paid. I don't give a rat's ass what I got to do and who gets killed getting it done."

"Then why are you talking to me, Mr. ...."

"Captain Marco Jemison of the FPV *Stormcrow*. Why? Because, though I would like to come over there and put your ass on a spit and roast you on an open flame, then sing songs and roast marshmallows, I'd just as soon not get my people killed doing it. Yes, I know I just said I didn't care, but consistency is the sign of a diseased mind, so sue me. Actually, I should say I don't give a rat's ass who gets killed on your side.

"So, I'm going to give you another chance. You and your people leave, right now. I know you got the facility accessed, just leave the door open. We won't mess with you. You can come back in a few days and have the town back. That's the deal. If you refuse, people are going to die starting with…"

Two mercs appeared at the door to the Town Hall. They dragged a hooded and bound figure out onto the portico and dumped him on his knees. Finally, a short, obese man in a spacer rig appeared in the doorway.

They walked to the edge of the portico and Jemison looked toward the church. "I'm pretty sure you got 'nocs, so you can see me."

He pulled the hood off the figure. Devlin gritted his teeth as the face of Nathaniel Jones was shown in the lights. His face was badly bruised, but they were fading. It looked like his nanis were already working. So, he hadn't been abused in at least the last several hours.

"I'm going to give you to the count of ten, and then I'm going to put a bullet through this young man's head. The only thing I'll feel is the trigger, so his blood will be on your hands. The choice is, as they say, yours." His wheezing chuckle came over the comm as he started counting. "One."

Devlin thought about taking Jemison out from here. He was sure Cho already had the fat wheezer in her sights. Suddenly a targeting reticule appeared in his vision. He realized that the suit's gestalt AI was "helping." *Not now,* he thought, and the reticle disappeared.

"Two."

"What's to stop you from just killing them and us as soon as you get what you want?"

"Nothing, really," the pirate replied casually. "Three. But I promise. Four."

Several of the recruits tensed and shouldered their weapons, preparing to fire, but Devlin broadcast a terse "no" across the platoon circuit.

"Five."

"Pony, where are you?" Devlin called.

"Six."

"Would you chill out a minute?" Devlin called desperately. "I'm trying to get this coordinated."

"Seven. Better work fast, mate." Jemison said.

But Nathaniel Jones took the decision out of everyone's hands. He burst upward, his shoulder crashing into Jemison, knocking him off balance. Jonesy, hands still tied behind his back, crashed into the pirate opposite Jemison, and lost his own balance in the process. Both soldier and pirate crashed to the ground. Jonesy popped to his feet and then his head exploded as Jemison fired a single shot from his railpistol.

Devlin took a sharp intake of breath, but that was his only reaction. He zoomed his glasses in at the body of his teammate. There wasn't much left of Jonesy's head. Devlin fought the urge to puke, then directed his gaze at the face of the pirate captain. The man showed no more than an annoyance at a plan gone awry. Devlin felt his rage building.

Jemison blew out a breath. "Well. I hoped we could have gotten this done. Ah well. Prepare to die, Mr. Devlin. We'll be coming over there shortly."

Devlin seethed as the entourage on the porch moved back toward the doors.

"I'm going to break you in half, you sonuvabitch!" Devlin grated. The targeting reticule came up again, and he raised his arm. He could feel the suit making minute changes, sighting in the railgun. The telltale showed green, and he fired.

* * *

Jemison had just passed through the door of the building as the rounds from Devlin's auto-gun stitched the porch. A pirate who was covering him jerked, then exploded as the rounds turned his unarmored body into paste.

"Shit!" Jemison snarled as the heavy blaststeel door closed. He wiped blood and probably brains off his face. "Shit! Shit! Shit! That asshole; I'm gonna roast him. I'm gonna find his body and roast it just like I said!"

He turned to Mangone. "Get your men out here. And bring me Longo's armor. You're gonna fit me in it!"

"But..." the mercenary sergeant started to protest, then decided better of it. "Whatever you say...Captain."

Jemison stalked off, snapping orders to the mercs as he went.

* * * * *

Chapter Twenty-Two

Devlin sat in one of the pews of the church looking at the altar at the front. He wondered if the residents had actually used this as a house of worship rather than just a façade for a place that made weapons.

At any rate, the artwork in the church—he was pretty sure it was a church and not a temple—was very well done. Starting at the entrance and culminating in the chancel area behind the altar, scenes depicting the history of Man, from the creation of Man to the Exodus from Earth were shown in holographic detail and beauty.

Devlin never considered himself religious. His mother had been moderately so before the plague. He was never sure whether she had kept the rituals and prayers from faith, devotion to tradition, or for appearance. He wanted to think it was faith. That seemed to fit with his ma.

If there was a God or Gods, they must be having a farking field day over the twists and turns of one Nikolai Devlin. He wasn't sure if he should thank them or curse them. But then, he supposed, that was the way it was supposed to be, wasn't it? Believe or Not, Obey or Not, Worship or Not, the Heavens would remain immutably silent. Man was free to choose.

He had made a lot of choices, questionable and otherwise, in the last several months. Choices that led to this church. To this fight.

After everyone had gotten fitted that could be, they had planned, folded, spindled, and mutilated what they each could and would do when the fighting started. The sergeant major was right, he thought as his armored hand absently flicked the ammo cover on the prototype rail gun designed to be used with the CRATOS armor.

It was larger than the M294. It could still be used by an unarmored trooper, but the weapon's power was probably more than a trooper would want to deal with.

Its capacitors fed off the micro-fusion reactor that powered the suit. There was a feed tube that snaked up his arm and into the variable ammunition pod attached to a hard point on the back of the armor. The pod also housed a small number of property denial rounds for the personal grenade launcher on his right shoulder. For the moment, that was in the upright and locked position.

He realized what he was doing—woolgathering—and took his hand off the rifle. Time to get the game face on.

"Squad," he said over the comms. "Sound off and go/no-go."

* * *

McCarthy placed the ammo boxes on the ground.

"This is a whole lot of ammo, 'Stasia," he said as he opened one of them and began laying it out on the ground.

"It is not normal ammunition, Thomas," the diminutive sniper countered. "As I understand it, and our Artificial Intelligences can correct me if I'm wrong, these rounds are capable of self-controlled homing and flight. As such, the rounds are more massive than the ammunition for an M289. Is that correct, Gangrim?

"You have an effective range of twenty-six kilometers or line of sight to horizon."

McCarthy frowned. "Don't you go getting yourself killed, Little Flower," he warned. He saw her back stiffen, then she went back to setting up equipment.

"I shall not," she said. "I trust that you will take the same care."

Tom McCarthy nodded and closed his visor.

Devlin's voice came over the comm, "Squad. Sound off and go/no-go."

McCarthy walked out to the rocky ledge and turned back one last time to look. "Pigpen inbound to position number one. Pen is *go*."

Cho looked up, saw McCarthy disappear over the ledge and spoke, trusting her armor to pick up her voice. "Ninja in position. Go."

* * *

Joe Harold watched as Cat and Kilmeade got the refugees moving in the right direction. There were a lot of scared faces. He wasn't happy. He and Kilmeade had spent the last four years running from fights. That was all right, he supposed; he had originally deserted over a no-win fight. That's what you do when your entire outfit gets wiped out due to "intelligence failure." Such a nice clinical word. He preferred negligent murder himself. If he ever found the intel asshole that had screwed them, he might commit premeditated murder. But whatever.

Now he was running again and, strangely, he didn't want to. He wanted to be back in that church with that boy, Devlin. *No,* he thought, *not a boy. He was making decisions like a man; what's more, a commander.*

Harold felt conflicted. He was in armor, dammit. Devlin had made him and Paddy suit up. The kid/man needed combat vets, and the two he had, he was sending away with the women and kids. "If they buy it," Devlin had said, "all of this is for nothing."

He watched as Cat picked up one dark-skinned little girl and gave her a hug, whispered in her ear, then walked with her to the gathering area.

"Paddy?" Joe said into his comm.

"Yeah," his partner answered.

"What the Hells are we doing?" He watched Kilmeade make a few final inspections, then turned and walked toward him.

"The right thing, Pard. The right thing."

Joseph Harold looked over his shoulder in the direction of Weyland Station and the kids being asked to do way more than they should.

"Squad. Sound off and go/no-go."

"Mutt and Jeff. Cargo is secure. We are *go*."

* * *

Anne Marie Decker was slightly miffed. She didn't get any of the really high-tech armor. But only slightly. She wasn't big on being enclosed in the armor, to be honest. She was always a little tense when she couldn't see the outside with her own eyes.

She looked around her. Everywhere there were memory modules and processors. In the center of the room on a raised column of nanocirc was a round enclosure.

"Weyland?" she asked.

"Yes, Anne," the voice acknowledged. She was the only one of the Hellions, or she guessed they were now the Devil's Choir, that the AI called by name. She thought that was nice. She and the AI had gotten to be pretty good friends in the last day or so. She'd spent every waking moment working on this moment with Devlin and the Cybernetic Assistant Facilities Manager.

"Are you ready?"

"As ready as I can be, Anne. It's been interesting trying to condense myself. I think you fleshies would compare it to trying to fit a two-meter-tall man into a half-meter-cubed box."

"Is that possible?" Anne asked, keying in a sequence on the terminal across from the dais. Lights flashed on the dais, and one bank of processors went dark.

"Well, it was before the Exodus. There is archaic holo footage of a 'yogi,' someone who practiced a semi-religious art of body control, who could do it. He was able to stay in the box for hours."

Anne shuddered. She really didn't like that mental picture.

She keyed in another sequence from her implant. Another bank went dark.

"We need to hurry, Anne."

"Rush a miracle worker and get a lousy miracle," Anne muttered.

"No pressure," the voice in her head said.

"No pressure," she replied and keyed in the last sequence. The last bank of processors went dark.

On the dais, the lights on the central pillar blinked in a cascade of lights that culminated at the top. Anne Marie watched as the lights performed a momentary dance of various colors and patterns, then went dark themselves.

The cylindrical container at the top of the pillar split and the top slid aside.

"Okay, Anne Marie. Please remove me from the cradle." Weyland's voice was no longer in her implant but came from a small vocoder at the base of the processor cradle.

Anne looked in and saw a nanocirc processor core about 20 cm by 30 cm. She raised her eyebrows. "Can you still hear me, Weyland?" she asked.

"Yes, but only so long as I am actually in the cradle. My core is just that, it has no sensory organs per se, and it is just my core programming and certain memories. The data logs from the facility for example. I regret that I will not be able to save all of the data files from the CRATOS project."

"Well, there's no help for that," Decker said. "The powers that be should be able to salvage something from the armor and the AI's in there."

"Possibly." Weyland sounded doubtful and...

"Are you afraid, Weyland?"

"I'm a little...apprehensive," the AI answered. "I have never been this cut off from everything since I came online. I already feel blind. Is this what it's like to die? To have everything you are just start to go dark."

"I think you're being a little melodramatic," she said. "But yes, sometimes. Dying is little like that. I can't say from personal experience, having never done it, but I've heard it's like having everything go out. I suppose that would be scary.

"But then sometimes you're surrounded by people who love you and you just go to sleep. And when you wake up, it's in a much better place, and you're happy."

"That sounds pretty," the AI said. "I think that's a good idea, Anne. I'm going to go to sleep. I'm going to shut down my core and wait for the awakening after this is all over."

"You do that," Anne said. "And I'll be there when you awaken."

"I would like that. Good night, Anne Marie Decker."

"Good night, Weyland."

She watched as the processor core detached itself from the cradle, then a moment later, all sign of activity in the nanocircuitry stopped.

Decker reached out and took the core and placed it in her carry sack. She exited the core room and nodded to Chapis. He was in armor. He scooped her up in his arms and started moving up the empty grav shaft toward the exterior entrance to Shack Number Six, Weyland Station.

"Squad. Sound off and go/no-go."

"Alice and Sniffer," she said. "Package is secure. En route to rendezvous. We are *go*."

* * *

Kenyon watched as the ground trucks came out of the motor pool. Even loaded as they were, they didn't ride lower on their field effects, but they were going to be slower than Moses.

"Squad. Sound off and go/no-go."

Once they were all out, she approached the rearmost truck, got into the passenger side of the driving cab and transmitted.

"Sparkle Pony. Trucks are loaded and en route. We are *go* here, Shaitan."

* * *

Devlin's head cocked at Kenyon's call. "Shaitan?"

MacBain touched him on the shoulder. "We figured it fit. You never give yourself your own handle, dude. You said your old man's handle was Old Nick or Satan. Shaitan is just…"

"Got it," Devlin said. He mulled the name over in his mind. Then he shrugged. At least it wasn't "Buttsniffer" or "Dammit Carl."

"Squad, this is Shaitan. We are on the clock. Countdown commences!"

* * *

"What are they doing?" Jemison demanded. He stood just inside the portico for the Town Hall, with two of his officers beside him. The sergeant of the mercenary group, already in his combat exoskeleton, looked in the direction of the church through the combat glasses in his helmet.

"Nothing at the moment. There appears to be no movement. I'm getting vague heat signatures from the church, about five or six at the moment, but they aren't regular human heat signatures nor are they APEs. And they aren't moving."

Sergeant Mangone really did not like Jemison, and he really didn't like this situation, but he had a duty to the men in his platoon to get them home, which meant dealing with this piece of filth, even after the piece of filth had murdered his colonel, the XO, and the platoon leader. Somebody was going to pay for that. Pay in cash and pay on delivery, but that was for getting home.

Jemison looked at his XO. "What's the status on *Stormcrow*?"

The XO consulted his tablet. "Punching Shuttles Six and Seven in fifty-five minutes. ETA, punch plus twenty-nine minutes."

Jemison grunted. "So, what do you say there, soldier boy? Should we go ahead and kick off? Or should we wait for my guys to get here and do your job for you, heh?"

Mangone really wanted to take the short, fat son of a bitch by his head and squeeze until he popped like a zit.

"It would be unwise to attack while we don't know what they are bringing to the dance." Mangone said formally. Then as an afterthought, he added, "Sir."

Jemison didn't even notice.

"Fine, fine," he said, exasperatedly. "But when they get here, you're going to lead the charge, and you're going to be the one to breach the entrance. Once you've done that, you'll wipe out everybody in that the farking facility. I don't want a cockroach living. My boys will come in afterward and clean the place out. We need to be out of here in twenty-four hours. We'll hit the hyper limit well before any Impy ships arrive, and you'll be collecting your paychecks in two weeks."

He grinned like a father regarding a child. Mangone didn't think it was a natural look. It looked more like a father who had an unwholesome attraction for his child.

"Yes, sir." He turned. "I would like to go and make sure the squads are ready to go."

Jemison waved his hand, and the NCO bounded off toward the shuttle.

Jemison turned to his XO. "Once they've killed the last one, I don't want a single one of them assholes getting on the shuttles, you understand?"

Justine, the XO of *Stormcrow,* dimpled brightly. "It will positively be my pleasure, boss."

* * * * *

Chapter Twenty-Three

It started with a single shot.

From his position, Devlin allowed the feed from the sensor drones he and the rest of the team had deployed to play in his display—or rather that's how he perceived it. It was really relaying directly into his consciousness through the implant modification that allowed him to gestalt with the CRATOS Armor. The AI sensed his eye movements, interpreted that as a desire to shift attention and shifted perspective.

Devlin watched as a sentry on the northwest corner of the settlement sprouted a hole in his chest and toppled from his perch. His partner, recovering from the shock quickly enough to duck and thus avoid the rail gun round meant for him, turned and fired in the direction he believed the round had come from, as did just about everyone else who saw the sentry fall. What they didn't know was that the shooter was no longer there.

Streaks of fire licked at the hills surrounding the settlement as rounds poured out of mercenary weapons. Devlin smiled ferally inside his helmet. "Okay, boys and girls," he said over the squad push, "light 'em up."

* * *

The first rounds from Devlin's railgun punched a fist-sized hole in the outer wall of the church. As the debris cleared, Devlin used the sensor feed to target. He sensed, rather than felt, the AI complete the aiming process, and Devlin started unleashing hell on the startled mercenaries and pirates approaching the church.

Through the feeds, he saw the other members of the squad in the church begin firing as well. As he thought, a tactical map split off from his main vision and icons arranged themselves in his mind's eye—the blue icons of the Choirboys and the red of Jemison's troops. He watched as two groups of red icons split off, one going north and one going south, using the buildings to find cover.

"Watch your sectors," Devlin said, shooting and taking out a pirate peeking out from the same bridge strut he had used to infiltrate the settlement.

"Hold your own pecker!" MacBain responded, laughing. "I'm getting mine stuck in." He fired a burst into a housing unit that had a duo of pirates taking shelter.

"Dammit? You got leakers on your flank."

"On it," Weber acknowledged. Devlin thought he heard, "Dammit," under the soldier's breath.

A line of fire streaked out from the northeast corner of the church, stitching into a cluster of buildings. It hit a power sump, and the building burst into actinic fire and exploded.

"Oooooh. Break out the marshmallows!" Carl Curran yelled.

"Shut the Hell Up, Carl!" every voice in the squad replied in unison.

"You're all just jealous that you didn't think of it first!" Curran grumped.

"Shut Up, Carl!"

The soldiers laughed as they poured fire into the oncoming troops.

* * *

Town Hall was like a kicked-over hive. Jemison bullied and pushed his way through the corridor and finally burst into the command center.

"What the fark is going on?" he demanded. "Mangone! Where are you, your gutless maggot?"

The mercenary NCO's voice came instantly over the comm. "I'm outside getting shot at, you fat bastard! It seems our friends have kicked off the party a little early!"

"Where the hell did they get heavy weapons?" Jemison raged.

"One would surmise that there were weapons aplenty in a *military research facility!*" Mangone was losing patience with the imbecile. He didn't care if he had to turn his people over to the farking Avalonians. Breaking rocks was better than this shithead.

"Did they…did they…" Jemison asked, his voice nervous, his hands gripping the console.

"I have no farking clue at this point, Captain. They aren't showing themselves. I don't know."

The mercenary paused while he took a shot and ducked behind cover. "At this point, it really doesn't matter, does it? We have to get into that facility and get what we can or this whole trip is a bust. If they do have what we came for, I suppose we could try and kill them and take what's left back."

"How the hell are we going to do that?" the obese pirate screamed into the comm. "They're shooting at us. They're killing anyone who gets close."

"No shit!" Mangone grated as a group of railgun rounds hit ten meters away, showering him with rubble.

"Why don't you convince them to stop that? Maybe get your flier up in the air and pin them down while I get some troops in place to flank them."

Jemison's eyes snapped to where Tijiit Rhombo stood. "Rhombo!" he said, straightening. "Get the flier up in the air. Don't sweat the ammo. Kill them! Or at least keep their heads down! Get them to stop shooting at us!"

"On it, Cap'n!" Rhombo acknowledged, hitting the door at a run. "Make a hole!"

* * * * *

Chapter Twenty-Four

The flier climbed, spiraling up and out of the settlement. Rhombo juked it from side to side, trying desperately to keep away from the railgun rounds streaking out from the church on the other side of the settlement. The second he appeared above the level of the buildings he saw one of the streaks of fire disengage from what they had been firing at and begin tracking toward his precious flier.

"Oh, hell no!" he said, jamming his controls to the side. The flier banked, his compensators not quite absorbing the movement. He jammed the controls to the other side and added power to the drives, clawing for as much altitude as he could get. He flew toward the church as he climbed, figuring the closer he got to the church as he rose, the angles might become difficult for the fighters to get a clear shot at him.

Suddenly, he was free of fire and rising above the hills that formed the perimeter ring around the Aberdeen Settlement. He continued to climb in order to circle around and get a clear angle for a strafing run. *That ought to keep their heads down,* he thought, his mouth twisting into a rictus grin.

As he leveled off at five hundred meters and began his wide bank, something caught his attention out of the corner of his peripheral vision. He banked quickly and trained his flier's visual pickups in the direction of what he'd seen.

"Holy shit!" he yelled. "Captain! We've got a convoy heading southwest away from the settlement at a distance of fifty klicks!"

He angled up and gained another two hundred meters. He zoomed in. "Three vehicles. Transports. They look like they're loaded."

He only had to wait a minute. "Take out those trucks! Disable, don't destroy. They might have what we came for!"

"Roger." Rhombo poured power into the drive and screamed in pursuit of the trucks.

* * *

"Flier has lifted off," Devlin said to Kenyon. "Looks like you'll have company soon." He continued to fire into the settlement as Nicki Kenyon's face appeared in his display.

"Roger. I was wondering how long I was going to have to drive forward before putting them in reverse." She grinned ferally. "I get to use this nifty new launcher." Then she pouted. "But I didn't get you anything."

"That's okay, Pony," he said grinning. "Make that farker plasma, and I'll consider us even."

"Squeeeeeee!"

* * *

"Dammit!" Jemison grated as the tactical plot showed the flier screaming off toward the convoy. "We've got to get those farkers to stop! Justine! God's dammit, do something!"

"Like what exactly, Marco?" his XO asked curiously. She was watching the battle on the vid screen, as she didn't want to be out there. She liked to kill, but only when the other guy couldn't fire back.

"I don't know, you stupid bitch, figure something out."

She looked at the feed then the tactical scanners. Fire was coming in, and then she saw it. Her pulse quickened; she drew in her breath. She tapped the icon, highlighted what she saw on her screen, and hit "Fire" on the terminal.

From underneath the combat shuttle, a single missile streaked out, and the Church of the Fundamental Way exploded.

* * * * *

Chapter Twenty-Five

"What the hell did you just do?" Marco Jemison screamed, his face livid. Justine noticed the vein standing out on the side of his forehead.

"I just took care of our problem," she replied calmly. "You said, 'Do something;' I did something."

"But I wasn't talking about destroying our only way into facility, you stupid bitch!" the pirate captain raged, turning even more purple.

She looked at him over the top of the console. "You'd better calm down, Marco. I'd hate for you to have a stroke or something." She didn't put any particular emphasis on the last word.

Jemison recoiled from the console. He suddenly had a vision of a fire serpent preparing to strike. He took a breath, tried to calm down, and said in a much quieter tone. "It's not like you to panic, so I'm going to assume you figured something out."

"Smart boy," Justine muttered. Then she smiled, an expression that unnerved Jemison even more. She swiveled the vid screen around so he could see. "Look."

Jemison craned his neck to get a proper view. Then he saw it, and he smiled.

* * *

Mangone's boots crunched in the rubble of the church. Segments of it were still smoking and burning from the blast. What had possessed that cold-eyed bitch to use a missile on the church was beyond him, but he wasn't going to complain about results.

Where the church hadn't simply exploded outward from the blast, the collapsing roof had formed discrete piles where the four corners used to be. In addition, the debris had fallen away from the object of everyone's attention from the outset: the lift entrance to the facility.

In some ways, they all had Devlin and his people—whoever and whatever they had been—to thank for this moment. Mangone supposed the only reason Longo had decided NOT to try this avenue from the outset was the lift was locked down. Devlin and his guys coming up to defend the church had left the lift in the upright and locked position. Now that the church was gone, as were Devlin and Company, Mangone and his boys and girls could just enter the facility and get what they came for.

"All right, boys and girls," he broadcast, "time to get it on. There's room for everyone, so no grabass. When we get down there, two-man teams. We'll split up and search the facility. If we come across any resistance, kill them. Trash any facility security. Comm if you run into anything or find anything useful."

He got the requisite number of acknowledgments, and the squad entered the lift.

* * *

Tijiit Rhombo was in his element. He was in flight. He was fire. He was death.

He poured power into the drive plant of the flier as he pursued the fleeing trucks. In the back of his mind, he knew the trucks were likely filled with the same refugees that had been rescued by that group of Avalon army types and that he was about to kill them in cold blood, but at altitude, he didn't have to look any of them in the eye.

That's what he couldn't stomach about the crew of *Stormcrow*. They could look you in the eye as they pulled out your entrails. Tijiit hadn't quite gotten to that point yet. He hoped he never would. As long as he couldn't see their faces, he could just pretty much lie to himself that he didn't know anyone was actually in those trucks. He didn't know he had killed anyone.

And for Tijiit Rhombo, that was good enough.

The convoy had started as a small group of dots on the horizon, something that had required his visual gear to make out clearly. Now, it was growing steadily, quickly becoming larger in his view. He readied his guns. No need to waste another of the captain's precious missiles on them. He was going to gun the farkers and keep the guns on them until the trucks were just so much wreckage.

He placed the crosshair icon in his HUD on the rearmost truck, watching the icon go from green to red with a circle that contracted around it as the range closed. As the circle reached its smallest diameter, the icon flashed, and Rhombo pulled the trigger on his flight stick.

Twenty-millimeter railguns whined into life as the guns cycled the rail capacitors dozens of times in the space of a heartbeat. Rhombo watched the rounds tear into the earth and then walk into the trucks of the small convoy.

He saw the rearmost truck flash into flame as the power plant took a hit and exploded. The next truck was luckier, it avoided total destruction and ground to halt as its drive was destroyed. The lead truck swerved a bit and the rear of the truck took a couple of hits, but it was still functional.

He pulled back on the controls and felt the tug of inertia as the flier screamed into the sky. He leveled off and then banked, bringing the flier around for another pass. This time he would get all of them. He grinned. Well, even if he didn't, he could just keep coming back around. He had plenty of ammo.

Tijiit Rhombo was in his element. He was in flight. He was fire. He was...

* * *

As the flier came back around for another pass, Nicki Kenyon hummed, "Friendship Is a Lot of Fun," the theme song to the latest season of *My Friend the Pony*. She watched the range counter on the flier tick down, and the firing data poured into her mind from the armor's sensors. As the flier opened fire again, chewing into the rearmost truck, Nicki dropped the stealth field on her armor and the slaved six-pack rocket launcher.

At a range of about one thousand meters, she saw the targeting icon flash red, and she keyed her fire command. Six missiles reached out to Tijiit Rhombo's flier and introduced him to fire and death. He never even noticed the trucks were empty.

* * * * *

Chapter Twenty-Six

Even before the lift doors completely opened, the point man was out and sweeping the corridor for threats. He advanced, training his weapon to the front, trusting in his teammates to cover their sectors.

Mangone was last off the lift. The lift doors closed quietly as he exited. He gave a ten count, then followed the rest of the squad up the corridor.

He entered a common area approximately fifteen meters from the lift doors. His squad had already swept the room and cleared the three entrances to the common area. Mangone frowned. No helpful placards on the walls to denote, "This way to the secret weapons cache." Damn.

"Smitty, you and Clark take three o'clock," Mangone ordered. "Ivanova and Drayven nine o'clock. Werner and Goetz, you get the nooner."

"Been a while, Boss," the basso rumble of Goetz came back as he chuckled. "But I'm not sure that a nooner with Werner would be a satisfying experience."

"Fark you, Goat."

"Ah, you wouldn't like it, Little Man," Goetz said. "I'd just lay there and sweat." More chuckles. Mangone smiled inside of his helmet. The routine between Goetz and Werner was so old, everyone had forgotten how it had gotten started.

"Just check out the corridor. If you're both good, I'll give you a pogie treat," Mangone growled.

"Ooh," Werner said. "For one of those, I'll even put up with Goatfarker."

"That's the spirit, Little Man," Goetz rumbled, laughing. "It's all about incentive." The pair peeled off toward their assigned sector. The other teams went their way, and Mangone leaned against a wall.

"Sarge!" Susan "SusieQ" Quinones said over the comm a few minutes later.

"Whatcha got, Q?" Mangone called back. He started walking toward the passage she and Drayven had disappeared down.

"Dray and I have a set of doors; one is marked Facility Admin and Control."

"Bingo!" Mangone crowed. "We should be able to zero in on where our package is from there. On my way. Do not attempt to enter until I get there."

"Roger," Quinones said.

"Goetz and Werner, Smitty and Clark. Mangler. Unless you've found the Lost Ark or the Space Beast, meet me in the nine o' clock corridor. Dray and Q have found the admin office."

"Roger!" the other two teams said in unison.

Mangone entered the passageway and saw his team seventy-five meters ahead of him. As he advanced, Quinones approached him and popped her helmet. Mangone checked the air sensor and verified the air was indeed breathable—old habits made for old mercenaries—then popped his own.

"Doesn't seem to be anyone home, Boss," the woman said. Mangone felt a pang of pain at the subtle reminder he was now the titular head of Longo's mercenary company. It was a promotion he never wanted. He felt himself grimace but nodded.

"Probably in that convoy that guy Rhombo reported before we hit the lift. If they took what we came for, we should hear about it when he stops the convoy."

"Yeah, assuming he doesn't destroy the convoy."

"Point," said Mangone. He activated his comm. "Death Crow, this is Mangler. Death Crow, Mangler, over."

No response. Figured. Comms would be useless down here. He sighed. "All right, boys and girls, let's get what we came for. Smitty? Crack that door."

"Roger," the trooper replied, slapping some "boombutter" on the door actuator. Everyone backed way the hell up. Suddenly, Mangone had a thought.

'Hold up, Smitty." The trooper looked up quizzically.

"Has anybody actually tried to, ya know, open the farking door?"

Quinones actually managed to look abashed. "Boss, we just—"

"Can it, Q. You did exactly what you were supposed to," Mangone replied. "I just was wondering." He looked at Smith. "Well, go ahead and try it before you blow the door into dust bunnies."

Smitty shrugged, his lip curling into a disappointed grimace. He reached out to touch the activator pad. Drayven and Quinones covered him with their weapons.

The door hissed open. Dray and Q were first through the door, sweeping for hostiles.

"Clear!" Drayven called, echoed by Ivanova. Mangone stepped through the door, his eyes sweeping the room—old habits—then his eyes were drawn to the main viewer. A moment later, his face went pale.

"Boys and girls," he said, "it's been a pleasure and an honor…" as the countdown timer on the main viewer reached zero.

And the world came to an end.

* * * * *

Chapter Twenty-Seven

Weyland Facility was comprised of a central facility and five separate cells, each situated several kilometers from each other and from the central facility located underneath the vale that contained Aberdeen Settlement. Each of the facility cells was powered independently by a fusion reactor, similar to what powered Avalonian destroyer-sized warships.

Normally, a fusion reactor is designed not to detonate under even the most catastrophic conditions. The way fusion works, it's nearly impossible for it to explode on its own. Contrary to the holodramas, if a ship loses containment on the fusion bottle, the reaction dies within moments; it's somewhat anticlimactic.

However, military people are by nature both paranoid and ultimately pragmatic. In the not-so-ancient past, it was realized that starships that are disabled are just big hunks of target waiting for a place to happen, and that in most space battles, an enemy isn't going to stop at disabled. So, some engineering—pardon the pun—soul got the brilliant idea that if a starship wasn't destroyed, but might soon be, there was still one contingency the crew could undertake. Sure, it was suicidal, but in some cases, death is not the worst thing imaginable. Starships were fitted with hardware that could enable the power plant to do the one thing that power-plants weren't supposed to do—go boom in a spectacular supernova way.

The containment bottle is powered by a small fission pile. When a self-destruct order is given, a huge amount of reactant is dumped into the bottle, then there is a sudden, catastrophic, earthshattering kaboom of a thermonuclear explosion.

Weyland Facility was comprised of five separate cells and a central facility...that was located directly under the vale that contained the Aberdeen Settlement.

* * *

Jemison tapped his railpistol against his fleshy thigh and gloated. The remaining pirates of FPV *Stormcrow*'s initial assault were scattered over the grounds of the now destroyed and smoking church, while the mercenaries went below to secure the property. When they came back topside, they would be met with a little over a dozen railguns, shot as they exited the lift, and Marco Jemison would take what they had come for, go back to their contact on Alphonse Station, and regretfully hand over the property that Longo's company had "given their lives to obtain."

His reverie and anticipation of payment yet to come was interrupted when he was violently thrown to the ground beside the little bridge leading to the ruins of the facility entrance. As the earth bucked and heaved beneath them, Justine and Plahm nearly fell on top of him.

An expanding shock wave radiated out from where the church stood. Jemison watched in horrified amazement as the bridge shattered and the buildings and houses of Aberdeen Settlement fought the twisting and shifting ground beneath them.

Then as quickly as it had happened, it was over. In the stillness, Jemison could hear their breathing, the creaks and moans of tortured buildings behind him, and a low, almost indistinct, rumble.

Plahm recovered first, realization making his face go completely white. "Holy shit!" he gasped. "We gotta move! *Now!*"

"Wha—?" Jemison wheezed as armored hands grabbed him unceremoniously by the collar.

"The farking Facility blew the fark up!" Plahm yelled, pushing Jemison toward the stream and grabbing Justine. The rumbling became louder, and, as they ran for the stream, Jemison could feel the ground shifting again, but this time in the other direction. "We gotta move before the ground—"

He was cut off as the ground slid out from under him again. Plahm caught him and tossed him; this time his armor lifted the fat officer completely off his feet and launched him through the air.

Jemison landed in the cold stream, his indignation at such rough handling by his subordinate muted as he watched the water of the stream abruptly change direction and start flowing toward the ruined church and the entrance to the facility—which was sinking into the ground!

"Captain!" a voice called. "What the hell just happened? The shuttles and the command center rocked like Justine's bunk." The cold-eyed second officer looked daggers in the direction of the shuttles but said nothing as she picked herself up off the ground. "Shit is all over the place here."

"Apparently that idiot Mangone and his grunts blew up the facility!" Jemison grated. *Nothing!* He seethed inwardly. *We did all of this for nothing!*

Then a thought struck through his brain. "The convoy," he said, almost to himself. He got ponderously to his feet and started in the direction of the command center. He keyed his comm.

"Did that farkwad Rhombo stop the convoy? Has he called in yet?"

"Nothing yet, Captain," the technician replied.

"Well try contacting him!" Jemison snapped.

"Aye, aye," the tech answered.

* * * * *

Chapter Twenty-Eight

In the White Room, Devlin looked at the rest of his team. The faces of Wolf, the Carls, and MacBain regarded him. "You boys ready? This is just like APE exercises. Kill them all and let the Gods sort them out. The difference is, we *have* to stop them. We can't afford to leave even one of them combat effective. You got this?" he asked his virtual reality counterparts. Everyone nodded.

A figure blurred into "existence." It was Kenyon. She still appeared in her iridescent sparkle pony armor. Devlin shook his head.

"Flier is a ball of atoms, Devlin," Kenyon said. "I'm on my way to your position, but I may be a bit behind schedule." She frowned.

"What happened?" Devlin asked, his brow furrowing.

"Shrapnel. A big piece caught me," the woman replied. "Took my six-pack and part of an arm. I'm still functional…sort of. I'm heading back, but I don't know how much help I'm going to be."

"Gotcha," he said, concern in his voice. "If that's the case, see if you can link up with Cho or Pigpen. I haven't been able to reach either one. BFTs haven't gone off so I think they may just be busy."

"Okay, Devlin," Kenyon said. Then her face twisted into a feral grin. "Ya know, shrapnel tearing an arm off smarts rather severely, at least for a second. Then Spark Butt shut it down and I'm driving on. I'm starting to really like these suits, Devlin. Plus blowing the shit out of that flier asshole was very satisfying."

Devlin grinned back and saw the others grinning hungrily as well. They were all going to get some payback in a few moments.

"Well, drive on, Private Kenyon!" he said.

"Aye, aye, Cap'n Heroic!" the woman in purple armor said as she faded out.

Devlin stood up from the chair he was in. The others were already on their feet.

"Let's do this!"

* * *

The White Room disappeared, and he was by himself again in his CRATOS armor. He felt the reassuring presence of CALI in the back of his mind. *Don't worry about what you need to do,* the thought came into his conscious mind. *Just do. I'll fill in any gaps.*

The sensor balls he had deployed at the beginning of the battle had been destroyed with the church, so he mentally told the backup balls they had guided to various points on the hills surrounding the vale to wake up.

Instantly his mind filled with sensory data, which CALI dutifully filtered and cataloged. He cycled through the sensors, bringing the scene outside the church into different perspectives. He queued the tactical plot. Red icons denoting enemy combatants sprang into being in his "vision."

It's almost god-like, he thought, and that actually frightened him a bit.

Underneath the rubble of the Fundamentalist Church of the Way, servos activated and whined to life, shifting the individual "shell-ters" that had kept the rubble from crushing the suits when the church collapsed. As the missile struck the church, shaped charges had directed their energy to keeping the lion's share of the rubble from falling on the shell-ters. What had fallen on them had served to obscure and bury, but not enough that the enhanced armor musculature couldn't shift it aside.

As the armored forms emerged, they brought their gun systems online. Targeting reticles bracketed the pirates nearest them, and they opened fire. Railgun rounds impacted flesh and bone, and matter exploded as the hypervelocity rounds tore into the pirates. Between trying to pick themselves up after the upheaval and shock at what had just transpired, the pirates of *Stormcrow* were caught completely by surprise by the apparitions materializing out of the rubble.

Devlin charged up the middle of the formation, his weapon reaching out and killing. He saw Jemison and his first officer but couldn't immediately draw a bead on them. He would get to them, but he had other targets to service first.

"Get 'em boys!" he yelled into the comm. "Don't let them get their feet under them. Keep up the 'Skeer.' I'm going right up the middle and taking out the command group!"

He fired a burst and watched as a somewhat pretty, but cold-faced, blonde woman came apart under the hail of fire from his railgun. As he continued to advance, he saw the remaining pirates in his sector get their shit together and start returning fire.

Without any cover, he took fire as he advanced on them, his own weapon laying down an answer to the oncoming storm.

Devlin felt a sharp pain as a railgun round penetrated his armor and ripped out a piece of his thigh. He felt the momentary pain, but it was over quickly as the suit's AI shut down his pain receptors, anesthetized and stanched the wound, and sent a fresh injection of medical nanites to begin the healing process, all within the space of a heartbeat.

He felt the second round graze his arm. It stopped him as effectively as the first round. He kept going. As hypervelocity rounds picked off the last of the regular crewmen, a lone round struck him on the suit connection to his railgun. He saw the system flash yellow, then red as it went offline. He had the suit jettison the useless weapon and continued stalking toward Marco Jemison and a taller figure in armor like an implacable juggernaut. He felt a couple of rounds glance off his armor, but none penetrated. The tall pirate finished a reload and started to bring his weapon to bear as Devlin closed the final distance between them.

One sweep of his arm took out the railgun, ripping it from the armored grasp of the tall man. Devlin closed in and brought his armored fist up and drove it into his enemy's armored cuirass. While it didn't actually hurt the other man, the blow served as a catalyst for Newton's First Law of Motion. The force of Devlin's augmented blow knocked the exoskeleton off balance and forced it backward.

Flailing, the pirate tried to keep upright as Devlin rushed him raining blow after blow. Repeated strikes dented and crushed the armor. After the fifth blow, the armored exoskeleton lost its coherence under the hail of Devlin's gauntleted fists.

The pirate stumbled back, trying to get his feet under him, but Devlin had none of it. Another blow fell, and pirate's helmet was ripped from its magnetic mounts. The second officer of the *Stormcrow* quit trying to fight back and started trying to get away from the furious juggernaut trying to kill him.

He almost succeeded, but just as he thought he was out of the reach of the young recruit, an armored fist grabbed him by his armored wrist and tugged, hard.

The taller man set his feet and resisted the pull in the opposite direction. Devlin closed in again and the two locked with each other and went to the ground.

Servos whined and popped as the two men wrestled for control in the rubble. The pirate managed to get upright and pinned Devlin's arm while he reached down and pulled a railpistol from its holster.

"I'm going to splatter your brains, you little shit," he spat between clenched teeth.

"Don't...think...so...asshole. Rule Forty-One," Devlin panted. Then he pushed the combat knife into the groin juncture of the pirate's armor.

Pain exploded through Thomas Plahm's brain as the monomolecular combat knife sank deep into his thigh and severed the femoral artery. Plahm didn't have an autodoc in his armor. He didn't have military augmentation. All he could do was bleed. Which he did, throwing himself backward off the knife piercing his groin.

He tried to rise as Devlin got up and stalked toward him. He fumbled for his pistol which he had dropped fleeing the Devil. He could feel his life draining from the severed artery in his leg. He continued to resist feebly as his vision blurred, and he felt himself being picked up.

He screamed as Devlin's armored hand came down on his head, the fingers digging into his skull. Devlin's gauntleted hand came up, and the borrowed kukri of his sergeant major flashed in his hand. Devlin stared at the corpse for a moment, then dropped the severed head of the pirate to the ground.

He felt something slam into his back. He turned and regarded the fat pirate commander. Captain Jemison, commander of the FPV *Stormcrow*, held a railpistol in his trembling hand. He started to back away from the raging hulk in front of him and stumbled.

Devlin watched the panicking bully scrambling away. This was the fat farker who had shot Jonesy, who had ordered the rocket launch that had killed Tamman. He stalked toward the cowardly pirate.

For the first time in probably decades, Jemison ran. He ran for his life. He ran for the shuttles. One was burning, but the other was just damaged, not destroyed. If he could make it to that shuttle, he could hole up until the reinforcements arrived, then he'd show them. He would nuke this entire farking site. He could make it. He knew it. Plahm had wounded that farker Devlin. He turned his head, the farker was just walking. He was even limping. But he was still coming.

And so Jemison ran. He ran like he never had before. The shuttle was closer; he was going to make it. He started laughing. He was going to make it.

The laugh turned into a scream as steel-fingered gauntlets grasped his skull and picked him up off the ground. The scream was cut short as his head was ripped from his body.

* * * * *

Chapter Twenty-Nine

Devlin dropped the pieces of the former captain as a railgun round tore through his side. He stumbled and the ground next to him exploded as another round hit where he had been a moment before.

He rolled behind a piece of a rubble and tried to see in the direction the shot had come from.

He saw an unarmored man stalking toward his position. Several things fell into place in his head.

He reached down for…nothing. No weapons, no knives. He sighed. He could always throw a rock, he supposed. He tried to reach out and realized that both of his arms didn't really want to move.

Great, he thought, the autodoc must be keeping me awake just enough to get to safety so it could send me nighty-night and activate my beacon.

He watched as his would be attacker came to where he lay. He smiled. "Hello, Marty. I see you survived."

Martin Atwell sat down on a neighboring piece of rubble, covering Devlin with a large rail rifle.

"I guess I shouldn't be surprised," the young man said. "How did you figure it out?"

"Didn't completely figure it out until just now. I sort of suspected, but I suppose I really hoped you had gotten eaten."

"How is Natalya?" Is she with you guys?"

"She burned in. Bax, too."

Atwell looked stunned. "Damn, man. I'm sorry. They were both good women. I really did like Nat. And I know you had a thing for Bax." He sat there for a moment, then shook his head. "But you were saying..."

Devlin licked his dry lips. "I originally thought she might be a hitter. Sure, the gun misfire might have been just an accident, but I'm paranoid, I guess. And yeah, the guidon tip happening to come off and hitting me in the head was a coincidence..."

"Hey, Dev," Atwell held up a hand, "that was, as far as I could tell, an accident. I didn't have anything to do with that. You were just unlucky with that one."

Devlin looked at the other "recruit" for a few moments. Then he shrugged his good shoulder. "Okay, fine. For what it's worth, I'll take your word on that one. But let's just say I was extra careful after that."

"So, what clued you in with this?"

"Well, the last several days, I thought that if anyone was going to try and do me, this would have been an excellent time and way to do it. Take the long approach, and even if we hadn't had this cock up, it would have been relatively simple to do me on the exercise while no one else was around. It's a big planet. I could have a real convenient accident. So, let's just say I was extra paranoid. Seems like I was right."

"How did you figure out I had survived?"

"Didn't really until I saw you. I figured someone had. That the pirates clued in on our mission to rescue the town's survivors clinched it for me, as I knew someone had to have survived and contacted the bad guys. And remember, I used to be in that life, so I know there are ways for people in the community to prove their bona fides if they run into one another. I actually know a few. How did you survive and make contact, especially with people looking for you?"

Atwell smiled again; it was not particularly warm smile. "Well, although I'm pretty good at what I do, I will say I did learn a few things from this whole experience. I may have to branch out and use them.

"I hid for a few days, putting things together. I figured we were shot down, but I wasn't sure why. Then about three or four days after the crash, someone came near where I was hiding. It was one of Pringle's people. I clubbed him over the head and when he came to, I questioned him. I found out about you, the attack, the split up, and how you were heading for the settlement."

"You didn't…"

"Well, I couldn't exactly trust he didn't know who got him, and I couldn't leave a witness…"

"You're gonna pay for that," Niko grated, but Atwell continued like he hadn't heard.

"Then I set off to follow you. You had a day start on me, so I ran for a bit. I still didn't get there until a couple of hours before your little rescue mission. Thanks, by the way, for repeating your mistake with the coms. That idiot captain would never have believed me if I hadn't been able to drop the dime on you. Oh, and sorry about Tam and Jones."

"You can quit being sorry, asswipe," Devlin snarled. "I'm not really sure I can take it at face value, what with you trying to kill me and all."

"Aw hell, Devlin. Just because I'm going to kill you doesn't mean I didn't like them," the killer replied. "They were unfortunate collateral damage."

"Fark you."

"Aw, don't be like that," Atwell said. "I will say, those suits are something else. And I'm not going to kill you. Jemison already contacted his ship; they are sending reinforcements in another shuttle. I'm going to nighty-night you and take your body and the armor with me when they get here. We'll drop a KEW on the site afterwards to take care of whoever else may be wandering around. I'll get a share of the money for the armor, which is why they were here in the first place. Then I get to take your carcass back to Caliban and collect the bounty. I'm going to be a pretty wealthy boy for a while. My family will be real happy. Family business, you know."

Devlin snorted. "Family that slays together…"

Atwell looked pleased. "That's pretty good, Devlin. I'll have to tell Da." Then he looked puzzled. "If you knew someone might have made it, why in the Hells did you broadcast your orders? I mean, it's not like you to repeat a mistake."

Devlin said nothing but spread his hands. "I guess we just came close."

Atwell got up and walked over to Devlin. "Thanks, by the way for taking out that fat bastard, Jemison. He was a disgusting asshole." He pointed the gun at Devlin. "You came close, old boy," he said taking aim, "but Rule Number Seven."

Then his head exploded.

Devlin smiled as the contract killer's headless corpse collapsed beside him. "Close only counts in horseshoes and atomics. But I was thinking more like—"

Cho's voice came over his com. "Rule Number Five? 'Never assume?' Rule Number Twenty-Two? 'Always remember someone may be listening in?'"

Devlin coughed a bit and said, "I was thinking about Rule Number Eighty-Four."

"Rule Number Eighty-Four?"

"If you're gonna kill someone, just kill them."

"I can work with that. I'd prefer that. But I hadn't heard that one."

"I just made it up."

"Oh."

MacBain's voice came over the com. "Is he really dead? I can't see from here. I'd like to come down and shoot him again, and maybe again just for good measure," he finished savagely. "I never did like that effete asshole."

A few minutes later, the Hellions appeared on the outskirts of the town. Kenyon was missing her lower arm, her armor was pocked in several places, and her beloved rocket launcher was gone. Cho came bounding up, cradling her odd-looking railgun. MacBain came over a pile of rubble, using his railgun as a crutch, his left leg in tatters below the knee. There was still no sign of McCarthy. Devlin supposed they were going to have to go looking for him.

He tried to roll and get up, but it wasn't going well. Just moving hurt. His guts were on fire. His leg throbbed. Suddenly, he felt hands under his shoulders helping him. Dammit Carl was on one side, Shuddup Carl was on the other. "Come on, 'mano," Dammit said. The little group met in the middle of the destroyed settlement and grinned at one another.

Suddenly, Kenyon stood stock still, her eyes going blank. Her face drained of color.

"We've got shuttles inbound. ETA, five minutes!"

Devlin brought up his tactical plot in his mind. CALI, sensing what he wanted, zoomed out. Two more assault class shuttles were entering atmo on a trajectory that would bring them in on them. The ETA was exactly what Nicki had said. He watched the numbers tick down.

Devlin started to give an order, but a sound got his attention.

The town was a shambles. The collective fire from the Hellions, Jemison's group, and the mercenaries had pretty much trashed the buildings. That was okay; nobody was coming back here. The facility had self-destructed. The cover was blown. The two shuttles that had carried Longo's mercs and the pirates from *Stormcrow* were burning in front of the Town Hall, or at least one was.

It would never fly again. Whatever McCarthy had done to it had completely gutted the thing, as well as killed whoever had been on it. Every once in a while, some part or piece of munitions on board would cook off, giving a really impressive show.

The other shuttle was a different story. The drives were trashed, again thanks to McCarthy, but it was otherwise intact. Now the missile pods on it were moving, rotating.

Devlin watched in horror as the pods rotated and stopped when they were pointing in their general direction.

"Get down! Missile! Missile!" Devlin yelled as the missile pod started disgorging its payload. The entire team threw themselves forward onto the ground, Devlin's wounds screaming as he landed. He almost passed out. He felt the air ripple as the drive systems drove the missiles past the team's position.

They streaked past the team and arced into the sky. Everybody watched as the plumes went up and over the mountains and into the dark night.

The team looked at each other, then in the direction the missiles had disappeared, and then back at the damaged shuttle.

McCarthy's voice came over the comm. "Sorry about that!" A moment later, he appeared on the loading ramp to the shuttle. While his armor had scorch marks and was still smoking in places, he was relatively unscathed. He jogged over to where they were standing.

"You asshole!" Kenyon fumed, rounding on the young man. "You could have hit one of us. You could have at least WARNED us!"

McCarthy held up his hands. "S-s-s-sorry, Pony!" he stammered. "I was busy, and I didn't realize you were standing there until after I hit the initiate key!"

Devlin watched Nicki start to swell and build up steam for an epic rant. McCarthy saw it coming as well and sidled toward Cho. From her stance, he could see she wasn't going to be an ally, and he started backing away. "D-d-d-devlin?"

"Don't look at me." Devlin chuckled, though it hurt. The pain was really starting to break through the neural blocks. "I'm not getting in their way; I already got the shit kicked out of me."

"Do not bother running, Thomas." Cho said. "You will only die tired..."

"Oh shit. I'm sorry! I didn't mean to—" He was cut off as the two women tackled him and laughingly proceeded to thump him lightly on the cuirass.

Then Cho did something Devlin had never seen her do. Anastasia Cho smiled.

* * * * *

Epilogue

"Enter," the gravelly voice called from the other side of the door. Devlin keyed the door and entered Sergeant Major McClellan's room on Asclepius Station.

"You wanted to see me, Sergeant Major?" he asked as he entered the room and came to a position of attention at the foot of the NCO's bed.

McClellan waved his hand. "Bloody Hell, Devlin, at ease. This isn't the blinking parade ground, and I ain't the bloody Prince of the Blood Royal."

Devlin grinned in spite of himself. "As you say, Sergeant Major." He got another glare from the sergeant.

The Imperial frigate carrying the MUSTX forces had gotten a piece of the message McCarthy had tried to send via WHISCR and was at full battle stations when it encountered the FPV *Stormcrow* in orbit. It hadn't been a match.

Three of the pirates hadn't been killed in the fighting and had surrendered almost immediately. MacBain put Pringle and Kenyon on guard for the trio.

The next morning, the transports carrying the survivors of the shuttle crash and the settlement inhabitants entered the pass into the valley. While most of the settlement had been leveled by the destruction of Weyland Facility, there were still a couple of structures left standing. Plus, they still had the intact shuttle.

Decker, Chapis, Teresa Monath, and her friend led the efforts to get everyone if not comfortable, then at least content.

Kilmeade and Harold, along with Cat, had tended Devlin's injuries to the point where they thought he could stave off hibernation, which he did until he was able to report to Colonel Gries later that day, when the first shuttles from the MUSTX advance force touched down in the ruins of Aberdeen Settlement. He then spent four days in the tank while dedicated nanites worked on his injuries, essentially healing him from the inside out. Of the Choirboys, as they had become to be known, Devlin was wounded the worst. Severed limbs and such would be regrown but weren't generally life threatening. Gotta love modern medical tech.

Kenyon was fitted with a temporary prosthetic until her new arm could be grown and attached. Then she'd have a couple of weeks of training while she got used to the new limb. It was the same with many of the others. The new limbs would be a few months in the making.

For some reason, the sergeant major wasn't walking around on his own prosthetics. That confused Devlin to a certain extent. Maybe the old NCO had been more badly damaged than Devlin had thought.

As if reading the younger man's face, McClellan sighed. "They're taking me today to get fitted for a set of 'fake' legs. Between that and the eye-patch, I'll probably be looking like one of those farking pirate wannabes on holo. After that I'm back in the saddle—lightly—until your graduation."

"We're actually going to graduate?" Devlin asked, slightly confused. "I thought—"

"Let me guess," the older man interrupted. "You thought because you didn't actually go through the MUSTX you'd be recycled?"

Devlin nodded soberly.

McClellan guffawed. "Boy! You just led a force of seventy-nine people away from a combat crash, survived in the wilderness for seven days, staged a rescue and a rearguard fighting engagement, took over an enemy-held installation, then mounted a forlorn hope assault and ultimately won. Hell, you've done more than some combat commanders currently *serving*.

"As far as it goes, I'm trying to lobby the colonel to let me write this up as a possible MUSTX scenario. Since we lost half you pathetic shits, he's a little reluctant." He grinned, but then it faded into seriousness.

"You did an outstanding job, Devlin," he said. "PBJ's gonna be proud when he hears. I know I am."

Devlin cocked his head. "Sergeant Major?"

McClellan shifted his position on his bed. He looked the younger man in the eye. "I told you before, I look for men and women who not only can take an order, but can expand, react, adapt, and overcome in any circumstance. People who can not only follow, but lead. Get people to follow them. Those are critical people in any military, Devlin. The King and this Empire sorely need them.

"But warriors aren't born, and they aren't actually made. They are a combination of factors, the most important of which is the mind and will of a man or woman who will not sit idly by while others suffer or die. It all boils down to choice.

"Will you choose to take up the struggle? Will you choose to do your very best in service to King and Country? I can take a raw recruit and turn him into a soldier, a weapon. I can hone that weapon, but it is the mind of the warrior that is truly dangerous, if he chooses to be.

"That is why I pushed you so hard, lo those many weeks ago, boy. If you'd stayed that boy who joined up to avoid prison and getting killed, there may or may not be an Alpha Company right now, short staffed though it may be. I made you choose. And you chose well, if I do say so myself.

"I can't sit here and blow sunshine up your ass and tell you that it's all you; it's not. But you, and Kenyon, and MacBain, and the others all contributed, just like a unit of His Majesty's military should, and it is precisely the reason the colonel has decided to push graduating you lot. The ones who were wounded in the crash will be recycled, but the ones that made the march to Weyland or populated the rearguard camp will graduate as Alpha Company, Third Battalion, One Forty-Ninth Training Legion. All seventy-three of you." He paused. "Including Tamman and Jones," he said, his eyes boring into Devlin's. "Wanna fill me in on how that is supposed to work?"

Devlin regarded the older man levelly. "Are we on record or off, Sergeant Major?"

"Oh, definitely off. I don't think we could get any more off on this one. Jesus Marimba, boy, did you honestly think somebody wouldn't notice?"

"No, I was pretty sure you would notice. I was sure Captain Glass probably would, too. But I'll choose to call this an on-the-fly reconciliation."

"Wanna run that by me again? Feel free to use words of more than one syllable. I'm going to have to sign off on this, so I want to know what I'm getting into."

"Joe Harold and Patrick Kilmeade were former Army and Marines, Sergeant Major. They individually deserted after various little screw-ups that you and I know happen once in a while," Devlin said waving a hand to indicate present surroundings. "They removed their BFT's and were living off the grid, generally trying to stay out of trouble when they met Miss Schrodinger." Devlin had come up with the moniker for the little data-slicer, and while she wasn't thrilled outwardly, Devlin had thought it funny as hell.

"Given her...talents...and lifestyle, she kept them even more off the authority's grid. As you are quite aware, AWOL or desertion during time of conflict carries a few stiff penalties, as in rigor mortis stiff. Since they were carried as MIA in the records, their families were not penalized, i.e. survivor benefits, etc. However, were they to show up now, it would carry said penalties for them, and their families would be penalized as well. I think that's a fairly farked up situation. And since they were somewhat instrumental in helping us, I figured I would help them out."

"By 'giving' them the identities of two of your slain comrades?" McClellan said, a deep frown on his face. "You realize that you are denying—"

For once, Devlin interrupted. "No one of anything. Tamman was a crèche baby on Typhon. He had no family or ties. He joined up so they wouldn't put him in a workhouse. Jonesy was similarly without relatives. And to be honest, Kilmeade is almost a perfect body match for Tamman and Harold is close enough for Jonesy. You said there are rules, and rules. They actually have wanted to come back, Sergeant Major, but after a certain point, what would have been the point? Go in front of the firing squad just so you know you died honest?

"I don't know, Sergeant Major. Maybe it's because I was a crook when I was a kid. I have a little different perspective. At any rate, you don't have to sign off on anything."

"No?" McClellan asked, his eyes narrowing again. "Just why the hell not."

"Because the records have already been changed. Miss Schrodinger reports that two individuals were caught in the blast that destroyed the Aberdeen Weyland Research Facility. Although identifying individual remains is impossible, we have accounted for all remains, including those research personnel lost during the initial raid by the pirates, the pirates themselves based on the numbers given to us by the three who surrendered, and Miss Schrodinger's associates—which the pirates were courteous enough to vouch for and are willing to testify that they were contractors who had been dragooned into this little fiasco.

"Due to exigencies of combat, Privates Jones and Tamman sustained bodily damage that resulted in the loss of their BFT devices which have already been replaced and programmed to their genetic codes…"

"Wait a sec…" McClellan interrupted. "Whose DNA?"

Devlin's face was completely blank. "There was a glitch in the medical database during Privates Jones and Tamman's in-process to the medical facility. Since Miss Schrodinger is a data retrieval expert, she was able to piece the medical records sufficiently that Tamman and Jones were able to get their proper medical treatment for their injuries as well as receive new BFT and nani pack updates."

"She what?" McClellan raised an eyebrow. "Pieced the—"

"DNA and medical records data out of the machine, Sergeant Major. Miss Schrodinger is an accomplished data—"

"Retrieval expert. Yeah, I get it," the NCO growled. "You're taking an awful chance. They could wind up screwing you, Devlin."

"We take a chance every time we get out of the rack in the morning, Sergeant Major." He shrugged. "Let's say I know a little about second chances. Let's say I'd like to pass one along, or two in this case. What's the worst thing that could happen really? They go AWOL again? They'd just be screwing themselves. If not, His Majesty gets a couple of pretty damned good soldiers who had made stupid decisions when they were younger back into the fold. Rule Number Ninety-Nine."

McClellan frowned and looked blankly at the recruit. "I know I didn't come up with a number ninety-nine…"

"Never hesitate to use good material just because of a past misuse. Or do not throw something useful away because of a past misuse, and you'll have something when you need it. Or waste not want not."

"Smart-ass," the Sergeant Major said without heat.

"By the way, Sergeant Major, I have something of yours," he said, drawing a package from his tunic. "I made sure they didn't take it from me and do something stupid." He held out Moon of Death.

"I will have you know that while it did not kill the asshole responsible for all of this, it did take out one of them. The captain, I tore his head off."

McClellan seemed to take that in stride. "You need to work on your anger issues," he said, grinning.

Devlin grinned back. "So, they tell me."

* * *

Glass looked from Devlin to McClellan and back. "Seems to me we have way too many of these explanatory meetings, gentlemen."

"I don't know why you'd think that, Captain," Sergeant Major McClellan drawled. He smiled. "Just trying to make the captain's life a little easier and make sure he's up to speed on current events and all."

"I'm sure," Captain Glass said as he closed out the individual files on his tablet. "At any rate, we put into port tomorrow, and Colonel Gries will be meeting us at Battalion HQ. He has a few words to say to Private Devlin and the rest of the company. Then the MISS people will be taking everyone's occupational specialty choices in preparation for graduation. After that, you and Alpha Company—those who are ambulatory—will be involved in final prep, IE turn-in, and so forth and so on."

He looked at Devlin. "Out of curiosity, Private, have you decided what branch and specialty you will ask for as first choice?"

"Armored Infantry, sir!" Devlin barked.

Glass carefully tried to hide a smile. "You do realize you can't take those shiny toys you found with you?"

"Yes, sir," Devlin admitted. "However, hope springs eternal, sir. I *am* one of the few who can work with the suits as they currently are, sir. I have been made aware that the Weapons Research Board is going to be dragooning—I mean encouraging some members of the squad to volunteer to work with the WRB on replicating the suit's AI interfaces."

"Well," Glass said, lips firmly pressed together. "I'm going to be the bearer of bad tidings, sort of.

"While I have it on good authority you will get your desired choice, you will not be one of the ones working with WRB." Devlin's face fell. Glass laughed. "Don't look so glum, Devlin. You look like I just kicked your favorite puppy. You're not going to work with the WRB because you're going to go get some proper armor training and experience. Each of the squad members will be transitioning in and out over the next couple of years. Some of the work is going to involve medical procedures to work on the interfaces *in situ*. Not incredibly invasive, but it can't be done from the field. So rather than subject one to all the poking and prodding, they're going to poke all of you. Besides, it will help them, as I understand it, to see how the interfaces conform to different people. It's all terribly complicated, and I only have two PhDs. The Sergeant Major probably understands better with his five."

Devlin blanched and looked over at McClellan. "Seventy-five years is a *long* time," the older man said.

"The suits are going to be there when you get done. I realize those suits are…addicting. However, pirates and Nords we have a-plenty, so conflict isn't going away any time soon. So, while you're gonna have to wait for your next 'fix,' you will probably get it."

"Yes, sir," Devlin said.

* * *

Nikolai Devlin folded his uniform tunic and placed it neatly in the bag. They had entered the Wellington System and would be docking at Glalco Station in a few hours. Devlin and the rest of the surviving members of Alpha and Bravo Companies would disembark and go back to camp where they would begin the process of out-processing and graduating Basic

Training. They had all chosen their branches and service. Nicki Kenyon, Mike Chapis, and Kilmeade and Harold—or rather Tamman and Jones—were taking the initial round of duty with the WRB. Somehow, he smelled a Cat in that decision, but he wasn't going to bitch. MacBain had chosen Armored Cavalry. He, by God, was going to drive a tank for him *and* Kuz.

Wolf Gartlan and the Carls were assigned to Armored Infantry with APEs on Al Bakkar. Devlin wasn't sure who he felt sorrier for, the enemy or whichever commanding officer got them.

Decker had been seen in the company of a captain with Intelligence insignia. She hadn't said, but he got the impression that she was going somewhere else after graduation.

Cho and McCarthy were on their way to more training as a sniper and insertion duo—SAID. Devlin felt sorry for the enemy with those two. On second thought…

"Private Devlin?"

Devlin looked up from his packing.

Standing in the door of his room was a tall, older man in an admiral's uniform. The slight epicanthic folds, different but not totally dissimilar to Devlin's own, and the darker cast to his well-worn complexion indicated he was from the New Nepalese part of the Empire. Startled, Devlin snapped instantly to attention.

"Admiral on deck!" he said to an empty room.

"Oh please, Private. As you were," the admiral said. Devlin relaxed slightly. "I am Admiral Mitul Mujumdar. I am the father of Captain Sanjay Mujumdar. I am given to understand that you were using the armor my son had worn. And before you worry, I am read in on CRATOS and what they were doing there."

Devlin bowed his head and nodded. "Yes, sir. I had that honor. I got the sense from everything I learned about the armor that he was a superior officer. I would like to have known him."

"He was a good son and a good officer, but I may be biased," the Admiral said, smiling faintly. "On second thought, no, that is a proper assessment. And it seems his armor acquired a wearer that added to his honor."

"Thank you, sir," Devlin said.

"I was also given to understand that you avenged his death and rescued his son and daughter."

Again, Devlin nodded. "I tried to avenge a lot of good people who lost their lives, sir. But I was but one. I lost a couple of good people rescuing your grandchildren, but that was a price we all agreed to."

The admiral looked at the young man for a full minute, sizing him up. "I heard that you carried one of our kukris, but it was not yours?" He looked disapproving. Devlin's sphincter puckered a little. The sergeant major hadn't indicated there might be an issue. He did know Gurkhas could be "funny" about their knives.

He gulped. "Yes, sir. I was given the knife for safe keeping by my sergeant major."

"Ah yes, Sergeant Major McClellan," the older man said. "Does he still call his knife by that silly name?"

Devlin attempted to keep a straight face. "I believe he does, sir."

The admiral finally dropped the stern mien and regarded Devlin warmly.

"Private Devlin. I came here mainly to thank you for saving my daughter-in-law and my grandchildren. They were the apple of my son's eye, and he would have given himself many times over to save them. I'm glad they are alive because of you and your teammates.

"But that is not the only reason. I also had something I wished to give you." He held out a package similar to the one Devlin had given to McClellan a few days before. Devlin looked a little puzzled.

"Sir?"

"It is my son's kukri. The recovery teams found it among the bodies. I would like the man who helped complete his mission, and who saved his children, to have his knife to remember him and his family by. I would have that knife wielded by a man of the same type of courage."

Devlin took the package humbly. "Sir, isn't this something that one of his children...?"

"His children, should they join the service when they are able, will earn their own. In fact, they were insistent you be given their father's knife."

Devlin was stunned. The knives were made on New Nepal by master craftsman. It would be a lie to say the methods were some deep dark secret, but the Gurkhas had lobbied the Imperial Legislature to limit the use of the knives. They were not sold; you couldn't even get a knockoff in the bazaars. The crescent-shaped knives were the exclusive property of the New Nepalese Gurkhas.

McClellan was the only non-Gurkha he had ever known who had one.

"I will try to bring honor to it, sir."

The admiral reached out and clasped the private on the shoulder. "I'm sure you will, Private."

He smiled, his aging face showing real warmth along with a little sorrow. "And should you ever come to the home of my people, I would invite you to stay with my family and know more of my son. And should you ever have need, I will do whatever I may. Thank you again, Private Devlin. Be well."

He turned and walked out of the compartment.

* * *

Teresa Monath coughed gently at the still open compartment door a few moments later, and Devlin spun around. "Thought I stayed on Aberdeen? Not hardly. While you were in the tank, Colonel Gries contacted Command, and we were given passage back with the fleet to Tir Na Nog. Most of us will be taking some time while the military and our employers and such iron out little things like settlements for getting shot at, imprisoned, etc." She smiled somewhat sadly. She walked up to him. "I lost some good friends," she said, her eyes misty.

Devlin put his hand on her shoulder, and she embraced him. Somewhat surprised and more than a little awkward, he put his arms around her and held her.

"Me, too," he murmured. They stayed like that for a while, each taking comfort from the presence of the other. Finally, she pulled away and smiled, a few tears remaining in her eyes. "But I also still have some friends that I might not if you hadn't helped us. I wanted to thank you."

Devlin wanted to say something, but just hung his head. She lifted his chin with her hands and looked him in the eye. "Private Devlin, thank you. Thanks to all your 'Choirboys.'" She kissed him lightly on the cheek and winked at him. "We get into station in a few hours, and I asked your sergeant major what was going to happen after graduation."

Devlin furrowed his brow. "Okay," he said. "I could have told you—"

"He said you weren't going to have leave or anything, right off the ship. He said you'd be going back to your base and getting ready for graduation. He then said I could attend it if I so desired, and I do. Athena, Sheellah, Joy, Christine, Sharon, and all the others want to as well. He said while most of the recruits had put in for leave, you hadn't, so he didn't know what you had planned."

Devlin's brow furrowed even more. "What does that have to do with—"

"I wanted to come down here and thank you, personally," she said. He nodded his head like he understood what she was saying, but his face betrayed him, and she laughed and took his hand.

"Nikolai Devlin, I would like you to do two things."

He looked even more confused.

"One, I would very much like it if you would spend some of your leave with me. I want you to show me around where you and the rest of your unit trained. You guys are fascinating. I might even decide to join up," she said, grinning.

"You said two things."

"Well, we have a couple of hours…" She pressed the door control and closed it.

* * *

Nikolai Nikolayevich Devlin always knew he was going to wind up with his name on the board. He looked up at the list of shuttle boarding calls to see if he was there yet. Nope.

All the survivors had left already, most going home or somewhere on leave. Devlin was the last person to leave after spending a few days with Teresa. First a transport straight to the jump point, and then on to Zanzibar, where he would be joining the 439th Armored Infantry Legion in the fight to liberate that system from the Nords. From what he had heard, the hard part was already complete on Prime; they were just mopping up pockets of resistance and the occasional insurgent. *No big deal,* he thought. *You take a risk just getting out of the rack.*

He looked out on the tarmac and watched a group of recruits being chivvied off by McClellan and his minions. *The cycle goes on, world without end, reprieve, or rest.*

He'd gotten a letter from Jadwidzik just before graduation. He'd apparently heard about the "survival" exercise. After expressing his relief that Devlin had survived, he went on to say that he had made arrangements so Victoria would be taken care of in comfort until the day she passed away. Devlin was relieved by the news. His mom was the only tie he really had to Caliban, apart from the justiciar. Now he could concentrate on his life and what he needed to do.

And what he needed to do right then was get on the shuttle as he looked up at the board and saw, "Devlin, N. PFC—HMS *Pertwee*—Gate 14."

# # # # #

ABOUT THE AUTHOR

Chris Maddox started reading science fiction and fantasy as soon as he could read. He's been looking up to the stars ever since. When he's not writing, he works as an electronics technician in the Aerospace Industry. He lives in Delaware with his wife, Christine and their three dogs.

* * * * *

The following is an
Excerpt from Book One of the Earth Song Cycle:

Overture

Mark Wandrey

Now Available from Theogony Books

eBook and Paperback

Excerpt from "Overture:"

Dawn was still an hour away as Mindy Channely opened the roof access and stared in surprise at the crowd already assembled there. "Authorized Personnel Only" was printed in bold red letters on the door through which she and her husband, Jake, slipped onto the wide roof.

A few people standing nearby took notice of their arrival. Most had no reaction, a few nodded, and a couple waved tentatively. Mindy looked over the skyline of Portland and instinctively oriented herself before glancing to the east. The sky had an unnatural glow that had been growing steadily for hours, and as they watched, scintillating streamers of blue, white, and green radiated over the mountains like a strange, concentrated aurora borealis.

"You almost missed it," one man said. She let the door close, but saw someone had left a brick to keep it from closing completely. Mindy turned and saw the man who had spoken wore a security guard uniform. The easy access to the building made more sense.

"Ain't no one missin' this!" a drunk man slurred.

"We figured most people fled to the hills over the past week," Jake replied.

"I guess we were wrong," Mindy said.

"Might as well enjoy the show," the guard said and offered them a huge, hand-rolled cigarette that didn't smell like tobacco. She waved it off, and the two men shrugged before taking a puff.

"Here it comes!" someone yelled. Mindy looked to the east. There was a bright light coming over the Cascade Mountains, so intense it was like looking at a welder's torch. Asteroid LM-245 hit the atmosphere at over 300 miles per second. It seemed to move faster and faster, from east to west, and the people lifted their hands to shield their eyes from the blinding light. It looked like a blazing comet or a science fiction laser blast.

"Maybe it will just pass over," someone said in a voice full of hope.

Mindy shook her head. She'd studied the asteroid's track many times.

In a matter of a few seconds, it shot by and fell toward the western horizon, disappearing below the mountains between Portland and the ocean. Out of view of the city, it slammed into the ocean.

The impact was unimaginable. The air around the hypersonic projectile turned to superheated plasma, creating a shockwave that generated 10 times the energy of the largest nuclear weapon ever detonated as it hit the ocean's surface.

The kinetic energy was more than 1,000 megatons; however, the object didn't slow as it flashed through a half mile of ocean and into the sea bed, then into the mantel, and beyond.

On the surface, the blast effect appeared as a thermal flash brighter than the sun. Everyone on the rooftop watched with wide-eyed terror as the Tualatin Mountains between Portland and the Pacific Ocean were outlined in blinding light. As the light began to dissipate, the outline of the mountains blurred as a dense bank of smoke climbed from the western range.

The flash had incinerated everything on the other side.

The physical blast, travelling much faster than any normal atmospheric shockwave, hit the mountains and tore them from the bedrock, adding them to the rolling wave of destruction traveling east at several thousand miles per hour. The people on the rooftops of Portland only had two seconds before the entire city was wiped away.

Ten seconds later, the asteroid reached the core of the planet, and another dozen seconds after that, the Earth's fate was sealed.

* * * * *

Get "Overture" now at:
https://www.amazon.com/dp/B077YMLRHM/

Find out more about Mark Wandrey and the Earth Song Cycle at:
https://chriskennedypublishing.com/

* * * * *

The following is an
Excerpt from Book One of The Progenitors' War:

A Gulf in Time

Chris Kennedy

Available from Theogony Books

eBook, Paperback, and (Soon) Audio

Excerpt from "A Gulf in Time:"

"Thank you for calling us," the figure on the front view screen said, his pupil-less eyes glowing bright yellow beneath his eight-inch horns. Generally humanoid, the creature was blood red and had a mouthful of pointed teeth that were visible when he smiled. Giant bat wings alternately spread and folded behind him; his pointed tail could be seen flicking back and forth when the wings were folded. "We accept your offer to be our slaves for now and all eternity."

"Get us out of here, helm!" Captain Sheppard ordered. "Flank speed to the stargate!"

"Sorry, sir, my console is dead," the helmsman replied.

"Can you jump us to the Jinn Universe?"

"No, sir, that's dead too."

"Engineer, do we have our shields?"

"No, sir, they're down, and my console's dead, too."

"OSO? DSO? Status?"

"My console's dead," the Offensive Systems Officer replied.

"Mine, too," the Defensive Systems Officer noted.

The figure on the view screen laughed. "I do *so* love the way new minions scamper about, trying to avoid the unavoidable."

"There's been a mistake," Captain Sheppard said. "We didn't intend to call you or become your minions."

"It does not matter whether you *intended* to or not," the creature said. "You passed the test and are obviously strong enough to function as our messengers."

"What do you mean, 'to function as your messengers?'"

"It is past time for this galaxy's harvest. You will go to all the civilizations and prepare them for the cull."

"I'm not sure I like the sound of that. What is this 'cull?'"

"We require your life force in order to survive. Each civilization will be required to provide 98.2% of its life force. The remaining 1.8% will be used to reseed their planets."

"And you expect us to take this message to all the civilized planets in this galaxy?"

"That is correct. Why else would we have left the stargates for you to use to travel between the stars?"

"What if a civilization doesn't want to participate in this cull?"

"Then they will be obliterated. Most will choose to save 1.8% of their population, rather than none, especially once you make an example or two of the civilizations who refuse."

"And if *we* refuse?"

"Then your society will be the first example."

"I can't make this kind of decision," Captain Sheppard said, stalling. "I'll have to discuss it with my superiors."

"Unacceptable. You must give me an answer now. Kneel before us or perish; those are your choices."

"I can't," Captain Sheppard said, his voice full of anguish.

"Who called us by completing the quest?" the creature asked. "That person must decide."

"I pushed the button," Lieutenant Commander Hobbs replied, "but I can't commit my race to this any more than Captain Sheppard can."

"That is all right," the creature said. "Sometimes it is best to have an example from the start." He looked off screen. "Destroy them."

"Captain Sheppard, there are energy weapons warming up on the other ship," Steropes said.

"DSO, now would be a good time for those shields…" Captain Sheppard said.

"I'm sorry, sir; my console is still dead."

"They're firing!" Steropes called.

The enemy ship fired, but the *Vella Gulf*'s shields snapped on, absorbing the volley.

"Nice job, DSO!" Captain Sheppard exclaimed.

"I didn't do it, sir!" the DSO cried. "They just came on."

"Well, if you didn't do it, who did?" Captain Sheppard asked.

"I don't know!" the DSO exclaimed. "All I know is we can't take another volley like that, sir; the first round completely maxed out our shields. One more, and they're going to fail!"

"I...activated...the shields," Solomon, the ship's artificial intelligence, said. The voice of the AI sounded strained. "Am fighting...intruder..." the AI's voice fluctuated between male and female. "Losing...system...integrity...krelbet gelched."

"Krelbet gelched?" the DSO asked.

"It means 'systems failing' in the language of the Eldive," Steropes said.

"The enemy is firing again," the DSO said. "We're hit! Shields are down."

"I've got hits down the length of the ship," the duty engineer said. "We're open to space in several places. We can't take another round like that!"

"That was just the little that came through after the shields fell," the DSO said. "We're doomed if—*missiles inbound!* I've got over 100 missiles inbound, and I can't do anything to stop them!" He switched to the public address system. "*Numerous missiles inbound! All hands brace for shock!* Five seconds! Three...two...one..."

* * * * *

Get "A Gulf in Time" now at:
https://www.amazon.com/dp/B0829FLV92

Find out more about Chris Kennedy and "A Gulf in Time" at: https://chriskennedypublishing.com/imprints-authors/chris-kennedy/

* * * * *

Made in the USA
Middletown, DE
30 November 2022